Light Shining in the Forest

Paul Torday burst on to the literary scene in 2006 with his first novel, *Salmon Fishing in the Yemen*, an immediate international bestseller that has been translated into twenty-eight languages and has been made into a film starring Ewan McGregor, Kristin Scott Thomas and Emily Blunt. He is married with two sons by a previous marriage, has two stepsons and lives close to the River North Tyne.

Also by Paul Torday

Salmon Fishing in the Yemen
The Irresistible Inheritance of Wilberforce
The Girl on the Landing
The Hopeless life of Charlie Summers
More Than You Can Say
Breakfast at the Hotel Déjà vu (ebook only)
The Legacy of Hartlepool Hall
Theo (ebook only)

Light Shining in the Forest

PAUL TORDAY

Weidenfeld & Nicolson
LONDON

First published in Great Britain in 2013
by Weidenfeld & Nicolson
An imprint of the Orion Publishing Group
Orion House, 5 Upper St Martin's Lane,
London WC2H 9EA
An Hachette UK Company

3 5 7 9 10 8 6 4

This book is a work of fiction. Some of the details about
Northumberland and the Kielder Forest, and horrific crimes
perpetrated upon children in the past, are true, but all the details of
the story and all the characters that appear in it are imaginary. Any
resemblance between the fictional characters and real people is
entirely coincidental.

A CIP catalogue record for this book
is available from the British Library

978 0 297 86747 0 (cased)
978 0 297 86748 7 (trade paperback)

Typeset by Input Data Services Ltd, Bridgwater, Somerset

Printed in Great Britain by Clays Ltd, St Ives plc

The Orion Publishing Group's policy is to use papers that
are natural, renewable and recyclable products and made
from wood grown in sustainable forests. The logging and
manufacturing processes are expected to conform to the
environmental regulations of the country of origin.

www.orionbooks.co.uk

Catherine Meyer, founder of the children's charity, Parents and Abducted Children Together, said: 'The truth is we don't know how many children go missing, which is an appalling state of affairs. But the best estimate we have shows that every five minutes a child goes missing in the UK. It is really quite shocking,' she added.

—Mike Sullivan, Crime Editor, the *Sun*, 11 October 2007

One

Kielder Forest lies along the English and Scottish Borders. A few hundred years ago, all this part of the world was a desolation of mires and low, heather-covered hills. Its inhabitants – more then than there are now – were once considered masterless men, who acknowledged no king and lived by violence and cunning. The Border clans were known as 'reivers' and they lived on either side of the Border: in Liddesdale, Teviotdale, Redesdale and Tynedale: clans such as the Armstrongs, Bells, Charltons, Dodds, Elliots, Kers, Nixons and Scotts. They stole from each other and fought with each other. The Border region was difficult for any king to control, whether he was king of Scotland or England. For a while, it was known as the Debatable Land.

It is an empty and silent country. Even today, on this crowded island, there are spaces along the Borders where you can walk for a day without ever seeing another human being.

The country itself has changed. Once there were grey-green hills, covered in rushes and heather. Steep-sided denes scored the hillsides; thick with birch, alder, willow, oak and pine. These ancient woods have now been replaced by a patchwork of huge forests: Wark, Kielder, Redesdale, Harwood, Newcastleton, Craik, Tinnisburn, Spadeadam and Kershope, spread across hundreds of square miles. Tens of millions of trees: Sitka Spruce, Norway Spruce, Lodgepole Pine, Larch, Scots Pine; a dark host only occasionally relieved by avenues of broadleaves. Who lives there now? A few forestry communities, scattered villages and isolated hamlets. Foxes, deer, buzzards, goshawks, jays, magpies, ravens and crows far outnumber the human inhabitants. Once there were red and black grouse living in the heather-clad hills, and grey partridge in the white grassland. But the predators that live among the trees, the hawks and the foxes, have dealt with most of these. Nothing much else lives here; nothing except the trees themselves.

Intersecting the forest is a labyrinth of graded roads. Each year several million trees are planted and as many more are extracted, taken by road down to the chipboard factory in Hexham, or to the Tyne docks, or to the stockyards of timber businesses and fencing contractors. Most of what is logged is softwood, not suited for joinery or cabinet-making, and destined for some industrial purpose. The roads are cut through the forest as they are needed, and then abandoned, chained off to prevent access, quickly overtaken by weeds, and then by regenerating pine and fir. Kielder Forest alone covers two hundred and fifty square miles, and its siblings cover maybe twice that area.

Before the trees came, this was a land of marshes and rolling grass hills. Across the hills ran the old droving roads along which sheep were driven to markets further south, or else to the strongholds of the local clans. The place names recall the former nature of the land and its people: Haggering Holes, Bessie's Bog, Bloody Bush, Foulmire Heights, Gray Mare Moss. The mires and moss were a perfect protection for the reivers who once inhabited this region.

It was a landscape of a thousand soft colours: the subtle shades of heathers, bog myrtle, sphagnum moss, cotton grass,

4

lichens and the whites and browns of the grasslands: an infinitely varied palette, changing with every shift of light from the cloudy, windy skies above. Now only corners of this older world can be glimpsed in places where it has not yet been submerged in the sea of conifers.

Many of the trees were planted in the 1920s as part of a national undertaking to replace timber consumed in the trenches in France during the First World War. Much later, an enormous lake appeared in the forest. It was created by damming the headwaters of the North Tyne – seventeen miles of it between tree-clad banks – to provide water for industry further east. A drowned village lies beneath its waves. As for the trees, it is difficult to know what purpose they now have: they have become an end in themselves, a reason for their own existence. The trees are there because the trees are there.

Geordie Nixon has worked in forestry for most of his life. His father and his grandfather were woodmen. His father tended the private forestry of a local estate. In those days trees were still worth money: ash, beech and oak for furniture; larch was once cropped for ship's masts. Now a tide of cheap timber from Eastern Europe and the former Soviet Union has made home-grown woodlands close to worthless. His father was made redundant and died young, aged sixty. His mother died a few years later, still working as a cleaner.

Geordie began by helping his father during the school holidays. When he was sixteen, he left school and started work as a fencing contractor. He's done fencing, planting, weeding amongst the young trees. Now he's registered as a lone worker and he harvests the trees in Kielder for the Forestry Commission.

He has known nothing else. He visits Hexham, the nearest

town of any size. He's been to Newcastle, the nearest city, twice. He's never been to London, and has no plans to go there. He barely knows where London is. What he does know is the forest, and the birds and the animals that live there. Almost every day he sees the deer lifting their heads to look at him as he drives deep into the forest in his truck. In their season he hears the vixens shouting. He knows where the badger setts are. From time to time, he hears the scream of a rabbit being taken by a hawk. These sounds and shapes and sights are his company when he works in the forest. He works in all weathers: in the faint sunshine that sometimes filters down through the trees; in driving rain; sometimes in the soft and soundless fall of snow, when the forest seems to go to sleep under its white blanket.

You don't find men like Geordie Nixon in towns. You find few men like Geordie anywhere. He's a big man, over six feet tall, and he looks as tough as the trees he cuts down. He has a square, pale face and grey eyes under thick black eyebrows.

His life is work. The money comes in and it goes out even faster. Geordie knows he won't die a rich man. He doesn't think much about the future. He knows he has to meet the lease payments on his vehicles and his HP on the forty-inch HD television in the flat. He has to pay his girlfriend, Mary, his share of the rent on her flat, and his share of the food and heating. He owns nothing except the clothes he stands in, his chainsaw and his mobile phone.

At first light, Geordie Nixon is working with the chainsaw and is already well into the area of forest marked out for clear-felling. He cuts away the small trees and other bits of rubbish to allow the harvester to reach the bigger trees that have to be felled and logged. By eight-thirty, he is cutting down trees in his harvester, a second-hand Valmet 941. It is tracked, to cope with the soft ground. Rubber tyres would just dig in and sink. The whole of this forest grew out of bottomless mires, or else fell land full of sharp rocks.

Geordie is contracted to cut down a block of thirty-year-old Sitka Spruce. The harvester grinds and chugs and whines as its hydraulically powered jaws grab a tree and then bite into its base. In a few seconds the tree has been cut, but it is not allowed to fall: instead the harvester tilts the tree over in its jaws and strips off the branches and most of the bark, then cuts it to length before placing it on top of a growing pile of poles beside the forest track.

Geordie works alone. It's what he prefers. There isn't the money in the job to pay the wages of another man. Once he would have had a lad helping with the stacking of the felled timber, so that he didn't have to load up his truck at the end of the day. Now he has to do it himself. But even Geordie knows about market forces. He's seen the price of timber go down year after year.

Every now and then, he stops to take a nip of lukewarm tea from his Thermos, or else to light a cigarette. When he switches off the engine of the harvester, the silence of the forest is uncomfortable. At midday he stops again and eats the packed lunch – his 'bait', he calls it – that Mary has put up for him the night before: processed cheese slices in a bap, with not enough butter. He eats the dry food mechanically, and swallows the last of his tea. Although it is only early April, there is a hatch of midges. These trouble him whenever he opens the door of the cab. Around him a soft light filters through the forest canopy: a hint of the sun far above the clouds, just enough to gleam on the wet cobwebs on every branch, on the wet bracken by the edge of the wood, on the pools of water lying everywhere. From his cab, Geordie can see down into the shallow valley on whose upper slopes he is working: nothing but spruce and pine, nothing but trees in their endless dark tangles. The light turns greyer in the afternoon as the cloud thickens. Dusk comes early to these places: beneath the shadow of the trees it never really leaves.

At four o'clock he locks up the harvester and walks down to the forest track where he's parked his truck. This is a big Scania tractor-trailer, with a jib-crane at the back for loading up the timber. That and the harvester are leased to him by a finance company.

He has a girlfriend, Mary, whom he thinks of as his 'lass'. Once they had a child as well.

He begins loading the stacked timber from the roadside onto his truck. This is a hard task that requires patience: stack it badly, and it might start rolling and then the whole trailer could tip over. After an hour or more, he's finished the job and he's finished too. He's absolutely shattered. It's not just the one day's labour. It's the unending labour of a hundred days, a thousand days. He's grateful for the work, but it's killing him. Then he remembers the pills Stevie sold him in the pub a couple of nights ago. He doesn't know exactly what they are: 'Man, ye can gan forever on these' was how Stevie made his pitch. Amphetamines, Benzedrine, Mephedrone – who cares? As long as they sort him out.

They do something to him, that's for sure. Half an hour after taking them he feels less tired; but also a whole lot worse, as if something has changed inside him, or something outside has changed, but he's not sure what.

Maybe it's the pills, maybe not. As dusk approaches, his sense of unease grows. All his life Geordie has worked alone. He's used to being in the middle of nowhere. This *is* the middle of nowhere: a remote area of the forest between Kershope Rigg and Blacklyne Common. Walkers and farmers rarely come here. There is no reason to: no grazing, no paths that go anywhere, nothing to see except trees. There's nobody here; not at this time of day. He has heard the barking of foxes, the alarm calls of birds and often he has heard the screams of buzzards overhead as they float sideways in the winds that never stop blowing across these Border hills.

Now all he hears is the silence, and it is getting on his nerves. When the trailer has been loaded and the huge stack of wooden poles secured, he climbs into the cab of the big Scania and turns the key in the ignition.

He knows that the pills have done something weird to him. He wishes he hadn't taken them, but it's too late for that. His heart is pounding much too fast and he can feel the sweat beading on his forehead. He flicks on the headlights as he enters the dark tunnel of trees, following the intricate and confusing maze of forest roads down into the valley of the North Tyne, to Leaplish and on down to the chipboard factory in Hexham to drop off his load. When he's done that he will drive to the village beside the Tyne where Mary and he live in their flat. There's something else getting into his head: something he thinks he has seen rather than heard.

He switches on some music to drown out these odd and unwelcome thoughts – not really thoughts, but flashes from somewhere arriving in his brain like radio signals. Then the huge truck meets blacktop road, and he pushes the accelerator to the floor. Headlamps on full beam, the trailer sways dangerously as he drives much too fast down the valley. Only when the lights of the first villages appear does he slow down a little. As he drives through them, images come to him: images of children. In many of the houses, lights glow from upstairs windows. He imagines that those lights are illuminating bathrooms and bedrooms. He imagines children at their bath-time; children having stories read to them by their parents, sitting on the side of the bed, turning the pages in the gentle glow of a bedside lamp. He imagines the children turning over sleepily in bed and murmuring goodnight. He imagines – so clearly – the father and the mother smiling at each other as they close the door softly on the sleeping child. He imagines it; he remembers it.

Mary is watching television when he arrives home. She stands up as he comes through the door, but does not offer him a kiss or greet him in any way. Instead she puts the kettle on. She knows he won't eat straightaway. He is too tired to eat, almost too tired to speak. He accepts a mug of tea from her and asks how she is.

'All right.'

A little later, he stands up, as if uncertain what to do next. Mary asks: 'Will I get you something to eat?'

'No – I'll do myself a fry-up in the morning.'

She leaves the room. He hears her running the tap in the bathroom and then the door of her room shuts. It isn't really her bedroom. It used to be the nursery, where the boy slept. He disappeared just before Christmas, when most buildings in the street had fairy lights hanging over the door and Christmas trees visible through the windows. He disappeared while they were starting to wrap his Christmas presents, while Christmas carols played incessantly on the radio and Christmas jingles played over the public address systems in the supermarkets.

That was four months ago, and more. Mary hasn't changed anything. The toys are all still in the cupboards. The ceiling is still pasted with stars and crescent moons that glow a little in the dark when the lights are switched off. Mary moved in there a few weeks after the boy went. She and Geordie haven't shared a bed since. They haven't shared much else either: not their thoughts, nor their worries. They have plenty of those, but they no longer talk about them.

It's one of those things. She doesn't particularly blame Geordie for what happened; that's to say, she blames him equally along with the rest of the human race.

An hour or two later, Geordie switches off the television. He has no idea what he has been watching. He goes to the bathroom and brushes his teeth. He goes to their bedroom and strips off to his boxer shorts and climbs into bed. He sleeps in the middle now; it's less lonely. After a few minutes he falls asleep, but it is not the dreamless sleep of the tired man. His hands twitch and he moans once or twice. Then he mutters to himself: '*Light in the forest. Light in the forest.*'

There is no one to hear him, and when he wakes in the morning he doesn't remember his dreams. There is no one beside him to ask how he slept, or nuzzle against him for a moment before he steps out of bed. He showers, then dresses laboriously, for the tiredness from the day before hasn't left him. He goes into the kitchen and puts on the kettle. He raps gently on Mary's door to see if she wants a cup of tea bringing in. There is no answer. They still love each other, he tells himself, although it's hard to say why, or how you would know, they see so little of one another these days. He cooks himself a good breakfast: two fried eggs, beans, tinned tomatoes, bacon, a mug of hot tea with two sugars. After he has eaten, he experiences a rush as the glucose and the fats surge into his bloodstream – an illusion of energy; an illusion of purpose. By the time he has climbed into the truck and started it up, that flicker has died down again and he already feels weary as he heads north, back towards the forest.

Two

Mary and Geordie have lost a child. Why should they think themselves anything special? Why should they feel entitled to grieve? It's so commonplace. Abusing and losing children is something the nation excels at. Look at the headlines in the newspapers most weeks: children are tortured as witches; they are tortured for recreational purposes; they are abandoned, abused, trafficked, exploited, or just lost. It's hard to believe how many simply disappear. Presumed runaways, presumed to have gone to live with a relation, presumed to be someone else's problem.

It's a profound philosophical question as to why we do this to our children. Some blame it on the decline of the family. Others bridle at this suggestion; what's so special about families? Why should marriage be the only valid framework within which to bring up a child? It's an interesting debate.

There's a benefit system in place that rewards the production of children with money, housing and other prizes. Children are produced and nobody knows quite what to do with them. They go on the streets. They disappear. Or their economic value is recognised by entrepreneurs who know that children can provide services that will earn their owners money.

There are nameless children on the streets of every big city in the country: un-persons without family or even nationality.

There are children by their thousands in care homes. Some of them encounter compassion or even love; some of them receive less attention than rescue dogs.

A few of them encounter other kinds of love: a twisted, touching, groping kind of love that is hard to distinguish from hatred.

Every now and then some fresh crime against children is reported in the newspapers and the debate leaves the rooms of policy-makers and special political advisers and think-tanks and sociologists, and acquires a brief flicker of urgency. People are interviewed on television and say things such as: 'It's the twenty-first century. And we still live in a society that can't protect its own children from harm.' The statistics are dusted down and trotted out: the tens of thousands of children who go missing every year; the sixty-five thousand children placed in care homes. And everyone knows that's the tip of the iceberg.

Then some especially gifted adviser whispers in the ear of the secretary of state. He whispers that this could become an issue for voters. Something needs to be done. There has to be an initiative.

This secretary of state is keen on initiatives. He senses his career is on an upward trajectory. Five years ago he was a back-bench MP, whose previous employment was as an actor in a long-running soap opera on television. Then his talent at histrionics resulted in him being plucked from obscurity and appointed as a parliamentary private secretary. He would never have dreamed, when he first stood for parliament, that one day he would be secretary of state for the Department of Children, Schools and Families. Now – who knows where he might end up? The voters want action? Using all his vast ministerial powers he proposes, as with the twitch of a magic wand, a network of Regional Children's Commissioners. They will be known as 'Children's Czars'.

Something like this has been done before, but it's going to be different this time. That's what the secretary of state argues. In a major speech that receives wide coverage in the media, he talks about the importance of his department's role. He refers to the recent conviction of a perpetrator in a case that shocked the country, and asks for more resources for his department to support his initiative. These *new* children's czars will be individuals of the highest possible calibre, and paid a fortune. They will have undreamed-of powers and enormous budgets.

'The new children's czars will get rid of the culture of compliance within social services,' intones the secretary of state on a BBC morning chat show. He has forgotten that, in response to an earlier crisis, he himself introduced many of the new compliance requirements that are keeping social workers behind their desks; filling in risk assessments; training in epidemiology; or engaging in 'reflective practice' sessions.

'They will help get social workers back on the front line. They will set new intervention targets. They will cut through the red tape and make things happen! We will pilot this scheme and then, as soon as possible, we intend to roll it out nationally.'

It sounds good. A children's czar! And who will be the first to be chosen? Who is this kindly person, muffled in furs, travelling everywhere by sledge and rescuing children trapped in gingerbread houses?

It is not some benign autocrat who is appointed to run the pilot scheme, but Norman Stokoe.

Norman Stokoe, Children's Czar! Who would have thought that Norman could ever aspire to such a position? He started his working life in a North London Local Education Authority.

Then an opening appeared for an administrator in the Social Services department. It soon became apparent that Norman was a clever man. He always did his homework. He always turned up at meetings on time. He spoke well. He was considered to be sound. And it wasn't too long before he began to rise effortlessly through the great new industry of child protection.

Norman Stokoe, Children's Czar. You wouldn't get a job like that without knowing your business. And Norman does know it. He was involved in the second intergovernmental conference on Violence against Children. He is familiar with the UN Convention on Rights of the Child. He did sterling work for the Safeguarding Children review that was sponsored by Ofsted, the Care Quality Commission, Her Majesty's Crown Prosecution Chief Inspectorate and other august bodies. He can reel off the annual statistics from the British Crime Survey: half a million children recorded as the victims of violent crimes in England and Wales; forty-three thousand the subject of child protection plans, thirteen thousand of them under four years old; twenty-one thousand children the victims of rape, gross indecency or incest; one in seven of those children under the age of ten; eight thousand violent attacks against children under the age of ten.

It is a problem on an industrial scale and it requires an industrial response. The UK leads the world – but whether in measuring the problem or solving it, it is harder to say. The UK has some of the most stringent codes of practice of any country regarding the exploitation of children in sweat factories in Thailand or Vietnam. It is sometimes less effective at preventing the abuse of children within its own shores. But successive governments have studied the problem. They may not have solved the problem; perhaps it is a problem nobody will ever solve. But they have certainly studied it.

Norman has spent many happy hours in the thickets of reports by commissions of inquiry, by charities, by government agencies both national and international. He knows his way around. He can quote the numbers. He can provide the references. He speaks the language: the special, anaesthetising language that is used to neutralise the stark truth of the figures. Norman is not shocked. He is not in favour of violence against children. He considers it – directly, and indirectly – a serious cost to the economy. The indirect cost is the hardest to quantify: all those children growing up – if they survive – to become damaged adults. It's a shame, Norman used to think, but all the same he is in some sense grateful for the industry – industry is definitely the right word – that provides him with a living. For every few thousand crimes there must be a report and there are a lot of reports produced every year. For each report to be produced, there must be meetings. Norman likes those meetings: he can shine, he knows his stuff, he drinks the coffee and he eats the complimentary biscuits.

He knows the child protection industry like few others. He's never put a foot wrong. He has worked for the Child Wellbeing Group, the Safeguarding Vulnerable Groups Group, the Child Protection Steering Group, and the Independent Safeguarding Authority.

Norman Stokoe is an obvious candidate to be the first regional children's commissioner. Checks reveal that he is squeaky clean. He went to a good church school and the right sort of university. He has never caused anyone a moment's trouble. He is a safe pair of hands. Nobody knows what he does, or has ever done. He is perfect.

In all the due diligence that is done on Norman, nobody comments on the fact that Norman isn't married, has no male or female partner, and there is no recorded instance of him ever having actually met a child.

Of course he met children at school, when he himself was a child. He was a clever boy whose academic parents had taught him to believe that cleverness was everything, more important than good looks, more important than athletic prowess. He was not the most popular boy in his class. However, Norman knew he was the cleverest and therefore the most important boy in his year. His classmates made a point of never asking him to be on their team and rarely asked him to come home to tea with them. Perhaps it was that experience that turned him away from the idea of having children himself.

Who can say? But it is a fact that in all his years working in and around the social services, Norman has never been directly involved in an intervention. He's never tripped over a bicycle in the hall of some dingy flat. He's never encountered the smells and sights of some barely furnished living room, graced only by a huge television set, where a mother and father sit in semi-stupor, drinking Special Brew and rolling joints, while an unregarded and unwanted child sits in a corner in a nappy that should have been changed the day before.

It hasn't hindered his career so far. He is driven by ambition. He sees life as a ladder that clever people can climb and stupid people cannot. He evaluates his own worth as a function of his pay grade and the size of his office. When, after a number of interviews culminating in an expensive lunch in St James's Street, he is offered the job of Children's Czar, he accepts with gratitude. The salary is prodigious. He could afford to take the prime minister out to dinner rather more easily than the prime minister could afford to take him.

And so Norman's life begins to change. He sells his flat in North London and purchases another, larger and much cheaper, in a market town near Newcastle-upon-Tyne. From there it is only half an hour to his smart new office in a complex of glass and steel by the shores of the River Tyne. Norman hires a removal firm to do the tedious work of packing and transporting his worldly goods, and drives north in his Honda Accord. As he drives, he contemplates his prospects with pleasure. He will be a shark in the fishpond of the North East. They won't have come across an operator of his calibre before. Norman knows, without having met any of his new colleagues for more than an instant, that he will run rings around them.

He smiles as he drives. He sits low in his seat, one hand on the steering wheel, listening to *The Food Programme*. From time to time, he plucks a wine gum from a bag and inserts it between his lips. He is not in uniform today. His twenty suits have gone ahead of him. Today he wears a (rather tight-fitting) pale-blue pullover and an open-necked pink shirt and cream-coloured trousers. He might be on his way to play golf somewhere, except that Norman doesn't play golf. He doesn't play golf; he doesn't play tennis; he only likes watching sport on TV.

It is early evening when his car approaches Newcastle. He turns on to the Western Bypass and the first thing he sees is a giant crucifix, an iron cross silhouetted against an orange sky. A crucifix a hundred feet high, spreading its arms over the motorway like a warning. Then he sees it is not a crucifix but a gigantic iron angel, unfurling its protective wings above the warehouses and factory units below. It is the enormous metal sculpture called 'The Angel Of The North'. Norman has arrived.

His new appointment doesn't quite turn out as Norman expected. He has forgotten what he should not have forgotten:

that nothing lasts for ever in these fast-changing times. This is a government of action. It wants progress in all directions. It wants change. It *loves* change. Only a matter of weeks after the announcement of Norman's new position, before his first salary cheque has even hit his bank account, new priorities are set for the government department for which he works. The enabling legislation that is required to implement the network of Children's Czars is put to one side for the moment, in order to free up parliamentary time to accommodate some other initiative. But Norman Stokoe has already been hired. He has already moved north. It is too late to reverse the decision to employ him, and he will no doubt be needed soon. So he is given a PA and the office he was promised and he settles down in his new leather chair behind his new desk to wait for the green light to begin his mission.

At first the inactivity does not bother him. He is used to the odd hiatus in his career, while the rest of the world catches up with his next promotion. But, after a while, he begins to wonder when word will come from London confirming it is all systems go.

The green light never comes. There has been a cabinet reshuffle and another secretary of state has been appointed to replace his predecessor, who promised so much. His old boss has been moved to the Home Office: a promotion. The new incumbent at the head of Norman's department has many things to think about and enormous problems to resolve. Children's czars were not his idea. He will get no credit for implementing someone else's initiative. It never occurs to him to worry about Norman Stokoe. So Norman is left high and dry: no department, no budget, no terms of reference, nobody reporting to him, nobody to report to.

Norman cannot believe he has been forgotten. It is not

conceivable they would pay him and not ask him to *do* any-thing. His new office is located close to the Tyne in an elegant, airy complex where once there was a dirty, unpleasant power station. In the vast atrium are works of art by a well-known and extremely highly paid Finnish sculptor: twisted metal shapes that look like a clutch of vultures glued to the wall. There is a coffee bar serving espresso and different kinds of latte. Outside his large and comfortable office is an ante-chamber where his PA sits. It is hard to know what she does all day, because Norman has nothing for her to do. Not yet.

Norman spends pleasant hours in his new office getting to know his neighbours, having lunch with future colleagues, and visiting local government offices to introduce himself. His time will come. Word will arrive from Whitehall. His day in the sun – his new lifetime in the sun – is about to start. Except that nothing happens.

Norman has been overlooked. In the new organisational structure of his department, his name is nowhere to be found. The administrative system to pay him is the only mechanism that has been established since his appointment. That ticks like a Swiss watch: his salary arrives monthly without delay. Norman's salary is a footnote to a footnote in an appendix attached to a vast document describing the operation of his department of state, and absolutely no one remembers that he still exists. Norman has business cards printed at his own expense, for which he files a claim. Still he waits. He is a patient man.

Three

Becky Thomas, nine years old and small for her age, goes out to play. It is eleven o'clock in the morning and Mum is sitting in the kitchen drinking vodka from a mug. Becky should be at school but isn't, because Mum can't remember the name of the school; she can't remember where it is; she can't be sure she even remembers the name of her daughter. But she knows how to deal with little crises of this sort. She calls out for her daughter. Becky comes into the kitchen, her long, fair hair hanging down her back, her blue eyes watching her mother with apprehension.

'Goo't an' play,' Mum commands. Her words are slurred, and Becky knows that outside is the best place to be for an hour or two, until Mum goes back to sleep. She would rather sit in her room and read, but now is not a good time to be hanging around the house. Becky goes out to play. It means stepping out of the back door, crossing a little alleyway and entering a small park garlanded with old plastic carrier bags and ambushed by dog faeces. But there is a wooden roundabout there, and Becky likes to play on it until it is safe to go back home.

This has been Becky's life for a couple of years now. There was Before, and there is Now. Before, they were a family. Mummy didn't drink then, at least not all day long. The house was tidy and meals were regular and Becky, an only child, felt secure in her home, at the centre of the universe.

Now, they are not a family. There is her mother and there is Becky. Becky's no longer at the centre of the universe. She's on the edge of somebody else's universe, and it's not a good place to be. Her mother has gradually upgraded from the odd drink before lunch and several drinks in the evening, to a life where she has her first shot of vodka at breakfast. That is breakfast, as far as Becky's mum is concerned. And it goes on from there. Once the whole house was warm and safe and clean. Now the house is always cold, because there isn't the money to pay for the central heating. Becky's mum has her own internal central heating, and that doesn't leave anything over for Becky. The house isn't clean any more. It's filthy. It's never cleaned, unless Becky is allowed to have use of the vacuum cleaner and dustpan and brush when she comes home from school. But sometimes when she starts to tidy up around her mother, she's shouted at. Perhaps Becky's mum realises that she's the one who should be doing some of the housework. Perhaps it's a guilty conscience; or perhaps she just likes shouting.

Nowadays, if Becky's mum won't take her to school, she doesn't go to school. The streets around here are not always safe. Questions are asked at school to which Becky has no answers. Once or twice a social worker's been to call, but Becky's mum doesn't answer the door. Becky's probably on a care register somewhere, marked down for fostering. But nobody's got around to taking her away from her mother so far. Meanwhile, if Becky's mum tells her daughter to go out and play, then that's the best thing to do. It's by far the safest course of action.

She goes and stands on the wooden roundabout, one foot on the roundabout, one foot pushing at the concrete pad until she has momentum and is whirling around and around. As the roundabout revolves, Becky thinks – but it is only her fancy – that she can hear the shouts and laughter of other children, as if she were in the school playground in the morning break, where she should be. She imagines her friends, jumping on and off the roundabout. She gives a quiet little smile. Becky is a quiet sort of girl. She knows she is on her own.

At first, nobody stops to talk to her while she plays. At first, nobody asks her what a little girl like her is doing, playing in the streets of the small town where she lives, when she should be at school. Afterwards, nobody can remember seeing her there, except one old lady driving to the shops on her mobility scooter. She says later that she remembers seeing 'A little girl playing on the roundabout. She looked lonely, poor little dear.' When the old lady comes back from shopping at the Co-op about half an hour later, she notices that the little girl is no longer there, and assumes she must have gone back home.

The old lady isn't the only one in the street that morning. It has other inhabitants. They are not all drunk, or asleep. They are inside their houses cleaning; or hanging out the washing on lines strung across backyards; or standing at the fence in front gardens talking to their neighbours. A few of them have jobs and have gone to work. None of them notices little Becky Thomas. Maybe fifty cars and vans go up and down the street that morning. The post never comes until half past ten, so the postman should have seen her. Parcelforce makes a delivery to number fourteen. The driver doesn't remember seeing Becky. Others go about their business as they do every day, but nobody notices Becky Thomas, and nobody talks to her.

Except that somebody sees her. Somebody, after all, does stop and talk to the lonely little girl. There are no eyewitness accounts to colour in the details of the person who stops and talks to Becky. Nobody can say that he or she was wearing a tracksuit, or a hooded top, or a grey suit. The unknown person has no identifying features or shape or personal characteristics with which we can tag him, or her. But whoever it is, there's speculation it must have been somebody familiar to Becky because she's been trained at school, if not at home, never to talk to strangers. It would have been easy, if she had been scared, for her to run back across the alleyway to the relative safety of her home. So the assumption is that she wasn't scared. Not at first.

'Are you happy playing here all on your own?' this person might have enquired.

'Oh, I am,' Becky might have replied, not wanting to talk to the familiar person. She knows him or her, she's seen him or her around before and she doesn't want to be rude either. She has found that some grown-ups hit children who are rude to them.

'Don't you get bored?' the familiar person asks.

'No, I like being on my own,' answers Becky. And she does. She recognises her interlocutor, and in a way she even likes him or her. But why's he or she here now, all alone, without the familiar van? There's something going on here. Something is not right. It is easy to imagine that, at this point, Becky is beginning to wish the familiar person would go away and leave her alone. It isn't normal for someone to appear out of nowhere in the alleyway next to the playground. It isn't normal for someone to get out of a car and come and talk to her. CCTV pictures show all the regular vans and buses that go down that street; they also show a Mitsubishi Shogun with tinted windows in the area that morning. It is one of two or three vehicles the police would like to trace in order to eliminate it from their enquiries, but the number plate is spattered with mud and unreadable.

'Would you like to come for a ride in my car?' asks the familiar person. Presumably Becky says no and presumably by then she's been grabbed and, before you know it, Becky is gone, her companion is gone and the car (that might or might not be a Mitsubishi Shogun with tinted windows) is also gone. Becky Thomas has gone missing.

When Becky's mum wakes at about three o'clock that afternoon, with a dry taste in her mouth and the television turned up too loud, she isn't thinking of Becky. Then she sees the clock on the mantelpiece and it tells her it is nearly time to go to the school gates and collect her daughter. She wonders if she can bring herself to stand up, to straighten herself out so that she looks a little less like an old drunk who has just woken up, and make the effort to walk the half mile to the school gates. Then she remembers that she didn't take Becky to school that morning. So that's OK, then. Becky's mum is very slow to realise that, no, that is not OK. It is very far from OK, because Becky is not in the house. She is not in the park. Becky Thomas isn't anywhere.

And, after a while, Becky's mum realises, with a sick feeling that is worse than any hangover, that while she's been asleep her little girl has disappeared. With a great effort she manages to find her way to a neighbour's house, where there is a phone that is still connected, and she calls the police.

The police send a car, and two officers interview Becky's mum. They can't get a lot of sense out of her. They make a few house-to-house enquiries and get nowhere. It isn't until late evening that a formal search gets underway. These things take time to organise. It's not like on TV. There aren't many spare bodies at the local nick. Men have to be drafted in and a search plan has to be agreed. It doesn't make any difference. Becky's far away now.

The local papers make a fuss, and the disappearance of Becky Thomas even makes the national news, for about two days. But she is only one little girl. Her single mother appears on BBC's *Look North* at a press conference a few days later. She is not sober. It is not an edifying spectacle. When she's given her moment to speak to Becky's abductor, she can't find the words or, if she finds them, she can't articulate them. She looks like an old scarecrow with her creased-up, red face.

'My Becky,' she manages to say. 'Come back to me.' She wants to say to somebody out there: 'Bring her back to me', but she can't, she just makes swallowing and gulping noises. It is obvious by now that swallowing and gulping are what she does best. The senior policeman sitting beside her touches her arm and takes over. 'If someone took Becky away without her mother's knowledge or permission, that person may have friends, or family. If anyone you know has been behaving oddly recently, or you think might in any way know something about this missing little girl, please contact us.'

A telephone number comes up on the screen. But the person who took Becky doesn't have friends and no longer has family. The person who took Becky doesn't watch television and doesn't need to. He or she has other interests.

The private view of the police is that Becky's a runaway. Having floated the theory that some unknown person may have stopped and talked to Becky and then grabbed her, the more they see of Becky's mum, the more they're inclined to discount the possibility of abduction. 'With a mother like that,' says a DI, 'who can blame the poor little thing? She'll be in

Newcastle somewhere. Or even London.' Officially, they say the case is still open. Officially, they say: 'We haven't ruled anything in and we haven't ruled anything out.'

A missing child – you'd think the press would lap up the story, have a field day with it. But in this case there's too much ambiguity: is she missing or did she, as the police leak privately to journalists over a pint, 'do a runner'. The story starts to die. One or two more imaginative journalists try to think of a new angle. One of them discovers that there is a new arrival in the North East, a new addition to the panoply of regional social services: a children's czar. Surely he will have something to say about all this?

When the journalist rings, the children's czar is sitting at his desk, drinking a latte macchiato, with a sprinkling of chocolate and whipped cream. The drink has left a cream and chocolate moustache on his upper lip. He has a busy day ahead. No news from Whitehall, but meanwhile the local bureaucracy has become aware that Norman is a spare senior official with an impressive title. He receives lots of invitations: to exhibitions, conferences, workshops, break-out sessions – the kind of activities that fill the lives of so many these days.

This afternoon he is going to inspect a new art installation, a series of giant blue Perspex cubes which will be launched into the River Tyne and will float downstream. They have Wi-Fi on board and you can call them on your mobile as they float past and they can tell you things … recipes for salmon … information on water voles … information on canoe festivals. It is an important installation symbolizing … Well, it's a symbol of something, that's for sure, and Norman has been invited to attend the launch ceremony. Then this evening he is attending … But then the phone rings, breaking into Norman's review of the day ahead.

He wipes the moustache of fake cream and chocolate from his upper lip so that it won't smear the mouthpiece. 'Norman Stokoe speaking,' he tells the phone. The journalist introduces himself and asks for a comment on the case of missing Becky Thomas. Norman Stokoe can't think what the journalist is talking about.

'You know, the little girl that went missing last week,' prompts the reporter.

'Yes, of course, but I don't think I should comment while the investigation is ongoing,' says Norman. He has remembered now, he saw something about it in the papers.

'But as children's czar, you must have an interest in the case?'

'My job is not to hinder police investigations by unnecessary speculation,' says the children's czar. He hangs up a moment later and makes a note to himself to find out about Becky Thomas. You can't be too careful. Be prepared, that's Norman's motto.

He rings for his PA. She is one of a pool of ladies dedicated to making the lives of the workers in these government offices a little less stressful. She makes sure Norman doesn't have to bother with arrangements such as booking theatre tickets, arranging taxis or submitting expense claims. Even with all these demands on her time, she is surprised when the phone rings. It doesn't happen often. She puts down her copy of *Grazia* and answers: 'Yes, Mr Stokoe?'

'I want you to take a letter. Could you come through to my office?'

He dictates the letter. It is to be addressed to the Head of Human Resources in his department in London. After a short preamble, he says:

I would be most grateful if you could now forward to me, in writing, a copy of my Terms of Reference, as instructed by the secretary of state. There is, as a result of a recent missing child case, a growing interest in this region in the role of the new children's czar. It is important that in responding to enquiries from other government departments and, indeed, the press, that I speak with the knowledge that I have the full backing of the department and am in a position to clarify the precise nature of my role and the powers attached to it.

He hesitates before signing the letter when it is brought in to him. It is very *committing*, signing a letter like this. He hopes nobody will construe it as criticism. He is conscious that he has a generous salary and a comfortable office. All the same, he needs a letter like this on file just to show – if anyone ever asks – that he is keen to get on with his job. He has rolled up his sleeves and he is anxious to get on with it. The letter will be clear evidence that he is straining at the leash, not idling his time away at the taxpayers' expense.

It is some days before a reply arrives and, when it does, it is not helpful. Norman reads the letter. The principal private secretary has a terser literary style than Norman. He writes:

Unfortunately the enabling legislation for the proposed new network of regional children's commissioners was de-prioritised at short notice to enable other legislation to get into the Statute Book. Meanwhile, a select committee is considering the costs and potential long-term outcomes of the so-called 'Children's Czars' network. The committee is expected to report to Parliament next summer, in about fifteen months' time.

Norman writes 'Not helpful' in thick black ink across the letter and files it. At any rate, he can relax. He has asked, and he has received a reply. He can do no more. It is springtime now, and the leaves are budding on the trees. Norman decides to go for a walk along the river embankment in the sunshine and then find a nice little restaurant for a spot of lunch. He rings his PA and says: 'I'm going out for a meeting. I'll be back about two-thirty.'

'Oh, Mr Stokoe, I was just about to call you. A lady is asking to see you.'

Four

Norman Stokoe, children's czar, overweight and dressed in the uniform of the governing classes: dark-grey double-breasted suit, white shirt, a tie of gorgeous pink silk, a close haircut, gold-rimmed glasses. He looks like one of our ruling caste, but he isn't a full member yet. One day, he hopes he will be. Norman Stokoe sits at his desk and watches Mary Constantine in the chair opposite. From the neck down, she is a very attractive woman of around thirty, and as Norman appreciates this aspect of Mary, he does not know that his pink tongue peeks out of his mouth, like a tortoise poking its head out of its shell. Mary Constantine, from the neck up, looks weary. The weariness masks someone who might, in the right circumstances and in better times, be beautiful. She has put a photograph on the desk. She says: 'That's Theo.'

'Theo?' asks Norman. He glances at the photograph but does not pick it up. He is still wondering what this woman is doing in his office. He didn't invite her. She came in followed by the anxious PA, Miss Everbury. Pippa Everbury has failed in her duty as the watchdog guarding the entrance to the sanctum. She has let in a member of the public. Norman does not know if he can forgive her.

'Yes, Theo. My son. Theo Constantine. He has been missing

since just before Christmas. You have heard about Theo, haven't you? It was in all the papers.'

The name doesn't ring a bell with Norman. He waves to Pippa that she can leave them.

'Ah yes,' he says. 'I'm not sure how I can help?'

Mary Constantine says: 'They say you are the children's czar. I found you on the Internet. I didn't know about you before. I've tried everything else.'

'Tried everything else? I'm not sure what you mean by that?'

Mary tells him: 'I've been to the police. They say the case is still active, but they never tell me anything.'

'The police are very, very busy.'

'I've contacted Child Rescue Alert. I've rung the National Missing Persons Helpline. I've tried the NSPCC. Nobody can help. They talk, but they never *do* anything.'

All of a sudden, and without any warning, Mary is weeping. She weeps silently. She finds a handkerchief and dabs away the tears and blows her nose. This display of emotion makes Norman uncomfortable. He wishes the woman would hurry up and say whatever she has come to say, then go away.

'I'm sorry,' she says. 'I didn't mean to cry. It's just so frustrating. There's a child missing – *my* child – and people seem to be making less fuss about it than if a car had been stolen. I only came here because I thought – I hoped – you might be able to help.'

'Ah,' says Norman Stokoe. He doesn't know what to say. What on earth does she expect from him? His role is strategic, not operational.

'They say a child goes missing every five minutes in this country,' said Mary. 'The police say they can't possibly track down all of them. But Theo was only ten. He didn't run away. They think he might have run away, because of the bruising.

32

But that wasn't anything to do with us. They think it's our fault, but it isn't.'

She stops again. She sobs, then tries to get herself under control. She looks at Norman, who hasn't said anything further. She looks him straight in the eye and says: 'You haven't even picked up his photograph.'

Norman looks down at the picture on the desk. He knows that if he picks it up he might become involved in something he doesn't want to be involved in.

'Pick up the photo,' Mary tells him. 'Look at him. Look at my son.'

This is a watershed moment for Norman. What he is going to do now is shake his head in a kindly way and stand up. He is going to say, 'Dear lady, if there was anything at all I could do for you, believe me, I would help. But mine is a very new position. At this moment in time I have no resources to work with. I cannot become involved in an active police investigation unless I am invited to do so. And I haven't been.'

Then he will usher her out of the office with a little pat between the shoulder blades.

He hears himself say this so clearly in his mind that he is quite surprised to find that she is still sitting there, and that he has picked up the photo and is looking at it.

Norman Stokoe is not married. He never has been and probably never will be. It's not that he doesn't like women. He has had relationships – transactions – with women, but nothing has ever lasted. He suspects nobody is ever going to appreciate his company as much as he does. He enjoys the freedom a single life gives him. He's not lonely in the evenings. He's got his fridge, which he always makes sure is stocked with a range of delicious snacks; he's got his television and DVD collection; he listens to opera on his high-quality sound system.

It was never a conscious decision not to marry. He just didn't. He doesn't regret it. Marriage often means children. He does not like children: snotty, rude, ugly, ignorant creatures. His professional involvement with them is a separate matter. That does not require engagement at a personal level. Now he is looking at a photo of someone's horrid little child and he can't think what to say.

Except.

Except that the picture doesn't show a horrid, snotty child. It shows the head and shoulders of a young boy, nine or ten years of age. The boy's hair is dark and his face is handsome, calm. His dark eyes compel you as you stare at his picture. His eyes lock onto yours and hold them. Norman puts down the picture. It has an odd effect on him. He looks away from it and then looks again.

'He has the face of an angel,' says Mary. 'Doesn't he?'

Certainly there is something unusual about the child's face. But what it is, Norman would not like to say: angel or devil, there is some indefinable quality you would not expect to find in a photograph of a ten-year-old child. A photograph that was probably taken on a mobile phone, nothing special, nothing out of the ordinary. But once you have seen that face, you aren't going to forget it.

'You must help me,' says Mary. 'You really must. Someone must, and there's only you left.'

As she looks at Norman, her gaze has a little – just a trace – of her son's calm stare. It is enough. Norman realises that he needs a new plan to deal with this situation. Simple denial is not sufficient. Instead, he will write a report. It's what he has been trained to do. The writing of a report anaesthetises any discomfort produced by a recital of the facts. He opens a drawer in his desk and pulls out an A4 pad. He extracts a fat fountain pen from his jacket. He tells her: 'I will take some notes. I can make sure my report is forwarded to the Missing Persons Bureau. I will make sure it is on the Integrated Children's System PLATO database. More than that I cannot promise. Now, start at the beginning and tell me when Theo went missing. What happened, and whom did you inform?'

It is a thin little story. A boy goes to visit the mobile library with his children's library card a day or two before Christmas. He never gets there. Somewhere between home and the library he goes missing. The librarian never sees him. Nobody remembers seeing the boy walking the streets. He leaves home and then he is gone. The parents wait for him to return. They wait and wait. An hour has passed since Theo left the flat. Mary goes to where the library was parked. It has gone. She walks the streets. She and Geordie report to each other on their mobile phones while they search. They do not find him. They do not find anyone who has seen him. They return to their flat. Three hours have now passed since Theo left the flat. There is an argument about what to do. Geordie is going 'to tan the boy's hide' when he comes back. Mary wants to ring the police. They wait a little longer. They ring the police.

After an age, the police come. They ask questions that Mary thinks are stupid. They take away a photograph of Theo. They take away some of his clothing to try to capture DNA samples, in case it should be necessary to do a DNA match. Mary weeps. Geordie is pale, silent. They find it almost impossible to talk to each other; almost impossible to think. Six hours have passed since Theo left the flat. He does not return that evening. He never returns.

That night they do not sleep. They gaze at each other with the lights on. They go to bed and turn off the lights and gaze at the ceiling instead. Three times, Mary thinks she hears a noise, someone in the passageway outside the front door of the flat. Three times, she goes to the front door and opens it. Three times, there is nobody there.

In the morning, the police return. They tell Mary and Geordie that they want to talk to the school doctor. They don't say why. Mary signs a consent form. The police give her no information. They go away.

In the afternoon, the police come again. They tell Mary and Geordie that the doctor who looks after the school has informed them he has twice been called in by the school to examine the boy, because of concerns he might have been subjected to physical abuse. In each case the signs of physical trauma disappeared quite quickly, but the doctor photographed them before they did so.

'What about the bruising?' the police asked Mary and Geordie.

Norman looks up from his notes. 'The police asked what?'

'They asked me about the bruising on Theo's hands and feet and ribs. It had nothing to do with Geordie and me. The marks just appeared: on his palms and feet and once on the left-hand side of his ribs and sometimes on his forehead. We never knew how he got them. It didn't happen at school.'

Norman puts down his pen. Is it possible he is looking, for the first time in his life, at an actual child-abuser, right there on the other side of his desk? She doesn't look like a child-abuser. She looks worried, desperate, haunted: all of those things. But then Norman doesn't know what a child-abuser is meant to look like. He is strategic, not operational. He asks more questions about the bruising.

'The doctor called them stigmata,' said Mary. 'He said if we weren't doing it and they weren't self-inflicted, then that was the only explanation left. But the police thought it was us who did it, and I think the doctor did too.'

Stigmata: the Wounds of Christ. Appearing on a small boy in a small town in the middle of nowhere. Well, that's different, thinks Norman. A door opens in his mind that has been shut for a long time and memories of his own childhood begin to flood through.

He says: 'I'll write a proper note of this meeting. I'll make sure it is forwarded to the relevant organisations. I'm not sure there's a lot else I can do.'

He adds: 'We'll be in touch. Someone will be in touch. I hope they find your missing boy, Miss ... Mrs ...'

Mary Constantine stands up slowly, as if it is an effort to rise. She nods at Norman. She doesn't smile. She tells him: 'Someone had better find him soon. Otherwise I will go mad. I thought you might be able to help me. But you're just like all the others. All anyone does is write reports.'

It takes a while for the morning to right itself again. Norman sits motionless at his desk for several minutes after Mary Constantine has left. Then he rings through to his PA for another latte macchiato. And, very soon, everything is fine once more.

A little later, he walks along the riverside promenade to find somewhere for lunch. He has almost forgotten about Mary Constantine. He has given his PA a short lecture about admitting people without appointments. Now, as he walks, the fine, dry morning lifts his spirits. After all, life isn't so bad, he reflects. He is extremely well paid and no doubt in a month or two or three he will find something to do. Meanwhile, thinks Norman, the trick is to make the best of what you've got.

His mind goes back to the photo of the child he saw earlier

37

that morning. The woman said – someone said – that the child might be exhibiting stigmata. No doubt the person who said it was joking, but it is a joke that takes Norman back a bit. The memories released by that word, a word he hasn't heard anybody use for decades, are still washing through him. He can remember Father Adrian teaching them at the Catholic school in North London that Norman attended in his teenage years, before he saw the light and became an atheist. His parents, both academics working at The University of London, chose the school because it had a reputation for academic rigour. They had no objection to the religious aspects of school life. Norman could make up his own mind about all of that. 'Priests make natural teachers,' Norman's father had said. 'It's what they are trained to do.'

Father Adrian taught them to learn the Bible: 'In the beginning was the Word, and the Word was with God, and the Word was God.' He taught them about the Four Last Things: death and judgement, heaven and hell.

In Father Adrian's study at school, a picture hung on the wall. It was a full-size, high-quality reproduction of a work by Tintoretto. It showed the blessed Saint Francis in an attitude that suggested fear, anticipation and exaltation all at the same time. Norman can recall the picture as if it were hanging in front of him now. From behind a cloud, red rays of light stream out and fall down to earth where they strike the upturned palms of the Saint. Where the light touches them, the red mark of a wound appears in the centre of each palm. Underneath the picture the title on the gilt frame: *San Francesco riceve le stimmate.*

'I bear on my body the marks of Jesus,' Saint Paul had told the Galatians. Father Adrian read the passage out to them when they first saw the painting. He taught them about stigmata, as experienced by Saint Francis and many other blessed persons – mostly women – who had exhibited on their bodies signs of the Five Wounds of Christ.

In that period of Norman's life, if it was in the Bible or if Father Adrian said a thing was so, then it was so. In those days Norman thought of himself as devout. He always felt that he was more devout than the other boys. When Father Adrian said that such-and-such a blessed saint had exhibited stigmata on his body, Norman nodded his head enthusiastically, as if only he and Father Adrian really understood such matters. This behaviour irritated his classmates and occasionally they let Norman know how they felt by visiting him with mild physical violence. But Norman didn't mind. He knew he was different from the others. He suspected he would go to Heaven and they would not.

He doesn't remember when exactly he lost his faith. It leaked away, like water from a cracked glass. There was no violent rupture. It was just one of those things. Since then, Norman has read Richard Dawkins. He no longer believes that the universe has a Creator. He no longer believes that there is a God, or even a god. Professor Dawkins has argued that simplicity is anterior to complexity, and that it is simpler to explain a universe without a God, than to explain a universe with one. As Norman reads these arguments, his face assumes that Normanish smile, as if only he and Professor Dawkins really understand how people could have been taken in by religious propaganda. All the same, from time to time, he remembers how Father Adrian taught them the words that were spoken to Moses from the burning bush: I AM THAT I AM. He hears these words sometimes in the back of his head.

So when Mary Constantine mentions the word stigmata, it brings an uneasy memory of how he had once truly believed that such marks could appear on the bodies of other human beings; of how he once believed that when Father Adrian said these marks were the product of divine intervention, he really thought that it might be so.

Now he knows these are psychosomatic phenomena. On the rare occasions when such marks can be proven not to be self-harm, they are the product of hysterical personalities.

His attention is distracted from these memories of bygone days by a noise. A man and a woman, both wearing tracksuit bottoms and short-sleeved sweatshirts, are walking along the pavement towards him in the spring sunshine. The woman is wheeling an infant's pushchair, which is full of shopping, and a very small child is tagging along behind them. Norman has to step off the pavement to let them past. The man is shaven-headed and has tattoos on his bare forearms. He is arguing with the woman and the child, upset by the angry voices, starts to grizzle.

'*Jesus Christ*,' says the shaven-headed man, turning on the small child with extraordinary violence – a son, a daughter, Norman can't tell – 'will you shut the *fuck* up!'

Norman Stokoe, children's czar, walks on.

Five

Geordie Nixon, clear-felling his block of trees. How many trees must he cut before he is finished? They are infinite; new trees grow as fast as he cuts down old ones. Beyond each tree that he grabs in his harvester's hydraulic pincers stands another tree, and beyond that another. He is always tired now. He was tired before Theo left, or was taken, but it was a good sort of tiredness that came at the end of the day. Now he is tired all the time, a heaviness that makes it hard for him to lift his limbs, hard to breathe.

Two nights ago, in the pub he uses in the small town where he and Mary live, he said to Stevie: 'Those pills you sold me. You want to watch those.'

'How do you mean?' asked Stevie. Stevie is a little worm of a man, a little mouse, and when you sit him alongside a well-made man like Geordie Nixon, he looks like a pixie. He's a lucky pixie though; everyone knows he's a dealer, but he's never been busted. Stevie is too canny to be busted. That's what Stevie thinks, that's what his customers think. It's not what the police think.

'Because of how I felt after taking them,' replied Geordie.

'It wasn't my fault,' said Stevie. 'It was a bad batch. I had a word with my supplier. You know what? He won't be doing *that* again in a hurry.'

'You're the guy who sold them to me,' Geordie told him, knowing there was something wrong, but not sure what it was.

'Sure,' said Stevie in a hurry. Geordie's not a man to be mucked around. 'And didn't I say I would make it up to you? Cash back or free replacement. The replacement pills are good stuff. I've tried them myself.'

'The pills worked all right,' said Geordie. 'They just worked too well, that's what I'm trying to tell you. They're too strong. You should cut that stuff with something. You'll kill someone. Driving the truck after I'd taken them, I could have crashed a dozen times.'

Stevie started to laugh.

'Oh, man,' he said. 'Cut them? They were one hundred per cent cut anyway. They were just filler. There was nothing in them.'

Now Geordie is alone in the forest. He won't be taking any pills, new or old. He doesn't want to feel like that again. But the problem is, he does feel like that again. He hasn't taken any pills but for some reason his heart is pounding and there is sweat on his forehead. The trees loom overhead. His hands are shaking too much to go on working. He switches off the harvester and sits quiet in the cab, the engine ticking as it cools down.

Since Theo went, Geordie has felt like death. Theo isn't his child. The father was a Mr Constantine. Mary doesn't talk about him. But Geordie's been able to gather that Mr Constantine entered her life and then left it again almost immediately: he was the briefest of interludes. He wasn't with Mary long enough for them to become engaged, let alone married, but Mary took his name after the rest of him had left. For the sake of the child, she said. For when he left Mary, he left her a gift. The gift became Theo.

Theo wasn't Geordie's child but ... there was something about Theo. Geordie doesn't know how stepfathers are meant to feel about their step-children, but he felt like this boy truly belonged to him and Mary. He sometimes asked himself if he loved Theo. The answer was: he didn't know what he felt for Theo, but it felt like love ought to feel, and sometimes it felt more like awe than love. The way that boy looked at you, thinks Geordie to himself as he sits in the cab, it got inside your head. And once Theo was inside your head, you couldn't get him out again.

He sits in the cab shivering and thinking about Theo – not thinking anything in particular, but seeing an image of the boy, his wide, dark eyes staring straight at Geordie.

The forest is silent. There is no wind today, the branches are not rustling. There are few birds amongst these dark trees and any that are here are quiet. Downhill from Geordie are the shattered trunks of trees, stumps, broken branches, and deep ruts where the harvester has been. It looks as if the ground has been pounded by heavy artillery. Beyond the devastation is the forest track and he can catch the glint of the windscreen of his big truck, where it is parked behind another thin belt of trees. The road he has driven up peters out into a track not far beyond where Geordie is working. The track winds through the trees. Once it too was a forest road, but the trees have grown up again and encroached upon it since the last felling. It is fifty years since that road was last used. It doesn't lead anywhere; there's a locked barrier across it further up to prevent vehicles going on and getting themselves stuck. The track probably ends in a bog somewhere, for all Geordie knows.

It is a sunny day. There is no wind. The forest is silent. Geordie gets a grip on his nerves and unscrews his Thermos flask and has a mug of lukewarm tea. His heart isn't pounding any more. He wipes his forehead dry. He begins to feel himself again: he doesn't know what got into him. Maybe he should see a doctor. He will ask Mary. Then he remembers that he and Mary don't talk that much any more.

The silence of the forest is like a stage as the curtain rises, before the actors come on. The sun shines too brightly, the birds don't sing.

Around a bend in the forest track, an old ewe appears. Behind her are two lambs trotting at her heels. Where can she have come from? wonders Geordie. Maybe at the far end of the track there is some pasture: rushy grass and old heather. Maybe some farmer has taken the grazing way up amongst the trees and has left the ewe and its lambs unattended. Or the animals have pushed their way through a slack wire fence and somehow found their way to the track. They are following the track down to where it becomes a graded road. They are out of sight, but Geordie can hear the bleat of a lamb. If they follow the forest road, no doubt in an hour or two they will come to the metalled road that leads down the valley. Unless someone else finds them first.

Out of the corner of his eye, Geordie sees movement. Beyond the bend in the track there's a disturbance in the bracken. At first, Geordie thinks it is the wind that is making the fronds bend, but there is no wind. Something is on the prowl. Then a big grey dog trots out of the bracken, sniffs the air and looks down the track towards where the ewe and her two lambs have just disappeared. A big grey dog: a long-legged, bushy-tailed grey dog with pricked up ears and a shaggy, streaky blond and grey coat. It sniffs the air again, then drops its head down to the trail and lopes along the track after the ewe and her two lambs. Geordie shouts, 'Hey!'

The cab window is closed and the grey dog can't hear him.

If it could hear him, it doesn't look like the kind of animal that would take much notice of Geordie shouting 'Hey'. It trots down the track with a peculiar stiff-legged gait and is soon around the next bend and out of sight. Geordie fires up the engine of the harvester. It jerks and bumps down the hillside through the clear fell, until he is on the track. He turns down the track and drives as fast as he can, with painful slowness, until he has reached the truck. He switches off the engine of the harvester and looks about him. No grey dog. He climbs out of the cab and locks it up, then swings himself up into the truck. It is already facing downhill. He starts the truck engine. He drives down the forest road, looking for the grey dog, expecting to see strands of wool, rent flesh lying beside the track, pools of dark blood with flies clustering over them. He sees none of these things. There is no grey dog. There is no ewe. There are no lambs. After a while the truck comes to the metalled road. Geordie stops.

Did he imagine the whole thing? He couldn't have. There was the ewe with two lambs. He saw them. He heard them. Then there was the big grey dog. He doesn't want to say the word that comes into his mind to describe the dog. He sits in the truck and his face is the colour of the moon.

It is only one o'clock in the afternoon, but Geordie points his truck down the valley and heads home.

Six

Willie Craig: twenty-seven years old, youngest of three. One brother in the army has been guarding a barracks in Dorset for the last few years. Another brother is processing benefits claims in the DHSS in Newcastle. His mam and dad are still alive, but not so as you'd notice. Willie's the black sheep in a flock of grey. His career has gone backwards, sideways, every direction except forwards. He's not stupid, he just does stupid things.

Six GCSEs and a level four NVQ in journalism prove that he has a brain, not that he uses it much. At school he was noted for his idleness. The truth is, he used to fool around a lot. He didn't take anything too seriously and nobody took him seriously either. For four years after leaving school he never had a regular job. He partied hard and was in the habit of rolling home at four in the morning, dead drunk. His parents didn't appreciate it. They weren't well-off and to them it was an offence that someone with Willie's education and brains couldn't be bothered to work and continued to live off them.

Then Willie got a grip on himself and managed to land a job as a junior reporter for a local paper. If he's honest about the job, on a good day it's a dead end. On a bad day, it's an unspeakable torment. The boredom kills him. At the end of the month there's a salary that puts him firmly in the ranks of the lower-paid. It's better than being unemployed, but not by much. This last year or so he's begun to feel the itch. The itch is called ambition. He tastes it in his mouth, he feels it in his blood, but he doesn't know what to do about it. All he knows is that there must be more to life than this.

Willie Craig: journalist, destined to work on a national paper – some day. Just now he works for a local weekly: *The Northumbrian Herald*. He wants to be a columnist for the *Sun*. Or else he wants to be an investigative journalist for the *Sunday Times*. He wants to be able to take his pick. That's in the future – he hopes. What is certain is that, by this afternoon, he has to turn in five hundred words on the new five-year plan for a town in the Tyne valley. Headline: *New Town Plan for Hexham*. The sub: *Town to Remain Much the Same*.

That's the nice thing about rural Northumberland. Nothing much happens, most of the time. A few hundred years ago, he could have written: 'Scots Invade – Yet Again.' A couple of hundred years ago, he could have written, 'North East Man Boils Water, Produces Steam, Says it Could be Used to Power Public Transport.'

But, for the moment, it's local town planning that gets the headlines. He did have a sniff of a story the other week. The disappearance of Becky Thomas was well covered by the nationals, for a day or two. What nobody else picked up on was the existence of a children's czar, living in Hexham and working on Tyneside. Working at what? Willie Craig rang the guy and he didn't even seem to know that the little girl had gone missing. Children's czar: what does that mean? Willie thinks it would be interesting to find out. He rings a few people he knows in Social Services and the police. Nobody has ever heard of a children's czar, except for one man who says: 'The idea was mooted, but I didn't think it had ever got off the ground.'

Mooted? Mooted? That's how these people talk, thinks Willie. But maybe there *is* a story here: a Fat Cat sitting in an office doing nothing. He sounded like a Fat Cat when Willie rang him for a comment on Becky Thomas, which he didn't get. He likes the idea of an article with a headline that reads: 'Fat Cat Children's Czar: You Pay His Salary – What Does He Do for You?'

He takes the idea to Mr Naylor, his editor. Mr Naylor tells him he wants a piece on a new shopping arcade in Morpeth and how it's doing in the recession. He tells Willie not to waste his time worrying about children's czars.

Willie Craig: tall, thin, in need of spectacles; his long, brown hair is brushed across his forehead and falls into his eyes when he gets excited about something. Willie Craig: badly dressed in an old waxed jacket in the winter, worn over a brown pinstripe suit long past the first flush of youth. In the brief Northumbrian summers he wears a black T-shirt and jeans, with the suit jacket over the T-shirt, because he thinks it makes him look more respectable. It doesn't. Willie Craig: desperate to get the hell out of there and work on a proper newspaper. He can write. He can investigate. People seem happy to talk to him when he asks them questions. So why is he writing articles about shopping arcades?

Willie went into journalism because he thought one day he might write a story, the kind that changes people's lives, that people remember for ever after. He doesn't know what the story will be about, or whether he will ever find it, but he's not going to stop looking. It's what drives him on; what helps him to survive the tedium of his present existence.

Willie spends his morning visiting the shopping arcade.

When he returns to his desk, he bangs out a few hundred words and emails the article to his editor. Then he logs onto the server where the archives are kept: thousands of articles about shopping arcades and sheep being worried by stray dogs and all of the small histories of local life. Wille can only be thankful it wasn't his job to scan all this stuff when the newspaper went digital.

Just reading through the back issues is hard work.

He's trying to find out if this children's czar ever does anything, or ever says anything on the public record. He doesn't find anything about the children's czar. What he finds is a story from a few months back: 'Tynedale Runaway Still Not Found – Case Remains Open, Say Police.'

He reads the story and takes some notes. Theo Constantine, aged ten, disappeared.

'He only went to the library,' said distraught mother Mary. 'He went every week to get a new book out. He loved reading.' A police spokesman said they were treating the case as a runaway, but declined to give further details.

A missing child, a runaway child – or an abducted child? Willie Craig searches backwards and forwards through the archive, but finds nothing else. He checks the date: just before Christmas. A child goes missing just before Christmas – a boy. A child goes missing just before Easter – a girl.

Is there a connection? If there is, nobody has suggested it in print, not as far as Willie can see. Or maybe the police have made the connection, only they aren't saying. Willie thinks for a moment. Two missing children who live within twenty miles of each other: it could be a coincidence. Both about the same age, both vanished without a trace. It could be a coincidence, but supposing it isn't? And now there is a children's czar, sitting in his office in Newcastle and doing nothing about it.

Willie goes in search of his editor. His editor is sitting behind his large desk in his glass cubicle with the classified sales manager, haranguing him. Willie decides not to interrupt. He goes back to his desk, pulls out a phone directory and looks under 'C'. There's only one Constantine in the town he's interested in.

He dials the number. A woman's voice answers: 'Hello?'

'Mrs Constantine? It's Willie Craig, from *The Northumbrian Herald*. Can I come and talk to you?'

Willie explains his interest. The woman sounds doubtful, even a little hostile. Willie can tell she's about to hang up on him, so he says quickly: 'It would only be for five minutes. And it might mean fresh publicity to help find Theo.'

Then he's out of the office, before his editor can ring through to tell him to attend the opening of a new hairdressing salon. He takes the pool car and drives to the small town where Mrs Constantine lives. He finds the street. He finds the flat. A good-looking woman with a sad face opens the door.

'Mrs Constantine?' asks Willie.

She lets him into the flat. Willie looks around. There is a fair-sized living room, with doors opening off to a couple of bedrooms, and a bathroom and kitchen. In the living room is a big forty-inch television and a DVD player, and a laptop computer on an otherwise bare desk. There's a leather sofa and a matching leather armchair. A crucifix is hanging on the wall. Willie notices it because it is unusual. It's where most people Willie knows would have pinned up Newcastle United colours. In his own flat he's got a shirt signed by Alan Shearer pinned to the wall as decoration. No crucifixes. Willie recognises the leather furniture from the television ads – bought on hire purchase, nothing to pay for six months and then, watch out. The only other furniture in the room is a low coffee table covered in ring-marks. There are two photograph frames on the mantelpiece. Willie asks if he can take a look. Without waiting for an answer, he picks up the first. It is a picture of a tall, square-shouldered, black-haired man in a check shirt and jeans, holding a chainsaw and looking at the camera unsmiling. A good, tough face, thinks Willie.

'My partner,' explains Mary. Willie picks up the other photo. It is the very one Mary showed to Norman Stokoe, stuck back in its frame. Willie looks at it. He puts it down. Then he picks it up and examines it again for a full minute. He doesn't know what to say, but he knows she is expecting him to say something.

'Interesting face,' he says after a moment. 'Interesting' is the wrong word. There's something about it – he can't quite say what. He turns to Mrs C. 'Do you want to tell me what happened, if you can?'

Mary tells him the same story she told Norman Stokoe.

'And the police think Theo ran away because you were abusing him?' asks Willie. He doesn't pull his punches. He's found that most people prefer straight talking.

'Yes,' says Mary. 'It's the easy way out for them. One of the policemen told me that, on average, a child goes missing somewhere in the United Kingdom every five minutes. It was his way of saying they weren't going to get too excited about Theo.'

A child goes missing every five minutes! Willie writes it down. That's a good quote. He needs to find out where it comes from. Even if it is only half right, it's quite a statistic.

'And that's it? That's everything?'

'As far as the police are concerned. All they will say is that the case is still open.'

'Must be a nightmare for you,' says Willie sympathetically. 'Is there nobody else you can go to, Mrs Constantine?'

'I did go to somebody else,' says Mary. 'A man called Norman Stokoe.'

'The children's czar?'

'You know him, do you?'

'I spoke to him on the phone for two minutes. I've never met him. What did you think of him?'

'A waste of space.'

Willie can't think of any more questions. He stands up to go. It's one of his tricks. People tend to spill things they didn't mean to when the notebook has been put away and the interview appears to be over. It works again this time. Mary puts out her hand, doesn't quite touch him on the arm, says: 'You said something about new publicity.'

'Yes ... well. You link this story to the story of the other missing child ...'

'*What other missing child?*'

It's unbelievable. She hasn't seen the stories about Becky Thomas. She doesn't watch television any more; she hardly ever reads the papers; she hardly goes out except to work. Willie realises he's talking to someone who is well into a world-class depression. The sort of person who might end up taking her own life if someone doesn't drag her out of this. He tells her what he knows. He is amazed by the change in Mary – it's like Pinocchio coming to life, something wooden and puppet-like in its movements suddenly becoming fluid and animated. She listens. She is rapt. Her gaze transfixes him.

'You think there's a connection?'

'*I* don't think anything. I wonder what the police think, though. I wonder what the children's czar thinks. Or whether he'll ever do anything about it.'

52

'You'll print this story? About the little girl and our Theo both going missing. Will you?'

'Well,' says Willie awkwardly. 'That's up to my editor. But it's a hell of a story.'

She withdraws and the light goes out of her eyes again. Woodenly, she nods goodbye. Woodenly, she shuts the door in his face as he turns back, trying to think of a last, encouraging word to leave with her.

Back at the office, Willie does a mental stock-take: has he got enough to sell this to his editor and get his approval to work on the story? And what, exactly, is the story that he wants to write? That Willie has noticed something the police have overlooked? How unlikely is that? Or is the story going to be some kind of conspiracy theory? But who is conspiring to do what, and why? Why would anyone conceal a link between two missing children, if such a link exists? No, when it boils down to it, all he's got is a connection – that only exists in his own mind – between two missing children. And then there's the children's czar: the Fat Cat sitting in his office, ignoring it all.

The children's czar might be worth another call.

'Mr Stokoe, we now know that *two* young children have gone missing from the same area in the last four months. What is your office doing about it?'

The children's czar might complain to his editor. Then Willie Craig would be history. Plenty of people out there are waiting to fill his shoes: unemployed graduates of nameless universities with pass degrees in journalism or media studies, circling like sharks, looking for the first few drops of blood.

There has to be a story in there somewhere, though. Quite frankly, thinks Willie Craig, if he has to write one more brain-deadening hairdresser-salon-opens-in-North-Shields story, he might as well be history.

He knows the police won't give him the time of day. They will be on the phone to his editor for sure. No, if he wants a story, the best chance of getting one is with the children's czar. He's only been in the job a while. He might give something away. He might even help Willie. You never know.

Seven

Karen Gilby, aged nine, is dark-haired with a plump and smiley face. Karen lives in a village not far from Newcastle. It's a small village, with a primary school and a village hall and a chapel and a church. There are a few rows of red brick council houses and then a street of stone farm-workers' cottages which no longer house farm workers, but people who live in the village and work elsewhere. These houses all have porches, glass conservatories and pretty gardens full of pampas grass and cherry trees and sundials and stone bird baths. There's a pub, too, which offers twice-baked cheese soufflés and interesting New World wines on its list. It's a village of the old and the new. The newcomers live in the older houses and the original inhabitants live in the newer brick houses put up for them by the council in the 1950s.

That's where Karen Gilby lives and goes to school. Her father works in an office somewhere. Her mother stays at home and looks after Karen.

Today the new mobile library comes to the village, not the old County Council yellow bus, but a new blue van with white letters on the side spelling out 'B-O-O-K-W-I-S-E'. The new van has all the newest books and all the old favourites too. The yellow bus has books for grown-ups and just a few for children. The blue van *only* has children's books. And its driver knows that it is half-term, and his customers will be at home, not at school.

Last week, Karen's mum asked the van driver to keep a copy of *The Lion, the Witch and the Wardrobe* for Karen to read the next time he came. And now Karen is old enough to go to the mobile library on her own. It's only a few hundred yards from her home.

Karen Gilby, who loves kittens and hates maths, crosses the road. Looks right, looks left, looks right again. Now Karen is crossing the road to the lay-by where the bus always stops. She has her library card with her. It is a special library card and it says:

BOOKWISE.
Private Mobile Library Specialising in Children's Books.
Valid for two books at a time.

Underneath, there is a dotted line and a space where Karen has written her name and her mum has written the address. Now Karen is at the lay-by, waiting for the blue van to come. She is worried that someone else will get there first, and take out the book before she can, so she has formed a queue of one.

In the distance she hears the sound of an approaching vehicle. It must be the book van; it's the right time, she checked on the kitchen clock before she came out. The blue van has a chime, like the chime of an ice-cream van. As it approaches the village, the driver sounds the chime and in half a dozen houses children hear it and begin to make their way out onto the street. But Karen is already there.

The blue bus pulls up in the lay-by and, after a moment, the driver gets out, nods to Karen, and opens the doors at the back. A set of aluminium steps are unfolded to provide a staircase into the treasure chamber of books that line the inside of the van. A familiar face smiles at her. A familiar voice says, 'Good afternoon. You're here in good time. It's Karen, isn't it?'

'Yes,' says Karen. She has a slight lisp. She is wearing a brace on her front teeth.

'Are you alone, Karen?' asks the familiar voice. 'Is your mummy not coming today?'

'She said I could come and get the book on my own,' answers Karen.

'Well, hop inside and we'll look for your book together,' says the familiar voice. 'It was *The Lion, the Witch and the Wardrobe* that you wanted, wasn't it? Now I think I've got a copy right in the back here.'

Karen hops up the steps as she is told. The owner of the familiar voice puts a friendly hand on her shoulder. Just then another person speaks: 'Oh, good afternoon. I wonder if you've got that copy of *The Gruffalo* for my Helen?'

The friendly hand drops from Karen's shoulder. The familiar voice says, 'I believe I have, Mrs Hudson.'

Eight

It is morning.

Norman Stokoe inspects himself in the mirror in the bathroom of his new flat. He pats his freshly shaven cheeks with Eau de Portugal. He massages Ojon Hair Cream into his thinning hair and combs it until it lies down flat and sleek. He buttons up his collar (noting with concern that the laundry must have shrunk his shirt: his collar seems a little tight, the way his neck bulges over it) and knots his silk tie. Today it's a pale-blue one that looks good against the cream of his button-down shirt. And now Norman is ready to face the day. He slips on his suit jacket and dusts a few specks of dandruff from the shoulders. He studies his front view again in the mirror. He turns and studies his side view. All is well. He is suited and armoured against the cares and stresses of the day.

Today he is attending a regional sub-group meeting of the Safeguarding Adviser Network. He has been co-opted. He noticed when the agenda for the meeting was circulated, that he is described in the circulation list as 'Regional Children's Commissioner (Designate)' and the word 'designate' irritates him. But at least he is attending meetings. He doesn't have to say anything; no actions are ever minuted against his name, but he's there. People will see he is there. People know that one day soon he will be chairing meetings of his own. So they are polite to him; they are careful around him.

Sometimes Norman does indeed speak at these meetings, which are about Safeguarding (the current word for protecting vulnerable children). When he does so, he is brief, yet measured. He speaks only to agree with the last speaker, but he manages to do it in a way that suggests his own vast experience on the subject. He manages to do it in a way that suggests he is the opening batsman for the England cricket team who has found himself at net practice with a village eleven. When he speaks at these meetings and when he does not speak, he allows an amused smile to play about his lips from time to time, as if he is deriving interior enjoyment from the simple innocence of the other people around the table.

Norman crosses the atrium, sees his PA standing talking to the receptionist just outside the entrance to his own office suite, but is too far away to hear Pippa saying to the girl: 'Watch out, Fatty's about.'

He gives her his plastic smile and asks her to fetch him a double espresso from the atrium coffee shop. He starts his days with espresso; latte comes later.

She says with an air of casual unconcern that infuriates him: 'There's a gentleman from the press waiting in your office.'

Norman doesn't let his fury show. In his mind he starts composing the email he will send her later, reminding her in tones dripping with sarcasm that she is meant to keep people *out* of his office unless he tells her otherwise.

He manages to keep his smile in place. It might be someone wanting to do a profile of him: he enjoys talking about himself. He enters his office. The man sitting in the chair opposite his desk stands up as Norman enters the room, then sits down again. The man doesn't look like he writes many profiles. He looks as if he is six months out of school, and he is wearing the worst-cut suit that Norman has ever seen. Before Norman can speak, the man leans across the desk and holds out his hand saying:

'We've never met, but I spoke to you on the phone a week or two back. My name's Willie Craig, from *The Northumbria Herald*.'

'Good morning, good morning,' says Norman affably, ignoring the proffered hand and easing himself into his leather armchair.

'I'm sorry to drop in on you like this, without any warning. I hope you don't mind. I wondered if you had a few minutes to sketch out the work of the Children's Czar in the North East, for the benefit of our readers?' asks Willie politely. Norman decides Willie isn't quite as young as he first thought, and not quite as dumb as he looks. He steeples his fingers on the inlaid leather desktop in front of him and begins to talk. 'Children's Czar isn't really the proper job title. I'm actually the Regional Children's Commissioner.'

'I know our readers would love to hear more about the role. It's new, isn't it?'

'Very new,' says Norman. For a moment or two, he talks about the job, and how he will soon report directly to the secretary of state. Willie lets him ramble on. He takes out his pad and pretends to take a couple of notes. Then he asks in the same polite voice, 'So will you be taking an official interest in the cases of these two missing children?'

'What missing children?' asks Norman, 'Oh, you mean Becky Thomas?' Now he remembers the phone call: a rather impertinent young man, he decided at the time, and probably the same person who is interviewing him now. 'I'm not aware of a second case.'

'Theo Constantine is the other missing child.'

'The Constantine case was classified as just a runaway.'

Just a runaway, thinks Willie. In the United Kingdom, one child disappears every five minutes.

'Don't you think it's odd that two children have disappeared from the same area?' he asks the Children's Czar.

'You think that the two cases are connected?' replies Norman. 'Why is that?'

Willie notices how all of a sudden it is Norman who is controlling the interview and asking the questions. He decides Norman is a slippery fish.

'I'm just speculating,' suggests Willie. 'It seems like an odd coincidence. Two cases, twenty miles apart.'

'Well,' says Norman, 'you can speculate as much as you like. That's what journalists are paid to do, I suppose. My job is not concerned with speculation.'

'That's what I was coming to,' says Willie. 'What exactly *is* your job?'

'Coordination, liaison, strategic direction,' says Norman. 'Any more questions? You didn't make an appointment, Mr ... Mr ...'

'Craig,' Willie reminds him.

'You didn't make an appointment, Mr Craig, and I've a busy morning ahead of me.'

Willie has already checked with the PA when he arrived, who said loyally: 'Oh, he's free as the air this morning. I think he has one meeting this afternoon. He's nearly always free.'

So Willie doesn't stand up to go. Instead, he crosses his legs, jiggling his right shoe up and down, and asks: 'So the fact that two children have gone missing in your region in the last four months isn't of any particular concern to you?'

Norman says: 'As a private individual, as a human being, I am very concerned. But cases such as these are a job for the police. My input is strategic rather than operational. Now I really have to bring this interview to a close, Mr Craig.'

Willie Craig gets to his feet. He can't believe this guy. What is a children's czar for, if not to look after children? 'My input is strategic, rather than operational.' He can use that quote. He puts out his hand again and Norman responds this time with a moist handshake. Willie tries another 'end-of-interview' trick, spiced with a sharp dig. He remarks: 'Well, you are handling your anxiety for these children very well, Mr Stokoe. I'm sure if I was in your position, I wouldn't be as calm as you are.'

Norman withdraws his hand. He stares fish-eyed at Willie. Too late, he understands. This is to be a hatchet job. He can read Willie's mind. He can almost read the piece Willie is going to write.

'Goodbye, Mr Craig,' he says in a cold voice.

At the reception desk, Willie winks at the PA. 'I'll be back,' he says in a good imitation of The Terminator's voice. She's a good-looking girl and she gives him a nice smile. Outside, the temporary lift from this flirtation deserts him. What has he got from this interview? Nothing. One quote, but where's the story? He needs more.

Willie finds a pub on Newcastle's quayside that is already open – and busy – in the morning sunshine. He sits outside at a table with a view of the river, and drinks a bottle of lager from the neck. What he needs is a story. Norman Stokoe is definitely working his ticket. He's sitting there drinking his espresso, doing nothing and collecting a fat salary. When the PA brought in Norman's espresso, Willie noticed two things. The first was that nobody offered *him* coffee. The second was that Norman took some change from the girl and a receipt, and he put the receipt in the drawer. He's sitting in his office, doing nothing, and claiming his coffee back on expenses, thought Willie. But that's not a story, it's just a bit of colour. Willie drinks some more lager and the chill liquid must be giving him inspiration because he suddenly thinks, What about Mrs C? Was she telling me the truth?

He remembers her telling him about the bruises on the child. Could that be the story? Perhaps she *is* a child abuser, and perhaps the child did run away. Willie pulls out his mobile and rings an old school friend who now works for the police. After a bit of banter, Willie asks: 'Any way you can get me copies of the photos of the Constantine boy who disappeared? You're treating it as a runaway, apparently.'

'Who?' asks the old school friend. Willie explains. The school friend says he'll call back in five. Willie finishes the lager, thinks about a second bottle and decides against it. The mobile on his table rings. He puts it to his ear.

'No fucking way,' says his old school friend. But he doesn't hang up. Willie thinks fast. How badly does he want a story? Badly. He says: 'I've got a ticket for the football on Monday night.'

'It's a big ask.'

'So's a free ticket to St James's Park.'

They agree to meet the following day, when the old school friend will give him five minutes with the photos of Theo Constantine and Willie will hand over his ticket to the game.

Willie parks his private project at the back of his mind and goes back to the office. Mr Naylor pops out of his glass-walled lair as Willie walks past.

'Where have you been?' asks Mr Naylor. 'I was looking for you.'

'Just checking a couple of things for that story,' replies Willie, hoping that Mr Naylor won't ask what things he was checking for which story. For a moment he fears he hasn't got away with it, as Mr Naylor lowers his spectacles and peers over the top of them with a look that can only be described as cold. Then he says: 'I want you to go to Temple First School this afternoon. The children in the second year are putting on a play. I want a couple of hundred words on it, and a photo if you can get one. The headmistress is expecting you.'

Willie knows better than to ask why the readers of *The Northumbria Herald* would want to read about a play staged by tiny tots. He knows without asking that one of the paper's major advertisers will have a son, or a daughter, in that class. He sighs. 'Yes, Mr Naylor.'

'It won't bore you, I hope?' asks his editor.

'No, not at all.'

'And you're not too tired after your recent exertions, whatever they were?'

'I'm raring to go,' replies Willie. Mr Naylor disappears again, like a genie back into its lamp, and Willie goes off on his new mission, after arranging to meet Nick the photographer at the school gates. Never work with children or animals, that's my motto, he tells himself.

At the Temple First School, the headmistress greets them and takes them along to a classroom full of small, giggling children. Stuck to the wall are pictures of Easter lambs, white cut-out figures gambolling across a green cut-out field against a blue cut-out sky, left over from last term.

'We would like to have done an Easter play,' explains the headmistress, 'but some of the parents objected to the religious theme. So instead, this term we're doing a play about a little girl who wins a talent contest and becomes a pop star.'

The little girl will be why he is here, thinks Willie. The little girl will be the daughter of a local car dealer, or whomever Mr Naylor is courting for business at present.

'That sounds like fun,' he says. He asks questions, takes notes. Nick the photographer snaps a few pictures; Willie makes sure they are mostly of the little girl whose father sells cars. When they are done, Nick says: 'Fancy a quick half before we go back to the office?'

Willie is about to say yes when a thought strikes him.

'Next time,' he says. 'You go on, anyway. There's something I need to do here.'

Nick leaves and Willie goes back into the school to look for the headmistress. She's in her office and seems surprised to see him return.

'Yes?'

'Did a boy called Theo Constantine attend this school?'

'Theo? Poor Theo? Yes, he did.'

'What was he like?'

'Excuse me, but what's this about?'

Willie thinks for a second. Then he smiles and says: 'It's in connection with another story we're thinking of doing: about missing children.'

'I don't want the school brought into this,' says the head-mistress. She is not smiling any more.

'It won't be. This is just background. And I'm interested anyway.'

The headmistress relents a little. She says: 'Theo was a spe-cial boy. He wasn't particularly good at games, or especially bright, I don't think. But everyone liked to be with him.'

'Why? Did he tell jokes? What was it, particularly?'

The headmistress looks perplexed.

'I don't know. It was just how he was. He made people smile. He seemed to exert an influence over the other children. They were calmer and happier when he was around. It was a most extraordinary thing.'

The headmistress seems to feel she has said more than she intended to, and stops speaking.

'Is he missed?' asks Willie.

'We all miss him very much,' replies the headmistress. 'The children were devastated when he went.'

The next morning, Willie and the old school friend meet up. The old school friend is nervous. He's behaving as if he's about to hand over the design specifications of a nuclear weapon to the Iranian ambassador. He looks over his shoulder. He pretends not to see Willie. Then he pretends to see him. He pretends to be very surprised. They sit down at a table outside the pub they have chosen. The old school friend slides a flat envelope across the table with the nuclear weapon information and Willie slides across his ticket to the Newcastle United game.

'Be quick,' says the old school friend in a nervous voice. 'There'll be hell to pay if anyone sees us.'

Willie takes his time, looks at the photos one by one. They were taken in a well-lit room with walls painted white: a doctor's surgery? The photos are very clear. There are close-ups of the right and left hands. A dark-blue bruise, roughly circular, shading to deep red at the centre, presents itself on each palm. There are photos of the ankles. A dark-blue bruise, roughly circular and shading to red at the centre, presents, itself just where the foot joins the ankle. Bruises? Willie supposes they must be, although they don't look like the bruises you would expect if, for example, someone had kicked the boy on the shins. He can't think how these marks have been caused.

A fifth photo: the head and shoulders of the boy, the dark

hair and the calm, handsome face. Willie remembers them with a strange sense of familiarity, as if he has been staring into the boy's eyes inside his mind ever since he saw Mrs C's photograph of him. More marks: a series of lacerations in a bracelet shape across the forehead that looks as if it continues under the boy's hair.

'What on earth made those marks?' asks Willie. He hands back four of the photos but keeps the fifth.

'His mum beat him up. His stepfather beat him up: one or the other. That's why the boy ran away, isn't it? What do I care? It's not my case. Now give me the other photo. I need to get back.'

Willie stands up. He puts the fifth photo, the picture of the boy's face with that strange series of welts and lacerations across his forehead, in the inside pocket of his suit.

'I'll hang onto this for now. You'll get it back later.'

'Give me the fucking photo,' hisses his old school friend. Willie walks away.

Nine

Geordie is back home early. The flat is silent. He wonders if Mary is asleep in the boy's room, but there is nobody else in the flat. She is out somewhere. She must be at work. She works odd hours. Or maybe she is shopping: there's no food in the house. Geordie sits at the kitchen table, clutching a mug of cold tea, and wonders what is happening to his life. Four months ago he would have said things were as good as they were ever going to get. He had Mary; they had Theo, and if Theo wasn't his own child it never seemed to matter. He never thought about Theo in that way at all. He was a strange child, but Geordie liked having him around. Liked was the wrong word. While Theo was around, Geordie didn't realise what a terrible place the world is and what a useless life he led. It is only since Theo went, that Geordie started having these thoughts. Now he has them all the time.

When Theo was around, Geordie had Mary and they all had each other; they were a family. Geordie had a job. It was a hard job, but he was independent and he could work when and where he liked. Life was not perfect, but it was better than Geordie could ever remember.

But after two years of living together, not married, but as close as two people can be, Geordie realises he still knows so little about Mary. When he met her at a party, the attraction between them was sudden: he felt like an iron filing being pulled towards a magnet. That's how Geordie remembers his first meeting with Mary – it was as if he had no say in the matter. He saw her. She was standing talking to another girl, whom Geordie knew well enough to speak to. The other girl was called Frieda Robinson. She wasn't a particularly attractive girl, unlike her companion, but Geordie saw his chance and went up to Frieda and greeted her and at the same time smiled at Mary so that Frieda would have to introduce them. He looked into Mary's eyes as they shook hands. Her touch was cool, and firm. And that was more or less it. In a minute he had put himself between the two girls, with his back to Frieda, and was talking to Mary. Not very polite, but there you were.

He remembers talking to her the next time, in a crowd of people all having drinks together at Jimmy's house. Not a party exactly, a social gathering. Jimmy was just having a few friends in as a change from going to the pub, taking advantage of that week's special offer at the supermarket on premium lagers and New Zealand Sauvignons. That was how Jimmy MacDonald liked to do things. He'd call up a few friends at the last moment and ask them over. He asked Geordie because they had been at school together. Just a couple of dozen of Jimmy's mates there in the house, including Geordie, and a few wives and girlfriends.

And Mary. Geordie remembers feeling as if someone had stabbed him when she turned and talked to someone else, as if he couldn't believe she wasn't feeling what he was feeling.

He remembers the first time he called at her flat, to take her out on their first date. Mary presented Theo to him and the two of them shook hands. He remembers the sensation – like a mild electric shock – as he took the boy's hand in his for the first time. Later that evening Mary told him, 'If you want me, you have to have Theo as well.' He's never regretted what he did next, which was to take her in his arms and kiss her.

What did Mary feel for him then? At times he was bewildered by her passion. It was more than he had a right to expect. She clung to him as if he had rescued her from something unguessable and terrifying. He didn't know if she loved him or not. She was grateful for the affection he showed her child. It's not every man who can cope with someone else's offspring, but Theo didn't diminish their relationship. He added to it. Sometimes Geordie didn't know whether the best thing about Mary was that she had brought Theo into his life. They weren't just a couple. They were an instant family.

She was beautiful then: dark hair, dark eyes, a clear complexion, a stunning figure. That was before Theo went. Now her face looks half-dead. Now her skin is tired and pale. Her eyes have dark rings underneath them. Her hair, which was so smooth and shiny, has become flat and dull. In the bathroom he sees clumps of it tangled in the hairbrush. It's falling out. He wonders if she is slowly dying.

He doesn't know who Theo's father is: the guy with the Greek name. He gets the impression it wasn't anything more than a one-night stand. Mary doesn't talk about it. He respects her for that. All the same, from the things she *doesn't* say, it seems to him that the guy with the Greek name came and went. Went without ever knowing his son, presumably without ever even knowing that he had a son. More fool him.

Geordie believes that the first two years with Mary, before Theo vanished, were the happiest of his life. He never expected to be so happy before he met her. He never expected to be able to tell his friends in the pub that he had to be going home now: 'Wor lass will be cooking me tea,' he would say, and how pleasant those words sounded in his own ears. He had a lass. His lass had a child, and yes, he loves them both. He loved them both.

He almost wishes he had never known what that happiness was like, because if he hadn't, he wouldn't miss it so much. It's like a spear in his side when he thinks of it.

Now they have a non-life together. They have their non-conversations, they exist in the same building, the same space, but that's it. He doesn't know when, or why, it will ever get better. He only knows that he cannot leave her. He's decided to stick around. He's decided he's in it for the duration. He's in it for better or for worse; for worse or for worst.

Geordie drives to the forest to start another day amongst the trees. Another day alone: another day thinking about the pointlessness of what he does. Another day of realising that this existence is all he knows. What else can he do? All his life he's knocked in fence posts, tightened strainers, tidied up stone walls. All his life he's planted trees, weeded the plantations, beat them up, thinned them and then cut them down again when they've grown to maturity. That's the sum of his abilities and his knowledge. He doesn't know any other kind of work, doesn't think he could ever learn to do anything else, doesn't in his heart believe that he could ever be employed by anybody. His fate is to spend his life amongst dark trees. Once he accepted that. Now he hates it. Now Theo isn't there any more. When he went, it was like a silent earthquake. The ground between him and Mary cracked, then widened into a chasm. He doesn't know why it has to be like that. Surely she wants to be comforted; surely she must see that their love for each other is their only hope of salvation. But Mary doesn't see it like that. She's still there; but she's not his. She barely speaks to him or to anyone else.

He's kept on working throughout, but now his job weighs on him. It crushes him. He cuts a tree down; another one grows. He cuts down dozens of trees every week. When he's not cutting down trees, he is planting them – the planting season has just ended – but it's the same. It's pointless. He looks into Kielder Forest and he knows its infinite monotony, the vastness of it, will bury him one day.

And now his nerves are going. Did he see that ewe? Did he see those lambs? Did he see that grey dog? And something else has been troubling him, but he can't remember what. He can't stand being on his own any more. He's on his own in the trees and he's on his own when he comes home. He needs to see a doctor. He needs to talk to someone.

He sits at the table with his untouched mug of cold tea. He remembers the day after Theo was taken as if it were yesterday. He knows someone has taken Theo. Mary knows it too. The police don't agree. They have their own theory. The boy's face and body showed bruises on not one occasion but several: angry bruises on his hands and feet, other marks of severe trauma. The police interviewed Theo's teachers at the school. They interviewed the GP who examined Theo after the bruising was first observed. They looked at the photos that the GP took. They interviewed Mary and Geordie, again and again. The interviewing officer, a detective sergeant, was very persistent. He sat in this kitchen, in the chair opposite where Geordie is sitting now, and he asked: 'Did you cause these bruises on Theo's face and body, Mr Nixon?'

'Of course not.'

'You're his stepfather, aren't you? Don't you get on with him?'

'I am very fond of him,' says Geordie. The sergeant writes something with painful slowness in his notebook, and then looks up and asks: 'Has Theo ever run away from home before?'

Before Geordie can answer, Mary answers – Mary almost screams at the sergeant: 'He hasn't run away. Someone's taken him. Why can't you understand that? Why aren't you out looking for him?'

'Oh, we're looking for him, Mrs Constantine. Don't worry. We are looking for him. We just want to have a better understanding of the circumstances in which he left you.'

'He didn't *leave* us,' says Geordie. 'Someone *took* him.'

The police knew better. Theo was a runaway: 'He'll probably turn up in London, sir. That's where these runaways usually head for.'

They suggested to Geordie and Mary that they should contact the Missing Persons Helpline and the NSPCC. Geordie and Mary went to the press. For a couple of days they got some airtime on BBC *Look North* and other local television shows. They got a few column inches on the front page of the regional papers: for one edition only. Then another story bumped Theo off the front page to an inside page, and soon after the story died.

It was Christmas, after all. People didn't want to read about missing children; they wanted good news in their local paper at that time of the year. They wanted pictures of snow falling; of sprigs of holly; of a golden glazed turkey just out of the oven; of mince pies dusted with sugar. They didn't want to worry about parents who couldn't keep hold of their children. Mary rang the editor and complained that the story had been dropped. She asked for more publicity. The editor said: 'Tell you what, I'll diary it. If he hasn't come back in a year's time, we'll run an anniversary special on him. I can't say fairer than that.'

Geordie and Mary didn't know what to do. They arranged to have some leaflets printed, using an old photo of Theo. They went to the main shopping centres on Tyneside and handed them out to passers-by. Most people ignored them. A few took a leaflet, glanced at the photo on the front as they walked away. Their glance lingered on the photo, but not for very long. On the way back to the car park, Geordie and Mary saw their leaflets lying on the ground, blowing this way and that in the wind. Dozens of discarded leaflets:

Have You Seen This Boy?

Nobody had. A social worker called to interview Geordie about the bruising on Theo's hands, feet and forehead. She was a small, thin person wearing a tweed jacket and skirt with thick-green tights and carrying a large leather bag. She wore spectacles. When she came into Geordie and Mary's flat, she looked around with distaste, as if she could already see evidence in the sparsely furnished room to confirm her unfavourable judgement of Theo's parents. She sat down on the leather sofa without being invited to and pulled out a file from her leather bag. She read the case notes to remind herself of the situation she was examining, then she got up and asked Mary to show her the bathroom. But she didn't use it. Instead she examined the door handle.

'What are you looking for?' Mary asked, in bewilderment.

'The bathroom is a typical place of refuge for a frightened child. It's usually the only room with a door that can be locked. We look for signs of attempted violent entry. Can you show me his bedroom?'

In the bedroom, she made the same examination of the door frame and handle. Then she returned to the sitting room and made a note of what she had seen. Once she was satisfied with her notes, she started the conversation in a brisk manner: 'I see one of my colleagues has already visited you to talk about Theo.'

'Yes,' replies Mary.

'Was there a quarrel?' she asks. 'Is that how Theo received those bruises?'

'It was us that took him to the doctor when the bruises started to appear,' says Geordie. He wants to pick up the social worker and shake her, but he can just about manage to bottle his frustration. He knows it will only make things worse if he loses it.

'If Theo comes back, we will need to interview him,' says the social worker. 'Confrontation within the family, especially where physical violence may have occurred, is very traumatic for a young child. We need to hear his side of the story.'

'Theo's been taken,' says Geordie. 'Why isn't anyone doing anything about it? If I'd lost my dog, there'd have been more going on.'

'You do appreciate, don't you,' replies the social worker, 'that if our investigation gives us reasonable grounds to believe there has been abuse in Theo's case, we may need to take him into care?'

'But he's not here!' shouts Geordie, losing control at last.

'I know,' says the social worker. 'But if he *were* here.'

Mary and Geordie went to the police again and again. At first they were treated with sympathy, but very quickly it all changed.

'We'll let you know if we hear anything, of course,' said the case officer. 'You must bear in mind that this sort of thing happens a lot more often than people think. There's one child goes missing in this country every five minutes on average.'

'Theo didn't run away,' says Mary. 'He's only ten.'

'Well, there you are,' replies the case officer. 'It's just one of those things.'

Geordie sits at the table remembering. He hears Mary's key in the door. She enters the flat, sees him and says: 'What are you doing home so early?'

'I packed it in. I didn't feel too good.'

'Oh,' says Mary. Geordie wants to tell her about the grey dog; the ewe; the lambs. But the sound of that 'Oh' discourages him. There is no interest in that 'Oh'. There is no sympathy in that 'Oh'.

Mary crosses the room towards the kitchen. 'Do you want a cup of tea? Will I put the kettle on?'

Geordie sits up straight and looks at her. He says, without thinking about his words: 'I can't stand working in Kielder much longer. It's driving me crazy.'

Mary is silent for a moment and then answers: 'You can't sit at home all day. That won't pay the rent. I can't earn enough for both of us. Anyway, I don't want you hanging around the flat all day.'

It's Mary's flat, not Geordie's. He pays a share of the rent and the household expenses. He realises that, suddenly, they are very close to breaking up. He realises that Mary has lost interest in him, just as she has lost interest in everything else since Theo disappeared. It's as if she had invested her whole life, her reason for existing, in Theo. Now he's gone, what's left of her? Geordie realises that, between them, in another couple of sentences, they could quite easily throw away everything they have ever had together. It's one of those conversations that could go downhill very fast.

Geordie doesn't want to lose Mary. He still loves her. She needs him, even if she doesn't realise it. That's what Geordie thinks. Geordie thinks that if he left the flat for good, Mary would turn in on herself. She'd go to bed and never get up again. Or she'd do something far worse. He forces a smile onto his face and says: 'Come on, let's have a cup of tea.'

Ten

Willie Craig sits in his flat looking at the photograph of Theo Constantine. He sees the boy's forehead – a patchwork of bruises and scratches, as if his head has been wrapped in barbed wire. Some of the marks have flecks of red in them as if the skin has been broken. You would think Theo would be in pain, but the eyes are calm and the mouth is firm: neither smiling nor frowning and certainly not wincing. There is no sign that the boy was feeling anything when the photo was taken. Certainly no sign that he was aware of, or in any way troubled by, the marks on his face.

The photos are weird. That's Willie's first thought, and the word isn't quite adequate. It doesn't begin to describe the inference of pain and the aspect of tranquillity. The photos aren't just weird; they are disturbing. When he gets up and walks around the room, trying to think what he's up to, why he's wasting his time with this, the image he has borrowed stays in front of him. When he shuts his eyes for a moment, the boy's face with its bracelet of bruises is right there on the back of his eyelids. So what's he going to do about it? Give the photo back? After all, what use is it? He's struggling to see what the story is here.

There's something going on. Was Theo the victim of abuse? Is he a runaway, as the police claim? Willie doesn't know what abused children look like, but he imagines they look fearful, haunted, traumatised. Apart from the inexplicable bruises and scratches, the boy in this photo exhibits none of these things. He looks – Willie gropes in his mind for the right word – he looks serene.

Willie needs to share this with someone. He needs to talk it over. As he thinks about this, he realises that there's only one person he can talk to who might have an opinion and who might be in a position to take it somewhere. It's not his editor. Not the police. It's Norman Stokoe, the children's czar. He puts the photo to his face. He smells jasmine.

Norman Stokoe doesn't want to take his call, but Willie's persistent. He gets put through to the PA.

'Your boss might as well pick up the phone. I'll just keep trying until he does.' Then he asks her, 'What are you doing on Friday night, anyway?'

'Wouldn't you like to know?'

That's not a 'no', then.

'We'll speak later. Go on, put me through to Norman.'

She puts him through and Willie says quickly, 'It's Willie Craig, Mr Stokoe. The journalist. Now, don't hang up on me. I've found something interesting. Something you ought to see.'

'I can't imagine what that could be.'

'I have a photograph of Theo, one of the missing children. He's got some strange marks on his forehead, like bruises, only not. You'd have to see them, I can't describe them any better.'

'Ah,' says Norman Stokoe. It's a long intake of breath, as if he is inhaling the scent from a flower. He says nothing else. Willie fills the gap.

'Well, do you want to see the photo? I think you should. I

think someone should look at it. There's something strange about all this.'

There is another pause.

'Well. I suppose it would do no harm to have a look. Bruises, you say?'

'When are you free?'

Willie knows Norman is probably free right now, and will probably go on being free all day, but he doesn't say anything when Norman suggests the following morning except, 'Thank you. I'll be there.'

He's outside Norman's office the next morning on the stroke of nine. He pauses to chat to the pretty girl who is Norman's PA.

'We can't go on meeting like this,' he says. 'People will talk.'

'Well, let them talk,' she answers. 'I'll buzz him.' Pause. 'You can go in.'

In the office, he gets the treatment. Norman is writing something on a pad with his fat fountain pen. He doesn't look up for a moment so Willie just stands there. Then Norman lifts his head and says in a tone of mild surprise, 'Oh, Mr Craig.'

'Good morning, Mr Stokoe.'

'You'd better sit down.'

Willie sits down. Then he slides the envelope containing Theo's photo across the desk. Norman looks at the photo for several minutes without speaking. When he does say something, it is a word Willie doesn't recognise. 'Stigmata.'

'You what?'

'It really does look like stigmata. Who took this photo? Could it have been faked?'

'It was taken by Theo's GP in his surgery. I got it from a police file. Don't ask me how.'

They stare at each other. Then Willie asks, 'What does "stigmata" mean?'

'Stigmata are said to be the visible signs of the Five Wounds of Christ as experienced by ecstatics or saints. St Francis of Assisi had stigmata – wounds on his hands and feet, in the same places where nails would have been driven in when Christ was crucified. And sometimes a stigmatic might have a wound in the left side, where the Roman centurion was said to have pierced Jesus with a spear. The marks on Theo's forehead might be interpreted as coming from a crown of thorns.'

'How do you know all this?' asks Willie.

'I was educated at a Catholic school,' says Norman. 'We were taught about such things. Sixty-two saints and blessed persons have been recorded as having mystical stigmata. There was St Francis, of course, and Anna Katherina Emmerich, and Padre Pio, and many others. At the moment I can't think of a previous example of a child suffering stigmata, but there's no reason why not.'

So Norman had a religious upbringing. He seems too secular a man for that. Norman sees something in Willie's expression that makes him say, 'I was educated as a Catholic, but I no longer attend church. Even if I were still a religious man, I wouldn't allow my faith to interfere with my work.'

'I'm sure not,' says Willie. There's a silence. Norman looks as if he wants to say more about how un-religious he is these days, what a free-thinker he can be when he gets going, how well up he is on A.C. Grayling and Richard Dawkins and how, in Norman's universe, God has been relegated to a relatively low-grade job. He can't quite abolish the idea of God altogether, because then he hears Father Adrian's admonitory tones some-where in the back of his mind. But, in practical terms, Norman has joined the ranks of those who believe it is important not to believe. There's no doubt it wouldn't have helped his career if people had thought he was still a religionist.

But Norman only thinks all this, doesn't say any of it aloud. His mind comes back to the matter in hand.

'Was this the only photo?' he asks.

'There were four others. They showed similar markings on both hands, and on the ankles and feet.'

Norman stares at Willie again. His mouth opens. He doesn't say anything, but Willie guesses that Norman is regretting the decision to allow Willie to show him the photograph. Norman is stuck. He can't leave this alone. He can't pretend to himself that he has never seen this picture. But what is he going to do about it?

'I've an idea,' says Willie.

'What?'

'Either these photos are fakes, or they are real. But who would fake them? Why bother? I think they are for real.'

Norman gives a non-committal grunt: he lets Willie have that point, whilst reserving his position. He looks down at the photo again and asks, 'So?'

'If those bruises are real then, whatever caused them, I don't believe it was Theo's parents. I might be wrong about that, but say I'm right. If I'm right, then Theo had no reason to run away from home. He might have run away from school, if the bruises had been inflicted on him there, but he wouldn't have run away from home. I think he was abducted.'

Norman nods and purses his lips to show he can just about accept this line of argument.

'And so?'

'So we've probably got a serial child abductor operating in the region. If another child goes missing, we'll know for sure. But even as it is, two missing children is two too many.'

'Yes. I see your point,' says Norman. To see someone's point is not the same as agreeing with it.

'You see my point. The police don't see my point. The social services don't see my point. If I'm right, we've got a major predator working right under our noses. In your region, Child Commissioner.'

Norman starts to say something, but Willie cuts him off. He says, 'I want a new job. I want to get out of here.' Willie waves his hand to include Norman's office, the silver ribbon of the Tyne glimpsed through the window, the industrial sprawl beyond, the housing estates, the bypasses, the whole of the North East of England. 'I want a job working for the *Sun* or the *Daily Mail* or the *Daily Mirror*. I'm fed up with reporting on agricultural shows and shopping centres. If I break this story, I've every chance of being noticed by the national press. I might receive job offers from other papers. At any rate, I would be a million times more likely to get away from my present job than I am now. But first I need to know for sure that I'm onto something, that there really is a story behind the disappearance of Theo and Becky. I need to do some investigating and I know my paper won't back me. But if you and I do this together, we'll get a lot further.'

Norman digests all this. He says, 'What is it you want me to do, Mr Craig? And why should I?'

'I've asked around about you, Mr Stokoe. What I hear is that you've been put in an office up here with no budget, no resources, and no proper job. Am I right?'

Norman cannot bring himself to admit this, but he does not contradict Willie, so Willie presses on.

'Suppose that, between us, we get to the bottom of what is going on? Suppose we persuade the police to investigate Theo's disappearance more actively? Suppose we get some sort of result?'

'Suppose we do?'

'Then I would write an article telling the world how you achieved this despite your lack of resources, and despite your lack of official recognition. They'd have to do something then, wouldn't they, Mr Stokoe? They'd have to set you up in business properly.'

Norman leans back in his chair. Willie knows that, at last, he has his attention. Norman is listening. Norman is thinking. But he hasn't made up his mind yet. Willie can see that Norman is a cautious man.

'I will give this my serious consideration, Mr Craig. Where would you propose we start?'

'By going to see Theo's parents,' says Willie promptly. 'They might refuse to see me again, but they won't refuse to see you.'

'I will mull it over,' says Norman. 'I will undoubtedly mull it over. I will call you tonight with my decision.'

For Willie, it's a done deal. But let the man mull away, thinks Willie, he needs to think this is his party.

'I won't take up any more of your time just now,' says Willie, standing up. He stretches out his hand. 'The photo, please.'

Norman is still pinning it to the desk with one finger. He hands it back to Willie with reluctance. On the way out, Willie stops by the PA's desk.

'What's your name?' he asks.

'Pippa.'

'A beautiful name, Pippa. I'm Willie.'

'Willie. Not William, or Bill?'

'Willie is what my parents christened me,' says Willie, then he realises she is mocking him. He blushes. She smiles. He leaves.

Norman is mulling things over in his office. One part of him, the cautious, professional civil servant part, is shrieking at him not to get involved. He can see Willie is an accident waiting to happen: an over-confident, inexperienced young man who will undoubtedly get himself into trouble and, by association, Norman too, if they join forces.

But he can't get that picture of Theo out of his mind. He wants to understand what made those marks. He wants the comfort of knowing there's been a fraud, or some other explanation that doesn't challenge reason.

He has to know. And working with Willie might be the only way to find out.

Eleven

Karen Gilby's mum is going to bake a cake. It will be Karen's birthday tomorrow. This will be a special cake, with two layers, and icing on the top, and candles. Karen's mum realises that she has run out of self-raising flour. She says to Karen, 'Darling, will you do something for me?'

'Yes, Mummy, what?'

'Will you run – no, I don't mean run – will you *walk* down to the village shop and ask Mrs Beesley to give you a bag of self-raising flour?'

'Self-raising flower,' repeats Karen.

'Yes. Can you do that for me?'

'Yes, Mummy.'

Karen likes doing errands. The village shop is a few hundred yards from the Gilbys' house. The Gilby family lives in a house of dark stone: not much more than a cottage and standing on its own in a pretty garden with cherry trees just coming into blossom. Mr Gilby is out at work doing whatever Daddies do in their offices. Karen has been back from the village school for half an hour and is helping Mummy in the kitchen. Now she is going to help Mummy with her shopping.

She takes a wicker basket from the hall table and steps out of the front door. As she does so, she hears Mummy say: 'Now, be careful, Karen, and watch out for traffic. You don't need to cross the road. And come straight back.'

Karen trots down the garden path with her basket over her arm. It is a lovely late afternoon in spring. The air is cool, but not chilly. The sky is clear with a few high clouds in it. There are no houses directly opposite Karen's house. On that side of the street the houses don't begin for a few hundred yards. Instead there is a field with sheep and now they have lambs too, suckling or else racing around in lamb gangs. Karen loves to watch them hop and skip about. She skips herself, mimicking the lambs, as she walks down the street past the church in the direction of the village shop.

A Mitsubishi Shogun with tinted windows cruises past her. Karen doesn't know what the car is called, but she recognises it. She has seen it before, travelling in one direction or the other through the village. About five hundred yards further down the road it slows down, and turns into a side road. Karen walks along to the village shop. Mrs Beesley hears the bell tinkle as the door opens. She turns around, sees Karen and says, 'Now then, what can I do for my favourite girl?'

'Please, Mrs Beesley, can Mummy have some self-raising flower?'

Mrs Beesley finds the self-raising flour and puts it in Karen's basket. She marks it down on Mrs Gilby's account. A few more words are said, and then Karen leaves.

'Bye, Mrs Beesley.'

'Goodbye, Karen.'

Karen steps out into the street and starts walking home. Behind her, a Mitsubishi Shogun with tinted windows pulls out of a side road and drives behind Karen on the same side of the road.

As she walks past the gate to the churchyard, the vicar comes out and falls into step beside her.

'Good evening, Karen,' he says. Karen can't remember his name so she just says, 'Hello.'

'Can I walk with you a little way?' asks the vicar. 'I'm going to visit old Mr Johnson next door to you.'

Behind Karen, the Mitsubishi Shogun speeds up, drives past her, and continues on out of the village until it is lost to sight.

Twelve

Norman and Willie have become temporary allies. Norman has mulled over Willie's suggestion that together they do some digging into the Constantine case. Norman can't see the downside. Yes, somebody might accuse him of interference – the police, probably – but when the day comes that someone asks him what on earth he has been doing for the last few months to justify his very substantial salary, Norman thinks he will have a better answer to give than he might otherwise have had.

Norman and Willie meet in the early evening at the same Newcastle quayside pub that Willie drank in a few days earlier. It is convenient for Norman's office. It is another cool, bright spring evening and quite a few people are sitting outside, despite the chilly air. It is high tide and the river is full and flows swiftly past. On the opposite bank is the shiny silver outline of the Sage Music Centre, and the old flour silo that has been converted into the Baltic Art Centre. On this side of the river, groups of early-evening revellers and late shoppers are gathering here and there along the quays. Willie arrives ahead of time, and orders himself a lager. He assumes Norman will keep him waiting, but Norman is prompt. He is wearing a double-breasted dark-blue overcoat to keep out the cold, with a blue snood wrapped around his neck. Willie is wearing his brown pinstripe, with a V-neck pullover underneath the jacket.

'What will you have?' asks Willie.

'A glass of Sauvignon, please.'

Willie goes off to get the drinks in and Norman has a moment when he thinks he ought to get up and walk away while Willie is gone. What is he doing, sitting in a pub with this young man? How could he have allowed himself to be drawn into this situation? But then Willie is back with the drinks, a glass of white for Norman and another bottle of lager for himself.

'Cheers,' says Willie, raising the bottle to his lips. Norman suppresses a shudder and sips delicately at his glass of wine.

'So, are you up for this?' asks Willie.

'I am prepared to spend a little of my time looking into the Constantine case. Those photographs require explanation.' He licks his lips. 'What would be an appropriate first step?'

Willie takes out his mobile, scrolls through the phone numbers, and then punches Dial.

'It's ringing,' he says, handing the phone to Norman. 'Why don't you ask Mrs C if we can come out and visit them?'

Norman looks alarmed by the speed of events.

'Now?'

'No time like the present,' says Willie. 'I've got a car parked near here.'

In some confusion, Norman takes the phone, and then Mary Constantine is on the line. Norman pulls himself together and suggests a meeting.

'You can come if you like,' says Mary Constantine. 'I can't stop you.'

'We have a new photo of Theo we'd like to discuss with you.'

'A *new photo of Theo*. When was it taken? Where?'

Norman explains, 'It shows markings on his face. You talked about bruises when you came to see me. These aren't bruises. We want a better understanding of what happened.'

Mary says, 'Oh, that photo. It's an old photo.'

She hangs up without saying 'Goodbye'.

'Well done,' says Willie. 'Game on.'

They find Willie's car and drive through the dusk to the commuter-belt town where Mary and Geordie live. Where Theo used to live.

When they ring the doorbell, it is not Mary who answers, but a tall, well-built, dark-haired man. He has a strong, square face heavy with beard. There are dark circles under his eyes. Willie recognises the man from the photograph that he saw on his last visit.

'Is Mrs Constantine at home?' asks Norman, as if he were speaking to the butler.

'Aye. You'd better come on in.'

Inside the flat, Willie introduces himself to Geordie. Geordie doesn't take much notice. He seems dazed. Mary appears in another doorway.

'Will you all be wanting a cup of tea?' she asks. No one does. There is an awkward silence – four disconnected people staring at each other. Then Willie Craig sits down on the leather sofa. He pulls out an envelope from the inside pocket of his brown suit. He takes out the photograph of Theo, bent around the edges, and puts it on the low table in front of him.

'Let's talk about Theo,' he suggests. The boy stares up at them from the table, his brow a bracelet of scratches and bruises: a bracelet of thorns, thinks Norman. He sits down heavily beside Willie, the leather sofa squeaking under his weight. Mary crosses the room and picks up the photo, stares at it hungrily. Geordie flops down in the only other chair, and sits there as if he's waiting in a surgery for an unpleasant interview with the doctor.

'I've seen four other photos,' says Willie. 'I've seen the

bruises on his hands and feet. What made those marks? And when did you first see them?'

Mary speaks first. 'The first time we noticed them was at bathtime one night. A couple of years ago, wasn't it, Geordie?'

Geordie looks surprised that he has been spoken to, and lifts up his head. It was bathtime right enough, he agrees.

'You must have asked him how he got the bruises? What did Theo tell you?' asks Willie.

'He said he didn't know. We asked him if someone at school had kicked him, or grabbed his wrists. He said no. We told ourselves he must have banged into something. You know how boys of that age are always running about, scraping their knees, playing together too roughly.'

She looks at Willie as if he might still be young enough to remember this aspect of childhood.

Suddenly Norman asks, 'Was he a very religious boy? Did he pray a lot?'

Everyone looks at Norman in surprise.

'No,' Mary answers.

Geordie gives a short laugh and says, 'He was more interested in football than prayers. I don't think he ever went into a church. Not with me, anyway.'

'You said "the first time we noticed them",' says Willie. 'Did the bruises appear on more than one occasion?'

'Yes,' answers Mary.

'So what did you say to Theo the second time the marks appeared?'

'It was at school the second time it happened. His teacher told us about it, but by the time I picked him up the marks had disappeared.'

'We asked, who did this to him?' says Geordie. 'I said I

would go and speak to his teachers if he didn't tell us what was going on. I thought he was being bullied. The marks that time were only on his hands and feet. It wasn't until the last time that the marks on his forehead appeared.'

'What did the teachers say?'

Geordie starts to respond, but Mary interrupts him: 'They told us they had noticed the bruises again and had called in the school doctor. The doctor took photos. The marks faded away very quickly. If you looked at Theo the next day, and then looked at the photos, it was hard to believe it was the same boy.'

'Did Theo say whether he was in any pain?' asks Norman.

'Theo never complained,' says Geordie.

'About anything,' adds Mary.

'The next time it happened, the school reported us,' says Geordie. 'We had the Social come round.'

The school reports Theo's bruises to the council, a Domestic Violence Prevention officer comes to see them to carry out a risk assessment and suggest a Violence Prevention plan. Then a social worker comes to interview the mother and the step-father. No one is any the wiser. The marks have disappeared. It is a mystery, and a worry, but the problem has ceased for the time being. The school and Social Services do not feel able to take the matter further. Theo is not in pain. He is not exhibiting any of the behaviours of a child who is being beaten or abused in any way. The photographic evidence is contradicted by the appearance of Theo himself. He seems a normal, happy, well-adjusted child. In fact, more than happy. On the end of the autumn term report his teacher writes:

Theo has a calming effect on the other children in his class and is a valued member of our little community.

Mary finds the report in a drawer of the desk that stands in the corner of the room and shows it to Willie and Norman.

Then the bruises reappear, just before Christmas. This time Theo has the strange circlet of bruising around his forehead as well as the marks on his hands and feet. This cannot be ignored. Mary takes Theo to their GP. The GP takes Theo's temperature. He looks in his eyes and ears. He takes more photos of the bruises – the same photos that Willie has seen. He cannot offer any explanation.

'You told me that your doctor referred to the marks as "stigmata",' says Norman. Mary doesn't look at him. She replies: 'Yes, he said that. When we asked him what that meant, he said it was how a sixteenth-century priest might have explained the markings. He said he preferred a more modern explanation.'

'What modern explanation?' asks Norman.

'He wouldn't say. I think he meant that Geordie and I were producing these marks on Theo ourselves. That we were child-abusers.'

'Were you?' asks Willie.

'No,' says Mary.

'No,' says Geordie.

Then Norman, in Willie's view, spoils everything.

'Tell me about Theo's father?' he says.

Geordie raises his head and gives Norman an unfriendly glance.

'Why do you need to know?' asks Mary.

'Because sometimes the fathers of children who have been separated from the mother have been known to take the law into their own hands. And take the children away with them. They abduct them. Could that have happened here?'

Geordie says, 'Don't bother her with these stupid questions.'

'Could it?' persists Norman. 'Could that have happened, Mrs Constantine?'

Willie is watching Geordie carefully. He reminds Willie of a bull that is being teased. He's lowered his head. He might just charge, and then Norman will be in deep trouble.

'Theo's father never met Theo. He was long gone before the birth.'

'Constantine – that's a Greek name, isn't it? Could Mr Constantine have abducted Theo and taken him back to Greece?'

'It's not like that. It wasn't like that at all. You don't understand. You couldn't possibly understand,' says Mary. She's almost in tears.

'Out,' says Geordie, standing up. He's a big man and he looks enormous in this small room. Willie stands up too.

'We're on our way,' says Willie. But Norman is still pursuing his question. 'All right, I don't understand,' he says to Mary. 'So if it wasn't like that, what *was* it like?'

Geordie steps forward. For a moment, Willie thinks he's going to hit Norman, and he steps between them, grabbing Norman by the arm.

'Time to go,' he says. Norman looks up and sees the expression on Geordie's face.

'Out you go now, you fat bastard,' Geordie says. 'Before I punch your lights out.'

Willie and Norman leave.

Thirteen

Willie and Norman don't talk much on the way back to Newcastle. The faces of Mary and Geordie remain in their minds: full of pain, full of longing, and empty of deceit. At last Willie speaks.

'I don't believe they had anything to do with Theo's bruising.'

'I agree,' says Norman. 'The man is obviously capable of violence, but I don't believe he was violent towards his stepson.'

'Then what did cause the marks?'

'I really couldn't say,' replies Norman, but there is something in his voice that makes Willie think that Norman really *could* say, if only he dared to. Willie thinks that Norman has a theory, but he doesn't want to voice it: not even to himself.

'Whatever caused the bruises is maybe not the point,' Willie goes on. 'The point is: I don't believe Theo ran away.'

'It doesn't seem likely,' agrees Norman.

'They seemed like loving parents as far as I could tell.'

'Of course, some people can be very clever at getting you to think what they want,' says Norman.

'Do you believe those two beat their child?'

There's a pause, then: 'No.' Another pause then, 'I don't have much practical experience of this. But they don't look capable of abusing their own child.'

'So if they didn't beat him and he was happy at school, then he didn't run away. So somebody took him, right?'

'That's a logical conclusion,' replies Norman.

'What do we do now?' asks Willie.

'I don't know. I need to sleep on it. Drop me off here, my car is in that multi-storey.'

Willie drops Norman off on the quayside, not too far from where they met earlier in the evening. He watches the fat man walk away, wondering why on earth it seemed like a good idea to try to team up with someone like that. He goes home to his flat in Jesmond, an area of the town where students and impecunious journalists now occupy tiny flats crammed into the shells of once-gracious Victorian and Edwardian houses.

At first Willie thinks it would be nice to go out. There are a couple of bars not far away where the vodka and the white wine flow freely, and where it is not impossible Willie might find a girl. He's done it before. He doesn't want to be alone tonight. He wants lights; action; he wants alcohol. He goes into his bedroom and changes out of his suit into his other uniform: jeans, a clean white shirt, a dark-blue fleece. He is about to go out when he remembers the photograph of Theo is still in the inside pocket of his suit, which won't do it any good. He goes back into his bedroom and takes the picture out with the intention of putting a book on top of it to flatten it back out. It is becoming a bit dog-eared. He sits on the bed for a moment, looking at the boy's picture.

The bracelet marks crown the face: the wide-set eyes look into Willie's eyes and lock on. Willie swings his feet off the floor and lies full-length on the bed, looking at the boy's face, wondering what it is about it that is so strange. Why does it remind him of somewhere, a place he went to long ago and has forgotten about? It's a puzzle, and as Willie stares at the picture, his eyelids grow heavy and then close. Maybe he'll lie there for ten minutes before going out. Maybe he'll just doze for a moment.

He dreams.

In his dream, Willie is on a path in a dark forest. The trees surround him on every side. They lean over him. Their branches sigh and creak in the wind. The wind is blowing across the roof of the forest: Willie can't feel it but he can hear it, as if the trees are a great sea, their branches rippling and clashing together. Then, somehow, he is moving along the track, and climbing a low hill. He feels a great reluctance to keep walking, but his feet carry him onwards.

At first he can see nothing but trees, trees on either side of him, trees in front. But now there is something else ahead: a shape outlined against the night sky. He is in a clearing. The trees have fallen back, as if reluctant to come any further. He can see a few stars. It feels cold. This is unlike any other dream: he feels the chilly air against his skin. He wants to wake up, but he can't wake up. He sees a shape against the sky. It is a tower. Ahead of him is a tower house: an ancient place. It is uninhabited, a ruin, forgotten, buried in the midst of this huge forest. But no – it is not uninhabited after all. Willie sees a gleam of light in a window high up in the tower. He is at the foot of the tower now, peering up. He is almost close enough to touch its lichen-covered stones. He sees worn stone steps leading up into the darkness. The light – a candle, a lantern – appears at another window. Willie groans and mutters in his sleep: 'Light. Light in the forest.'

Norman too is back in his flat and in his bedroom. He has hung up his suit and changed into his evening costume: a yellow cardigan and a pair of chinos just back from the dry-cleaners. The routine of his evening has been disturbed. He feels unsettled. He cannot stop thinking about the boy. Those photographs! Norman has seen pictures of stigmata before now. In these post-religious days, stigmata can only mean one of two things: a confidence trick, like those dubious plaster statuettes of the Virgin Mary that weep; or else ... Or else he doesn't know. The 'or else' is something he doesn't want to contemplate. It means returning in his mind to the dark days at school, when Father Adrian told them what to believe. He is enlightened now. He doesn't have to believe in what Father Adrian taught him. Norman believes in his own abilities. He believes what his parents taught him, that a clever man will rise like yeast if he is careful.

He doesn't want to think about that 'or else'. Because, in his head, the sentence beginning with 'or else' ends with the words: 'it's the real thing'.

The real thing: if you are brought up as Norman has been, you don't choose what to believe in and what not to believe in. Faith is absolute, not relative. If Theo really were exhibiting signs of the Wounds of Christ on his body, then either his mother and his stepfather were proposing to make the boy into a commercial venture, or ...

Or, if he were still here to speak for himself, the boy could say, like Saint Paul: 'I bear on my body the marks of Jesus.'

Norman knows what the scientific explanations for these marks are: self-harm, or some complex form of psychosomatic disorder. He knows what he was taught to believe too. What he once believed. What a small part of him, buried deep down somewhere inside him, still believes. The boy is experiencing divine intervention. He has a direct relationship with Christ.

The boy must be found. He must be asked about this: what he feels, what he *knows*.

Norman's thoughts hit a wall: *if* the boy can be found.

For thirty years Norman has involved himself in the detail of the children's industry without thinking very much about the actual children. It hasn't been necessary to do so. He feels – he has felt – that empathy is the enemy of objectivity. Now, for the first time in his career, he is thinking of a child as something other than a statistic. Theo is his name. A dark-haired child with wide eyes, and a look about him that projects itself on to Norman's mind as clearly as if he were still looking at the photographs. He must find the boy. He must use the journalist and find the boy. He realises that the faith he once had, and the present needs of his job, have converged. He should find the boy and then his new job will be secure. If he finds the boy, he can ask him about the marks on his body.

Norman thinks: if the boy is still alive.

It is four months since anyone last saw him. How could he be alive? Except through divine providence. Except if God is keeping an eye on Theo.

At this time of the evening, Norman's thoughts usually turn to food. He likes to keep a few treats from Waitrose in the fridge to have with his glass of wine, a ready meal or two to put in the oven for afterwards. But now appetite has fled.

Norman lowers himself to the floor beside his bed. He is not hungry; he is not thirsty. He is in a state of mind he has not known since he was a child. He does something he hasn't done for thirty years. And even as he does it, he tells himself: 'Nobody can see me. It doesn't count. It can't do any harm.'

So he gets awkwardly down onto his knees and he prays. He prays for Theo. He prays that he will be found. He prays that his superiors and the secretary of state will notice, and confirm him in his new job.

When he has prayed, he gets to his feet and shakes out the creases in his chinos. But he doesn't, as he would on every other evening, go through to the kitchen to eat. Norman is too full of thoughts to fill himself with anything else. He sits in the armchair in his bedroom. He has not done much today apart from drive to the flat where Theo once lived, and then home again, but it is more than he does on most days. He feels tired. His eyelids feel heavy as he sits in the chair. Twenty miles away, Willie is lying on his bed in his flat, falling asleep. Norman's eyelids close and he too falls into a light doze. A pleasant torpor spreads over him: a warm, languid feeling spreading through his body like morphine. He sleeps.

He dreams. He is standing in a high place above a sea of dark trees. In his dream he feels the cold wind on his cheek. It is more real than waking. Now he is on a path. It leads into a clearing. At the far end of the clearing is a dark shape: the outline of a tower. It is abandoned, almost a ruin. Norman doesn't know why he is there; but he doesn't want to be there. A gleam of light appears at a window: a torch or a candle. Norman doesn't want to enter the tower, but his feet carry him in that direction. The light goes out and then suddenly reappears at another window. Norman cries out in his sleep: 'Light. Light in the forest.'

The dream changes. Norman is in a different place. It must be a different country, in a different time. He is walking up a stony path. He feels the intensity of the sunlight beating down on him. He feels sharp stones beneath his bare feet. Now a hot wind blows against his face. The sensations are so vivid, this cannot be a dream. A huge weight lies across his shoulders. He does not know how he can bear it any further, only that he must. The path is steep; he struggles for breath. He is in pain; worse is yet to come. He cries out at the pain. He cries out because he wants the dream to stop. He wants to awaken and find himself back in his armchair. No one takes any notice of his cries. The dream goes on.

Fourteen

The next morning, bright and early, Willie is waiting outside Norman's office. Norman has not yet arrived, but Pippa is at her desk.

'Morning, gorgeous,' says Willie. He makes an effort to sound brighter than he feels.

'Hello, yourself.'

'What are you doing tonight?'

'Staying at home and washing my hair.'

'And tomorrow night?' begins Willie, but just then he sees Norman approaching across the atrium. Norman looks wasted. His face is grey and his hair is not sleek but sticking up, suggesting that he has forgotten to brush it this morning. Willie turns to him and says, 'Good morning, Mr Stokoe. Are you all right? You look pale.'

'Good morning, Mr Craig. Good morning, Miss Everbury. Thank you for asking, Mr Craig, I had a restless night.'

Willie thinks about his own night's sleep, which wasn't so great either. Waking at three in the morning to find himself lying fully clothed on top of his bedspread. Kicking off his shoes. Pulling off a few clothes before climbing under the sheets, trying to recapture sleep. And then remembering the dream he had woken from, and lying awake for two hours with his eyes wide open trying not to fall back asleep until at around five, he must have sunk into a drugged and dreamless doze from which he awoke with difficulty about an hour ago.

Norman walks into his office, saying over his shoulder, 'Coffee, Miss Everbury, as soon as you like, please.'

He does not remember to offer Willie coffee, but a few moments later Pippa returns with two double espressos. Willie mouths his thanks at her with real gratitude.

'Ah, yes,' says Norman. 'A coffee for Mr Craig. How thoughtful.' He pockets the receipt that Pippa hands him. They sip the hot liquid and the caffeine does its work.

'What do we do now, Mr Stokoe?' Willie asks.

'I don't know. I don't know if there is anything more we *can* do,' replies Norman. He sounds dispirited. He sounds – he looks – as if he is regretting ever having met Willie or having listened to him.

'We go to the police?' suggests Willie.

'And say what? Say we've met the boy's parents and we don't believe they are child-abusers?'

'Something like that,' agrees Willie. 'We ask them whether they are sure there is no connection between Theo and the missing girl. Becky Thomas.'

At first Norman will not agree. Something is wrong with Norman today, thinks Willie. He seems scared. Or perhaps he is always like this. They argue for a minute. Then suddenly Norman says, 'Oh, very well. But don't blame me if we get thrown out.'

He calls Pippa to ask her to get Detective Chief Inspector Saxon on the phone.

'Who's he?' asks Willie.

'He's with NCACU,' replies Norman.

'Give me a break,' says Willie.

'It's the National Crimes Against Children Unit. They deal with child abuse and abduction cases, amongst other things. Chief Inspector Saxon attends the same meetings of the Safeguarding Advisor Network that I do. He's quite a senior policeman. We've met. He's not been in the region much longer than I have. He was transferred up here from London last winter, and works out of the local police headquarters.'

What Norman doesn't add is that Chief Inspector Saxon is what Norman thinks of as a player. He's like Norman. His rank is not a true measure of his importance. He keeps company with powerful people. Norman can scent the divine breath on him, the same breath that once breathed over Norman: the breath of government ministers. It's evident in the way the chief inspector takes his chair at meetings, the abstracted air he has, as if more important things are on his mind, the brevity of his replies when people ask him questions, as if he's not too worried about making friends. He already has friends, thinks Norman, powerful friends. Norman hopes that Chief Inspector Saxon might be someone he can do business with, now and in the future.

The phone rings. Norman picks up and Pippa tells him the chief inspector can take his call.

'Ah, Tom,' says Norman, in quite a different voice to the one he has just been using. His elocution has changed. He loses his Oxbridge twang. His speech becomes coarser: more hail-fellow-well-met. The speaker at the other end asks something and Norman says, 'Norman. Norman Stokoe. The regional children's commissioner. We've met a few times.'

They talk for a few minutes. Norman doesn't give much away, but he gets what he wants, which is a meeting later that day. Norman hangs up.

'Meet me at five tonight at Northumbria Police Headquarters, in Reception. Now, if you'll forgive me, Mr Craig, I've a lot of work to catch up on.'

Willie stands up and takes his leave. On the way out, he stops at Pippa's desk.

'Just one thing I want to know,' he asks, leaning towards her, and assuming a confidential tone of voice.

'What's that?' asks Pippa.

'What colour knickers are you wearing?'

Now she blushes, very prettily.

'Ask no questions and I'll tell you no lies,' she says.

'Come out for a drink tomorrow night?' suggests Willie.

'We'll see.'

'No, really,' persists Willie. 'I'll behave like a complete gentleman, I promise you.'

'I'll believe you, thousands wouldn't,' says Pippa.

Back at the office, Willie is summoned to go and see his editor, who has been asking for him. Willie swallows and goes into the glass-walled office.

'Where have you been this morning?' asks Mr Naylor. Willie mumbles something.

'What?'

'Just some personal stuff I had to see to,' repeats Willie.

'Well, it's not good enough,' says Mr Naylor. 'We don't pay you to wander around Newcastle looking in shop windows or hanging around pubs. I'm warning you about your time-keeping, Mr Craig, and next time it will be in writing. Do you understand me?'

'Yes,' says Willie, hanging his head and letting the storm blow over him. But Mr Naylor is really quite angry. He has a great deal more to say about Willie's work ethic, his general attitude and his appearance. It seems there is no particular redeeming feature about Willie that has caught Mr Naylor's attention. When his boss is in this mood, a prudent man keeps his mouth shut. Willie is feeling super-prudent.

'I want you to do a piece on personalised number plates in the region. Find a few good ones. Get onto the DVLA, or whatever you have to do. Find the owners and talk to them. I want a human-interest piece. Ask them why they chose that particular number plate. What it stands for. We're booking some advertising for a car sales special supplement in a couple of weeks' time.'

Willie takes it like a man. He smiles and says, 'I'm right on it, Mr Naylor,' and leaves the office. At his desk, he contemplates his career yet again. Now he is writing about car registrations. Could he sink any lower than this?

Despite Mr Naylor's threats, at half past four Willie slips out of the newspaper office, leaving a note on his desk saying: 'Out At Interview'. That may serve to cover him; or it may not. He heads towards Ponteland. There he meets Norman, and in a little while they are in a small office sitting on hard blue chairs facing a large man on the other side of a large desk. Chief Inspector Saxon may be a large man, but he is not fat. What hair he has left on his head is in tight blond curls shading to grey. He has white eyebrows, pale-blue eyes and a large, red face like that of a successful butcher who enjoys eating his own meat. His lips are thin. One look at him puts the fear of God into Willie. He's met policemen like Chief Inspector Saxon in his wilder days and the experience wasn't a happy one.

Norman doesn't seem bothered. He enters the office full of bonhomie that only wears thin when the chief inspector makes it clear that he scarcely knows, or cares, who Norman is.

But Norman keeps going. He does the talking, and he does

it well. He introduces Willie, says Willie believes there is a connection between the Becky Thomas case and that of Theo Constantine. Norman gives the strong impression that he is there only with the greatest reluctance. He says he is there only because his conscience will not allow him to overlook this possibility, however slight it might be.

'What possibility?' asks Chief Inspector Saxon. Willie thinks the policeman looks very sharp. He isn't making any effort to be nice to Norman.

'The possibility that the same person took both Becky Thomas and Theo Constantine.'

'I'm not aware that Theo Constantine is connected in any way with the later case. We have it on file as a runaway.'

'We don't think Mary and Geordie, Theo's parents, are child-abusers,' says Willie.

'You don't think?' repeats Chief Inspector Saxon. 'I'm very grateful for your *opinion*, Mr Craig, but this isn't a newspaper office, this is a police department. We have clear photographic evidence of abuse in this case. And we have every reason to believe that the most likely scenario is a runaway.'

Willie thinks about the photo, stolen from the police department, which is back inside his suit pocket. He wonders whether he should get it out, but decides there would be too many questions about how he obtained it. Chief Inspector Saxon has more to say. 'I'm surprised you are giving any credence to these suggestions, Mr Stokoe. I agreed to see you this evening out of respect for your position as regional children's commissioner, although I understand that this position has still not been confirmed.'

Norman blinks. No first names: no Norman, no Tom. The policeman is being barely civil.

'But I think you know,' Chief Inspector Saxon continues,

'that even if you were confirmed in your job, it is not part of your remit to involve yourself in an on-going police investigation.'

Then Norman surprises Willie. He surprises himself. He certainly surprises Chief Inspector Saxon.

'There may be another explanation for the bruises on Theo Constantine,' he says.

'Such as what? The boy did them himself?' asks the chief inspector, no longer bothering to hide his sarcasm, a sarcasm that is close to contempt.

'Exactly,' replies Norman. 'The boy did them himself. The injuries – the bruises – might have another cause. They could be what one might call psychosomatic in origin. They might be self-induced. How else do you explain those markings? They are not like any bruises I have ever seen.'

'We see a lot of things in this office that the public have never seen. The public are very lucky not to have seen some of the things we see in this department. Things we see on a regular basis,' says the chief inspector. 'You say I might call the bruises psychosomatic. What would *you* call them?'

'Stigmata,' says Norman, and Willie looks at him almost in admiration.

'Stigmata?' repeats Chief Inspector Saxon. Unlike Willie, who was at a loss when he first heard this word, Saxon knows exactly what the term means. 'I'll tell you what, Mr Stokoe. In this office, we find it helps if we leave our religion and our politics at home. We try to run a *professional* operation here, Mr Stokoe, without getting sidetracked by mumbo-jumbo.'

Norman is becoming red in the face as he listens to this. Chief Inspector Saxon continues, 'Don't think me disrespectful of anyone's faith. We're all well aware of the need to respect *diversity* in this police authority. But I really don't have time for this sort of thing. Both cases remain open. We are ready to consider any new evidence that may turn up. But we're not interested in your *opinions*, Mr Craig, and we're not interested in mystical theories, Mr Stokoe. Now, you'll have to excuse me, I've work to do.'

A few moments later, Willie and Norman are outside the office, walking towards the car park. Willie expects Norman to be chastened, humiliated. It's how he feels, anyway. He can't imagine why he ever thought there could be any other outcome to a meeting such as this. He needs to go back to his office and finish the article on car number plates, while he still has a job. But Norman has a different view. Willie sees him clench his fist. Norman Stokoe actually clenches his fist. Then he says: 'Diversity. I'll give him diversity. That man is prejudiced. The man has a closed mind. The case remains open? Not with people like that running it. By God, I'll show him where to get off.'

Willie realises that Norman doesn't like the way he has been treated, and that's fair enough. But there is something else, something that surprises Willie even more. He sees that Norman has begun to care.

He has begun to care.

Fifteen

It is a rainy afternoon when Karen Gilby leaves the village school on her own. She is a big girl now. That's what her mummy told her: 'You're a big girl now, and you don't need me to walk you home.'

Karen has noticed that Mummy still turns up on sunny days, or if some of Mummy's friends are also there to collect their children. Then Mummy and her friends can chat while Karen and *her* friends walk or run ahead. Karen has noticed that it's mainly when it is cold and raining that she is a Big Girl Now. But Karen doesn't mind. It isn't far. Sometimes she doesn't go straight home but instead goes to one or other of her friends' houses to play for a while. Sometimes if she has some money in her pocket, which isn't often, she might go into Mrs Beesley's shop to buy some sweets.

Today she has no money in her pocket. The rain has kept people off the streets. The other children's mummies have picked them up at the school gates in cars, even the ones who live quite near to Karen. That's not really fair, but Karen doesn't mind. Not really. She is only getting a little bit wet. It isn't raining very hard.

Behind her a Mitsubishi Shogun with tinted windows pulls out of a side street. It idles along behind Karen and at first she doesn't notice it. When it is quite close behind her she becomes aware of the sound of the engine, which she has been listening to for a moment without really thinking about it. She turns her head to see who or what it is. Now the Mitsubishi is next to her, and someone inside reaches across and opens the passenger door.

'Hello, Karen,' says a familiar voice.

Karen looks up in surprise.

'Oh, hello,' she says. She likes the owner of the voice. The voice says: 'I've got a new book that I want to show you. I haven't shown it to any of the other children yet. Hop in, and you'll keep dry.'

Karen hops in and the owner of the voice reaches across again and shuts the passenger door, then helps her put on her safety belt. The car moves off, slowly at first and then a little quicker. Karen is surprised to see that they don't slow down when they come to her house.

'Where are we going?' she asks.

'Not far.'

'Does Mummy know where we're going?'

'We'll have you back home in a trice. But the book is at my house. It's not far. Not very far.'

Karen thinks about this. Then she asks: 'What is the book about?'

'It has some very nice stories. Stories about some children, and what happens to them.'

This doesn't give Karen much to go on. They are quite a long way from her house now, and going at a steady speed. Mummy doesn't drive as fast as this. Karen feels a little nervous sitting in a car that is travelling so fast. Everything seems to be coming towards her too quickly and then it is gone. She asks another question. 'What's it like, your house?'

'It's very nice. You'll see.'

'No, but what *sort* of house is it?'

Karen means: is it a big house, a small house, a red house, a grey house. The answer is none of these.

'It's a tower house, Karen. A tower that has been made into a house.'

Karen has never seen a tower house. None of her friends live in tower houses. She tries another line of enquiry, because she feels she needs to keep the conversation going. Because if she doesn't keep the conversation going, they'll just be driving along in silence, getting further and further from her own house. She hasn't told Mummy where she's going. Mummy will be expecting her to walk into the kitchen any time now. She doesn't want to start thinking these thoughts, which are wheeling about her now like bats on a summer evening. So she asks another question. 'Where is your house?'

The familiar voice says: 'It's in the forest, Karen. In the middle of the forest.'

Sixteen

Willie Craig hears the news first. He's in the office writing his piece on car number plates when Dave Longland, the newspaper's senior reporter, takes a call from a friend at the local police station. A few minutes later, Willie hears the story too. He stops what he's doing and calls Norman Stokoe. He is too full of excitement to banter with Pippa and asks to be put straight through.

'Good morning, Mr Craig,' says Norman, in his measured way.

'They've taken another one,' Willie tells him. As soon as he has spoken, he realises that he is not being very clear.

'Who has taken another what?' asks Norman. 'I don't understand.'

'I'm sorry. I'll start again. I've just heard that a young girl has disappeared from a village near Hexham. The police have been called in. She's been missing for about eighteen hours.'

'Dear me.'

'But don't you see, if this is another abduction, then Chief Inspector Saxon is going to *have* to take us seriously. He'll have to eat his own words. There's a serial child-killer on the loose.'

'We must be careful to stick to the facts. We don't *know* that any of the children have been abducted and we certainly don't know that any of them are dead,' Norman points out.

'We don't know that they're alive,' replies Willie. 'If they're alive, where are they? Why haven't we heard anything? They are dead, Norman, and the same person killed all three.'

Willie stops himself in mid-flow. He has just called Norman 'Norman'. How will the children's czar react to being addressed by his first name? But the children's czar doesn't even notice.

'We must pray that you are wrong,' he replies. 'It's distressing news.' Norman sounds wary. Whatever pit Willie is dragging him towards, it suddenly looks a whole lot deeper. Yesterday it was still possible to dismiss the idea that the same malign force was behind the disappearance of Theo and Becky. It's harder to dismiss the idea now.

'Whatever else, it's a story,' says Willie. 'I'm going to get in touch with the missing girl's family, to see if they'll talk to me. Then I'll call you back with anything I've got.'

He hangs up without waiting for Norman's reply, then sits at his desk and thinks for a moment. His credit with the editor couldn't be lower, but he has to try. Even in the prelapsarian world of *The Northumbria Herald* where nothing really bad ever happens and most of the drama is about roads or dust-bins ('Council criticised for neglecting potholes'), the disappearance of Karen Gilby must count for something. The paper can't just ignore it. Or can it? Willie isn't sure. He has to try.

Mr Naylor is at first reluctant to allow Willie to cover the story. He says: 'Our advertisers don't like this sort of thing.'

'But it's happening right in the middle of our patch,' argues Willie. 'We can't ignore it. We need to give the family as much publicity as we can. It's the best chance of ensuring the return of their little girl.'

As he says this, Willie knows he is being less than truthful. He believes – he knows – that there is no chance that publicity will ensure the return of the little girl. Because he believes the little girl is gone for good, like the others. But he wants the story. He knows he has to be careful. He mustn't give away his theory that all three cases are connected. Mr Naylor would not allow it. Mr Naylor doesn't approve of 'investigative journalism'. In fact, he loathes that sort of thing. He believes that a local newspaper should concentrate on community issues and leave the rest to the national tabloids.

Then again, Willie doesn't want to give a lead to any of the national papers. This is his story, and he's going to keep his cards tight to his chest until he knows more. Mr Naylor asks: 'Who is it? What's the name of the little girl?'

'Karen Gilby,' says Willie, looking at his notes. 'She went missing sometime late yesterday afternoon. She left school at the usual time but never arrived home. Home is about five minutes' walk from the village school.'

'Karen *Gilby*?' says Mr Naylor. 'I know her father. He's in the Rotarians.'

This is a green light. Willie starts to leave the office, but Mr Naylor calls after him. 'Be tactful, Willie, if you know how to – I don't want to hear any complaints about your behaviour.'

Willie goes back to his desk and takes out the little Samsung digital camera he keeps in a drawer. He's very excited. Could this be the break he's been looking for? Three children snatched, all within twenty miles of each other: all about the same age. All lifted, if that's what happened to them, within a few hundred yards of their home. There's a *modus operandi* here, thinks Willie, relishing the term which he has read in a dozen crime thrillers. If only he could find out more. He looks up the Gilby number, calls it. No answer. He keeps calling. At last the phone is picked up and an irritated female voice asks: 'Who is it?'

'Is that Mrs Gilby?'

'No, it's not. She's not available.'

'Can I come and talk to her? It's Willie Craig, from *The Northumbria Herald*.'

A hand is put over the phone at the other end. Willie can hear a muffled conversation. Then the woman who answered the phone tells him: 'Neither Mr nor Mrs Gilby wish to speak to the press.'

'But my editor is a friend of Mr Gilby. Mr Naylor's his name. He wants to give maximum publicity to Karen's disappearance. I'd only need five minutes.'

'Wait,' says the voice, either a neighbour or else a Family Liaison Officer from the police. Another muffled conversation, then: 'When did you have in mind?'

'Now?' suggests Willie.

'Mr Gilby will give you five minutes, no more. Mrs Gilby is too unwell to speak to anyone at present.'

Willie is given directions to the Gilby house. He hangs up. Five minutes later he is on his way. The Gilbys' house is only twenty minutes' drive from his office. He finds it easily: the last house but one on the left on the way out of the village. A police car is parked outside. There is an Audi A4 in the driveway, and a couple of other cars pulled up on the pavement. He parks, and walks through the pretty little garden and presses the front door bell. An unfriendly-looking WPC opens the door.

'Mr Craig, is it?'

'Yes,' says Willie, showing his press pass.

'Come with me.'

He follows the policewoman into a small hallway. It opens onto a staircase, beside a door that leads into a sitting room. The sitting room is furnished with two sofas, covered in chintz, a small armchair and a large television and lots of ornaments parked everywhere: on the mantelpiece, on the television set.

Bronze dogs, glass vases, picture frames with family photographs. On the mantelpiece a digital photo frame is endlessly recycling pictures of a little brown-haired girl. That must be Karen, thinks Willie. On one of the sofas is a large red-eyed man in a beige pullover and blue suit trousers. He is unshaven. Willie guesses he has been up all night. When he sees Willie, he struggles to his feet.

'Don't get up, Mr Gilby,' says Willie, too late.

'Bob Gilby,' says the man, offering his hand. Willie shakes it. It feels rather odd to be shaking hands at a moment like this, but anyway.

'Willie Craig,' he says. Behind Bob Gilby's head he sees a kitchen/dining room area where two women are having a cup of tea. One is the policewoman. The other must be a neighbour, he decides. Willie can't see anyone who might be Mrs Gilby.

'Mr Naylor sent me,' says Willie, stretching a point.

'Teddy Naylor,' says Bob Gilby with a ghostly smile. 'Know him well. Old mucker of mine. Good of him to offer to help. Sit down. I won't offer you tea, if you don't mind. The wife's not well. I have to keep nipping upstairs to keep an eye on her. Can we be quick? I don't mean to be rude.'

Yes, thinks Willie, we can be quick if you stop babbling. Aloud he says, 'I just need a few details. We'll do everything we can to help. And I'll need a photo of Karen, please.'

'Can do,' replies Bob Gilby. 'Fire away.'

Willie coaxes him to tell the story of Karen's disappearance. It is told in fits and starts. Bob Gilby's narrative powers have been affected by last night's events, or perhaps he is always like this. He keeps wandering away from the main story into thickets of irrelevant detail. Or else he stops and stares into space as if he has forgotten who Willie is or why he is there.

The essential facts do not amount to much. When Karen didn't come home at her usual time, when she still hadn't come home ten minutes later, Mrs Gilby went out to look for her. She walked all the way to the school gates. No Karen. She looked in at the village shop. Mrs Beesley hadn't seen her. It was still raining and Mrs Gilby was damp by the time she returned to the house. Damp, and a little worried. Karen must have gone to Sarah's house after school. Now it was half an hour since anyone had last seen her. It had happened before and Karen had been told off for not letting Mummy know where she was. Mrs Gilby rang Mrs Cuthbert. No, Karen wasn't there. A pause. No, Sarah hadn't seen her go off with anyone else. When Sarah had been picked up in her mother's car, she had seen Karen walking home on her own in the drizzly rain.

'That's when the wife rang me,' says Mr Gilby. 'By then Karen had been off the radar for about an hour. Of course I told her not to worry, but it was a little odd. We couldn't think where she might be. It never occurred to us for a moment that she could actually be missing. That someone might have taken her.'

'What happened next?'

'I dare say we dithered a bit. In the end, I rang the police. By the time they came out – they were very good, I'm not criticising anyone – it was three hours since Karen had left school.'

Willie thinks it is just like the disappearance of Theo. Nobody wants to accept that the unreal can become real. Time slips by and with every minute the missing child is receding from the known world, receding from memory, receding into invisibility. He tries another line of questioning.

'Can you tell me a little about Karen herself?' asks Willie. 'Describe her for our readers, please. What she liked, her hobbies, how she got on at school?'

Mr Gilby clears his throat. When he speaks, his voice is unsteady: 'Karen's a very special little girl. Everybody loves her. She does well at school. She's a great reader. Her favourite day of the week is Wednesdays, when the mobile library calls. She's always got a book or two on the go.' Mr Gilby laughs. 'She reads more than I do. She loves animals. We promised her a kitten if she does well in her exams next year. She likes most games ...'

Mr Gilby becomes conscious that he is trying to recapture the essence of Karen. He is trying to recreate her, as if with his hands and his words he might conjure up a hologram of her: a bright image of his daughter standing there in front of him. But he can't do it. The words are so inadequate. They don't begin to describe his daughter; and yet he can't think of what else he can say. Mr Gilby bursts into tears. Willie looks away, embarrassed. There is a snuffle and the sound of someone blowing their nose. Willie looks up, and Mr Gilby is trying to smile.

'Sorry about that, old man,' he says. 'It's been a long night.'

'Just a few more details, and I'll go,' promises Willie. He jots down a few notes: Robert Gilby, aged forty, area sales manager for an insurance company. Elaine Gilby, housewife, aged thirty-eight. A framed photo of Karen is handed to Willie. Mr Gilby, aged forty, rang the police at half past five, when Karen had been missing for nearly two hours. When his wife was already in hysterics. The police came. They asked questions. They started doing door-to-door interviews around the village. By half past eight it was clear that Karen wasn't in the village. She wasn't anywhere and nobody had seen her go.

Willie jots all this down and then gets up to leave. The Family Liaison Officer has put down her mug of tea and looks as if she is about to throw him out anyway. As Willie goes into the little hallway, there is the noise of a door opening upstairs, a sound of muffled voices raised in alarm or warning. Then a woman in a nightgown appears at the top of the stairs. It is Elaine Gilby, housewife, aged thirty-eight. She looks as if she is aged fifty-eight. She clutches the banister rail. Her face is puffy and streaked with tears, her hair is a mess, and she seems bewildered. She sees Willie looking up the stairs at her and the Family Liaison Officer standing behind him grasps his arm just above the elbow. Elaine Gilby says in a loud and trembling voice: 'Ask them what monster has taken my child. Just ask them!'

Another woman appears behind Mrs Gilby, takes her hand and leads her back to her bedroom.

Willie exits the house sharply and walks to his car. He doesn't like scenes of raw emotion. All the same, he wishes he could have taken a picture of Mrs Gilby. Instead he turns back and photographs the outside of the house before climbing into his car. Then he drives off, the words of Elaine Gilby, housewife, aged thirty-eight, ringing loudly in his head: '*What monster has taken my child*?'

Back at the office, Willie calls the police. He is put through to the communications officer, and receives the official line: 'This is being treated as a missing person inquiry for the time being.' Willie rings off. He thinks for a moment and then calls his old school friend for the inside story.

'You bastard,' says the old school friend. 'Where's that fucking photo you walked off with?'

'You'll get it back,' says Willie. 'Don't worry. What's the story on Karen Gilby?'

'We're treating it as a missing persons inquiry for the time being,' says the old school friend. 'We can't classify it as an abduction until we have some evidence that another party was involved. We're checking Bob Gilby's laptop right now to see if Karen used it to get onto the Internet, maybe chatted to the wrong guy. But, between you and me, after forty-eight hours, the chances of her turning up safely go down pretty steeply.'

'Can I quote you as a "highly placed police source"?' asks Willie.

'Yes. But you owe me two favours now.'

Willie hangs up and writes a piece. It's tough and gritty. It's punchy. It's headed: 'Countdown – Missing schoolgirl Karen Gilby Now Gone for Twenty-Four Hours!' The sub, in bold, 'Police express mounting concern for fate of missing girl, aged 10.'

Mr Naylor crosses out the headline and rewrites it: 'Gilby Family Appeal For Help in Karen Search'. Then he edits the rest of the piece so that it ends up, in Willie's opinion, as exciting as an article about a church fete. When he sees the revised text, Willie bangs his forehead on his desk for a moment. Then he rings Norman Stokoe.

Seventeen

Norman and Willie meet in Norman's office. Willie is still high on the story: not the story that will appear in tomorrow's *Northumbria Herald*. He's looking ahead to the real story, the story about how a serial killer is at large in Northumberland. The story that will accompany the pictures and profiles of the two children from the Missingkids website, where Karen's photo will join them shortly. But Willie needs more. It's still not a complete story – it needs to go somewhere. He needs more information. The story he wants to write will point a finger. It will name a name.

'It's a great break for us,' he says to Norman. Norman doesn't see it that way. He grimaces in distaste.

'I can't share your enthusiasm for this poor little girl's disappearance.'

'I'm as worried for her as you are,' replies Willie. He tries not to sound defensive. He knows he ought to be more sensitive; or at least sound as if he cares a bit about what has happened to these children. But he's a journalist. The story must never get in the way of the story.

'If Karen's disappearance helps us persuade the police that these cases must be linked, then it's a break.'

'Tell me again what you learned from your visit to the Gilbys' house?'

Willie tells him again. He describes Robert Gilby and what he said. Then he repeats Mrs Gilby's line about 'monsters' and Norman winces.

'Poor woman,' he says. 'Perhaps she's right. I hope to God not.'

Willie says, 'There is a monster out there. I know it.'

'Well, we've nothing to go on,' says Norman. 'All these children are different. They have different family backgrounds; they disappeared from different places. If the same person took them, how did he or she know where and when to find them? It must have been very opportunistic.'

'Yes,' agrees Willie. 'It's hard to say how he picks them. Maybe he just cruises around looking for stray children. But then, you would think he'd be seen by someone? Someone would remember the car he was in, or he would have been seen talking to the children.'

They both fall silent for a while. Norman is doodling on a pad. Then he asks: 'What about Becky Thomas? We know a little bit about the other two children. We've met Theo's parents. You've talked to the Gilbys. We know nothing about Becky Thomas.'

'Shall we go and talk to the mother?' suggests Willie. Norman is still doodling on the A4 pad in front of him. He's drawing an angel. It has feathered wings outstretched and its head is tilted at a coy angle as if it has just said something rather amusing. Norman remembers the angel from somewhere: he has met it before. It used to hang on the wall in Father Adrian's study: *The Annunciation*. He sees Willie looking at the sketch upside down, a half-smile on his lips. Norman raises his head from his sketch and says: 'No, *you* go and talk to the mother. Then come and tell me what you have found out.'

Willie is dismissed. On the way out, he stops by Pippa's

desk and asks: 'What time do you get off work tonight?'

'Half-past five.'

'I'll pick you up outside here and we'll go for a drink, shall we?'

'Maybe,' replies Pippa.

'I'll see you then.'

Willie goes back to his office and sits at his desk for a while to ensure that Mr Naylor knows he's there. He Googles the names of the three children, gets a hit on Theo and another on Becky. But the hits are just articles from the local press he has already seen. It doesn't take him long to find Mrs Thomas's address. He walks past his editor's office with his head down, muttering to himself in a preoccupied way, holding some papers under his arm. He is the picture of an overworked journalist chasing a deadline. His editor doesn't notice. Then Willie is outside and in the sunshine. He buys a Mars Bar and unwraps it with his teeth as he starts up the car. Then he's driving and eating his Mars Bar, trying to remember the way to Becky Thomas's house and avoid getting melted chocolate on the steering wheel.

The drive doesn't take long. The former mining town where Mrs Thomas lives – it is larger than a village but not by much – is on a cold and windy ridge. As Willie drives towards it, a great escarpment falls away on the left side of the road towards a distant plain. In the plain below are other villages; the fleeting sunlight gleams on the fibreglass torpedo shapes of slurry silos; on the corrugated aluminium roofs of cattle sheds.

On the top of the hill a few hundred yards before the town are a dozen giant white wind turbines standing in rough pasture. The wind is blowing but the blades are not revolving. The road goes alongside this forest of static shapes and, as

Willie drives past, the sun comes out from behind grey clouds. Shadows spring up at the feet of the white metal structures. The nearest turbine casts a dark shadow like a cross over the road. Willie drives through it.

The Thomas family lives in Collingwood Street. It is a long row of terraced houses, with back gardens facing onto an alley. Willie drives along the front of the terrace until he has found number seventeen. Then he continues on to the end of the row, turns left, and left again into the alley at the back and drives along that. On the other side of the alley is rough grass and then a public park: a mournful-looking place with a couple of benches and a concrete pad on which stand a wooden roundabout, a slide and a row of swings. Beyond the narrow strip of parkland is a main road. No children are playing in the park. All the children are at school. How did anyone know that Becky Thomas wouldn't be at school, might be in the park playing all by herself? Or was it just random? Willie doesn't like random; he doesn't believe in it. If it is random, there won't be any connection between Becky and Karen and Theo – except randomness – and he will never write his story.

He turns back into the main road and cruises back to number seventeen where he parks the car. Number seventeen looks more dilapidated than the other houses: this is a Victorian terrace, and none of the houses are smart but, on the whole, they look cared for. Number seventeen is the exception. The brown paint on the front door is peeling. The curtains at the upstairs windows are drawn. Through the dirty window pane of the front window, Willie can see a dark and untidy room.

He pushes the front doorbell. It doesn't work, so he knocks. No answer, but somewhere he can hear a voice talking. It sounds as if it is coming from a radio or a television set. He knocks again a little harder, and the unlocked door swings inwards as he does so. He steps into the hall and calls, 'Hello-o? Mrs Thomas?'

A smell hits him. It is impossible to say of what it consists: there is a hint of old cigarettes; a strong suggestion of stale alcohol; grace notes of boiled vegetables. It makes Willie stop breathing through his nose and take in air through his mouth instead. On the floor, behind the door, is a great pile of leaflets, junk mail and brown envelopes. Most of these look like bills. The occupant obviously doesn't like opening letters.

'Mrs Thomas?' calls Willie again. He is already regretting coming here. Nothing good is going to happen in a house like this. Just then a door opens at the other end of the hallway. A figure is standing there in the dim light: a woman, short and stocky, her hair unbrushed, wearing grey tracksuit bottoms and a shirt.

'Who are you?' she asks. Willie introduces himself. He's not sure how much the woman understands of what he's said. She tells him: 'I don't want to talk to you.'

Closer up, her face is red and blotchy. Her eyes have dark rings under them. Her mouth is slack when she isn't talking. In the background is the sound of applause from the radio or TV. Willie isn't put off. He can't give up now. So he uses the same line he tried on Mary Constantine: publicity can only help, not harm. The disappearance of Karen Gilby will bring the subject back to people's minds. Willie knows he has no intention of writing a story linking Karen to Becky yet: that is the last thing he wants to do at the moment. He doesn't want to point the competition in that direction.

Mrs Thomas hasn't heard about Karen Gilby: she doesn't seem to care; she doesn't want to know. Her own loss is quite enough for her without bothering about anybody else's. She focuses on the young man in front of her. He wants something. Very well. She says: 'I've nowt to drink.'

Willie gets the message. 'What's your poison?'

'You what?'

'What do you like to drink?'

'Vodka.'

'Don't go away,' Willie tells her. 'I'll be right back.' He hurries out of the house and drives to the mini-supermarket he has spotted on the way to Collingwood Street where he buys a half bottle of Smirnoff. Six pounds fifty, and he can't claim it on expenses. He's back at the house in ten minutes. This time he doesn't knock. He walks through the hall, pushes open the door and finds himself in the kitchen. Mrs Thomas is at the table. She looks like someone switched her off; unplugged her at the wall. She's just sitting there, inert. Behind her, the sink unit is piled high with what Willie guesses must be every piece of crockery and cutlery in the house, all of it unwashed. On the table is a chequered linoleum cloth. On the cloth is a curled-up slice of white bread covered in margarine, with a bite taken out of one corner. It looks as if it has been there for some time. Willie puts the vodka on the table.

'There you are.'

Mrs Thomas reaches behind her, finds a mug, and pours a good measure of vodka into it. She sips. Then she looks up at Willie, finally registering his presence.

'What do you want to know, then?'

Willie goes into his routine: tell me about Becky, what sort of girl was she, what did she like, what didn't she like? Mrs Thomas starts to speak. She stops; then starts again. She wants to talk about Becky, Willie can tell, but all she says is: 'I can't remember her any more.'

Then she howls: 'I can't remember her. What she looked like. What she did. They've taken the photos.'

'Who took them?'

'The police. They said they'd bring them back, but they never.'

Willie tries to get her to tell him something. Anything. The answers are incoherent. It's painful to watch this woman trying to string words together, to string thoughts together. After a few more minutes, he realises he isn't going to get much information from Mrs Thomas. Not today, maybe not on any other day.

'Can I see her room?'

Mrs Thomas sips more vodka. She's calmer now, travelling to somewhere inside her head where none of this matters any more.

'It's upstairs.'

Willie slips out of the kitchen. He goes up the narrow stairs. The stale smell is stronger here. He opens a door. This must be the mother's room. He hastily retreats, shutting the door behind him. He tries another door.

This room is tidy. This room is neat. The bed is made. Willie wonders if Becky made the bed herself, thinks she probably would have had to. Propped against the pillow are two teddy bears. There is a wooden desk and chair, and a shelf with books and a reading lamp on it. On the desk a children's picture book is opened out flat. Willie looks at it. He reads: 'The princess went to the tower.'

Willie guesses Becky spent a lot of time in this room. He guesses she hid here, made this her own little escape from the chaos and despair downstairs. He thinks she probably spent a lot of time reading. He looks at the titles of the books: fairy stories, stories about little girls with ponies, stories about other places, stories about happy and well-cared-for children who live in houses that are clean and safe.

He extracts his digital camera and takes photographs of the neat little bedroom. Then he sits down on the bed for a moment. His own childhood was spent in a house much like this: not as dirty, but in other respects the same. His own parents were far from happy with each other: they quarrelled often. They quarrelled out of unhappiness with each other, and because they lived constantly on the edge of absolute poverty. Willie remembers the poverty more clearly than he remembers his own family. What drives him now is a desire never, ever to fall back into the way he lived then.

Suddenly he is overwhelmed. He feels a sense of desolation wash over him: a sense of despair. He imagines the life this child must have led, caring for herself and her alcoholic mother. He imagines, against his will, how this child's life might have ended. Or how it might be ending now. Or how it will end soon, if someone doesn't find her. Perhaps he is too late. He will write his story, but it will be too late for Karen, too late for Becky, much too late for Theo.

He doesn't have to imagine the sense of loss when the child disappeared. Now he feels it himself. He feels what the mother downstairs must be feeling. He understands that drinking has muddled her so much that she cannot remember the only thing that she loves. She doesn't know what to do or who to call. The only answer is more of the same: vodka.

He can't spend another moment in here. It's too painful. It's making him think too much. He doesn't say goodbye.

He leaves, banging the front door behind him.

Eighteen

His birth was not an easy one. Before he arrived, his mother had two miscarriages. After he was born, the doctors told his mother she must never have children again. It's as if her own body was conspiring against her to prevent her producing children. It's as if her body knew that the result would not be a good one.

He is born with a mild deformity. The medical term is *mandibular hypoplasia*. It is a mouthful. His lower jaw is undershot like an over-bred Labrador's. The top jaw overlaps the bottom. The teeth don't meet up properly. It's awkward when it comes to chewing. He has a tendency to oral secretion; he dribbles. It wasn't so noticeable when he was a baby. Babies don't have well-defined chins as a rule, and they dribble. But by the time he is six, he still doesn't have much of a chin, and he still dribbles. The deformity gives his face the look of a snout: a feral look. For a long while, he doesn't know that there is something odd about him. But as his self-awareness develops, he can see a reflection of himself in other people's faces. Not a literal reflection, not a mirror image; but he sees it in the way his mother lowers her gaze when she looks at him, in the way she turns her head to avoid eye contact. When he encounters other children, he sees it in their bright, cruel stares: he deduces that what they see, they do not like. His father pays him very little attention.

For a long while, he doesn't understand. His parents never talk about his condition in front of him. Sometimes his nanny gazes at him tenderly and murmurs, 'Poor little thing'; but for all he knows this is just what nannies always say. It's only when he starts going to nursery school that he begins to understand. The other children aren't comfortable around him. They call him names. He doesn't understand what he has done or why they should call him names.

One day, when he is six years old, his father's sister – his aunt – pays a rare visit. She is an outspoken woman who believes in calling a spade a spade. When she sees the boy for the first time since he was a formless shape wriggling in a shawl at his christening, she says: 'Oh, my dear George. What a hideous little thing!'

The boy goes and stands behind his mother. He's not quite sure what the word 'hideous' means, but it doesn't sound like a compliment.

'That's so unkind, Sarah,' he hears his mother say in a quavering voice.

'Well, Helen, you know I don't mean to be unkind. Perhaps "hideous" is too strong. But he is a very *ugly* little chap.'

He doesn't exactly know what the word 'ugly' means either. He asks his mother about it when his aunt has left. She bursts into tears and says: 'You're not ugly. You're just different.'

Different. He knows that he is different. He feels it. It isn't only his physical appearance. The outward deformity is not in itself the reason for his sense of alienation. It is a mask. It stops people looking beyond the physical aspect of the boy to the true nature of the boy. His true nature has nothing to do with his deformity. He is as different as could be. He feels no kinship with his parents, not with the children that he meets, not with any other human being. He feels as remote from them as if he had been born on another star. He understands mockery, but not love.

He learns about mockery when he goes to primary school. There's quite a mix of children there. Some of the older boys have a view about new boys. They have very strong views about new boys who look as strange as this one does. They make a point of teasing him. He doesn't like being teased. When they mock him, he looks at them. The way he looks at them upsets them, even the biggest and the toughest. They stop calling him names and leave him alone.

At home, he looks at himself in the mirror. He sees a face with a marked brow, a flat nose, and an upper lip that projects over a receding chin. His cheeks hang over his lower jaw like flaps. Snail-tracks of saliva appear at each corner of his mouth, no matter how often he wipes them away.

He doesn't like the way he looks, because he has been taught by experience to believe that his looks offend other people. When he goes to sleep at night, he prays that in the morning he will be reborn. He believes that if he prays hard enough, it will happen. As he lies in bed, he tells himself, just as the dark tide of sleep sweeps him out to sea: if I want to change, I can change. I can be born again with a different face. Each morning he awakes to discover that, if he has been reborn, then he has been reborn as himself.

He is a solitary child. His own parents treat him with reticence, as if they are wondering why all that pain and effort has led to this: has led to him. When he was very small, all he knew was that there must be something unusual about him. He made that judgement based on the way people looked at him, or on the way they wouldn't look at him.

Now he's a little older, his feeling of otherness is growing within him. It isn't just the way he looks; it's the way he feels.

He can see that certain responses are expected of him: that he should laugh when someone says something funny, that he should cry when someone says something sad. Funny and sad mean nothing to him. When his father becomes angry with him, which happens quite often, he doesn't feel afraid. He doesn't feel remorse. He just leaves the room, as soon as he is able. When his mother tries to take him in her arms, he wriggles and squirms until she lets go.

When he reaches the age of eight, his father takes him to see a consultant. His father introduces his son to the surgeon in an apologetic manner. The surgeon is interested in the boy's condition.

'The anatomy is aberrant,' he says, more to himself than the father. Aberrant: the word sticks to the boy's memory like a burr.

'We thought the condition would correct itself,' his father explains, 'but perhaps we were wrong.'

'You should have taken him to see someone years ago. I'm not sure how easy it will be to correct it now. We might be better off waiting until he is older.'

'What is involved?'

'Multiple surgical procedures. It can take some time to correct, and of course we cannot always be sure of the outcome.'

'So you think it is better to let sleeping dogs lie, for the moment?' the boy's father asks the surgeon. The surgeon doesn't answer directly. Instead he has another good look at the boy. He places a stethoscope on the boy's chest and listens.

'He doesn't seem to have any difficulty with his breathing. The airways are not obstructed.' He addresses the boy directly for the first time. 'Can you breathe all right, young man?'

The boy doesn't answer, but after a moment he nods.

'There, you see he can breathe all right,' says the surgeon, turning to the boy's father as if he is already claiming credit for at least this much.

'It doesn't look ... Well, it doesn't look normal,' replies the father.

'Of course not. Nobody is saying that he looks normal. But this is a very minor deformity in the grand scheme of things. He has all his limbs. His mental capabilities appear to be good. He can see and hear. He just looks a little odd. The important thing is that he should not feel stigmatised by his appearance. Many children with similar disadvantages compensate by developing a great sweetness of disposition.'

And the surgeon looks at the boy, as if he can already detect a sweetness of disposition. The boy looks at the surgeon. His glance reveals nothing about himself: nothing whatsoever.

They never return to the consultant, neither then nor later. His father has learned to live comfortably with his son's disability.

The boy himself finds contentment only when he is on his own. He has discovered that the best place to be is somewhere where he can control everything, and make everything just the way he likes it. He likes order; he likes silence. He likes beauty. When he is eight years old, he looks up the word 'ugly'. He finds a definition in a dictionary in his father's study: 'Unpleasant or repulsive in appearance'. He looks up the word 'beauty'. He finds nothing in the dictionary that helps him understand the word.

But he knows what beauty is. He looks for it and he finds it, in the most unlikely places. He knows that whatever he looks like, whatever he feels like, he can at least appreciate beauty. He can see it; he can feel it; he can touch it. He can *possess* it. If he surrounds himself with beauty, he will be beautiful.

His parents live in a big house in the country, with a large garden and fields and woods between the house and the nearest village. He likes being outside. It means he doesn't have to talk: he doesn't have to explain himself. He thinks that he cannot be explained.

He holds a dead bird in his hand. It is a goldfinch. Its beauty pierces him to the heart. He loves birds. By the age of eight he can recognise more different species by sight than many a fully grown birder. He holds the dead goldfinch in his hand and strokes its feathers, and talks to it in a low voice. What he tells it, nobody knows.

Beauty is all around him. He wants to preserve it for his own pleasure. He is always alone, but never lonely. He does not have friends. He does not need friends. Today he has found the body of a goldfinch. What other child has such a possession? He takes the bird home in his hand, back to the house. He enters the house from the garden, walking silently past the kitchen where Martha the housekeeper is cooking lunch, past the drawing room where he can hear his mother laughing and talking with friends that have come to visit, the smell of cigarette smoke reaching his nostrils. He climbs the broad oak-timbered staircase two flights to the upper floor where his bedroom is.

It is understood he is never to be disturbed when he is in his room. When he is in his room, it is his private place. He gets very angry if someone comes in and disturbs him with silly questions and wants to know what he is doing. He is only eight, but already those around him prefer not to see him when he is angry.

He enters the room and takes the goldfinch across to a chest of drawers. Inside are cigar boxes. They no longer hold cigars, but instead the bodies of other dead birds. When you open them, they smell of cedar wood and the faint odour of corruption. He puts the dead goldfinch alongside other specimens: a dead spotted woodpecker, a dead blue tit, a dead thrush. The older specimens are dried out: mummified. He strokes the still-warm feathers of his newest acquisition one last time, then puts it away. Summer is coming soon: he hopes to add swallows and house martins to his collection.

Nineteen

Willie meets Pippa outside the glass and steel palace where she works and takes her down to the quayside for a drink. He is a little nervous, he doesn't know why. She talks, she laughs at his jokes, but he can't quite work her out.

They sit down at a table in a bar Willie uses. It is too cold tonight to sit outside and the air is damp with a fret that has rolled up the river from the North Sea, blurring the outline of the Hilton Hotel on the other bank, and of the great arched iron bridge across the river. Inside, Willie asks Pippa what she would like to drink.

'A glass of white wine,' says Pippa. Willie gets the drinks in and sits down opposite her. She is examining her face in the mirror of a powder compact and dabbing at herself.

'Was His Lordship still there when you left?' asks Willie, meaning Norman.

'No way. He knocks off early most days.'

'What's he been up to today?'

'He went to see that policeman again this evening. The one you both went to see the other day.'

'Chief Inspector Saxon?'

'That might be his name.'

Willie sips his drink, leans forward and asks, 'So what's a pretty girl like you doing in a job like that?'

'How do you mean, "like that"?'

'Well, your Norman hasn't got a real job. So it stands to reason he hasn't got much to do. So it stands to reason you haven't, either.'

'It suits me,' says Pippa. 'I'm doing a home-learning course in IT. So when there's nothing to do at work, which is most of the time, I do my revision on the computer.'

So that's it. He knew there was something more to this girl. He doesn't appreciate, even now, how much he has under-estimated her. He thought she was just a pretty face who killed time reading women's magazines. But Pippa is much more than that.

'What, like a degree or something?' asks Willie.

'A diploma. With the Open University.'

Willie eyes Pippa with new respect. So she too has a dream. She too wants to get out of the dead-end job she's stuck in.

'Hey, you're a proper dark horse.'

Pippa smiles. She neither confirms nor denies that she is a dark horse. Pippa is a hard-working girl with good A levels and a degree in Economics. Academically, she is in a different league to Willie. She's working as a receptionist because she was made redundant in her last job as a graduate trainee in a bank. But Pippa never gives up: she would take any job to remain in employment. She's seen what unemployment does to people. There's a lot of it about in this part of the world.

Willie tells her about his own ambition: to become a Fleet Street journalist, even if it means working in Wapping. The big time, the bright lights. Scoops and exclusives. Stories, and more stories. Maybe one day *the* story that will change every-thing. They finish their drinks and Willie offers to get another round in. He looks at his watch and says: 'Why don't we go and have something to eat when we've finished these?'

'Oh, I don't know,' demurs Pippa.

'Why not? We both have to eat. Why not together?'

'All right then,' says Pippa.

As Willie goes to the bar to order the drinks, he finds that he is not quite master of his emotions this evening. His expectations for the evening were: worst case, a couple of drinks with an attractive girl; best (and least likely) case, he pulls her. But the girl he is sitting drinking with isn't remotely like the person he imagined she would be. She's a dreamer, like him. She wants more out of life, and she's prepared to work for it.

There's another quality to Pippa too. The more Willie talks to her, the more attractive she seems to him. He realises that it is an inner quality, something about her manner, that is what makes her so desirable. And he does desire her. His heart is fluttering as if this was his first-ever date.

Pippa, in turn, is attracted to Willie. She understands what he is: someone trying to find something that will give him more gravity. Willie is flippant, idle and ambitious. She suspects he will cut corners to get where he wants to be, and will use people and drop them along the way. But she likes him, all the same. And it's a while since her last boyfriend told her he had accepted a job in New York. They write to each other, sometimes. So she'll let Willie buy her dinner. Where's the harm in that?

A few hours later, Willie sits up in bed and looks down at Pippa's pale face and her neck and shoulders. The duvet conceals the rest. They are in the bedroom of his flat.

'That was very nice,' he says. The words sound inadequate, but it isn't Willie's style to show too much enthusiasm.

'You mustn't think I do this with every boy who buys me a hot meal,' says Pippa. She isn't smiling.

'I don't usually get up to this sort of thing on a first date myself,' admits Willie. 'It just sort of happened, didn't it?'

'I suppose you won't want to see me again, now you've got me into bed,' suggests Pippa.

'Of course I will,' answers Willie. 'As often as possible.'

Willie is as surprised as Pippa by the speed with which a date that was only intended as a couple of drinks together has developed into something much, much more. His track record with girls is mixed. Sometimes he wonders if he doesn't try too hard. Tonight he hasn't really been trying at all. It just suddenly took off. He's been known to score in the bars and nightclubs, but not as often as he would like: far from often. It is very rare that he manages to pull a girl as attractive as Pippa on a first date. In fact, it is so rare, when Willie considers the matter for a moment, it has never actually happened to him before. He looks at her as she sits up in bed. He finds that he likes looking at her. He likes being with her. He likes *her*. He hopes this isn't just a one-night thing.

Pippa clutches the duvet modestly to her throat. Her modesty is a virtue that comes and goes. She looks thoughtful. Then she surprises Willie by changing the subject completely. She asks: 'What are you and Norman going to do about those poor children?'

'How on earth do you know about that?' exclaims Willie.

'I listened at the door,' replies Pippa.

'You didn't!'

'I did. Because I couldn't work out what someone like you was doing with someone like Norman. It was too interesting. I couldn't help myself. Anyway, I haven't got anything else to do and I can't work on my Open University stuff all day.'

Willie frowns.

'Who else have you told about this?'

'Nobody, of course.'

'You mustn't.'

'Who else would I tell? Anyway, I promise not to.' Pippa lets go of the duvet for a moment to make the sign of the cross above where her heart ought to be, and Willie is distracted for a moment by her nakedness. Then Pippa pulls the duvet back up to her throat and says: 'But you never answered my question. What are you going to do about those poor children?'

'I don't know.'

'Why are you so interested? It's not your normal line of work, is it?'

'How do you know what my normal line of work is?'

'I looked you up on the Internet,' replies Pippa. 'After the first time you came in. You do local stuff. Articles about shopping centres and so on.'

'Did you fancy me the first time you saw me? Is that why you checked me out?'

'You'd like to think so, wouldn't you? So, what are you going to do about those poor children? Do you think there's any chance they might still be alive?' asks Pippa for the third time.

'I don't know. I want to find out what's happened to them. I want to try and find out who did it. Write a story about it. Get into the national press. That's the general idea.'

'Don't you want to try and find them first?' asks Pippa.

'Yes, of course I do,' says Willie, a little abashed.

'You think the same person took all three of them,' says Pippa. She shudders.

'I don't know. Yes, it's possible,' says Willie, not wanting to continue this conversation. 'I don't like to think about it.'

Pippa says, with an intensity that startles Willie: 'We have to find them soon.'

Twenty

Geordie Nixon drives to the forest. Every day it's harder to get out of bed and make the journey into the dark trees. The empty kitchen at half past six in the morning; the solitary breakfast; no answer when he knocks on Mary's door to see if she wants a cup of tea. She's either deeply asleep, or else pretending to be. He knocks on her door every day, just the same. He's hoping that one day she'll say 'Come in.' He's hoping that one day he'll go in and find her lying in bed, warm and sleepy, that she'll put her arms around him like she used to do. It never happens.

When he gets back home tonight, it will be just the same. She has a part-time job working for the council. Sometimes she's home when he gets back; sometimes she doesn't return until an hour or two after him. She'll cook him supper – if he's hungry enough to want it. She still feels she has to do that much for him. She'll cook him something – these days 'cooking' means heating up a ready meal from Tesco – and then she'll sit with him for half an hour. He tries to talk to her. She won't, or she can't, talk back. Her answers are monosyllabic. They verge on contemptuous. If it weren't for the fact that he believes she is suffering, that it is the pain that makes her behave in this way, he would walk out.

He doesn't know what she does. She says she works for the council. What does that mean? Which department? What does she do for the council? She never says. If he presses her, she'll say, 'What makes *you* so interested all of a sudden?' As if he's not interested in her. As if he hasn't always been. As if he deserves a reply like that. She comes and goes at odd times. She says it's flexi-time. He doesn't know what to think any more.

When Theo was alive he would never have dreamed of disbelieving her. It's only since he went that she's become indifferent to what he thinks. She barely notices that he exists. He doesn't know if her job is real, but the money she brings home is real. It's her flat. He pays his share of the rent. That was the deal when he moved in with her, and that's still the deal.

He drives north up the valley, past the great dam wall of Kielder Water. The metalled road takes him past the Tourist Information Centre at Leaplish, past Halfpenny Rigg and Matthew's Linn. Then he turns off the Tarmac onto a graded forest road. He drives into the forest in his Scania truck, going through the gears as the gradient steepens abruptly. The forest road runs alongside the Akenshaw Burn, then turns up Birtley Grain. By eight o'clock he has parked by the block of trees that he is clear-felling and has started up the harvester. The day's work begins.

It doesn't get any better, being alone amongst the trees. The sense of foreboding is always with him now. Geordie is becoming a mass of nerves. How could he not be with the life he leads? Alone all day and worse than alone at night. Except that he keeps feeling he is not really alone up here: that if he could only see a little further out of the corner of his eye, he would see something that he can't see when he looks straight ahead. He constantly checks his watch, which he has never done before, willing the seconds to pass; the minutes to pass; the hours to pass: until it is time to go home.

At half-past ten he stops the harvester and reaches down for the bag where he keeps his bait. He finds the Thermos flask and unscrews the cap, pours some tea into it, and sips. Around him is the devastation of his morning's work. Down by the side of the forest track is a growing pile of neatly cut poles. He sips his tea and looks through the dark trees to the dark sky above. It has been drizzling all morning and now it is starting to rain properly. The windscreen of the harvester is flecked with drops of water. He leans forward and flicks the wipers, which smear the windscreen. Through the blurred glass he can see two white shapes, below him and to the right. They weren't there a moment ago. The windscreen clears as the wipers do their work. Now Geordie can see two lambs standing side by side amongst the brash on the forest floor. Two white lambs, standing side by side, looking up at him.

Where have they come from? A minute ago, before the rain started, there was nothing there but the litter from his morning's work: nothing but the trees, and the forest track. Geordie slides open the side-window of his harvester to take a better look. His heart has started beating too fast again. Two white lambs looking up at him. He can see them quite clearly. He can almost smell the wet wool.

The lambs stare at him with their knowing, intelligent gaze as if they are waiting for him to say something. Geordie sees lambs every day on his drive up the valley, but not here: not now on a cool May morning in the middle of the forest. And he has never seen lambs like this, with eyes that are as bright and sentient as a human being's. Their gazes pierce him. Geordie cries out in his surprise and falls back in his seat, spilling hot tea over his legs. He picks up the cup and leans forward again to take another look. It's only two lambs.

But now there *are* no lambs. The forest floor is empty of anything except brash and dead trees. Geordie opens the door of the harvester, jumps down. He looks around him.

There are no lambs. He saw two lambs with eyes like human beings.

Geordie gets back in the harvester, starts it up and drives back down to the truck. He climbs into the truck and drives up the forest track until the ruts and pools of water force him to stop. Ahead of him, there is a padlocked barrier across the track, so he can't drive any further even if he wanted to, because he does not have a key. He makes a difficult turn in the big truck, and heads back down the way he came. He sees nothing: no lambs, nothing but the trees.

He can't stay out here a moment longer. At eleven o'clock in the morning, he heads for home again. He thinks he is sick: sick in the head. All his life Geordie has dealt in the real, the practical and the immediate. He's never troubled himself with the abstract or the imaginary. Now he's experiencing waking dreams, except they don't feel like dreams at all. Instead it seems as if he has somehow stepped out of the world he knew into a parallel one that mimics the world he came from, but is also peopled by phantoms: phantom lambs, phantom dogs. He is certain that something a lot worse than that is somewhere on the edge of his vision, at the back of his mind.

It's all happened since Theo went. He misses Theo so much. He can't understand why Theo, who united him with Mary by his presence, has divided them by his absence. Why can't she see how torn he is? It's as if Mary without Theo has been diminished, as if she had invested in him all her emotions and all her humanity. Now that Theo's gone, it's as if those aspects of Mary have gone with him. What remains is just the shell of who she was.

Twenty-One

Norman Stokoe calls on Chief Inspector Saxon. He knows the police officer can't refuse to see him. Norman might not turn out to be a star in the firmament of the child protection industry; then again, he might. That's the beauty of working for a department of state that reorganises itself as often as this one does: nobody can be sure who is at the bottom of the food chain, who is halfway up, and who will be one of the Big Beasts of the future. A Big Beast, who will stalk through the department devouring the plankton-like individuals of lesser importance. Chief Inspector Saxon doesn't rate Norman, not one bit. But he can't afford to take a chance that however impossible it might seem at the moment, this man might, after all, become a Regional Children's Commissioner.

When Norman is shown into Saxon's office, he finds the chief inspector on the phone. The chief inspector motions to Norman to sit down in one of the empty chairs opposite the desk. Norman remains standing and waits until the chief inspector has hung up. Then he leans forward, putting both hands on the chief inspector's desk, and says: 'So, now you've got three missing children. All within twenty or thirty miles of each other. It must be abduction, mustn't it? Don't you think it is possible, now, that all these disappearances are linked?'

'Do sit down, Mr Stokoe,' says Chief Inspector Saxon. He

waits until Norman has settled himself in one of the chairs before he continues: 'As you must know, after all your years in this business, we work to the rule book on this. The book says: "Anyone whose whereabouts are unknown will be considered missing until their well being, or otherwise, is established."'

'*Three* children have gone missing!'

'It wouldn't make any difference if it were ten children, Mr Stokoe. We are working very hard to establish the whereabouts of these two girls. And indeed the runaway who went missing last Christmas.'

'They can't all just have run away,' replies Norman energetically. 'Surely you must see that?'

'I'm not paid to speculate,' replies Chief Inspector Saxon. 'I told you that on the last occasion we met. Lots of children, unfortunately, go missing every year. Every week. You take the case of Becky Thomas. The mother's an alcoholic. The interviewing officers could hardly get a dozen words from her. More than likely, the daughter is a runaway. Or even a thrownaway.'

A thrownaway. The language of the children's industry is enriched by such terms. Norman Stokoe sits back in his chair, looks at Chief Inspector Saxon and asks: 'You're absolutely discounting the involvement of a third party?'

'Of course not. Abduction is another possibility we have to consider. We're ruling nothing in and we're ruling nothing out at this stage in our enquiries.' The chief inspector is twiddling a pencil in his fingers as he speaks. Norman understands why he has agreed to the meeting. The police officer wants to be on record as having met him, not once, but twice; of having listened to his concerns and made a note of them for the file. But he won't do anything. What *can* he do? He's a policeman, not a magician. Norman speaks: 'I think the common thread between the three children is stranger abduction. A stranger, not a member of the family.'

'We're investigating all the leads we have,' says Chief Inspector Saxon. Suddenly he sounds like a human being for a moment, although it won't last: 'Believe me, we want to find these children. But we've got to face up to the fact that in one case there is a presumption of domestic violence against the child. In another, the mother is an alcoholic, so anything's possible. But the probability is that either the child has left to escape from her mother or else her mother has dumped her somewhere. We haven't, by any means, ruled out third-party involvement. We're still trying to trace cars seen in the area at the time of Becky's abduction.'

The policeman stops for a moment to call up something on the screen of his computer.

'In the case of the other missing juvenile, there was no CCTV to help us. However, in the course of our investigations we took away Mr Gilby's laptop. We wanted to see if Karen had been accessing the Internet from there. Maybe she had been visiting chatrooms. Maybe she had been groomed by someone she had met in one of them.'

'Karen Gilby?' asked Norman with incredulity. 'She's not even ten years old. She probably doesn't even know how to switch on a computer.'

'You'd be surprised what a nine-year-old girl knows, Mr Stokoe,' replies the chief inspector. 'You're out of date. You don't have any children of your own, do you? They learn how to operate these machines almost as soon as they can walk. But, as it happens, we didn't find any evidence that Karen had been accessing the Internet. What we did find was some por-nography, mostly attached to emails sent to Mr Gilby's private account.'

Norman is startled. The chief inspector smiles and says, 'So, yes, abduction is a possibility. But we think it far more likely that we could be looking at a case of sexual abuse in the Gilby family. Maybe Karen found some of these images. Maybe her father did something he shouldn't have done. We're thinking that the little girl is another runaway. She may have run away and she may have injured herself. There's a fast-flowing river only five hundred yards from the village. We've been dragging it. At this point we haven't charged the father with anything, but we're keeping an open mind on that point.'

Running away on a cold and rainy spring day, thinks Norman. Aloud he says: 'I didn't get the impression Karen Gilby had an unhappy family life.'

'You've met the parents, then?' asks the chief inspector.

'No, but my colleague has.'

'Oh yes, the young reporter. Mr Craig. He seems to think he's some kind of investigative journalist. I very much doubt that he is. You might pass on a well-meant word of advice.'

'Such as?' asks Norman.

'Such as: he should keep his nose out of police business. There is a great deal at stake here. It doesn't make it any easier to run a professional operation if people like him keep interfering. I can't help wondering if his boss Teddy Naylor knows what young Willie Craig is up to. To be honest, your own involvement is not welcome either.'

The conversation is over. Norman leaves the building that houses Chief Inspector Saxon and walks through a cool and misty evening to find his car. There's something not right about the chief inspector's attitude. Norman can't pin it down, but he feels uneasy, as if he's not seeing the whole picture.

*

He arrives at the office early the next morning. For once he's there before anyone else. He has passed a wakeful night: more restless than the night Willie has spent with Pippa, but for very different reasons.

He has been examining himself and his life so far. And he has found himself wanting. Much of his working life has been spent in the world of the child protection industry. The nearest Norman has ever come to the front line has been delivering PowerPoint presentations. He never meets any children. He is wrapped up in a world centred on him, and he is the cleverest person in it. He is ambitious. He has always felt a sense of entitlement; that he should have a seat at the top table.

He is comfortable with the language of 'outcomes' and 'deliverables', words that often mean the opposite of what one would think they meant. He is familiar with the Dead Sea Scrolls of his industry: weighty reports by Commissions of Inquiry or learned judges, which lead to demands for yet more outcomes, yet more deliverables, and yet more reports. He is like a swimmer in the shallows contemplating the ocean, not wishing to step out of his depth, not wishing to explore the darker waters further out to sea: their swirling currents and abysses.

But he knows now that this is where he must go. It is where he must go if he wants to understand what might have happened to Theo Constantine, Becky Thomas and Karen Gilby. Now he is challenged by the disappearance of real children. They are no longer statistics. They are people. Norman realises that something has changed in him: he can't ignore what is happening, he can't pass the problem on to another department for clarification pending further action. He has to find out for himself what may have happened to these children. He has to understand. He cares.

Norman knows that the abduction of children falls under

two headings. Abduction by another member of the family is not uncommon, especially in cases where one parent has been born overseas. Every year Norman has seen instances of fathers (mothers less often) disappearing out of the country with their child, hoping to take them out of the reach of the British courts.

Stranger abduction is much less common, and unlike family abduction, almost always ends in the death of the child concerned. Now Norman wants to review the history of recent stranger abductions. Perhaps he may gain a better understanding of the minds of the perpetrators. Perhaps one of the perpetrators is out there again, though that seems unlikely.

In the Integrated Children's System network there are links to other systems and other databases. Norman has access to some of these. He has permissions and passwords to log into areas of the network that are closed to the public, also closed to many of his more junior colleagues. These are places one should not travel to without reason. There are servers locked away that contain secrets that should not be told, that should only be revealed as a last resort. They contain histories of child killers who have been caught, fragments of their lives, and clinical reports on their victims, or the remains of their victims; notes on file of the many unsolved cases.

And there are images: photographs of the murderers and of their victims. These are the worst of all to look at. In most cases the victims' photographs were taken before their fate overtook them: at a family party, on the beach, in a garden. There are photographs of smiling children and there are photographs of those who stalked them and seized them and took their lives away.

In a few cases there are photographs of the victims after they were visited.

The most common users of these directories and drives are senior police officers working on serious case reviews, or senior social workers, or a few elite forensic medical examiners. Only the most ardent researcher goes to these particular sites.

Here is John Staffen, his thin face twisted in an expression that is neither a smile nor a grimace, but which is not comforting to look at. Here are photographs of Brenda Goddard and Cicely Batstone, both aged five, whom he strangled. Here is a photograph of Linda Bowyer, whom he strangled when he escaped from Broadmoor. His motive? 'To annoy the police' he said, in a statement.

Here are Ian Brady and Myra Hindley, fellow workers in a chemicals factory in Manchester. There is a photograph of them together, smiling in a back garden. Here is a photograph of their first victim; a neighbour of Myra Hindley's, Pauline Read aged sixteen. The list of other victims follows: John Kilbride, aged twelve, Keith Bennett, aged twelve, Lesley Ann Downey, aged ten. There are others.

Here is the bespectacled and bearded face of Ronald Jebson. Here are the photographs of eleven-year-old Susan Blatchford and twelve-year-old Gary Hanlon, the 'babes in the wood', whose bodies were found, long after they disappeared, in Epping Forest. And then there is a photograph of Rosemary Papper, the daughter of his landlady.

Moving on to more contemporary figures, Norman finds Ian Huntley and Roy Whiting. Then, towards the end of the list, he finds William Latham and Gabriel Merkin.

Here is the photograph of William Latham, his long, black beard giving him the air of a Russian Orthodox priest, a faint smile on his face as if he is about to bless someone. Here is the list of his first victims: Michael Mountfield, aged nine, who was the son of a neighbour; Helen Smith, aged eleven, whom he saw waiting at a bus stop as he drove to work in the mornings. His victims were later reduced to the contents of a number of blue plastic carrier bags, weighted with stones and sunk in a pond on the site of an old colliery.

Then there is Gabriel Merkin. Gabriel Merkin, the son of a wealthy banker living in Hampshire. He has had many advantages in life: an apparently normal childhood, brought up by parents who remained married to each other; no obvious problems at school, despite his rather odd physiognomy. Yet in his early forties he began a career so grotesque it almost eclipses the others in this chamber of horrors.

He started with nine-year-old Jack Gryzbowski, worked his way through four other children and ended with Kevin McFall, aged eleven. The children were all killed by injections of diamorphine, then embalmed with glutareldehyde. Embalming is a difficult skill and one that requires practice to achieve the unnatural look of life-in-death that the true embalmer seeks. Gabriel Merkin did practise. Nobody can accuse him of indolence in pursuing his chosen hobby. He was caught, almost by chance, and received two life sentences, to be served in Broadmoor Hospital.

Norman Stokoe feels ill after reading through all this. What has he learned? Nothing, except that the human imagination is limited in its capacity. For who could have dreamed up creatures such as these, if they did not already exist? He wonders where they all are now and has a last scroll through the files. Staffen is dead; Myra Hindley is dead and Ian Brady is locked up. Jebson and Whiting and Latham and Merkin are serving life sentences in the true meaning of the word 'life'.

Except, no, when he clicks on Merkin to find his present whereabouts, the computer bleeps and a window comes up saying: '*Access Denied*'.

He clicks again. The computer bleeps again and the same window comes up saying: '*Access Denied*'.

Norman's first reaction is irritation. Who is this computer to deny Norman Stokoe access to anything? When he took the job he was told he would have universal access to files. People with information have power over people without information. People with more information have power over people with less information. Norman was told that he would be given the rights to all the information that was bound up in all of the servers and all of the networks in his department of state. Only then could he perform his job as children's czar with the relentless efficiency that is expected of him. He was to be granted the same access rights as his boss, the secretary of state. Even the prime minister would not have greater access than Norman Stokoe. He clicks the mouse again.

Access Denied.

Twenty-Two

Willie and Pippa arrive together in the atrium of Norman's office block. Then Pippa walks ahead while Willie waits around, counts to one hundred in his head so that it doesn't look as if they have arrived together, and then follows her to her desk.

Pippa is doing something with her make-up. She looks up when Willie arrives and says, 'Oh, good morning, Mr Craig,' in a bright voice. In an equally false tone, Willie says, 'And good morning to you, Miss Everbury. Now, is Mr Stokoe available?'

'I'll just see, Mr Craig,' says Pippa. She buzzes through and, after a moment, says, 'Mr Stokoe will see you now.'

'Thank you,' says Willie. Pippa blows him a kiss. He winks, and goes into Norman's office.

Norman greets him. He is morose and it doesn't take long to work out why. He tells Willie about his conversation with Chief Inspector Saxon. He tells him about his trawl through the database.

'What did you learn?'

'Surprisingly, I couldn't get access to all the files I wanted. But I looked at most of them.'

'And?'

'We need coffee. I need coffee. I'm too tired to think straight,' says Norman. 'Miss Everbury,' he calls into the intercom. 'Two double espressos, please.'

They wait in silence for coffee. Willie drums his fingers on his knees. He is not good at silence. Norman is staring up at the ceiling, through the ceiling, through all the ceilings beyond and into the deep-blue sky. Coffee arrives. Suddenly Norman lowers his gaze and says, 'None of them started as random.'

'How do you mean, random?'

'All of the child murderers I've looked at. The first victim was usually someone they knew, or else someone who lived nearby, or who they saw every day. The first victim is nearly always specific. In some cases the later victims might have been chosen at random, but there was always a connection with the first one.'

Willie asks, 'How does that help us?'

'I don't know – except that if the same person took Becky, Theo and Karen, then the same person had probably met or at least seen all three of them before. They weren't just picked up off the street.'

Willie scratches his head.

'You said you couldn't get access to all the files you wanted. Who couldn't you get access to?'

'Gabriel Merkin,' replies Norman.

'Oh, *him*. I remember.'

Most people old enough to read newspapers at the time of his conviction would remember Gabriel Merkin's name.

'I could see his file up to the date of his conviction. After that, nothing.'

Norman explains the 'Access Denied' problem. 'It shouldn't happen. I'm meant to be able to see all the files.'

Willie can't see that it matters. Norman says, 'It's a missing

157

bit of the jigsaw. All of the others on the files are either dead or serving life and I can see all of them, except for Gabriel Merkin. If I can't find out where he is now and what's happened to him, I at least need to know why.'

'Ring your boss,' suggests Willie.

'I haven't got one. Technically, it's the new secretary of state, but I doubt he knows that I exist.'

Willie is quite sure that the new secretary of state neither knows nor cares about Norman's existence.

'So complain to someone else.'

'Put in a request under the Freedom of Information Act,' says Pippa. Both men turn their heads in surprise. She has been standing quietly by the door all this time. She had delivered the two cups of coffee and then melted into the background, but she did not leave the room.

'Really, Miss Everbury,' begins Norman, but Willie shushes him. It is remarkable how familiar he has become with Norman in the last few days, but Norman doesn't seem to notice, or mind.

The truth is that, all his life, Norman has longed to be on a team. When he was at school he found that, most of the time, he would be picked last or not at all for teams playing football, cricket and all the other sports that most of the school could play and Norman could not. Now the idea of being part of a team appeals to him in a way he finds hard to resist: even a team that has Willie on it.

'She has a point,' says Willie.

'I couldn't help overhearing,' says Pippa.

'She knows what we're talking about,' Willie tells Norman. 'I told her. She's bright. She's doing a degree in IT. She can help.'

Norman looks from one to the other. Some inkling of what

has been going on occurs to him. A few weeks, or even days, ago he would have considered Pippa's indiscretion treachery of the worst sort and deserving of instant dismissal. Or perhaps it is Willie who has been indiscreet. They're both in it together, he decides.

'How do we do that?' he asks.

'We download a form and fill it in,' says Pippa. 'When you serve the notice on a government department, the department concerned has to reply within twenty days. It's the law.'

'Twenty days is a long time,' says Norman. 'If this does have anything to do with Gabriel Merkin, then in twenty days the missing children could be dead. They probably are already.'

'I know, I know,' says Pippa. 'It's horrible. But we *don't* know who did this. I don't see how it could be Gabriel Merkin. He's in prison, isn't he? We've got to look for the children ourselves, and not wait a moment longer.'

'Look for them?' asks Norman. 'We don't know where to start. It's only the fact that I can't get access to Gabriel Merkin's file that makes me feel we ought to see it. It may have some bearing on all of this.'

'We don't know that,' says Willie.

'We don't *know* anything,' says Norman. He turns to Pippa and instructs her to submit a Freedom of Information request in his name for the whereabouts of Gabriel Merkin. Glowing with enthusiasm, Pippa leaves the room.

'You've a bright girl there,' Willie tells Norman.

'An inquisitive one, anyway,' replies Norman. But he is not really thinking about Pippa.

'You've talked to all the parents of the children. There must be something to connect them,' he tells Willie.

'Well, I can't see what it might be,' replies Willie. 'The

parents are totally different. Theo's mother and stepfather are a council worker and a forester living together near Hexham. Becky's mother is an alcoholic living outside Newcastle and there doesn't seem to be any sign of the father. Karen's parents are an insurance salesman and his wife, living in the North Tyne valley. Whatever they have in common, it isn't their social life. They've never met.'

'You're talking about the parents,' says Norman. 'I'm asking you about the children.'

'I've never met the children,' says Willie.

'Obviously,' says Norman. 'But you've been to the homes of all three. You must have learned something about them.'

But Willie is shaking his head.

'Then go back to their homes and look again. Go back to Karen's house and to Becky's. And visit Theo's mother again. I don't suppose the stepfather will make much sense.'

Norman hasn't forgotten that Geordie called him a 'fat bastard'.

'All right. But it won't be today. I'm hanging onto my job by a thread as it is. I'll have to produce some pieces for my editor. I'll try and see all the parents tomorrow.'

Norman remembers Chief Inspector Saxon's threat to complain about Willie to his editor. He sees no advantage in sharing this information with Willie. But he senses that Willie, unemployed and broke, will be less use to him than Willie still in a job and with the access that his press card can give him.

'Maybe you're right,' he agrees. 'We'll meet here tomorrow afternoon. Before that, try to see the families of Theo and the two girls. Get into their homes and look around. Ask their neighbours about them. Do a bit of digging. You're a journalist, after all.'

'Oh, so that's what it's called,' says Willie. He goes out, whistling, hands in pockets.

'Tonight,' he says to Pippa on the way out.

'Don't be greedy,' she tells him. 'Maybe tomorrow. We'll see.'

Twenty-Three

One day the boy is walking back to the house when he meets Evan, the old gamekeeper who is living out his retirement in the lodge cottage at the end of the drive. In the boy's hand is the body of a mistle thrush he has picked up, still warm. It fell out of its nest when he shot it with his airgun from a bedroom window.

'What are you going to do with that?' asks Evan. The boy doesn't like his actions to be questioned by anybody, especially this old man from the lodge. He answers as briefly as possible: 'Keep it,' he says.

'Keep it how? Like that? It will rot.'

'I'll put it in an old cigar box,' he tells Evan. 'I've done it before. They dry out after a while, you know.'

'It won't look like much after all that,' says the old man.

The old man has never bothered the boy much in his comings and goings. To tell the truth, the boy has barely acknowledged his existence before. So it's a surprise when Evan says, 'I'll stuff it and mount it for you if you like. Keep my hand in, it will,' says Evan.

'Stuff it? Mount it?'

'Yes. I used to do a lot of that. Some of the shooting guests where I worked before used to ask me to stuff birds for them. Or beasts. Pheasants, ducks, stoats, rabbits: I've done them all in my time.'

The boy is fascinated. He drops his habitual cold demeanour and says, 'Can I see?'

It turns out that stuffing and mounting means doing something with the dead thrush so that it looks as if it were still alive. It won't dry out and shrivel, like the specimens in his cigar boxes. It won't smell. It will look just as he first saw it, perching on the rim of its nest, feeding its young.

The idea entrances him.

He goes back with Evan to his cottage. He has never entered it before. Why should he have been? Evan doesn't interest him any more than anyone else around the place. People don't interest him. But inside Evan's cottage he sees wonders he has never even imagined: a stuffed red squirrel on a branch, holding a hazelnut between its paws. A stoat, in its white winter coat, crouches on a rock. A pheasant sits in a glass case. A grouse nestles in a sprig of dark-brown heather. A mallard is suspended on a wire frame that makes it look as if it is just taking off from the water, forever frozen in its first few wingbeats of flight. The boy has never seen anything so beautiful: alive, yet dead.

He asks Evan how he performs these miracles. He is so interested that Evan, who has never even seen the boy smile before, who has hardly ever exchanged two words with him despite living a few hundred yards away for the last five years, is touched. He had thought that the boy must be simple in some way. He didn't like to ask. But now it turns out the boy can speak, can even smile. His enthusiasm is infectious.

So Evan tells the boy about mounting birds and animals.

'First we must skin it,' he says. 'If you give me a few minutes to find my bits and pieces, I'll show you how.'

He makes them both a mug of tea, and then they go through to a little back kitchen in the lodge. Evan lays the thrush on a wooden chopping block. He looks in a drawer and pulls out a small Swibo skinning knife, a scalpel, a pair of fine-pointed scissors, tweezers and pliers. He makes a cut in the thrush's breast down to the root of its tail. The boy watches as Evan cuts away the skin from the bird, removing and cutting away the flesh inside and throwing it into a bin. Then he skins around the head of the bird. The work is delicate and intricate. He scoops out the eyeballs and throws them into the bin as well.

'You have to be careful you don't get the eyes leaking onto the feathers,' he warns the boy. 'Difficult to clean up afterwards.'

Then he goes to some bottles on a shelf, and mixes a solution of a strong-smelling fluid in a large glass bowl.

'That's to stop 'un from rotting,' he tells the boy. 'We'll leave it to soak for a while. You come back tomorrow and I'll show you how to finish the job off.'

The boy is fascinated. He can hardly contain himself. He comes back the following afternoon. Evan shows him how to stuff the thrush, and how to insert two glass eyes in the bird's empty sockets.

'A number five glass eye should do the trick,' he says. The boy watches with an intensity that impresses Evan. The boy misses nothing. He watches Evan as he pops clay into the eye sockets and then takes two tiny glass eyes from a drawer full of glass eyes of different shapes, colours and sizes and sets them into the clay base.

It is not a great piece of work. Evan hasn't taken his time over it. Normally he would fit the skin over a polyurethane form, or onto a moulded resin shape. But this is just a lesson, not an object prepared for one of Evan's friends or customers. He shows the boy the finished job. The stuffed thrush is not particularly lifelike, but the boy is thrilled. He hugs it to his heart as if it were still alive. He says, 'Thank you, Evan.'

His parents would have been stupefied to hear him say that. As far as they know, the boy has never thanked anyone in his life so far. Evan is touched. He says, 'Tell you what, I've got an old cock pheasant in the freezer I've been meaning to stuff for a while now. Never got round to it. You come down here tomorrow afternoon, and you can have a go. I'll show you what to do.'

The following afternoon the boy turns up and the two of them have a go at the pheasant. Evan is pleased to see the boy is not squeamish. With a little difficulty at first, the boy uses the Swibo skinning knife and pliers to skin the pheasant. He doesn't tear the skin and his cuts are neat. He peels the dead pheasant like an orange. He is a natural.

The next day he comes back, and Evan has made a resin form for the skin. The bird is recreated. It is a pheasant again, not a floppy pile of skin and feathers and meat and bones. It is resurrected. It is more beautiful dead than it ever was alive. The boy walks back to the house carrying the mounted pheasant in his arms. Evan thinks his face when he leaves the cottage is a picture: a picture of longing.

Evan believes that in time, and with practice, the boy could become a fine practitioner.

By the time the boy is in his teens, he has become an accomplished taxidermist. Evan is a good tutor, and within a few years the boy learns everything Evan can tell or show him. During that time, the boy goes to Evan's cottage two or three evenings a week. Evan enjoys his company. He doesn't mind his looks. He accepts the boy's sarcastic manner without question. Maybe that's how they all speak up at the big house.

The boy learns the craft of skinning animals and birds. He

learns how to build polyurethane forms. He learns how to take moulds, and how to cast resin shapes resembling the dead animal over which the hide or fur or feathers can be fitted. His parents are pleased. It's good to see the boy has a hobby. It's good to see he has a friend at last, even if the friend is a retired gamekeeper in his seventies.

The fact is, before this development, the parents were worried about the boy. His mother worried that the boy's appearance was preventing him from making friends. There was a feeling that everything wasn't quite right. She didn't understand then, that how the boy was had nothing to do with his looks. She didn't understand that her son looked at the world with a vast ironic detachment that contained not one shred of humanity in it.

So she's pleased. The boy has a hobby. The boy has a friend.

The parents give the boy commissions. The parents' friends give the boy commissions. He mounts pheasants. Evan helps. Evan tells him where to buy the glass eyes, the resins and other tools of the trade. The parents buy everything that the boy asks for. They even buy him a small-calibre rifle for collecting the materials he needs for his new hobby. They are so relieved to see him *taking an interest*.

The boy mounts a pheasant couched in bracken. He stuffs squirrels, stoats and ducks. He is familiar with the full range of taxidermy – or almost the full range. On his own initiative he kills and mounts a rabbit, dressing it up in miniature garments he sews together using scraps from his mother's needlework box. The stuffed animal bears a strong resemblance to Peter Rabbit.

Evan is entranced. When he sees what the boy has done with the rabbit, he tells him: 'My word, that's good. You've got a good imagination. I never had much imagination. I'd never have thought of dressing that rabbit up like that.' He shakes his head and repeats, 'My word.' And then he adds, 'You know, I don't think there's much more I can teach you. I don't know that there's anything I know that you don't know.' He smiles with pleasure at the thought.

The boy listens to this statement, then smiles back. His smiles are disturbing, but that's just the way he is. He rises from the chair in Evan's cottage he has been sitting on and says, 'Well, it's kind of you to say so. I think I'll be going now. Goodnight.'

Evan doesn't see the boy again. Not to speak to. He never quite understands what he did or said to make the boy drop him like that. He's convinced that somehow he has upset him, or else the boy's parents have decided they disapprove of their son spending so much time in the gamekeeper's cottage. After all, he's just an old man, and the boy ought to be mixing with his own kind instead of spending every other evening stuffing dead animals.

It's not his fault. That's just the way the boy is. There are one or two things he doesn't understand about other people: their feelings, for example.

The boy drops the old gamekeeper, but he doesn't drop his new hobby. He carries on with it in a quiet way. His skills grow. His curiosity grows. His mounted creations are life-in-death. He sees only the beauty. The animating spirit that has deserted the objects he treasures is of no concern to him.

The years pass. The boy grows up. His relationship with his parents doesn't change. His father takes no great interest in him, but lets it be known that he wants the boy to become a banker one day. He encourages him to go to sixth-form college and study Economics. Leaving school is a great release. The boy's life has not become any easier with the passage of time. He is avoided – he is shunned – by most of the other pupils. He doesn't do well. It is unlikely he will ever do well at any academic subject. He is quite lacking in motivation. He knows something his father cannot understand: he will never, ever be accepted anywhere. Whatever life he leads, his education will not have fitted him for it.

Sixth-form college is not a success. The boy doesn't mix well with the students here, either. He doesn't enjoy the subject. He doesn't like the other people he studies with – although like and dislike are concepts he might not recognise. He doesn't feel *comfortable* with these people, but he is good at masking himself. He gets by. He does it because his father wants him to, and because he hasn't any ideas of his own as to how to earn a living. He doesn't much care what he studies or what he will become. All he knows is that he will need money to be independent. He needs money to pursue his interests. If he does what his father asks, maybe his father will give him some money.

Then his father dies. Nobody expected it. His father wasn't expecting it. The boy knocks on the study door one afternoon after lunch, because his father has said he wants to talk to him. No doubt another boring lecture about his lack of application to his studies. His communication with his father is limited to exchanges of this kind.

Receiving no answer to his knock, he pushes the door open and sees his father sitting in his armchair. He looks different, somehow. He doesn't respond to the boy's presence in the room. He doesn't answer when he's spoken to, but he isn't asleep. His eyes are wide open. The boy touches his face. It is cold. His hands are cold. His head lolls to one side when the boy touches it. His eyes don't blink when the boy waves his hand in front of them. After a moment, the boy realises his father is stone dead.

He decides to go upstairs to his room to read a book, but on the way it occurs to him he ought to tell someone. His mother is in the sitting room, gazing at the television. The boy puts his head around the door and says, 'Mama?'

He knows this form of address, which he has borrowed from a Victorian children's book he once read, irritates her. She looks up and asks him what he wants. She's watching her favourite soap, a medical drama.

'I've just been in to see Papa. I think he's probably dead.'

The fuss and the drama that follow this announcement make the boy wish he had never spoken, that he'd left it to someone else to find his father's body. His mother is devastated.

'I'm very sorry, Mama,' he tells her when she is in a condition to speak again. He tries to look sorry but it doesn't work. It is a grimace. His mother doesn't notice, doesn't hear anything he says. She has long ago given up hope of recognising any of the young man's emotions.

The funeral is held. The will is read. The young man learns that he is the sole beneficiary of his father's estate. His mother is the life tenant. Within weeks of the grant of probate, he has put the family house on the market. He will buy his mother a nice flat, he tells her. She doesn't like to argue. She finds it easiest to agree with what her son tells her. She can't think straight. Maybe a flat would be best.

The house is sold. The mother is installed in a small flat in a sheltered housing development in a nearby village. She is not yet sixty, but her son – by now a young man – has stuffed her into a colony of people in their eighties and nineties, a place where people go when they are too old to live unsupervised. The young man also takes charge of her income. He gives her a pittance to live on. Why would she need money, he thinks, what would she spend it on? He accumulates the rest of her income in a savings account, for emergencies. He's hoping there won't be any emergencies. Those savings will be his when she dies. He goes to see her once or twice after he has moved her to the flat. Then he stops going. What's the point? If she needs anything, she can call him. She doesn't call him. Without the bulwark of her husband, her son frightens her.

How does the young man occupy his time in the years that pass? He buys himself a small house in the suburbs of a nearby town, and invests the balance of the sale proceeds of his parent's house. He doesn't try to get a job. He has just about enough money to live on, if he's careful. And he continues to pursue his interest in taxidermy. Before his father died, he used to receive a few commissions from old family friends who had heard about his talent. These dry up after his father dies. There appears to be some disapproval of the way he has treated his mother.

But word has spread. Other dead and frozen animals arrive at his new house, for re-creation: for resurrection. He doesn't charge much but, all the same, it is an additional income. He gets some odd enquiries. They fascinate him. At first he sets them to one side. They are too absurd for him to consider.

Then, one night, he goes out after dark with his rifle. A few hours later, he returns with a dead cat and a dead dog. He goes to work. It takes him a long time. There is nothing intrinsically more difficult about this job than many others he has done, but it has to look right. The detail has to look convincing. Otherwise it would simply be grotesque.

At the end of three days he produces the first in a new line of creations: a black and white mongrel dog that has somehow mutated and has the head of a tortoiseshell cat. He is enthralled by what he has done. If he can produce something like this, what boundaries can there be?

He has entered the world of freak taxidermy.

Twenty-Four

These days, Geordie is spending less time in the forestry and more time in the pub. One evening he comes home long after the usual hour for supper, red-faced and with a sheen to his eyes.

'Where on earth have you been?' Mary shouts at him. But Geordie has sunk into his chair, and his head is down.

'I'm sorry,' he says. He doesn't want to argue with her.

'You're sorry?' replies Mary. 'You look as though you've spent the day in the pub, when you should've been at work.'

'You don't understand,' says Geordie.

She folds her arms across her chest.

'Try me,' she says. 'I'd really like to know what's going on.'

So Geordie tells her. He stumbles over his words sometimes because the drink is still in him, but he tries to explain how he feels. How he can't stop thinking about Theo. About the loneliness of his life since Theo went. How he feels cut off from her. About the loneliness he feels when he is at work. He stops and raises his head and looks at her. By now Mary has unfolded her arms. She has sat down on the edge of the sofa. She is listening. It's the first time they have had a conversation in five months. Her attitude is not friendly, but it is no longer remote.

'Go on,' she tells Geordie when he stops. 'You might as well say it all.'

'You won't believe me,' he replies. But he starts to talk again. He tells her about the feelings he has, a sense of dread that comes upon him at certain times.

'And ...' His voice trails off. Mary waits. Then he tells her about the old ewe and the two lambs and the grey dog that followed them. It sounds silly when he describes them. He can't convey the horror he felt when he saw the grey-dog-that-looked-like-a-wolf. He tells her about the two lambs with human eyes. He can't convey the disbelief he felt when they vanished. Or maybe he can. He must be conveying something, because Mary is no longer angry. If there is any emotion in her eyes, it is closer to pity than anger.

At last he says: 'I can't face it any more. I must be going mad.'

Suddenly his shoulders start shaking. He buries his sobs in his hands. He is ashamed of his own weakness. Then a small miracle happens. Mary crosses the room and kneels beside the chair in which Geordie is sitting. Sitting and crying, like a big baby.

'There,' she says. 'There.'

She puts an arm around his shoulders. In a muffled voice he says: 'I just want our lives to be like they were before.' He feels Mary stiffen.

'Don't,' he tells her. 'Don't take your arm away. I miss you so much. Can't we be together again?'

'I've got nothing left to give,' says Mary. But the coldness in her voice has softened. 'You can't understand. You've never had a child of your own. I feel dead. I feel worse than dead.'

'Will you always feel like that?'

'I don't know. If Theo came back it would be different, perhaps. But he's never coming back.'

'What will happen to us?'

'I don't know.'

All the same, Mary doesn't take her arm away. He loves the warmth of her next to him. It is such a long time since he felt that warmth: so many centuries. He doesn't want her to leave. He just wants to be held.

Then she removes her arm. She gets slowly to her feet. She crosses the room towards the kitchen. She asks: 'Will I put the kettle on?'

A bridge has been crossed. Mary has gone back to her corner of the room. It would be hard to say what has changed; but something has. She has listened to him. She has touched him. She has – so briefly – put her arm around him. She brings Geordie a mug of tea. He pulls himself together. He says, 'It'll be all right. I'll get back to work tomorrow.'

'You should see a doctor.'

'A doctor can't help.'

'But these things you say you've seen …' Mary can't quite finish her sentence.

'You mean I should go to the doctor and tell him I've been seeing things?'

'Well, if it bothers you that much. If you're not feeling right.'

Geordie laughs without humour.

'You think there are pills for what I've got? Pills that stop you seeing sheep? I don't think so.'

He stops talking. Mary doesn't speak again. The silence is creeping back like the front edge of a glacier, returning them to the deep freeze from which they had both emerged momentarily. Then Geordie says: 'It's to do with Theo.'

'What's to do with Theo?' asks Mary.

'What I see. The way I feel.'

She doesn't answer. A little later, she stands up to go to bed. Geordie stands up too. He says, 'Come back to our old room.'

'No. I can't. Not now.'

She leaves. An hour passes as Geordie sits in the silent room without moving, then he goes to bed.

In the middle of the night Geordie is woken. He can't think what it is at first. Then there are sounds: creaks, the faint clunk of a drawer being closed. He sits up in bed, trying to work out what he is hearing. Then he realises that Mary is moving about in the next room. He switches on his bedside light and looks at his watch. It is quarter to four in the morning. He hears a door opening. He flicks off his light. He hears Mary's steps across the sitting room, then the sound of the front door being opened and gently closed again.

He turns the bedside light back on and swings his legs over the side of the bed. He spots his jeans lying on a chair, pulls them on, fits his bare feet into his trainers and puts on a fleece over the vest he has been wearing in bed. He is out of his bed-room and across the sitting room in a moment. He puts the front door on the latch and then goes down the stairs into the hallway as silently as he can. This hallway provides common access to a number of flats. It is a concrete tunnel, with safety lights set in the ceiling. At the bottom, an archway opens onto brick steps that lead up to the street.

What is Mary's council job, that it requires her presence at four in the morning? Geordie looks up the main road and sees her in the distance, heading uphill. It is not yet light and the street lamps are still on. Geordie avoids the pools of orange light as he stalks Mary. He doesn't know why he is doing this. He doesn't know why he simply didn't go into the sitting room when he first heard Mary moving about. Why he didn't just ask her where she was off to at that time in the morning?

A car goes by, its headlights on full beam. Geordie is dazzled and for a moment he loses sight of Mary. When his eyes adjust again, he catches a glimpse of her turning into a lane that winds further up the hill. That's not the way to the council offices. He comes to the turning and follows Mary. He cannot see her any more but he hurries on. The lane straightens out in front of him and then drops back towards the town. Mary isn't visible. She can't be that far ahead of him. Where did she go?

Above Geordie looms the bulk of the Church of St Joseph of Arimathea. Stone steps lead up to a wooden gate, which has been left open. Beside the gate is a wooden crucifix under a sloping timber roof, fixed to a wooden board. On the crucifix is the plaster image of Christ. Someone has knocked the head off. At the head of the crucifix, the inscription in black script: 'IESVS NAZARENVS REX IVDAEORVM'.

Below the crucifix is a goblin's scrawl in red ink, in which only a familiar four-letter word is recognisable.

A flagged path between two rows of Irish yews leads up towards the church. Has Mary gone in here? Did she see him behind her, and has she hidden until he goes past? He doesn't think she can have seen him, even though it is getting steadily lighter. He goes through the wooden gate. He walks as soundlessly as he can up the yew avenue towards the church. He reaches the doors and tries them softly. The church is locked: locked by night and empty by day.

He walks around the side of the building. There is the graveyard, a forest of dim stone shapes. This side is further away from the glow of the street lights. He stops for a second to allow his eyes to adjust. Then he sees Mary.

She is sitting on a gravestone, her knees drawn up to her chin. She is half turned away from Geordie and doesn't see him standing there amongst the yew trees. She isn't doing anything, just sitting on the cold grave marker, her chin touching her knees. Geordie doesn't say anything. He takes a step back into the shadow of the yew trees so that he can't be seen. He waits. It is very cold.

Dawn is approaching. As it becomes lighter, he can make out the expression on Mary's face. It is a familiar look, a look that is not the particular property of Mary: it is a look seen on the faces of people who are straining to hear. She is intent, her face tilted upwards towards the dawn. There can be no doubt about it. She is listening to something: sounds or whispers that must be barely audible to her and are certainly inaudible to Geordie. They are sounds that seem to be arriving from a great distance. If they are words, they left the lips of the speaker millennia ago, and are arriving only now like the light from dying stars. She does not alter her position, though she must be cold.

Then he hears her speak for the first time. Her voice is so low it is barely audible, but Geordie hears the words in the still air: 'Why did you give him to me, if you were going to take him away again?'

As he watches her from his concealment, Geordie shivers. There is something alien about Mary, and a chill buzzes in his blood, as if thousands of spicules of ice have invaded his veins and arteries.

He lacks the courage to call out to her or to show himself. He doesn't understand what she is doing here, but he suspects he's better off not knowing. The expression on her face is so private. Slowly he retreats back down the yew avenue, treading as delicately as a cat. He goes down the stone steps and turns homewards.

A few hours ago, he had thought that the gap between them might be closing: that perhaps in a few months or a year or two the gap might be closed. Now he realises it is wider than ever: it may take eternity to cross it.

Twenty-Five

Willie Craig has tried calling Mary Constantine, but nobody answers the phone. He's been round to her flat, but nobody answers the door.

Instead he goes to call on the Gilbys. He leaves a Post-it note stuck to his computer monitor that says 'Out at Interview'. This might get him off the hook if his editor decides he wants to see him. Or it might not. Willie knows that his boss is losing patience with him. He knows that it will take just one more thing for his editor's temper to snap. He goes anyway.

When he arrives at the Gilbys' house, the Audi A4 isn't in the drive. There are no cars in front of the house. Willie parks, walks up the garden path and presses the doorbell. There is a series of chimes: a cheerful little cascade of silvery notes. Nobody answers. He tries again. The house is silent. A sound behind him makes him turn. A woman is standing by the garden gate, her bare arms folded. She asks, 'What do you want?'

'Do you know if the Gilbys are at home?'

'She's in the hospital, Mrs Gilby is.'

'And Mr Gilby?'

'He'll be with her. Or at the police station. What do you want?'

Willie smiles pleasantly.

'I'm a journalist. I've been before.'

'Well, they're not here.'

The woman – next-door neighbour, possibly – stands with her arms folded giving Willie an unfriendly stare until he gets back in his car. He drives down the street until she is out of sight, then parks the car and walks around the back of the houses. Here there is a field of young wheat. He climbs over a fence and walks along the headland. He hopes that nobody is watching him. When he reaches the back of the Gilbys' house, the last but one in the village, he climbs over the fence into the garden. He tries the back door. It is locked. He walks around to what looks like the kitchen. A window has been left open on a catch. He snakes an arm inside and frees the catch so that the window swings open, then he sits on the windowsill, swings his legs over and drops down on the other side. He's in. The Gilby family have not been exercising their usual care in locking up the house.

He takes off his shoes and pads through the kitchen, through the sitting room where he met Mr Gilby and into the hall. Up the stairs he is confronted by various closed white doors. One of them has a cardboard cut-out of a baby elephant pasted on it. He tries this one and, sure enough, finds Karen's room. Neat and tidy like the other one he saw, although Willie thinks Karen probably doesn't have to make her own bed like Becky Thomas does. Or did.

What's in the room? There are soft toys and some notebooks that look as if they are for schoolwork. There's a single shelf screwed into the wall filled with children's books propped up against a china bookend in the shape of a large owl. On the bedside table, underneath a lamp, is a copy of *The Lion, the Witch and the Wardrobe*. He opens it. Inside is a library stamp. The book is due back in a week. The library is called

Bookwise. A good name for a library, thinks Willie, putting the book down. He inspects the other books. He sees books about ponies; a set of Eva Ibbotson books; picture books. So Karen is an enthusiastic reader, a lover of cuddly toys. What other clues are there in the room? There is a gold star certificate for having the tidiest desk in her classroom, stuck to the wall with Blu-Tack. There isn't a games console or a computer. There are two posters: a picture of a cat playing with a ball of string, and a picture of Shrek.

Willie searches the room for a few minutes more. He takes a few pictures with his little camera and then sits down on the edge of the bed. He's come here, but for what? Has he somehow absorbed some element of Karen's personality while he is in her room that will help him to understand what has happened to her? He doesn't think so. He's none the wiser, really. Except that he does feel something.

The house feels dead. It feels as if nobody has ever lived there, or ever will again. The tragedy has sucked the air out of it. It doesn't feel like a home any more.

Willie wants to leave. Suddenly he hates being here, spying on the fragments, the remains of this young girl's life. For that's what he believes: that life and Karen have parted ways. He's still thinking about this when the front doorbell rings. Is it the neighbour? Has she seen something, or somehow heard him moving about?

He's out of there as fast as he can go on his stockinged feet without making a noise. He slithers into the kitchen and puts his shoes back on, then climbs out of the window. He climbs over the garden fence into the field and walks back along the edge of the wheat. A voice shouts from a back garden: 'Oi! What d'you think you're doing there?'

Willie turns an anxious face towards the person who has

shouted, a large man wearing army surplus trousers and jacket who is staring over his fence at Willie.

'I've lost my dog,' says Willie. 'A little golden cocker. Have you seen her go past?'

'No,' says the man. 'Didn't come this way.'

'Oh dear,' says Willie, hurrying on. 'I'll check the other end of the village, then.'

He quickly walks back to where his car is parked, and he's off.

Willie decides to check in at the office and show his face there for a few minutes, just to make sure that he hasn't been missed. Then he'll nip out again and visit Becky Thomas's house once more to see if anything there rings any bells.

But events don't quite work out as planned. When he walks past Teddy Naylor's glass-partitioned office towards his desk, the boss sees him and catches Willie's eye. He waves, indicating to Willie that he should come in. Willie's heart sinks. It sinks a little further when the boss gives him a pleasant, friendly smile.

'Willie,' says the boss. 'Oh, Willie, where have you been?'

'Checking out a couple of things for that story you asked me to do,' replies Willie, trying to remember what the current story is that he's supposed to be working on. Was it the car number plates? The straw bales fire? The school play?

'What couple of things?' asks his boss in the worryingly friendly manner he has adopted. Willie scrambles mentally, tries to think of what on earth he can say, opens his mouth in the hope that somehow his brain will find a few words for him to say. The boss gets in ahead of him.

'I've had Chief Inspector Saxon on the phone,' he says. 'You remember the name?'

Willie thinks, Oh God, but doesn't say anything. Tries to raise an eyebrow in a quizzical sort of way.

'I've heard a lot about Chief Inspector Saxon since he was seconded to the local force,' says Teddy Naylor. 'They say he's very professional. *He* says you've been wasting his time with half-baked theories about the missing child, Karen Gilby.'

'Missing children,' Willie corrects him.

'What I can't quite recall,' says Teddy Naylor, his voice acquiring a little more edge, 'is when exactly I asked you to go and interview Chief Inspector Saxon?'

'I ...' begins Willie, but he is cut off.

'I agreed to let you go and interview Karen Gilby's parents. And that was all I agreed to.'

'But ...' says Willie, then he's cut off again.

'Hardly a day goes by without you vanishing somewhere for reasons I know nothing about. You're apparently working on some story I know nothing of, and which I have no intention of printing. And yet, when I do ask you to do a piece for me, you appear to find even the most basic forms of writing a struggle. Do you think you really are cut out for a job on the *Herald*?'

This is the question Willie has been hoping he won't be asked. Because he may be able to lie about a lot of things, but when it comes to this question he knows he has to tell the truth. There's only one answer he can give.

'Maybe I'm not, Mr Naylor,' he answers.

Mr Naylor, who has been looking increasingly bad-tempered, switches on his smile again.

'Good,' he says. 'That settles it nicely. Now I'm sure you will agree, young man, that it would be best all round if you were to write me a polite resignation letter. I'll accept it, of course, and then you won't have the bother of being fired, which wouldn't look good on your CV.'

'Fired?' asks Willie. That seems a bit strong. Mr Naylor is nodding.

'Yes, fired. We can go through procedure and I can write a final warning letter. Or you can write me a resignation letter and then everything will be sweetness and light.'

There's a silence. Willie is thinking about a lot of things at once: his overdraft, the fact that the rent on his flat is overdue; the fact that he has promised to take Pippa out to dinner tonight. He's thinking about the fact that a bad job with a pay cheque is better than no job. He's thinking that without being able to use the cover of the *Herald*, he's going to be even less use to Norman, who might very well drop the whole affair of the missing children without Willie there to stiffen his backbone.

'Well?' asks the boss.

'I'll resign,' says Willie.

'Do it now. Ten minutes should be all you need. Then collect your belongings and drop the letter off in my office on your way out.'

Willie heads back to his desk. He has no real choice. If he tries to stick around until he's fired, it will be embarrassing and painful and word will get round. It's the end of an era. He feels as if he is about to step off a cliff and, for a moment, he is frightened by the prospect. He writes a brief letter of resignation, prints it off and signs it. He drops it on his boss's secretary's desk together with keys to the pool car he's been in the habit of using. Then he puts his few personal belongings in the plastic liner from his wastepaper basket and leaves. He doesn't say goodbye to anybody: too embarrassing to have to explain. Maybe they have guessed anyway.

He neglects to hand back his press card and digital camera.

An hour later and Willie is in the pub. It's a warm afternoon and today his choice of drink is not lager, but vodka and tonic. A few vodders should sort him out. He sits at the table sipping his drink and reflects on the life of Willie Craig so far. It is not a happy story.

For some years after leaving school Willie was a mess: his room was a mess, his life was a mess. Then came the break-through: a job on *The Northumbria Herald*. As Willie pointed out to his mam and dad, and to anyone else who might listen, papers like the *Herald* are the classic training ground for anyone with an ambition to write for a national newspaper. The day he got his offer letter, Willie told his audience – his mam and dad and Bruce the family dog who looked like a croissant on legs – that he planned to hang around for a year or eighteen months and learn a few tricks of the trade. Then he'd be off to London: the bright lights and the big stories.

His mam and dad asked if he'd ever thought of going to live in his own flat?

Five years later, he's still stuck in the North East, and the only trick of the trade he feels he's really learned is how to pad out his expenses claims. But he had a wage, a room of his own, and the use of a car. Now, as of this afternoon, Willie tells his third vodka and tonic, he has no wage, no car and no money in the bank. At least his mobile phone is his own, although the paper paid the rental. He wonders whether he should call Norman, but decides he can't face it. He wonders whether he should cancel Pippa. He can put dinner on his credit card, just like he's going to put these drinks on his credit card, but he doesn't know how long it will be before his credit runs out. After some more thinking, which is becoming quite hard work, Willie has another vodka and tonic.

A few hours later, Pippa calls Willie on his mobile. He's in his flat and lying on his bed, staring at the ceiling; not quite asleep, not quite awake. He's got room spin. He definitely wishes he was dead. It takes him a while to answer his mobile and when he does all he can say is: 'Hello-o-o.'

Even to his own ears, his voice sounds like someone trying to communicate from beyond the grave.

'Willie? Is that you?' asks Pippa.

'Hello-o-o?' says Willie, not quite sure what's going on.

'Where are you? I thought you were going to pick me up at the office. We were going to have dinner together?'

This is too complicated for Willie. Too many concepts here, all at once: concepts like 'picking up'. Picking up who? Where? What for? He can still remember how conversations work, though. Someone says something and you have to say something back. He attempts this formula and remarks: 'I lost my job today.'

'Oh, Willie, you didn't!' exclaims Pippa.

'Oh, Willie, I did.'

'Where are you now?' asks Pippa, beginning to grasp the situation.

'I'm here.'

He drops the mobile on the floor and closes his eyes. A while later, he notices Pippa is in the flat. She is straightening him out and washing his face with a damp cloth. Has he been sick? He doesn't remember. Then he feels his suit trousers sliding off his legs.

'Here, don't do that,' he says, waking up for a moment. 'I can't go out to dinner with no trousers on.'

But his trousers come off and then he finds he is lying under his duvet, feeling warm and comfortable and strangely remote, as if he and his duvet are on an asteroid somewhere, far away from all his troubles. He sleeps.

Twenty-Six

For a while, the young man is absorbed by the creation of strange animals: two-headed rabbits, cat-dogs. He learns to cruise the Internet for rogue taxidermy sites, where freak galleries can be visited. Sometimes the grotesque pseudo-creatures are treated as 'Art', sometimes they are just for fun. He constructs mythical creatures: a griffon, a chimera, a basilisk. He explores other ideas: a dead cat with the head of a doll; a calf's head sewn onto the body of a sheep. He prepares little tableaux of double-headed animals or birds, all mounted in a big glass case. His new clients are *thrilled*. His work commands good prices. There's an offer of a show, a suggestion that he might win a prize. He turns it down. He prefers to operate out of the light and in the shadows. None of his new clients have ever met him. None of them knows what he looks like, or what his real name is, or where he lives. He uses a bank account and post office box in the name of Gordon Martin. His productions are created in his house and then dispatched from another town.

As the years go by, he realises he has reached the limits of what he does. The aesthetic is shallow, and familiarity with the subject has diluted its effect on him. Once these bizarre creations made his blood race; now it feels like tepid water travelling through his veins. His subject matter is too confined. It lacks flair. Then comes a moment of revelation.

His mother – whom he has not seen for nearly a year – becomes forgetful. Her short-term memory is going. At first this refusal to live in the present is simply irritating. It's not clear whether she is suffering from dementia, or whether she has retreated so far into herself that the result is almost the same. But then his mother starts to wander. Sometimes she forgets to put on her clothes. She is found – luckily at least partially clothed on this occasion – in the middle of the village, in tears, with no idea of how she has come to be there or how to get home again. The warden of the sheltered housing project rings the man up. She's becoming too much of a liability, he explains. She needs full-time care.

The man at first resists the idea, because it would involve a significant increase in expenditure. But it soon becomes obvious that his mother needs a carer, day in and day out. The man looks for the bright side and finds it: he can sell his mother's flat.

He does so, and arranges for her to be transferred to a care home. His mother doesn't really notice what is going on or, if she does, she keeps it to herself. She is far too frightened of her son to let him think she is complaining about anything.

After all, the care home is inexpensive as far as these things go. Maybe they cut a few corners now and again, to keep costs down. The man thinks they are very efficient. They use chemical restraints on their more demented patients, and they work a treat. He doesn't want to be bothered by his mother, and his mother doesn't bother him. After only a few months she sickens and weakens. The man receives a phone call from the manageress of the home.

'Mrs Merkin is very ill, Mr Merkin.'

The man replies, 'Oh dear. I'm sorry to hear that. Thanks for letting me know.'

He's about to hang up when the manageress says quickly, almost as if she could see what he was about to do, 'Don't you think it would be a good idea if you visited her? It's been some months since you were last here.'

The man is annoyed, but he has plenty of common sense. It may be irritating to have to visit his mother, but it would be a lot more irritating if she died and he hadn't been to see her. People would start murmuring about him, as they did when he sold the family home a few years ago. The man does not want to be the object of gossip and speculation. He dislikes attention more than anything else.

'Of course. I've been terribly busy. But I'll come this afternoon.'

When he visits his mother, he is interested to note the changes in her. She once weighed about ten stone – not a plump woman, but a well-built one – now she looks as if she'd be lucky to break eight. She looks as if, were you to put her on a weighing machine, she would hardly make the needle flicker. Her eyes are red-rimmed, her sockets shadowed. She has the confused look one might see on the face of a dog that needs to be put down.

'How are you, Mama?' asks the man. He doubts it will make much difference to his mother whatever he says. But someone might be listening.

'Gabriel?' asks his mother. 'Why are you here? What do you want?'

A number of possible replies pass through the man's head, none of them kind or sympathetic. In the end, he says: 'I think you're looking very bonny, Mama. In the pink. You've lost weight. It suits you.'

He gives her his curious smile. His mother closes her eyes. He chats to her for a little while longer, getting some harmless fun by asking her what parties she has been to recently. Then he gets bored and leaves her. A week later, his mother dies.

The doctor says the cause of death was anorexia and nervous exhaustion brought on by her dementia. Her son thinks that perhaps she just gave up living. Arrangements for the funeral are made, in which he barely takes an interest until the funeral director asks him if he would like his mother to be embalmed.

Embalmed? He hasn't given it any thought. He had been thinking along the lines of a low-cost funeral: an eco-friendly cardboard coffin and a quick burst from the flamethrowers at the crematorium. The funeral director's suggestion catches his attention.

'What does embalming involve?' he asks. The funeral director tells him a little bit about it. The man listens, fascinated. He's learning about something quite new, something he ought to have found out for himself. When he's heard what the funeral director has to say, he decides he would like his mother to be embalmed after all. He would like it very much. He says to the funeral director: 'I'd like to watch while you do it.'

The funeral director is shocked. It is not a request he has ever received before from a client. It doesn't seem right to him. He starts to explain why such a thing would be impossible. The man tells the funeral director: 'Of course I'll buy your best casket. And I'll pay you a bonus if I'm satisfied with the result of the embalming.'

A brief negotiation takes place. The funeral director says, 'You may find the experience upsetting. After all, it is your own mother.'

'I'll manage,' replies the man.

Later, when he is back home, he reads what he can about

embalming. He reads about the ancient Egyptians, who eviscerated corpses and removed their brains with hooks pushed up through the nose. The main organs were extracted through a cut in the left side of the body and kept in jars packed with sodium carbonate. The body was drained of its fluids and washed in oils to keep the skin elastic. Then it too was packed with sodium carbonate, and finally covered in linen bands. The man wonders if all this will happen to his mother.

The next day, he goes to the funeral parlour. The funeral director looks as if he is regretting the bargain he has made, but lacks the nerve to say anything.

The man's mother, in a grey plastic body bag, is wheeled into the room on a gurney and placed on a slab. The body bag is unzipped. Inside, his mother is naked apart from a modesty cloth over her middle. The man notices with interest how emaciated she has become. He has seen more meat on a sparrow.

The funeral director sprays his mother from head to foot with disinfectant and then starts work. There is a tray of instruments and devices on a table to one side of the slab. The funeral director picks up an electric razor from the tray. A humming sound fills the room. He shaves the body and the face. He places eye caps on the eyeballs to stop the eyelids sinking into their sockets. He rubs the eyelids with cream. He picks up an implement that looks like a small chrome-plated hand drill. It turns out to be an injector. He places it against Mrs Merkin's cheek and shoots needles with fine wires attached into the lower and upper jaw. He twists the wires so that the jaws will not fall open. He forces open the lips of the corpse and pushes a little mastic inside to give the mouth the plump shape it once had in life.

The man watches, fascinated, as the process of arterial embalming begins. A machine like a vacuum cleaner is brought to his mother's side. A cannula is inserted into the jugular vein and the machine begins its work of draining the fluids from the arteries. The funeral director goes to the tray and brings back a sharp bladed instrument he calls a 'trocar'. He attaches this to a hose and cuts a hole in the abdomen of the man's mother. His mother's body gurgles and twitches a little as more fluids are aspirated through the aperture. A flesh-coloured plastic screw is inserted in the hole the trocar made, in order to plug it. Another machine is switched on and embalming fluids are injected into the arteries of the corpse. The smell of formalin fills the room, overpowering other odours.

When all this is done, the funeral director says: 'Now we wash her hair. Do you want it styled and set?'

The man says he doesn't care. They should do whatever is customary and he'll pay. He's seen what he came to see. He's electrified. This is going to be what he does next. With a little research and a lot of practice, he may be able to embalm corpses that will last for years, perhaps for centuries. This is so much better than taxidermy: so much more fulfilling.

He goes home and for days he thinks about what he has seen. He almost forgets to attend his mother's funeral, and hurries away as soon as it is over. He knows his life is about to change. He knows he has to take some very big decisions. What he is contemplating will not be without risk. Because he is going to need a steady supply of human corpses to work with. He doesn't pretend to himself that this new skill will be easy to acquire. And the corpses need to be alive when he finds them. He needs to see them alive to know how they ought to look when they are dead. He needs to know them and under-stand them as living beings before he translates them into death-in-life.

The planning alone will be a joy. The execution will be very difficult, but he is looking forward to it. This is what he has been preparing for all his life, without realising it.

Then he happens to read a newspaper. It is the *Sun*. An article by Mike Sullivan, Crime Editor, catches his eye. He is writing about a new TV programme that will be launched 'to help trace some of the 150,000 kids who go missing in the UK every year.'

Catherine Meyer, founder of the children's charity Parents and Abducted Children Together said '... the best estimate we have shows that every five minutes a child goes missing in the UK.'

He has the answer. A child goes missing every five minutes. No doubt most of them return a day later; a week later; months later. But some of them never return. How can the police possibly investigate such huge numbers of missing children? What difference will it make if, next year, the statistic is one hundred and fifty thousand and one? Or one hundred and fifty thousand and five? No difference. Nobody will mind. Nobody will notice: not if he is careful.

He has learned to be careful. He will be very careful. It will be a challenge.

He loves challenges.

Twenty-Seven

Willie Craig feels awful. At first he can't work out why he is still in bed at nine on a weekday morning. Was there a party? He doesn't remember a party. He pulls off the duvet, notices he is still wearing his socks and shorts. His mouth feels like— Well, it doesn't feel good. He staggers to the tiny bathroom and looks at himself. Hair all spiked up, unshaven cheeks and red eyes. He drinks a glass of water and almost brings it straight up again. What the hell has been going on? He sits on the edge of the bath and tries to remember.

Pippa. Pippa was here. His suit has been hung up on a coat hanger. He would never bother to do that, so Pippa must have been here and he thinks he remembers her sponging his face. Then everything comes back to him as if someone has opened a door in his mind and he can suddenly see the whole awful mess that is his life.

'Oh God,' mutters Willie.

No job, no prospects. His whole career has been thrown away because of a stupid story about some missing children. Worse still, it is a story that will probably never be written. Or, if it is written, will never be published. Willie has stepped off the edge of the world in order to write a story about a serial killer. But the serial killer probably doesn't exist, except in Willie's imagination. He's become involved with Norman

Stokoe, Children's Czar: a man Willie doesn't like and doesn't trust. He's even managed to involve himself with Norman's personal assistant, for God's sake.

Pippa. She was here last night, looking after him. He can't have been a pretty sight. She didn't have to come here to his untidy flat, and somehow manage to put him to bed. Yet she did. Willie realises that, in Pippa, he has met one of those rare people who give rather than take. And she has given: she has given her time; she has given herself. Willie doesn't know whether to feel suspicious, or grateful. His previous relationships haven't qualified him to judge someone like Pippa, he realises. He isn't used to people being so good to him.

'What's in it for her?' he asks himself.

Willie showers and dresses. He doesn't know what to do next. He looks for his car keys, remembers he hasn't got a car, and remembers that if he had, there's nowhere in particular to drive it to. He knows what he ought to do. He ought to start looking for a job. Right now. He should buy all the local papers and look through the job ads. He should go to the job centre and sign on. He needs income and he needs it very soon, because otherwise, Willie thinks, he'll be living in a cardboard box underneath a railway arch. His mam and dad won't have him back. They're too old and too poor to help him anyway.

His mobile rings. It's Norman. He says, without any preamble, 'I hear you've lost your job.'

Bad news travels fast. Willie admits it is true.

'What are you going to do now?'

'Look for another one.'

'No, I mean what are you going to do about our project?'

Willie sighs. 'I was sacked after I came back from visiting the Gilbys' house. There was nobody there. I didn't get an interview. I was sacked anyway.'

'I'm sorry to hear that.'

'I've no car. I've no money coming in. I can't afford to spend any more time on this story. Much as I'd like to.'

'You're the one who got me involved. Now you're saying you want to give it all up, just when we're getting close. I thought you wanted to be an investigative journalist.'

That stings Willie. He replies: 'I need to be realistic. We're going nowhere with this story. The missing children are almost certainly dead by now. The police won't talk to us. We're just wasting our time. It's because of all this that I lost my job. When in a hole, stop digging.'

There's a silence and then Norman says: 'You can borrow my car. Go and see Becky's mother again. See what else you can find out. Then come back here and let's put together what we know and what we don't know. If we can't make any more sense of what's been happening then, fair enough, you can quit. But you owe one last effort.'

Willie doesn't think he owes Norman anything. Perhaps Norman means he owes it to himself. He's finding it difficult to think of a reason why he shouldn't do as Norman suggests. It will put off the moment of having to sign on the dole. He isn't looking forward to that. And he realises he still has a few vestiges of pride left: he doesn't want to leave the job unfinished after all. He still believes there might be a story, and that he will write it one day, and write it well.

'I'll come round to your office, then, and get the car keys,' says Willie.

When he arrives at Norman's office, Pippa greets him with an anxious smile.

'How are you feeling?' she asks.

'Was I in a state last night?'

'You could say so.'

'Thank you for looking after me, then.'

For a moment they look at each other and Willie is conscious of a warm, unfamiliar feeling spreading through him as he looks at Pippa. It's gratitude. There's something else as well, some other emotion he can't identify. It has to do with wanting to make love to Pippa, immediately, right there in the atrium. It has to do with wanting to be with her so badly that the thought of leaving her almost gives him physical pain.

Then Pippa holds up a bunch of keys.

'He said to give you these,' she tells him. He takes the keys from her and she hands him a plastic card. 'His car's in the multi-storey next door, in bay thirty-seven. The card gets you through the barrier.'

Ten minutes later, Willie is driving Norman's Honda Accord towards the little town where Becky Thomas once lived. He checks out the sound system and hears the choir of King's College, Cambridge. He helps himself to a couple of Norman's wine gums. Then he's in Becky's street and parks outside number seventeen.

He walks up the path. If possible, the garden looks even more derelict than before. It's full of rubbish: abandoned Coke cans, an empty Smirnoff bottle, the remains of someone's fish and chips. The place looks as if it has become a convenient dumping ground for local people too tired or pressed for time to make it as far as their bin.

The door is open and there's a smell of smoke inside the house. It overpowers the other odours that Willie remembers from his last visit. The hall is full of more trash. There is broken glass on the floor. A burned-looking spoon lies beside the kitchen door with a residue of something like gum on it: Willie wonders if someone has been using it to cook crack.

'Mrs Thomas?' he calls. There's no answer. The house feels

empty. He pushes open the kitchen door. That's where the burned smell is coming from. Someone's tried to set fire to the kitchen. There is a pile of ash, a large black mark on the floor in one corner and black stains going up the kitchen units. The paint has bubbled and cracked on the cupboards and the legs of the kitchen table have charred. The chairs are all overturned or broken. Crockery is smashed on the floor. There's no sign of Mrs Thomas. Willie takes a couple of shots with his camera.

He leaves the kitchen and goes upstairs. There's more rubbish on the staircase: empty bottles; a pair of stained jeans; a pair of knickers. There's a used hypodermic needle on the top step. With some hesitation, Willie knocks on the door of what he thinks is Mrs Thomas's bedroom. There's no answer, so he pushes it open. The room looks as though Attila the Hun has dropped by. All the drawers have been pulled out of a chest in the corner. The mirror on the wall has been smashed, and someone has given the wardrobe a good kicking. The bed has been stripped of its bedding and the mattress is badly stained. Willie shuts the door. He is trembling with shock or disgust, he's not sure which.

He goes to Becky's room. It, too, has been visited. Every book has been pulled off the shelves. Most of them have had their pages torn out or have been ripped apart. The desk that stood there is on its side, the top broken off. The book that was on the desk has vanished. The soft toys have gone and all the bedding has disappeared. There is a star-shaped hole in the window.

Willie goes back downstairs. The house isn't a house any longer: it's the lair of wild animals. He can't stand being there a moment longer. He goes outside and down the garden path and then knocks on the door of the neighbouring house. After a pause, a man opens the door. He's wearing a vest but no shirt and brown trousers that look as if he's had them on for at least six months. He looks Willie up and down and asks, 'Yeah?'

'I was looking for Mrs Thomas.'

'She's flit, hasn't she?'

'Flit?'

'She owed rent.'

The man looks as if he feels he has said all that could be expected of him and starts to close the door in Willie's face. Willie puts his foot in the door and asks: 'Do you know where she's gone?'

'Nah.'

'What happened to the house?'

'Well, it's kids, innit?'

'Children did all that?' asks Willie, incredulously.

'Well they've nowt else to do, the little tinkers.'

Willie leaves. There's nothing more he can do here. There are no clues; nothing remains of the room Becky once lived in. His trip has been a waste of time.

He needs to stop worrying about missing children. There's no story after all. He needs to get on with his life.

Twenty-Eight

He drives through the streets in search of a suitable workshop. He finds one in the town a few miles from his home: a row of business start-up units beneath the arches of an old stone railway bridge. They have 'To Let' signs up. None have been taken, so far. He makes a note of the letting agent's number.

He still has the postbox and the bank account in the name of Gordon Martin that he set up in his dealings with taxidermy clients. He uses these for his next transaction. He arranges to take a lease on one of the workshops. Then he uses the Internet to purchase the tools of his new trade: a trocar, a Porti-Boy embalming machine, a reverse-flow hydro-aspirator. He buys skin-preservation creams, mastic, and a supply of embalming fluids. These are all ordered from different sources, mostly from outside the United Kingdom, and shipped one by one to his new business address.

He installs a sturdy second-hand wooden table. He has posters printed advertising 'Restoration of Church Furniture and Altar Fabrics' and pins these up in the windows of his new workshop. It is impossible to see in from outside. He supplements the security with additional padlocks for the front door, and for the roller shutter that can be raised to allow anything up to a medium-sized van into the workshop's small unloading bay. Then, still using his alternative identity, he rents a van from a company keen to do business and undemanding about documentation if hard cash is produced.

When all this is done, he checks through everything and is satisfied with his work so far. He is ready. The scene is set. Now the real work can begin. But he's in no hurry. He has to be careful.

He finds Jack Grzybowski by chance. He is the son of the cleaning-lady who comes twice a week to clean his house. It's an easy job for her. He is a fastidious man. He lives an orderly life and a solitary one. He never entertains. He doesn't like clutter. Mrs Grzybowski comes twice a week and cleans and dusts and does the washing and the ironing. Once, at half-term, she brings her son with her. There has been a domestic crisis in the Grzybowski home; it seems the Grzybowski marriage is tempestuous and the father is not available to look after the boy at present. While Mrs Grzybowski is upstairs, the man comes silently into the kitchen where the boy is sitting, mute as a piece of wood. The boy stands up when the man appears – it is hard to say whether it is good manners or unease at the man's appearance. The man knows he makes a poor impression on people. He wipes the corners of his mouth with his handkerchief to remove the perpetual threads of saliva that form there. Then he smiles and asks if the boy would like something to eat: a biscuit, perhaps?

'No thank you,' says the boy. His face is pale and set. The domestic drama, whatever it was, has affected him.

'A banana, perhaps?'

The boy accepts. Perhaps he thinks the man will go away once the ownership of the banana has been transferred to him. But he doesn't. The man asks a few questions. How old is Jack? Nine. Where does Jack go to school? The boy names the school. Is it a nice school? The boy says it is OK. Does Jack go to school on the bus? No, there is no bus, he walks: it takes about fifteen minutes. Mrs Grzybowski comes into the kitchen and says to the man that she hopes Jack isn't being a bother. The man says no, he's no bother at all; he's a credit to his parents. The man leaves the kitchen, anxious not to leave an impression of too much interest on his part. The next time the boy comes to the house, the man doesn't offer him a banana. He ignores him.

But he hasn't forgotten him.

He goes and collects his white Mercedes van, rented and insured in the name of Gordon Martin. He picks Jack Grzybowski up in the van one morning when the boy is on his way to school. He offers him a lift, and the boy, after a moment's hesitation, is persuaded by the friendly smile and the coldness of the morning to climb into the van. The man says he will drop Jack off at the school, but the destination is elsewhere.

In the van the boy tries to undo his safety belt when he realises they are not heading towards his school but somewhere entirely different. The man places a large gloved hand on the boy's thigh and the boy gives him an awful, sick look. He thinks the man is a paedophile. It is a word he cannot yet spell but, unfortunately, he is familiar with the concept. He does not realise for a moment that what is happening to him is something quite different: and a great deal worse.

The man restrains the boy for a moment. Then he removes his hand and says: 'Be still, and I won't hurt you. But you must stay absolutely still.'

The boy stops struggling. He is terrified. The man reaches into his pocket with his left hand, the right hand on the steering wheel. He pulls out a hypodermic. It is full of liquid diamorphine. He bought the diamorphine on the Internet. What can't you buy on the Internet? Before the boy can react in any way, he has stabbed the boy in the thigh with the needle. The boy shrieks and jerks with shock. The man injects him with a solution that is five times the recommended adult dose. The boy screams again and starts to struggle. The man is very strong and is able to hold him down without losing control of the van. Quite soon the boy stops squirming. His head slumps to one side and he starts to breathe heavily, almost snoring, through his open mouth.

By the time they reach the workshop, the boy is scarcely breathing at all. The man jumps out of the van and checks the street. There are one or two people about, but nobody is taking any notice of him. He unlocks the padlock on the roller door and presses the control on his key fob that operates the electric motor. The door rolls up, he drives in and clicks the control again. The door rolls down. They are in darkness, the man and the boy, but the boy is far away now.

The man finds the switch and puts on the lights. He lifts a box from a shelf and puts it on the table. He takes out a set of medical scrubs: a plastic set of overalls, plastic shoe bags, a cap and a face mask and surgical gloves. The man has read up on the subject of forensics and he's keen not to leave any evidence behind. He is aware of his tendency to produce oral secretions. Then he walks around to the passenger side of the van and opens the door. He unfastens the boy's seat belt, takes him in his arms and carries him into the workshop. Tenderly he lays the boy out on the makeshift operating table he has prepared.

His own pulse rate is raised and his breathing is irregular. He stands quite still until he feels calm again. Jack Grzybowski, on the other hand, appears to have stopped breathing. It doesn't matter whether he is or isn't breathing, because quite soon all the blood in his veins will start to drain out through a cannula that the man will insert into the boy's jugular vein. Everything is under control. It is very peaceful in the workshop. The man's hands are steady now. He is ready to start work.

He has printed out instructions, a do-it-yourself guide to embalming based on his own recent observations, and on various other sources he has visited on the web. He is hopeful that this will work, but if it doesn't, he plans to keep a careful note of everything he does and then review his method for mistakes afterwards. The boy is too young to require shaving. He needs to be undressed and sprayed with disinfectant. Then the work can begin.

The man feels more alive than he has ever done before.

Twenty-Nine

Norman has never really known any children, since he ceased to be a child himself. He has seen them around, of course. And what he sees he doesn't much like. Children cost money. They take up time. They disrupt one's routine. He sees no inconsistency between this view, which is after all a personal one, and his professional life.

In the recent past he has studied – as have many members of his profession – the Serious Case Reviews of children who have fallen through the elaborate safety nets constructed to save them from harm. He has read up on Victoria Climbié, whose guardians hit her with hammers and bicycle chains, and burned her with cigarettes. He has read up on Kyra Ishaq, who was starved by her mother and her mother's boyfriend until she weighed only 2 stone 9lbs at death. He has read endless reports on Baby P, whose mother and boyfriend sliced off his fingertips with a Stanley knife.

When he reads these, and many similar case notes, Norman's reaction is not so much disgust but dismay at the system's failings which meant these perversions went undiscovered until it was too late to save the child. If Norman is honest, and in his own way he is honest, he feels relief that no such cases have until now been discovered in any department for which he has had responsibility. He doesn't feel the revulsion that some others, for example most parents, would feel. These are anomalies. These are the exceptions that prove the rule that – on the whole – the child safeguarding networks in this country are effective.

He doesn't consider the fact that no systems and no senior manager anywhere, ever, can legislate against pure evil.

Now, for the first time, Norman has met, not children, but the shadows of children. He has encountered the traces left by three children that once existed. They are like the shapes traced by smoke rising from bonfires. They are like the fragments of clouds dissolving in a hot summer sky. He experiences them as the faintest of images in the words of Willie Craig, in the words and in the expressions that passed across the face of Mary Constantine. These phantoms are now more real to him than all of the statistics he has studied over all the years of his career.

Norman knows his life has reached a point of transition. He cannot go back to being the safe and sensible Norman that he was. It's Willie Craig's fault. That callow young man has marched into his office and thrown down a challenge that Norman has picked up. 'Let's find out what's happening to these children' was Willie's challenge. The irony is that Norman doesn't think Willie cares that much about the children himself. He's using the opportunity to advance his own career, if he can. Willie will use Norman, he'll use Pippa: he'll do anything to get on in life. Norman knows about getting on in life. He can sense that drive in himself and he can smell it in others. Although so far, Willie's efforts seem to be propelling him backwards, not forwards.

But the encounter with Willie has changed Norman. He can't go back to how he was before. He's become involved. He's not going to let go of this problem. He's going to find out what has happened to these particular, non-statistical children, and he's going to stop it. He's going to find out what happened to Theo. He wants to trace every movement that Theo made, every thought that Theo had, right to the end.

Norman's reverie is interrupted by Pippa buzzing him from next door. She says: 'I've a Chief Inspector Saxon here to see you, Mr Stokoe. He says he hasn't got an appointment, but he needs to speak with you.'

Norman is surprised. He hadn't expected to see Chief Inspector Saxon again after their last meeting. The man had made it very clear that he didn't have any time for Norman and even less for Willie. He made it clear that he thought their theories were rubbish. Now he is outside Norman's office. Norman wonders what's brought him here.

The next moment Chief Inspector Saxon is in the room. His eyes are light blue and uncomfortable to stare at for any length of time. His face has no more expression than a house where all the windows are shuttered. He sits down heavily in the chair opposite Norman and says: 'Well now. Thank you for seeing me at such short notice.'

'Not at all,' replies Norman politely. As if he had a choice.

Chief Inspector Saxon seems to be in a hurry because he is breathing a little heavily, and yet appears in no rush to explain why he is there.

'How can I help you?' asks Norman, after the silence has lasted a little longer. He is expecting the chief inspector to complain about Willie again. He has a faint hope that the chief inspector might have had a change of heart, or might have been presented with new evidence in one of the missing children cases. Maybe he is here to tell Norman that he was right all along. The chief inspector's answer is not what he expected to hear.

'You filed a Freedom of Information request a day or two ago,' says Chief Inspector Saxon at last. He looks at Norman as if he expects him to deny any such thing.

'Yes, I did,' agrees Norman. Then he looks surprised. 'How do you know about it?' He doesn't ask: what's it got to do with you, although that's what he thinks.

'I've been asked to have a word with you about it.'

Norman doesn't answer. Instead he presses the button on his phone that connects him with Pippa and asks her to bring in the FOI request. A moment later, Pippa is in the room. She has printed off the form and now Norman studies it.

'This is a request for information about the whereabouts and status of Gabriel Merkin, the child-murderer,' Norman tells Chief Inspector Saxon.

'I know. Why have you asked for that information?'

'Because I was carrying out some quite legitimate research and I found that I was barred access to his file.'

'The file is confidential.'

'Not to me. I am a children's commissioner and if I need access to files as part of a Serious Case Review, then I am entitled to see those files. Why not this one?'

'We'd like you to withdraw the request,' says Chief Inspector Saxon, without any further explanation. This is phrased as a demand, and not as if he is asking for a favour. The atmosphere in the room is growing a little tense. Norman notices that Pippa is still standing by the door, but he doesn't want to break off his duel with Chief Inspector Saxon to tell her to leave. Anyway, what does it matter if she overhears?

'Who is "we"?' asks Norman.

'I'm speaking on behalf of the National Crimes Against Children Unit, but I should also say that – at their request – I am speaking on behalf of the Ministry of Justice and the

National Offender Management Service. We want you to drop your enquiry.'

'Why?'

'Because it would create difficulties for the home secretary, and because it would interfere with current operations.'

Norman pushes his chair back from his desk. He leans back and spreads his hands out on the desk in front of him. He evaluates the latent threat in the chief inspector's words. If that is even half true – if one of the demigods known as secretaries of state really has heard of Norman's unorthodox activities – then Norman's career is history. He finds that he doesn't care quite as much as he once would have done. He answers, 'You'll need to give me a better reason than that.'

'This could be difficult for you. If we think you're being obstructive, the matter could go straight back to the home secretary.'

'*I'm* not being obstructive,' replies Norman in a reasonable tone of voice. '*You* are trying to obstruct my legitimate request for information, as far as I can see.'

Chief Inspector Saxon stands up. He is a very large man and Norman finds him intimidating, but he doesn't allow himself to show any discomfort.

'I find your attitude disappointing,' the chief inspector tells him. 'I would like you to reconsider your position. I shall come back and see you tomorrow and, to be quite frank, I shall expect a different answer. It is in your own best interests to cooperate.'

'If you come back and tell me what this is all about, I might understand. But based on the very little that you have told me, there's only one answer I can give. And that is no.'

The chief inspector does not say goodbye. He simply stands up and strides out of Norman's office, ignoring him and ignoring Pippa, who holds the door open for him. Pippa looks at Norman with admiration.

'You told him where to get off, Mr Stokoe. Well done.'

A week or two ago, Norman would have been amazed if Pippa had dared speak to him like that. Now he gives her a conspiratorial smile and replies, 'Yes, I did, didn't I?'

But when Pippa has left the room, Norman's faint bravado disappears with her. Who is asking the chief inspector to do this, and why? The chief inspector's demeanour is not just that of an irritated policeman. And Norman has the sense, once again, of slipping from the shallows into deeper water. And in the deeper water there are monsters whose teeth can rend flesh.

Thirty

Jack Grzybowski is the first and, if he's honest, the man has to admit his technique was lacking in finesse. The cadaver acquires the texture of a dried-out prune and the result is not good to look at. But it's all about practice. The man finds other children to take back to his workshop. They are all children like Jack. Children from broken or dysfunctional families; left on their own a lot, free to wander the streets, natural targets. The fifth is Kevin McFall and, by this time, the man's embalming technique has progressed. The results of his work on the first small boy were, frankly, inadequate. But the work he does on Kevin would stand comparison with anything you could find in any funeral parlour in the land. He is proud of himself. He begins to think about the next steps: groups of mummified children set in tableaux, illustrating themes from history or the Bible.

But something is wrong. The man doesn't know what. It's nothing specific. When he drove the van into his workshop to review his work on his latest trophy, the hairs on the back of his neck lifted as if he were an animal, scenting danger. When he has finished admiring Kevin, he locks up the workshop and drives the van to a disused petrol station where he can have the car valeted. He has the van steam-cleaned and waxed and polished. Then he drives to the city airport a few miles out of town, and drops the van off in the long-term car park. He throws away the parking ticket, then takes a taxi back to the city centre. Then he takes another taxi home.

He doesn't know what spooked him. Was somebody watching him? Was there an unfamiliar car parked in the narrow street in which his workshop lies? Did he hear something? He's not sure. He's very uneasy.

That night he watches the local news on television. He doesn't often do this. But tonight, for some reason, he feels compelled to do so.

The presenter says: 'And now an item of breaking news ...' and before she has said another word, the man knows that this is about him, that they have found the workshop. They have found his secret place. Policemen will remove his treasures. Forensic examiners will cut holes in them and poke them about. He won't be able to admire them any more. The months of secret pleasure are over. All that effort has gone to waste. He feels devastated. He's not afraid, not yet. He thinks he has been careful. He's as sure as he can be that he hasn't left any clues in the workshop. All the equipment was bought using a sanitised bank account. They can't connect Gordon Martin with him. If they find the van – when they find the van, he corrects himself – it will lead them back to the same dead end. He thinks he is safe. Although he's not one hundred per cent sure.

All these thoughts cross his brain in an instant, before the presenter has finished speaking. It's as if he has been preparing for this moment all his life. He finds that he's ready for it. Of course he feels a sense of loss, but that's not his only feeling. The camera cuts away to show Crime Scene Investigation officers going in and out of his workshop. It is raining in the street outside and three police cars, a police van and an ambulance are drawn up opposite the entrance. Their lights are flashing.

Outside he hears the patter of rain on his windows. He realises he's watching live feed.

He experiences a terrible curiosity. He wants to be there. He wishes he could be a fly on the wall, observing their reactions to what they find, listening to what they say. Like all artists, he longs to see the expressions on the faces of the people as they see his work. He wants to hear what they say about him. He wants to experience their fear, and their admiration. He wants to look close into their eyes and see his own reflection.

He could go back and have a look. He could just walk past, couldn't he? He could ask someone what is going on. The idea burns in him. To stand there, a few yards from the workshop, while the police begin hunting the entire country for him. But they won't find him. He's been careful. Five minutes later, he's driving his own car into the centre of town.

When he reaches the entrance to the street where his workshop is, he finds it has been taped off. Two police cars are drawn up so that it's impossible to go any further. There's quite a crowd: journalists and curious locals. There might even be a few people who, like him, have been prompted to come here by the piece on the evening news. Ghouls, he thinks contemptuously: creatures who look but don't do. It's still drizzling. The flashing lights have been turned off, but the ambulance and two police cars and the Crime Scene Investigation van are still there, their headlights reflecting off the wet road.

He leaves his car and joins the crowd.

'What's going on?' he asks a tall man standing near the barrier. The tall man is craning to see whatever is happening at the other end of the street.

'There's been a murder or something down there.' The tall man doesn't look at him when he speaks. He doesn't want to miss anything.

Someone else says: 'They're bringing out a body bag,' and four or five men with cameras and video cams surge forward, pushing the man out of the way as they try to get a shot. Not much else happens. The man thinks he'd better slip away while there is still a crowd. He can return when the street is open again, maybe cruise past in his car. He'll enjoy coming back for a look.

When he's arrested six weeks later, the arresting officer tells him that it was his frequent visits to the site that drew the attention of the police. Somebody remembered his face. His snout-like face, turning and looking out of the car window as he drove slowly past. Looking for what, he could not say. Somebody else took a note of his number plate.

The police don't tell him too much. They don't explain how they found him. They arrest him and bring him to the police station and take DNA swabs and fingerprint him. Then they start to interview him.

At first he tries to give the impression of outraged innocence, but he's not a natural actor. Even he can hear that he doesn't sound very convincing.

What was he doing on such and such a night?

He hasn't got an alibi: he lives on his own. Why on earth would he need an alibi?

Why did he keep driving down that particular street?

He didn't know it was a crime to drive down the street. If he had known, he wouldn't have done it. He was just curious.

Why was he curious?

It's human nature, isn't it?

After a while they cease questioning him and he's free to go back to his house. But almost as soon as he has returned home, the police are back again. They have obtained a warrant to search his house. Search away, he tells them. He can't tell what expression is on his face as he says that. He's trying to control of a bubble of laughter that is welling up inside him. He can't see the expression on his own face, but he can see the expression on the faces of the police officers. It's disgust, and something else. Do they fear him? He knows they'll find nothing. They suspect him, but they will never be able to prove anything. He's been far too meticulous.

Then there's a slip-up. They find a demand for water rates for the workshop in Harland Street. And he thought he'd been so careful.

Why have you got a bill for premises you say you've never been inside?

I picked it up one day outside the door. I was trying to look inside and I found it. I meant to hand it in in case it was a clue, but I forgot.

Why were you trying to see inside the workshop?

Just curious, that's all.

At that point the man decides to stop talking. He is getting bored and annoyed in any case. Least said, soonest mended. That's what his mother used to say, and it was one of the few things she said he could agree with.

He stays silent when they arrest him again. He stays silent when he's remanded in custody and all the way through the endless tedium of the interviews: weeks and weeks of them. There's one detective sergeant who wasn't in the Crime Scene Investigation team, but appears to have visited the workshop several times. He asks different questions to the others.

'Did you meet Jack when his mother came to clean for you? Was that it? Did you like cutting him up on the table? Did you?'

Stupid question. If he had cut him up, it must have been because he liked it. And if he had done, he wasn't going to say so. He answers with a look.

'You don't like questions, do you?' asks the sergeant.

The detective sergeant has been busy. He tells the man: 'I'm told you paid money to see your mother being embalmed for her funeral. Wouldn't you agree that's an unusual thing to do?'

No answer. The detective gives him a knowing look and says: 'You think you're going to get away with this, don't you? You think that we've only got circumstantial evidence. Your brief has probably told you he can persuade the jury that there's reasonable doubt.'

No answer. As a matter of fact, that is exactly the conversation the man has had with his defence counsel, a man younger than himself who won't look him in the eye.

'Don't celebrate too soon, will you?' says the sergeant. He leaves and doesn't return.

There are others after that, but with different lines of enquiry: police psychiatrists with their prying questions. He manages to put up with it. Now and then he asks for a cup of tea, or a newspaper to read. Otherwise he doesn't speak.

When the trial finally takes place six months later, it all goes to plan. Or almost goes to plan. The defence counsel might be young, but he is no slouch in a courtroom. For every item of evidence, he constructs a plausible alternative explanation to that favoured by the prosecution. The man can see the doubt creeping into the minds of the jurymen. They don't like the look of him, and for that reason they are making an extra effort to be fair-minded. Then the detective who questioned him earlier is called. He drops his bombshell.

The new evidence was entered after the trial had begun. A recent search of the premises at 6 Harland Street – the workshop – revealed an object that had been overlooked by the Crime Scene Investigation team. It is a used handkerchief. The man recognises it. The last time he saw it was when he tossed it into the laundry basket at home, for Mrs Grzybowski's successor to launder and iron in due course. He uses up one clean handkerchief every day, wiping the spit from the corners of his mouth.

The police sergeant is sworn in. He testifies that he found the handkerchief in a corner of the workshop. No, he can't explain how the crime scene team overlooked it, but these things happen. His colleagues are highly competent and meticulous, but things do get overlooked. That's why, in his experience, it's never a bad idea to keep going back to the scene of a crime. Just in case. Yes, the DNA taken from this object matches that of the defendant. Yes, that confirms the presence of the defendant at the scene of the crime some time before the bodies were discovered. After he has testified, the detective turns to leave the witness box. His gaze sweeps neutrally across the courtroom, across the man's face as he sits in the defendant's box.

The man smiles at the detective, showing all his small teeth. The trial ends with him receiving a sentence of imprisonment for life, to be served at Broadmoor Hospital, with no maximum term. The judge tells him: 'In view of the nature of the crimes you have committed, you will be detained as a patient at Broadmoor Hospital for an indefinite period.'

The man nods when he hears this. It's what he expected. He promises himself that if, by some stroke of good fortune, he should be set free before he is too old to walk and talk, he will pursue his hobby a little more vigorously in future.

Thirty-One

When Chief Inspector Saxon has gone, Pippa returns to her desk. A moment later, she comes back into Norman's office.

'Willie left your car keys on my desk. He must have returned them while the chief inspector was here.'

'Just the keys? No note?'

'No note,' says Pippa. Norman ponders for a few minutes and then rings Willie's mobile. Willie answers straight away.

'Where are you?' asks Norman.

'Standing in a queue at the job centre,' replies Willie. Norman doesn't know if this is a joke. He asks, 'Did you find anything at Becky's house?'

'Nothing. The house was empty. It's been trashed by a bunch of kids and crack-heads. You can imagine.'

Norman doesn't want to imagine. He changes the subject. 'We ought to meet and go through our notes together. You never know. And something else has happened.'

'What?' asks Willie. His voice sounds weary and uninterested.

'I've just had a visitor.'

Norman tells Willie about Chief Inspector Saxon's visit. He has to remind Willie about the Freedom of Information request.

'So?' Willie asks, sounding even wearier than before.

'So they are trying to hide something from me. Not just

from me, from everyone. And it's something to do with Gabriel Merkin.'

'And so?'

Norman controls his irritation. He says: 'This story could be huge, Willie: even bigger than you thought. They are trying to cover up something. I don't know what it is yet, but I want you to help me find out.'

There's a silence at the other end of the line. Then Willie replies, 'Look, Norman, I just can't afford to spend any more time on this. I'm broke, I've got no money coming in after the end of the month, and I need to get a job.'

Norman hesitates between anger and doubt: anger that Willie should be so spineless; doubt that he can deal with all this on his own. Then he makes a decision.

'I'll pay you for your time. Fifty pounds a day plus reasonable expenses, but check with me first if you're going to spend anything.'

'A hundred quid,' says Willie, 'and I might think about it.'

They settle on seventy-five. Willie sounds brighter now.

'So how do I earn my money?' he asks.

'Find out if Gabriel Merkin is still in Broadmoor,' he tells Willie. 'If he's not there, find out where. The only other two places they could send someone with his record are Rampton and Ashworth.'

'You tried to do that on your computer, right?' asks Willie.

'Yes, I did.'

'And with all your special databases and passwords you couldn't get any information on him? So what makes you think I can do anything?'

'You're the investigative journalist,' Norman tells him. 'Just get on with it.'

He hangs up.

Willie isn't at the job centre, as it happens. He was lying on his bed when Norman rang. When Norman rings off, he thinks: 'Seventy-five quid a day. I can claim five hundred a week if I work weekends. That's more than I earned on the paper. What the hell are they paying Norman?'

And he thinks bitterly about fat cats for a moment or two, and Norman's jibe about investigative journalism. Then he gets up and makes himself another mug of coffee. That's his new routine: lying on his bed drinking mugs of coffee and watching daytime TV. But this time he doesn't go back to bed. Instead it occurs to him that Norman might be right: what he's asked Willie to do is exactly the sort of task he would be given if he were working for the *Sunday Times*, or the *Sun*, for that matter.

He considers the project that he's been given. He needs to blag his way through this somehow. Then he picks up the phone and punches in a Directory Enquiry number. He is given a number for Broadmoor Hospital and calls it. After a number of false starts, he has the name and extension number of someone who will talk to him. He dials again and this time is put through.

'Hello,' coos Willie. 'I'm Willie Craig from Christian Action for Long-term Prisoners.'

Later that morning, he is in Norman's office. He is full of excitement as he sits down in the chair opposite Norman. Norman has given up even pretending to be busy. Pippa comes in with Willie and stands by his chair and nobody asks why she's there.

Nobody asks, because they have both changed their perception of her. She isn't just a pretty PA sitting at her desk, reading

Grazia and doing her nails. Both Willie and Norman have underestimated her. She's a bright, compassionate girl with a strong personality.

They're a team now – Norman, Willie, Pippa – and she's the reason they are a team. Norman can't quite analyse how it happened, but Pippa is no longer just an employee. She's become someone he has to take seriously.

Willie can't wait to drop his bombshell. 'Gabriel Merkin's not in Broadmoor any more.'

'Then where is he?' asks Norman. But Willie wants everyone to know how clever he has been so he doesn't answer directly. 'The first person I spoke to was some kind of communications officer. He was very cagey. He asked me why I wanted to know. I said that Gabriel Merkin was on a list of long-term patients that my charity was hoping to provide pastoral care for.'

Then Willie had to explain about Christian Action for Long-term Prisoners.

'I made it up, of course,' he said, 'but it sounds convincing, doesn't it?'

'You are clever, Willie,' Pippa tells him. Willie gives her a look that seems to say that he already knows how clever he is, but he's grateful to her for mentioning it.

'So get on with the story,' says Norman.

'Anyway, as I said, they were definitely cagey. The name Gabriel Merkin did it. As soon as I mentioned him, they clammed up. Wanted to ring me back, check me out. So I hung up and tried another tack. I rang through to the Nursing Department and got a Senior Therapy Assistant. She didn't know the party line. She just said, "Oh no, dear, he left ages ago. Not long after he arrived here. We didn't have him for very long at all." She told me he was discharged into police custody nearly two years ago. She doesn't know where he went after that.'

'What about Ashworth or Rampton?' asked Norman.

'I tried the same routine in both places as well,' said Willie. 'It was a bit more difficult. It was a lot more difficult at Rampton. But I'm as sure as I'm ever going to be that Gabriel Merkin isn't in either of those two places. I can't guarantee it, but I really don't think he is.'

'Then I can't think where else they could have sent him ...' says Norman, '... unless he died, that is.'

'You would have thought someone would have mentioned that,' Willie replies.

'How does this help us find the missing children?' asks Pippa.

'I don't know yet,' says Norman. 'I'd rather not speculate. But I think there's a connection, at least in Chief Inspector Saxon's mind. Why else would he have come to see me and tried to warn me off?'

Norman might have said he's not speculating, but he looks as if he has been, and isn't very happy about his conclusions.

'Well, oughtn't we to concentrate on finding them first?' persists Pippa.

'You're right,' agrees Norman.

'Then let's write down what we know about the children and see what they have in common,' she replies.

'They've nothing in common,' says Willie. Norman tells Pippa to get a note pad. Then Willie and Norman start talking at the same time. Pippa holds up her hand. 'Stop,' she says. 'Norman, let's talk about Theo first. Because he was the first.'

'I saw his parents too,' says Willie.

'Then you can add to anything Norman says when he's finished. Right, Norman.'

Willie sees Pippa taking charge like this and, despite his dislike of being told what to do, he is filled with admiration for her. He gives her a covert glance as she bends over the note pad, looks at the line of her jaw, the column of her neck, the smooth outline of her cheek under a wing of dark hair that she brushes away as she prepares to write.

'Theo liked games,' says Norman. 'His parents said he was very popular at school.'

'A calming influence, is what they said,' interjects Willie.

'Apart from the bruising, he was quite a normal boy.'

'He liked reading,' adds Willie.

'His parents didn't think he was especially religious, but I wonder about that,' adds Norman.

'His mother and his stepfather didn't get on very well,' says Willie.

'That's right,' agrees Norman. 'The stepfather – Geordie Nixon – looked as if he liked a drink. He was very uncivil towards me. I wondered if he might be another alcoholic, like Becky's mother.'

'He might be fond of a pint or two,' says Willie. 'But he's not a drunk. I've seen plenty of those, and he isn't one.'

For a few more minutes they talk about Theo, but can't come up with anything else of significance.

'OK,' says Pippa. 'Now for Becky Thomas.'

'I'll do this one,' Willie volunteers. 'Drunken mother, don't know what happened to the father. My guess is he's long gone.'

'Don't guess,' says Norman. 'If there was an abduction it could have been the father that did it. That's a very common thing. It's why I still feel we don't know enough about Theo's real father. Not Geordie, but Mr Constantine. It could be the same in the Thomas case.'

'I'll check on Becky's father,' Willie offers. 'Otherwise I get the impression that Becky was a solitary little girl. She played a lot by herself. No doubt the other mothers didn't want their kids hanging out anywhere near Mrs Thomas.'

'Likes and dislikes?' asks Pippa.

'I don't know about any dislikes. She must have liked order because her bedroom was tidy. The rest of the house was filthy, even before it was trashed. She liked soft toys. She liked reading. There were lots of books, and there was one open on her desk the first time I visited.'

'Just like any girl of that age,' says Norman.

'No it's not,' replies Pippa. 'No TV in the bedroom? No computer games? Is that right, Willie?'

'I shouldn't think Mrs Thomas could afford any of those things. The house was empty the last time I went – the neighbour said she'd taken off, with rent owing.'

'OK,' says Pippa. 'Now for Karen Gilby.'

So Willie describes his last visit to the Gilby house. When Pippa finishes writing her notes, she reads out a summary.

'She liked teddy bears; she wanted a pet kitten; she liked reading. Is that it?'

'She liked reading,' agrees Willie.

'Like the other two,' adds Norman. 'If they've got anything in common, that's it.'

'But so do thousands of children of that age. Millions,' says Willie.

'And millions more never open a book unless they have to,' replies Pippa.

'Well, I'm not getting any sense of where this is going at all,' Norman begins, when Willie interrupts him.

'Wait a minute.' There's something in his voice. Norman and Pippa both start to speak, but Willie holds up his hand.

'Wait,' he repeats. He's remembering something, something right at the back of his mind. The sense of loss, the sense of emptiness he felt in the three houses. The Constantine flat, the air leaden with despair; the Gilby house silent, vacant; the

223

Thomas house as alien as another planet, everything that was recognisably human gone from it. But there was something else. A connection.

'In the Gilby house,' he says, then stops, thinking. 'In Karen's bedroom there was a book. It was called *The Lion, the Witch and the Wardrobe*, I think. Yes.' He's staring at Pippa and Norman, but he's not seeing them. He's seeing Karen's room again, the warm, clean bedroom with no child to inhabit it. He can see the book on the bedside table. He can see himself picking it up and looking at the inside cover. There's a form pasted inside from a lending library. The library is called Bookwise. Willie remembers thinking: '*A good name for a library.*'

'Bookwise,' repeats Willie out loud. The others wait for him to explain. 'Karen got her book from a lending library called Bookwise.'

'Well, she had to get her books from somewhere,' says Norman in the reasonable tone of voice Willie finds so irritating.

But Willie is flipping back the pages in his spiral-bound notebook, until he finds what he wants. It was the very first time he heard about Theo Constantine. He came across his name by accident when he was trawling through the newspaper archives for articles on missing children. He wrote it down, he's almost sure. It was a quote from a local newspaper, not the one he worked for. He finds the quote scrawled across a page. He reads it out:

'He only went to the library,' said distraught mother Mary. 'He went every week to get a new book out. He loved reading.'

The three of them stare at each other.

'That's three out of three who liked reading,' says Pippa. As they all do, she speaks of the children in the past tense. It's become a habit.

'Two out of three got their books from a lending library,' says Norman. 'I shall call Mrs Constantine and find out which library it was that the family used. Willie, why don't you go back to Becky's house and see if you can find any of the books in her bedroom?'

'I've already been there twice. I really don't want to have to go there again,' complains Willie.

'Third time lucky,' says Pippa, standing up. 'I'll keep you company, Willie.'

After they've gone, Norman stares at the phone for a while. He very much wants to speak to Mary Constantine and ask her about Theo's father. But he's concerned that Geordie will answer the phone. Geordie frightens him a little. He checks his watch. It's just gone twelve-thirty. Geordie should be away working. He rings, ready to hang up if a man's voice answers. The phone rings out. There's no voicemail.

He gives it an hour and rings again. This time Mary picks up. Norman explains who he is, reminds her of their previous meetings.

'I remember you all right,' replies Mary. Her voice is unfriendly and he imagines she is about to hang up, so he says quickly, 'We've some new evidence I need to talk to you about.'

'What new evidence?'

The ferocity of her reply startles Norman so much that he almost drops the phone.

'Where did Theo get his books?'

'From the library,' replies Mary. 'What *new evidence*, Mr Stokoe?'

'Which library? The local council library? The school library?'

'No,' replies Mary. 'From the mobile library. It's a van. It specialises in children's books.'

'And what is it called, this van?'

'A funny name. I can't remember. It's on the tip of my tongue – hold the line a moment.'

There's a pause, then she's back.

'Theo still has one of the books in his bedroom. The library is called Bookwise.'

'Ah,' says Norman. 'Thank you, Mrs Constantine. That's been very helpful. Very helpful indeed.'

'So what new evidence?' asks Mary again.

'I'll tell you as soon as I can – we're still missing a piece of the jigsaw. But I also need to ask you about Theo's father. Do you mind answering a couple more questions?'

'Do you mean Geordie? He's got nothing to do with this.'

'I don't mean Geordie. I mean Theo's biological father, Mr Constantine. He couldn't have abducted Theo, could he? These things have been known to happen in other cases.'

There's a long silence. When Mary Constantine replies, Norman has the weirdest feeling. He thinks she is smiling. He thinks she is struggling not to laugh.

'Mr Stokoe, you can rule Theo's father out of your enquiries. I can say that with absolute certainty.'

'Thank you,' says Norman, and hangs up before Mary Constantine can ask him any more questions in return. After a moment the phone on his desk rings. It rings for a long time.

Then there's silence.

Thirty-Two

Geordie is running on empty. He doesn't know how much longer he can go on with his life the way it is now. He's back in the forest. It's a grey, windy day. As he drives up towards the forest, far away in the valley behind him there are patches of bright blue: sun shining on ripening wheat and barley; sun shining on those children still with their parents, playing in their gardens or in the streets and parks. Above him the forest: a grey sky threatening rain, but not raining. Where the dark trees meet the dark sky, there's a haze as if sky and forest are merging together. A wind sighs through the tops of the trees, a melancholy sound as the needle-clad branches swish and brush together.

He's not working like the old Geordie would have done. He keeps stopping and falling into his own thoughts. It's not a good idea when you're felling large trees. Already there have been a couple of disasters: trees snapped off halfway up because the harvester grabbed them in the wrong place. Another tree nearly falls on the cab: the modern-day equivalent of sitting on the branch while you're sawing it off at the trunk. Geordie knows he ought to give it up as a bad job. He knows he ought to go home before he breaks something.

But go home to what? Mary won't be there. Her hours of work are becoming more and more erratic, but chances are she'll be out at this time of the day. What does she do when she goes out? She can't always be in that grim churchyard – but then again, she might be. Geordie hasn't dared to follow her there again. He doesn't know how he got away with it the first time. She had only to turn her head to see him.

He doesn't believe in her job at the council. One or maybe two phone calls could establish for a fact whether she worked there or not. He thinks for a moment about ringing, but of course there's no signal in the forest, not until you get miles down the valley. How hard could it be to find someone in the council's Human Resources department who could answer a simple question? Does Mary Constantine work there? Yes or no? He's almost sure now that the answer would be no; never heard of her; Mary who? She's so vague about what she does there, it's almost as if she can't be bothered to think up a decent lie. But she always has money even though on some days it's clear that she hasn't been out at work. And the clothes she wears: really casual, jeans and tight tops, or the black tunic dress and leggings that she wears so often. Don't they have a dress code at the council?

Perhaps she's seeing someone else? The thought strikes him and he feels so sick that for a moment he thinks he's going to throw up right there, in the cab of the harvester. His vision blurs as sudden tears prickle in the corner of his eyes and he wipes his face with his hand. He halts the harvester in mid-operation, half a tree hanging from its jaws. He just has to stop for a minute. The thought of Mary with someone else is so absurd he doesn't know why he can't just blot it out. If she wanted to be with someone else, why didn't she just chuck Geordie out of the flat and move the other fellow in? Why would someone else be able to cut through her grief when he couldn't?

But he can't get it out of his mind.

If she were seeing someone else, he would have heard about it. There are a lot of people living in the Tyne valley these days, but it's still a village: a village consisting of a series of villages and small towns. They would know about it in the pub. Stevie the pill-pusher would have heard about it. Jimmy would know. He met Mary at Jimmy's house; Jimmy, whom he's known on and off since they used to try to thump each other in the play-ground at the local school. How did Jimmy know Mary? He's never asked. Jimmy's never said. Jimmy's known Geordie and Mary have been an item for ages, and Geordie's seen Jimmy around quite a few times since the night he and Mary met, but Jimmy's never asked: 'How's Mary then?' He's never brought the subject up, and that's odd. Jimmy's never mentioned her name.

But she couldn't be with someone else.

Geordie would have known it. He thinks: I may be bloody daft, but I'm not that daft. And then he thinks: but that would explain the irregularity of Mary's life. Out at odd hours, never volunteering any explanation of where she's going other than: 'I've got to go to work.' In recent days when Geordie has shown no signs of doing any work himself, she's added: 'Someone's got to bring the money in.' Maybe this other lad has a few quid. Maybe he's helping Mary out. That would explain the fact that she's never complained about being short of money. That would explain why she's avoided giving him any details about the work she does for the council, treating Geordie as if he's too thick to understand anything she might tell him. She could be leading a double life.

That might explain why, since Theo's gone, they've never shared a bed. She doesn't want to give herself away, he thinks. A sick little voice at the back of his mind squeaks: '*Because she's giving herself away to another lad. Everyone knows but you. You're a standing joke, Geordie.'*

The voice in the back of his mind constructs a scenario:

She was with another lad when she met you. When Theo disappeared, she went back to him. To stop herself thinking about Theo every waking minute.

Geordie shakes his head angrily. He starts up the harvester. He looks at the tree dangling from its jaws. He releases it and it falls to the forest floor: another wasted bit of timber. I've got to get my mind back on my job, thinks Geordie. It might be all I've got now. No Mary, no Theo. This job is all that stands between me and being homeless.

As he thinks of Theo, he forms a mental picture of the boy in his head. Mechanically, he adjusts the harvester's jaws around the base of another tree. He pictures Theo's face: the calm eyes looking at him. He can hear Theo's voice as if he were standing outside the cab: faint but not very far away, saying: 'Are you OK, Geordie? You look tired.' That's what Theo used to ask him sometimes when he came back from work. Theo wanted to know what sort of day *he* had had. What other boy of that age would think of asking how someone else felt about his life? He pictures his stepson (that's how Geordie thinks of him) walking alongside him on the way to the shops, or to the library to borrow a new book. That must be an invented memory, Geordie thinks, as he turns the harvester around and stacks the newly cut and trimmed pole on a pile of other poles. Did he ever go to the library with him? He can't remember. But a great calmness has come over him. He's stopped agonising about Mary: those thoughts seem dim and far away.

The calmness stays with him, a calm so deep that now Geordie's working like a clockwork toy. He cuts the trees; he trims the branches; he cuts to length; he turns the cab and stacks the pole with the other poles. He does it ten times. He does it fifty times. He's working like he used to when he first came into the forestry: in the days when tiredness was unknown; when he was certain about everything; when he earned a fortune, and spent it. He doesn't stop for his mug of tea. He doesn't stop for anything, and the pile of poles at the roadside grows larger.

All of a sudden, he realises with a shock that it is evening. He turns the harvester to drive back down the bank to where he's parked the Scania. As the harvester trundles downhill, his phone chirrups briefly in his pocket. A text. When the vehicle comes to a halt, he pulls out his phone and it automatically lights up. At first the message is hard to make out; his eyes are unfocused. Then he's able to read it:

im w8in 4u

He tries to see if it's from Mary. But there's no sender. It came from nobody and nowhere, but that's impossible. He reads it again:

im w8in 4u

There's a smell of perfume in the cab: the fragrance of some strange flower, faint but exotic. As Geordie becomes conscious of it, the jasmine scent fades, and is forgotten. The text must be from Mary, but he can't see any sign that it is. Then the screen goes blank. He thinks the backlight has timed out. He presses the select button, but the screen remains blank. He presses it again: nothing. He tries to dial a call. The phone's dead. It's not that he isn't getting a signal, although he knows from experience there's no signal up here. The phone's completely dead. Something has fried the electronics.

Thirty-Three

Willie and Pippa have borrowed Norman's car to go on their mission. Pippa's given up even pretending to work as Norman's assistant. Now she's off with Willie and they are returning to Becky Thomas's house to see if they can find any clues that might connect Becky with the other two children. Mrs Thomas didn't seem to Willie to be much of a book-lover herself, so there's a reasonable chance Becky obtained her books from a library. But which library? And who can they ask? Pippa is going to knock on the doors of neighbouring houses to see whether anyone is aware of a mobile library visiting the street. And Willie wants her to see if she can find out anything about Becky's father. It's proper detective work and Willie's mood is confident again.

Pippa is thrilled. After booking taxis and restaurants and theatre tickets for Norman for the last few months, she feels she's finally doing something real. She feels a sense of elation for a moment that is extinguished a second later as she remembers what this is all about: three children, presumed missing, probably dead. Dead or alive, they must be found, and she believes they can be found. She hopes they can be found.

She's a realist: she understands that a team consisting of Norman, Willie and herself may not achieve very much. They aren't super-heroes. She knows that, of the three of them, she is the only one with her feet on the ground. She likes Willie; more than that, she feels that Willie really likes her. 'Likes' hasn't turned to 'loves', and maybe it never will. She knows what Willie is: ambitious, self-centred, a dreamer and unreliable. She knows what Norman is too: she thinks he is timid, with a weak conscience and a strong sense of self-preservation. It's up to her to keep everyone concentrated on the task in hand. Without her, she believes Willie and Norman would simply waste all day arguing about who was in charge and what to do next.

Pippa has no illusions about the future. She wants to finish her Open University course and find a better job. It would be nice – no, much better than nice – if things worked out with Willie, if they developed into a real relationship. But all of that is background chatter: at the front of her mind all she can think about is the three children, and finding and saving them from whoever has taken them.

While Pippa and Willie are off on their mission, Norman is sitting alone in his office, staring at the ceiling. He finds he's doing that a lot these days. Staring at the ceiling, as if somewhere above it lies the answer. But the answer to which question?

He's brought back to wakefulness by a knock on the door. He manages to compose himself in time as Chief Inspector Saxon enters the room. Norman wonders for how long the chief inspector has been standing outside and whether he over-heard Norman's phone conversation with Mary Constantine. The chief inspector's face offers no clues.

'Good morning, Mr Stokoe. I hope you don't mind my drop-ping in like this again, but your secretary doesn't seem to be about. I'm not disturbing you, am I?' asks the chief inspector. Norman reassures him: no, not at all. The chief inspector sits down.

'Have you had a chance to think about what we discussed yesterday?' asks the chief inspector.

'I've no new information that would lead me to change my mind. Have you anything new for me?'

'I can only repeat what I said yesterday. Disclosure would compromise current operations. It would also create difficulties for the home secretary, something I imagine you want to avoid as much as I do.'

'So you've nothing new to tell me?' asks Norman. 'In that case, I fear my answer must be the same as it was yesterday.'

The chief inspector reminds Norman of Mount Etna on a quiet day: he can imagine wisps of smoke coming out of his head; he can imagine rumblings shaking the floor beneath the chief inspector's feet. But the chief inspector's reply is not at all volcanic. In a mild tone he enquires, 'Why on earth are you interested in Gabriel Merkin, anyway?'

'Because I was researching him and found that I was denied access to directories that are normally open to me.'

'And why were you researching Gabriel Merkin?' asks the chief inspector. 'For the life of me, I can't see what it has to do with your job. Why is your Department paying for you to occupy your time like this?'

This is below the belt and Norman just stops himself from wincing. He answers in an equally mild voice: 'As you know, I have an interest in the disappearance of three children in the region. We've spoken about this.'

The chief inspector raises his eyebrows but does not speak, so Norman continues: 'A quite legitimate interest, in my role as Children's Commissioner for the region.'

'Oh, I'm sorry. I thought you were still waiting for that position to be confirmed,' the chief inspector says. If anything, this is an even lower blow. Norman is becoming angry.

'The secretary of state has not yet found parliamentary time to get through the enabling legislation. Meanwhile, I am doing what I was employed to do until someone tells me otherwise: looking after the interests of vulnerable children.'

'Well, you can safely leave this part of it to the police. It's our role to find these children. Not yours, and not the boy detective's, either.'

The chief inspector must be referring to Willie. The contempt in his voice makes Norman glad Willie is not in the room. He opens a drawer to take out a file and while his hand is in the drawer, he flicks on the Dictaphone he keeps in there. Maybe it will pick up some of this conversation. It might be handy to have a record of what is said. He takes the file out, puts it on the desk and pretends to study it for a moment. Then he says: 'Gabriel Merkin is no longer in Broadmoor Hospital. He wasn't transferred to Ashworth. He wasn't transferred to Rampton. So where is he? You can tell me now and I'll withdraw my request and the matter will stay off the public record.'

Now it's the chief inspector's turn to be thrown off-balance. His mouth opens, but he doesn't say anything for a moment. Then he speaks in a very different tone of voice to any he has used before with Norman: 'Turn that tape recorder off, you little prick. I won't say another word until you show me it's switched off.'

Norman tries not to blush, fails, reaches into his desk and takes out the digital recorder, holds it up and switches it off. He waits.

'If you repeat what I'm telling you now to that journalist, or anyone else, your job is history. I guarantee you will never work for any government department again. Not even pushing the tea trolley. You're a bit old to retrain, aren't you?'

'If you can give me a good reason why I should retract my

235

Freedom of Information request, I'll do it. That's the only promise I'm making.'

'You heard what I said,' replies the chief inspector, 'and I hope you know I mean it.' After a moment, he continues: 'When Gabriel Merkin was on trial, his defence attacked the nature of the evidence, most of which was circumstantial. The plan was to convince the jury, not of Merkin's innocence, but that a guilty verdict could not be brought in safely because of "reasonable doubt". We'll never know if that would have worked, because late in the trial some evidence was produced – DNA – that linked Merkin to the scene of the crime beyond any doubt. That single item of evidence, found on a used handkerchief, was the cornerstone of the prosecution's summing up and led to Merkin being given an indefinite life sentence.'

Norman guesses what he is going to say next. Still, it's hard to believe.

'About a year after Merkin was sentenced, the officer who discovered the handkerchief was investigated by the Professional Standards Department, as part of an Independent Police Complaints Commission review. The officer admitted planting evidence in the case under investigation, which was a drugs squad case and nothing to do with Merkin. But, unfortunately, he also admitted planting Merkin's handkerchief at the scene of the crime, amongst other similar offences, in an attempt to plea bargain. You will see the implications, I dare say.'

'I'm not sure,' says Norman. 'The conviction would be unsafe, wouldn't it?'

'The new evidence had to be disclosed to the defence, who appealed immediately. The appeal hearing was held *in camera* – about the only bit of good luck we had, so at least it didn't get into the newspapers.'

'What happened?' asks Norman.

The chief inspector stops speaking and there is such a long silence that Norman wonders if he has fallen asleep. But the chief inspector isn't asleep. He's staring down at his hands. Without raising his eyes he says: 'Now I'm going to put to you a series of hypotheses. I won't admit to any of this if you repeat it. Instead I'll make sure that you regret it for the rest of your life. That's not a threat, of course, as we're only talking about a hypothesis.'

Norman nods to show he understands. He couldn't speak at the moment even if he wanted to.

'In my hypothesis, a court confronted with this sort of evidence would have no choice but to acquit Gabriel Merkin. So much of the other evidence in his trial was circumstantial. The original conviction would be unsafe. So let's hypothesise that he was acquitted. Someone in his situation would immediately be targeted by the press for his story, and possibly by vigilantes as well. Do you agree?'

Norman still can't speak, so he simply makes a noise in his throat.

'So let us continue with my hypothesis. Let's say a deal would be done. In return for his silence and comparative safety, the man who was acquitted would be entered into the Witness Protection Programme. He would be given a new identity and a new home and then he would vanish from the surface of the earth. By the way, the Witness Protection Programme is exempt from FOI requests.'

At last Norman finds his voice. 'That's outrageous.'

'You know quite as well as I do, that's how the justice system works,' says the chief inspector. 'But I haven't finished with my hypothesis yet.'

He looks up at Norman and Norman can see an expression

on his face that mixes pain and menace in equal parts.

'In my hypothesis, if knowledge of this were ever to become public, it would cause widespread revulsion. You would feel it. I would feel it. Every right-minded citizen would feel it. That would be regrettable because it might damage the reputation of a very good minister, who's now been promoted to be our home secretary.'

Norman had already begun to formulate his own hypothesis. But he is staggered to find that it is true. For a moment he doesn't know what to say next.

'There are those who say that he will be our next prime minister. He's certainly got the support of the police. It's unusual to find a senior politician with such a good grasp of policy on police pay and pension matters. So it's not in anybody's interest for anything to happen that could damage our new home secretary.'

Norman's had enough. With all the outrage he can muster he says, 'It must have occurred to you that it might be Gabriel Merkin who is involved in the disappearance of the three children? You must be investigating that possibility. Please tell me that you are.'

The chief inspector stands up.

'I won't comment on current investigations. As usual, the police will diligently investigate every case that is brought to their attention. You and I have only been talking hypothetically. I hope you understand why it is better for both of us if we decide this conversation has never taken place. I hope you understand why you must stop your interfering now, in order not to prejudice police operations.'

Without another word, Chief Inspector Saxon leaves the room.

Thirty-Four

Willie and Pippa stand outside number seventeen Collingwood Street, the former home of the Thomas family. The intervening day since Willie's last visit has not produced any improvement in the appearance of the house. The only change Willie can see is that the front door is now hanging off its hinges.

'Don't come in,' he tells Pippa. 'You don't want to see inside. It's not good. Why don't you try to find a neighbour who will talk to us?'

'Who shall I say I am?'

'Say you work at the regional children's commissioner's office. Or you work for the council. It doesn't matter, as long as they talk.'

'I'll just take a peek inside,' replies Pippa, and walks lightly up the short garden path, stepping over empty lager cans. She pauses at the threshold and pushes the door open. It swings drunkenly inward.

'Oh my God,' says Pippa. She puts her hand to her mouth.

'Told you,' says Willie.

'It's horrible. How could people do that?'

'I'll wait for you in the car when I've finished here,' says Willie. 'Or, if you don't have any joy, come and find me and I'll help.'

Pippa walks off up the street. Willie goes inside. The first thing to become apparent is that the hallway has recently been used as a lavatory by some person disinclined to make use of the one upstairs. The smell is awful. Willie gingerly crosses the hall and goes up the stairs. He enters Becky's room. This doesn't seem to have been disturbed since he was last here. The desk is still lying on its side. The floor is still covered in a blizzard of torn pages from books which have nearly all had their covers ripped off. Willie crouches down and starts sorting through the mess, looking for the front inside covers of the books.

Outside, there's a crash of breaking glass. Willie straightens up and looks out of Becky's window. Two small boys are running away up the alley, laughing. It sounds as if they've just put a brick through one of the downstairs windows. Willie resumes his work. He's quite confident he will find what he is looking for. It just has to be here. And he's right. Poking out from underneath the remains of the bed is the cover of a book splayed upside down. Willie picks it up. A half-hearted attempt has been made to rip the pages out, but most of them are still there. Maybe the people who trashed the house were tiring by that stage. This book looks newer than the others. It's more of a comic book than straight literature. It's called *The Penguins of Madagascar.* Willie turns the book the right way up and examines it. Pasted onto the inside front cover is a library plate. The library is called Bookwise.

'Bingo,' says Willie. He feels elated. Finding this book is like fitting the last piece into a jigsaw. Keeping hold of the remains of the book, he walks down the stairs. He can't wait to get out into the fresh air.

Outside in the bright sunlight, Willie heads for the car and sees Pippa walking down the street towards him. As he looks at her, his heart turns over for a moment. He's not in love with

Pippa, why should he be, he hasn't time for that sort of thing but, all the same, his heart turns over. He sees a pretty, confident girl walking down the street towards him and he knows that, for the moment, she's his. There's something special about Pippa: a wholeness. He can't explain it to himself, but he knows he is right about her. He also knows he has a tendency to let the few good things in his life slip through his fingers. He wonders if he will have any more luck with this girl.

'Any good?' he asks, as she approaches.

'Yes. It was dead easy. I just marched up to someone's front door and when I pressed the bell a woman came, and I asked her if she knew Becky's family. She couldn't wait to tell me all about it. I didn't even have to explain who I was. She didn't know anything about a mobile library and she's no idea where Mrs Thomas has gone. Nobody round here talked to her, she said, Becky's mother was always drunk. But I found out about the father.'

'Is he still around?' asks Willie. 'Can we get in touch with him?'

'He's dead. He was a soldier serving in Iraq and he never came home from his last tour. A roadside bomb got him. That's what started Becky's mother drinking.'

They get into Norman's car. As Willie starts the engine, Pippa adds, 'Poor little mite, she kept saying. Apparently that's what everyone in the street says about Becky: poor little mite.'

'Well, I've found what we were looking for too,' Willie tells her. He hands her the library book, slips off the handbrake and drives away.

A conference of war takes place in Norman's office. First of all, Willie shows Norman the library book.

'Three out of three children borrowed their books from the

same library, Bookwise,' says Willie. 'That's the connection.'

'A mobile children's library,' says Norman. 'It wasn't random. He checked the children out when they came to borrow his books. He watched them week in and week out until he had an idea of when and where he would find them unprotected.'

'So let's take this to the police,' says Pippa. 'Now we know who kidnapped the children, all the police have to do is find out who the driver of the mobile library is, and then they can find the children. Maybe they're still alive. If we hurry, there might still be a chance.'

Pippa stands up as she says this. To her the urgency is so great it almost hurts her. She can't bear the thought of those three children either buried in unmarked graves or, perhaps worse, still alive and at the mercy of some unknown monster. An image appears in her mind of two girls crouching in a room with rough stone walls. She cannot picture the boy. She can't bear to wait a minute longer. 'Shall I call the chief inspector?' she asks. 'I've got his number on my desk.'

'It's not as simple as that,' says Norman, and Willie's eyebrows go up. All the way back in the car he's been composing his story in his head. His idea is to wait until the police make the arrest, and then rush into print with the story of how Willie Craig made the vital breakthrough. Without him making the connection with the library, the police would be nowhere. They'd still be sitting in the police station twiddling their thumbs. He has a shortlist in his head of the papers he'll ring to see who wants his story. Maybe he can get an auction going: highest bidder is the one who offers a pile of cash *and* a job for Willie Craig. But now Norman is saying, 'It's not as simple as that.' It sounds like the typical civil servant's response to an emergency.

'Why isn't it as simple as that?' asks Willie.

'Because I think I know the name of the person who abducted the three children. I think it's Gabriel Merkin.'

The name brings with it a moment of silence. The trial was three years ago, but nobody who was living in Britain at the time could fail to know the name, and with it the awful memories, clinging to it like cobwebs, of the things that Gabriel Merkin had been convicted of.

'It can't be,' says Pippa in a voice that almost breaks. 'He was sentenced to life imprisonment, wasn't he? He must have been.'

Then Norman tells Willie and Pippa about Chief Inspector Saxon's second visit. When he's finished, Willie says angrily: 'Well, you may have promised to keep the story about Gabriel Merkin confidential. But I didn't. If it's him, if he was let out of prison and then did three more children, what a hell of a story.'

Pippa winces at Willie's choice of words.

And Willie's revising his ideas about what he'll ask for the story. It will be the biggest scoop in the last five years.

'Suppose for a moment that the Bookwise man and Gabriel Merkin are one and the same. Imagine if that story gets out in the middle of a police operation to catch Gabriel Merkin, and it spooks him,' Norman tells Willie. 'Imagine if he gets enough warning from your story to get away or to conceal the evidence, then you will go down in history as the man who sacrificed the chance of finding three children alive in order to get into print.'

When Norman speaks, his voice is like iron. He's transformed. His voice rings with passion. He stares at Willie until Willie drops his gaze.

'All right, I get it. But how do we know that the police really *are* after him?'

'Because Chief Inspector Saxon told me that if we disclosed what we suspect about Gabriel Merkin, it would endanger police operations. He wouldn't tell me any more than that.'

Willie replies: 'And you believe what he said?'

'I'm not naive,' says Norman. 'I know he'll say what he has to say to keep me quiet. But I cannot believe that the police aren't closing in on Gabriel Merkin, even if he is in the Witness Protection Programme. *Someone* must know where he lives. *Someone* must know his new identity. Surely there's some degree of coordination in police operations.' Even as he speaks, Norman doubts his own words. Maybe the operations aren't as joined-up as he would like to think.

Willie has his mobile out. He stands up and walks away from the other two, to the far end of the office. Over his shoulder he says, 'I'm ringing an old school friend who works at Northumbria Police Headquarters. He'll be able to tell me if there's an operation to catch Gabriel Merkin.'

'For God's sake, don't mention his name,' says Norman in alarm.

'I won't ... Hi, yes, it's me.'

Willie is silent while an excitable voice squawks at the other end of the phone.

Norman and Pippa can't make out what the voice is saying, but it sounds angry. Willie says: 'Of course I've got the photograph. I'll give it back to you tonight. I'll bring it round to yours about seven-thirty. I promise. But first you've got to do something for me.'

More squawking.

'If you don't, I'll drop the photograph off at your reception with a thank-you note addressed to the assistant chief constable.'

There's a pause and then Willie says: 'Can't you take a joke?

I need you to help me. I want you to tell me the current status of the operation to catch the person who abducted the three missing children. Theo Constantine, Becky Thomas, Karen Gilby. Fine. Ring me back in five.'

Willie comes back to the desk and sits down in front of Norman.

'He'll tell us. I guarantee it.'

There's a long silence. Each of them feels too tense to say anything. Then Willie's phone rings.

The old school friend has some news.

'The three names you mentioned are listed as runaways. What's this bollocks about abductions?'

'What, even Karen Gilby is a runaway? Come on – you must be joking.'

The old school friend checks something for a moment then says, 'Her old man had porn on his computer. The word is it was just email attachments. Jokes, really, like naughty post-cards. The sort of stuff you've probably got on your computer, Willie. But, hey, if the bosses say it's porn, then it's porn. They've been giving him a hard time. So Karen Gilby is listed as a runaway. Wanted to get out of the way of her dirty old man, I suppose.'

'Thanks,' says Willie. 'Yes, I'll see you tonight with the photo. Half seven at yours.'

He puts the phone away and looks at Pippa and Norman.

'There isn't any police operation to find Gabriel Merkin, or anyone else. All three children are listed as runaways and have been referred to the Missing Persons Task Force. Saxon has been having you on, Norman.'

Thirty-Five

Geordie returns home from the forest to find the flat empty. It's nine in the evening. Even Mary, with her odd comings and goings, is usually home at that time of night. But tonight, she's not. So Geordie leaves the flat again and goes to The Skinner's Arms for a pint.

The pub's not busy when he walks in. He orders his pint and finds an empty table to sit at in the corner of the room. All of a sudden, he feels tired to death. Whatever has been keeping him going these last few hours worked better than Stevie's pills, but now he feels hollowed out by exhaustion. He drinks his first pint quickly because along with the tiredness has come a raging thirst. When he goes to the bar to order a fresh drink, a voice beside him says: 'Mine's a pint of lager and a shot, Geordie.'

It's Stevie-the-pill. Geordie doesn't feel like talking to Stevie, much less buying him drinks, but the barman has overheard and produces the drinks anyway.

Geordie pays up. 'Now then, Stevie.'

'Now then, Geordie,' replies Stevie, lifting the lager to his lips. 'Where's your lass tonight?'

'No idea. She was out when I got back.'

'Hen party, is it?' asks Stevie. 'Out somewhere dancing round the handbags?'

He cackles and Geordie wonders if Stevie knows something he doesn't know. The paranoia comes flooding back: where is Mary? What is she doing? What does she do when she's not in the house? He frowns and Stevie remarks: 'You look well knackered, son. I've got something on me that would give you a lift, if you're interested.'

Stevie is talking out of the side of his mouth now, so that he won't be heard by anyone but Geordie. Stevie thinks it makes him look like the big-time pusher he'd like to be; Geordie thinks it makes him look as if he's had a stroke.

'Nah,' says Geordie. 'Not interested.'

'Go on, man. It'll do you good, put a smile on your face.'

'I *said*,' repeats Geordie. 'I'm not interested.'

He speaks with more force than he intended because Stevie winces as if Geordie had raised his fist against him and backs off.

'All right, son, keep your hair on.' Stevie knocks back his shot and picks up the remainder of his pint.

'Thanks for the drink, Geordie. I'll get them in next time. I've got to go and see a man about a dog now.'

Geordie picks up his new pint and goes back to his table. He still feels the anger in him that came like lightning a moment ago. Was it because Stevie offered him pills? No, he's bought from Stevie once or twice before now and there was no reason to be angry just because Stevie thinks of him as a customer. The anger was about Mary, wasn't it? It was about the wall Mary has built around herself since Theo disappeared. Maybe, if Geordie could see over that wall he wouldn't be so distrustful, he wouldn't be having these absurd thoughts about her.

He sits for a while thinking about this, trying to discover the roots of his anger so that he can pull it out. He finishes his pint and goes to the bar to order another. Nearby he can see Stevie plying his trade: cracking jokes and selling drugs, and not discreetly. He wonders why the landlord of the pub lets him do it. Maybe he gets a cut, thinks Geordie.

He takes his third pint back to the table and broods some more. Before Theo disappeared, there was no wall. Mary and he lived in an atmosphere of complete trust. And love, on his side at least. The wall came up when someone took Theo from them.

The person who is at the root of all his anger, all his exhaustion, all his confusion, is the person who took Theo.

Geordie's always known that, but somehow he hasn't expressed the thought to himself in quite that way before. It's as if for a long time he's been unable to think straight. Now that he can, he knows that the single most important thing for him to do in the world is to find that person, whoever and wherever he is, and kill him. He wants to kill him because he doesn't think Theo is alive any more.

But even if – by some miracle, for it would need to be a miracle – Theo was still alive, that person would have killed the Theo that existed before. The Theo that was left would be someone diminished, damaged, haunted for the rest of his life, distorted like a tree bent in the wind. He wants to punish the person who did this to Theo. He wants to punish the person who divided him from Mary. In a bleak moment of truth, Geordie realises that there's no going back to life as it was before Theo went. That world is lost to him for ever. And he doesn't much care what happens to him in this new world.

He drains the rest of his glass and stands up to go home.

Three pints is not a lot for a man like Geordie, but even three pints will have its effect on a man with an empty stomach and a tired brain. By the time he opens the front door of the flat, he knows he's had a drink or two. He sees Mary sitting in the armchair, a glass of white wine beside her.

'So where were you when I came home?' he asks. He meant to say hello, how are you, but the drink has made him forget and his words sound angry. He didn't mean to sound angry.

'And you've been in the pub again, from the look of you,' replies Mary. That's not an answer, thinks Geordie, but she's got him on the back foot straight away. It's a gift she has.

'Well of course I went to the bloody pub. There was nowt to eat in the fridge and you were out.'

'And now you've had a few drinks,' says Mary.

'You didn't answer my question.'

'What question?'

Geordie tries not to lose control of this conversation, or his temper. He repeats himself: 'Where were you when I came home at nine tonight?'

'Out.'

'I know you were bloody out. Out where?'

'Don't shout at me,' Mary replies.

Geordie loses it. He walks over to Mary and grabs her by the back of her hair. She gives a little cry of surprise and knocks over her wine glass as she reaches up behind her head to try and loosen his grip. 'Stop it, Geordie,' she says, 'you're hurting me.'

But the anger has kindled again and Geordie can't stop himself.

'Are you seeing someone else?' he asks, still pulling her hair.

'No,' she replies. 'But you would deserve it if I was. Let go of my hair.'

'Is that what you do when you say you're going out to work,' asks Geordie recklessly. 'Seeing other men? Is that where the money comes from? Is it?'

Mary has twisted out of his grasp and is on her feet in an instant.

'How dare you say that,' she tells him. 'How dare you!' She, too, is white with anger.

'Well then, where do you go?' shouts Geordie. 'How am I expected to know any different when you never tell me anything?'

'At least now I know what you think of me,' says Mary. She goes and picks up her handbag and takes her coat from the hook on the back of the door.

'Where are you going?' asks Geordie. He feels stunned by the pace of events, which is quite beyond his control.

'I'm going to spend the night at Frieda's,' says Mary. 'If she'll have me. I'm not staying here. I'm not staying with a man who calls me a tart.'

All the fire has gone out of Geordie. He looks confused. He gathers his thoughts enough to say: 'All I wanted to know was where you go all the time. You never tell me.'

Mary stops by the door, her hand on the latch. She tells him: 'I go and pray to God to return Theo to me. I go looking for Theo.'

'But why didn't you tell me? We could have looked together.'

'You never asked. You never suggested it. After the first couple of weeks you went back to work. You just gave up on him. It's all right for you, Geordie, Theo's not your child. But he is mine.'

Before he can say anything, she's shut the door behind her. He hears her quick steps on the concrete walkway and then she's gone. Geordie sits down heavily in the armchair she occupied a moment ago. He can still feel her warmth on the chair. He holds his head in his hands, trying to shut out the world. He should have gone after her, but perhaps it would only have made things worse. What hurts him most, of all the things that have happened today, is that last taunt: *'It's all right for you, Geordie, he's not your child.'*

Can't she see what the loss of Theo has done to him as well? Doesn't she think he cares? He can't believe how cruel she can be. She does know, he thinks, and she just wanted to use the most wounding words that she could think of.

For a long time, Geordie sits there. This flat is dying, he thinks, it started to die the day Theo went. If we found another place, maybe we could start again. But we'll never make it here. And she'd never move. He suddenly realises that Mary is quite capable of sitting here waiting for Theo to return for the next thirty years. She'll stay because if Theo comes back from wherever he's been, this is the place he'll return to. She'll stay until she is convinced beyond any doubt that Theo is never coming back. And it will take the sight of his dead body to change her mind.

Geordie doesn't know what to do. He can't bring himself to go to bed even though it's nearly eleven. He can't stand being here on his own, but he doesn't have anywhere else to go. The thought strikes him that this might be the last night he spends in this flat. Mary's bound to ask him to leave, after what has just happened. He crossed some sort of boundary tonight, the way he spoke to her. He blames himself. He knows what drink can do to him when he's tired. She'll never forgive him.

Geordie broods for a while longer and then it occurs to him that he knows where Mary might be. She may be at Frieda's, of course, but Geordie has no idea where Frieda lives. But there's one other place to look.

He leaves the flat and walks up the steps to the main road. He looks both ways but he's not surprised to see there's no sign of Mary under the street lights. It's drizzling now and his face and hair soon become damp. He walks up the road, following the direction he took a few nights earlier. At the top of the hill he turns left into the lane that winds below the crest and then down to the other side of the town. Halfway along the lane he comes to the steps and the wicket gate that lead up to the church. The rain is penetrating and Geordie hasn't got a coat on, but it's not cold, just wet. He walks quietly along the path between the rows of yew trees and then looks down to where Mary sat on a gravestone on that other, chillier night.

She's not there, of course.

He goes over to the gravestone anyway. He's not sure what he expects to see; perhaps he wants to know why Mary sat on this gravestone and not another.

He looks down at it. It is an old grave marker, half sunken into the grass that grows around it. There isn't much light to see by, but even under the high clouds that are producing this drizzle, there is the faint radiance of a northern spring night.

He can't quite read the name at first, but something makes him bend down and peer closer. The inscription is eroded by time and the sharp edges of the characters are blurred by grey lichen that has spread across the stone. But the characters are still legible:

Theo Constantine
2000–2010

Thirty-Six

Norman says: 'It's a political thing.'

The other two don't catch on for a moment. Norman's two steps ahead of them. He explains: 'It's the career of the home secretary versus three dead children. No contest.'

Pippa looks appalled. She says, '*We* must do something.'

'What do you mean, it's about the home secretary's career?' Willie asks Norman. Norman is sitting back in his chair. His hands are steepled on his lap.

'The present home secretary was secretary of state at the Department of Children, Schools and Families when Gabriel Merkin was caught,' replies Norman. 'He was very high profile during the trial. He made a speech saying that if more resources were made available to his department, there would be fewer children at risk and fewer opportunities for people like Merkin to snatch them. He completely drowned out the justice minister, whose department was responsible for Merkin's actual arrest and conviction. He managed to convince the public this was a war between him and people like Merkin, and he had just won the first battle.'

'I don't remember,' says Willie.

'Why would you?' replies Norman. 'I only remember because he was my boss at the time. Now he's home secretary, the last thing he wants is for the public to be told that Gabriel Merkin was acquitted in a secret hearing, then put into a witness protection programme at God knows what cost to the taxpayer. And then that he has kidnapped and killed again. It's not his fault, but the headlines would damage him badly if the story were to get out. They would damage the whole government.'

Pippa says, 'But the story *must* get out.'

'The thing is, we have absolutely no evidence that Gabriel Merkin *is* involved in any of this,' Norman chides her. 'We don't know, any more than the police do, that any of these three children have definitely been abducted. Just three children who were around aren't around any longer. No big deal. It happens all the time. All we have got is the suggestive coincidence that they borrowed books from the same mobile library.'

'Suggestive?' says Willie. 'I'd say it's absolutely fucking positive.'

Then all three are silent again for a while. Willie is dreaming of a headline: 'Political cover-up as mass-murderer slays three more children.'

The story will be far bigger than he imagined. The story will be huge. So huge that Willie can't yet imagine how much money he might ask for this, or who he'll sell it to. And if there's no police operation, then Willie can't prejudice it by breaking the story now. He's almost tempted to get up right there and then and go back home to write the story. But as he contemplates the detail, he realises that he hasn't got all the elements – not quite. He needs more evidence: what name is Gabriel Merkin hiding behind, for instance? What is his connection with the mobile library and can it be proved? He needs detail.

Pippa isn't thinking of newspaper headlines. Every fibre of her body, every brain cell, is screaming: 'Do something!' The picture in her head won't go away. When she shuts her eyes, she can see them: two small girls in a dark room with rough stone walls. They are out there somewhere. She must find them.

'It's an interesting conundrum,' says Norman. His voice is donnish, academic, as if he were in a breakout session at one of the conferences or team-building events that have formed such a large part of his professional life. 'We have evidence that we should take to the police. We have a duty to tell them. But we have a strong conviction that if we do, it will very likely be ignored.'

As Norman speaks, as he tries to detach himself from the problem – or detach the problem from himself – there is a sound. It's in his head; he's perfectly certain it is not external. It's as if he has tinnitus, but this sound isn't ringing and it isn't buzzing. More than anything else, it resembles the distant chime of a church bell. And it brings with it a vision of the dusty churches where he once worshipped, when he still believed in something. He can almost smell that peculiar musty odour that inhabits old stone buildings; he can almost feel the cushion under his knees as he kneels and prays; the rough wood of the pew in front underneath his clasped hands.

And inside his head, he imagines he hears words spoken, but spoken so softly that there is no sense of a voice, only a distant vibration in the dusty air: 'I'm waiting for you.'

He finds that he has shut his eyes. It's quite involuntary, as if his body is telling him he will hear better with his eyes closed where those words came from; he will know better what voice pronounced them. But there was no voice: only a vibration in the dusty air in the imagined church inside his head. The vibration is telling him many things, but as he swims back to the surface of consciousness again, the only words that he can remember are: 'I'm waiting for you.'

He opens his eyes to see the concerned faces of Willie and Pippa as they bend over him. They have come round to his side of the desk and Pippa is holding his wrist. His cheek tingles where Willie has slapped it.

'Are you all right?' asks Willie.

'We thought you'd fainted,' Pippa tells him. Norman finds he has slumped down in his chair, and makes himself sit upright.

'I only closed my eyes for a moment,' he says.

'You've been out of it for several minutes,' Willie tells him.

'We couldn't get an answer from you,' says Pippa. 'You're as white as a sheet.'

'I'm perfectly all right,' says Norman. As he speaks, he knows it is not true. Something has happened to him, but what? Did he fall asleep? Did he faint? Has he had a stroke?

'Shall I call a doctor?' asks Pippa anxiously.

'I'll be all right in a moment,' says Norman, but less confidently. 'What were you saying just now? Who is waiting for me?'

'I don't know what you mean,' replies Pippa. 'I thought we were trying to decide what to do next.'

'Do?' says Norman. He feels more alert now. His brain has started working again after the odd hiatus. 'It's perfectly obvious. We must try to identify the owner of that mobile library. What was it called again?'

'Bookwise,' says Willie.

'What are you waiting for?' asks Norman. 'Get on the phone to the county council and find out if they know anything about it. It doesn't sound like one of theirs, but I can't believe a private operator wouldn't require some sort of licence from local government. Or CRB checks.'

Willie and Pippa hit the phones. They work from Pippa's desk so that Norman can be left to recover from whatever has just happened to him. While they are sitting next door, Norman takes stock of his situation.

It's obvious to him that he is at some sort of crossroads in his life. If he goes on with this amateur detective work, there is only a very small possibility that it will do any good. Norman doesn't believe that the missing children will ever be found; and he doesn't believe that any of them will be found alive. So nobody's life is going to be saved as a result of anything he might do.

Except, he tells himself, the lives of Gabriel Merkin's hypothetical future victims if he is not stopped now. Although he can't be sure that this has anything to do with Gabriel Merkin. There's no *evidence*. He's going to wreck his career on a whim, on a fantastic story for which there is not a single hard fact.

He is sure that he will lose his job. If Chief Inspector Saxon finds that Norman has continued to walk down paths that the chief inspector has told him not to go down, then word will get back to his superiors. The pay cheques will stop. Or, at best, he will be offered a transfer to somewhere in the outback: as a deputy assistant director, Community Services, in some remote post-industrial slum where he can do no more harm. Either way, he will no longer be the children's czar. But then, he reflects, he never really was. It was all an illusion. It shone a bright light in his life for a short time, but it was still only an illusion.

Those children are waiting for me to find them, thinks Norman. Willie and Pippa can't do it without me. They're so young, almost children themselves. A grown-up needs to be in charge.

Norman stands up and walks back and forth about his office. Then he stops beside the window with its distant view of the river Tyne, silvery in the sunshine. He thinks: all my life I've been wasting time. I've never done a single thing that will be remembered by anyone, not even for a minute. I may not have done any harm, but I've never done any good.

The door of his office opens. Norman turns. There's Willie, in the doorway, with a big smile on his face.

'We've got him,' says Willie.

'What do you mean?'

'The mobile library called Bookwise? It's a licensed operation. The county council authorised it. The operator is a private individual specialising in children's books. We've got his name. We've got his address.'

'And who is it? What does he call himself?'

'George Mitchell. That's "G" for George, and "M" for Mitchell.'

Norman gets the point. He thinks: *George Mitchell. Gordon Martin. Gabriel Merkin.*

Thirty-Seven

In these bleak hills are towers.

Some are garrison towers, with a banqueting hall and an oratory and storage vaults and a well: designed to hold a troop of men in readiness for reivers coming over the Border. Some are bastle houses: much humbler semi-fortified dwellings with a space in the lower storey where cattle can be driven in for shelter, and a fortified upper chamber for the owner of the cattle. Some are pele towers. Once these fortifications guarded every valley in the Borders and every pass through the hills.

Few now remain except as piles of stone. The shell of Hermitage Castle still stands in Liddesdale, its ancient reputation as the haunt of a sorcerer infusing the atmosphere. Other ruins survive: Smailholme, Kirkhope, Hawkshawe and Greenknowe. Many more have been pulled down or else have collapsed, destroyed by neglect and time. Here and there stones stand like gaping teeth – the wall of a tower, the skeletal remains of an arch or a window that opens onto nothing except green pasture. Others have endured as a result of being absorbed into manor houses built in later and more peaceful times.

A few peles remain intact, in the corner of a village that has since grown up under the tower's protective shadow; in remote valleys on either side of the Border; by the gravelled shores of lochs and on the banks of rivers; or surrounded by the forests that were planted long after they had fallen into disuse.

At least one tower house survives deep in Kielder Forest. It was reinvented as a bothy for ramblers after the First World War. Whether the Ramblers' Association or the Youth Hostel Association did the work, nobody now remembers. It was not done in the manner that would be approved of nowadays by English Heritage. Mortar was slapped onto the crumbling stone in a clumsy attempt at re-pointing; some of the window openings were enlarged to accept window frames and glass. In one or two rooms rough plaster finished with a lime wash, or else timber planks, were applied to the walls. A few other simple amenities were provided and then the structure, salvaged for a moment from oblivion, fell into neglect once more. Its visitors went away to fight in another war and never came back. The Tower House was forgotten.

Some time in the 1950s, the National Parks became the owner of the Tower House. For a while the Parks administrators were unaware of or uninterested in this particular property, buried away in the trees. Then it became a store for fire-fighting equipment for forest rangers. The rangers didn't like using it. It was out of the way and had a dark, unpleasing look to it. For five decades it remained empty: an item on an inventory, another historic building that nobody cared about.

Then somebody had the bright idea of letting the Tower House as a holiday home. The accommodation was basic; but the feeling was that there might be someone out there who might rent the property: an eccentric individual or an adventurous family.

After a very long time, and when the agent responsible for the letting had more or less given up hope, a prospective tenant did express an interest. He made a very reasonable offer for the rent. Correspondence followed. An attempt was made to interview the new tenant, to make sure he was a suitable person to be entrusted with what was, after all, a listed building: even one of minor historical importance. But interviews proved hard to arrange, and the credit references were satisfactory. Money changed hands and the Tower House was let, without the letting agent ever having met his new tenant. The agent made a note to go and inspect the property some time, but then forgot all about it.

The new tenant was pleased with his acquisition, although it was not easy to reach. The best way in is to take the metalled road up the valley past Kielder dam, and then along a graded forest road for some miles. Then the road comes to a locked wooden pole barrier, put there by the Forestry Commission to prevent over-inquisitive drivers continuing too far up and becoming lost or stuck. Beyond the barrier the road dwindles again into not much more than a track, its edges crumbling, its ditches choked with foxgloves and willowherb, pools of water here and there that refuse to drain away. The track meanders for a long while between dark, overhanging trees until it reaches the clearing where the Tower House stands.

The new tenant cut the chain on the barrier and replaced it with a more robust one and a padlock to which only he had the keys. He took the precaution of fitting his car — it is a Mitsubishi Shogun with tinted windows — with all-terrain tyres. With the help of these, it is just about possible to get his car from the public road many miles away, along the forest roads and up the long track to the Tower, itself miles from the forest road. In wet weather he has to walk the last five hundred yards because he doesn't want to risk turning the track into a rutted quagmire.

His improvements to the Tower were few. His taste in

interior decoration must be remarkably ascetic, for he did little to make the interior more comfortable. Half a dozen oil lamps were purchased, and distributed around the house. With a huge amount of effort he managed to haul up a gas cooker and a number of gas cylinders. He transported some items of flat-pack furniture: beds, tables and chairs, and assembled these in the rooms that were more or less weathertight. He joined the flat-pack tables into one long table that he put in the largest room in the Tower. It was once the dining hall. He brought up some medical equipment, which he stored in a locked wooden outhouse that was erected by previous occupants between the wars. There was a fireplace and he gathered a pile of logs that he kept under a tarpaulin, so that he could have a fire when he was there during the cold months.

Over a number of journeys he brought up a store of jars and tins of food; enough to feed several people for weeks, one would imagine. His preparations were quite extensive, even excessive for a single man who only used the place from time to time. But he didn't anticipate that he would always be there on his own.

He was expecting guests.

The Tower House returned to life, although 'life' does not quite describe the solitary existence of the new tenant. When he was there, which at first was not so often, he was very quiet. He played no music – even though there was no fear of disturbing any neighbours – and he did not appear interested in outdoor exercise. He was waiting to see if anyone would come. He wanted to know if walkers ever visited this part of the forest. They did not. Nobody came. The Tower House and its tenant were left in peace.

Once he had made the building habitable, his activity slowed down and then ceased altogether. He sat alone in the Tower

House. Sometimes he climbed onto its roof, from where he could see a great bowl of dark trees extending in every direction, broken here and there by craggy outcrops. From there he could watch the buzzards, hunting for prey; he could hear their screams above the roof of the forest. He could feel the bite of the wind that blows forever in these Border hills. There were few other sounds that came to him over the constant sighing of the trees.

He made plans.

He prepares for the arrival of his first guest. To be accurate, it will be a collection rather than an arrival. His guest is to be the principal element in a really ambitious project he has conceived, and has been planning for the last year. He proposes to create an art installation that will pay homage to, and perhaps surpass, the original from which its inspiration is drawn. The latter is in the monastery of Santa Maria della Grazie in Milan and was painted nearly six hundred years ago. The painting was commissioned by the Duke Ludovic Sforza.

His first guest is to be the central figure in a grand composition of thirteen. The original work of art, the mural painted by Leonardo da Vinci, is known as *Il Cenacolo*. The tenant of the Tower House has several print reproductions of this picture: in English the title translates as *The Last Supper*. He envisages a unique form of still life. One by one, he plans to assemble thirteen figures and model them in the same attitudes as the figures in the great painting. The first group on the left: Bartholomew, James son of Alphaeus and Andrew. The next group – Judas Iscariot, Peter and John – are seated next to the central figure of Jesus. On the right: Thomas, James the Greater and Philip. Then, on the far right: Matthew, Jude Thaddeus and Simon the Zealot.

In the year that has passed since he first found the Tower House, the tenant has been doing his homework. He knows whom he would like to collect as Jesus. There is an obvious candidate, except that he is a child. But, of course, they will all have to be children. The tenant is a strong man, but not a brave one: he does not contemplate overpowering adult males for the sake of his art. Children are manageable, he knows that from experience. In his interpretation of *Il Cenacolo*, Jesus will be portrayed by a male child: a particular male child he has already met.

But there is a problem. To remain true to the original painting, he needs at least two models with long hair. Some of the apostles in the painting are short-haired or bald. That is easy enough and baldness can be achieved with the aid of a razor. But some are long-haired. For instance, the androgynous figure of John next to Jesus, which has sometimes been identified as Mary Magdalene and not the apostle. So for these figures he needs long-haired children: in other words, girls.

This is a major project. The tenant reflects that, in other circumstances, he might have been able to apply for an Arts Council grant. But the nature of the work is such that it is unlikely to be funded from the public purse; although, in one way, his whole existence is being paid for by the taxpayer – his new identity as George Mitchell and his smart semi-detached house on a new housing estate in Hexham.

It will be extremely difficult to do what he wants. The acquisition of thirteen models will be by a long way the most ambitious project he has ever undertaken. In other circumstances, the chances of acquiring all thirteen without detection and retribution would be slim.

But these circumstances are unique.

George Mitchell (one name does as well as any other for the

tenant) is well aware that the discovery that he has resumed his former hobby – his former *enthusiasm* – would be extremely inconvenient for the courts, for the minister of justice, and for the home secretary. He doesn't think the police will overlook the disappearance of thirteen children, if he ever gets that far. But he does believe they will be very slow to accept that he is at it again. He does believe the left hand will not tell the right hand what it is doing. He thinks there will be confusion, perhaps even a degree of reluctance, on the part of those investigating his crimes. People are not anxious to hear his name again, or to admit that he still exists. There will be endless obstacles placed in the path of anyone seeking to learn his new identity and location. He believes the admission even that an abductor *exists* – let alone any effort to find them – will be tortuous and slow and he may have several months, if not years, of fun ahead of him.

There's no point worrying about it. He hums a tune his mother used to sing when he was little:

> *Que sera, sera*
> *Whatever will be, will be*
> *The future's not ours to see*
> *Que sera, sera.*

In the dying month of his first year as tenant of the Tower House, George collects his first guest. It is easier than he ever imagined it would be. Nobody sees him do it; nobody notices him under their noses. The parents are too stupid to keep a proper eye on their child or, if they are not too stupid, he is too clever.

And when he brings the child to the Tower House, he drugs him but does not do anything else yet, because he wants to compare the still-living child with the central figure in the original painting – or at least the reproduction of it that hangs on one wall of the main room.

The child is perfect. There's something about him, even in his narcotic trance, some indefinable quality – it's almost too perfect.

George Mitchell thanks God for his good luck.

Thirty-Eight

They know what they have to do. Going to the police with what they now know – what they *think* they know – might lead to further delays. They can't be certain that the police will take any notice of George Mitchell. The police already appear to have decided there have been no abductions. The children are runaways. Their pictures have been posted on websites. The Missingkids website, for example, has their pictures below a headline that reads, in white script on a red banner, 'Have you seen these children?'

Underneath, a new statistic: 'In the UK, a child is reported missing every three minutes.'

Children are disappearing faster than ever before.

It might be irrational to rule out going to the police. It is certainly unwise. But it's what they think. They are in a state of mind approaching hysteria, incapable of doing anything other than being swept along by their emotions. Pippa is beside herself with anxiety for the children: it has been building up inside her like an electric charge. Norman feels the urgency too. And Willie is on the cusp of a life-changing moment. They are beyond caring about consequences. Now it is time for action.

Within a few minutes they are all in Norman's car.

They set off to Hexham. It's already early afternoon. Willie sits in the back of the car, writing his story in his head, uncommunicative almost to the point of being surly. Pippa is sitting, bright-eyed, in the passenger seat. A feeling of reckless elation bubbles up inside Norman. He is driving them into the unknown. At last, he is taking action.

He knows he will never be forgiven for what he is about to do: unmasking indifference, incompetence or worse, in the search for the missing children. But Norman's struggles with himself are over. He is quite clear that he will move heaven and earth until these missing children are found: alive or dead.

They arrive in Hexham. Norman's car has a SatNav. All they have to do is follow the directions to the street: a row of houses on the side of a hill, with views of the valley and the chipboard factory from which steam pours out every day as an endless supply of trees, delivered by people like Geordie, are rendered into products that will one day form part of a kitchen unit or a partition wall.

Halfway along the street is a clue. Outside one of the neat, semi-detached houses, parked on the drive, is a large, high-sided white van. As Norman drives along the street, the words in blue lettering are visible to them all:

Bookwise
A Mobile Library Specialising in Children's Books

'Hey,' says Willie. 'Looks like he's in.'

Norman pulls the car into the kerb and switches off the engine. He looks at Pippa and Pippa looks back at him, open-mouthed.

'What shall we do?' she asks Norman. She looks frightened.

'We should call the police,' says Norman. 'We should call Chief Inspector Saxon.' It is the opposite of what he was saying half an hour ago: now he has found what he was looking for, his enthusiasm for direct action has drained away. It has been too easy. They weren't expecting this: that they would actually come this close to meeting a real, live serial killer.

There is a silence. The semi-detached house on the hill looks down on them: the windows are blank; the front door is shut. There is no sign, one way or the other, apart from the van, as to whether this tidy little house is occupied.

Is Gabriel Merkin inside? Is he alone? Surely he could never have brought his victims here, thinks Norman. Everything looks so normal. Along the street other cars are parked. Cars come and go. A woman walks past with her shopping bag, heading for the bus stop they passed a hundred yards back. The row of houses sits on the hillside and everything looks so respectable, and so quiet, on this sunny afternoon. Nothing bad could happen in a street like this.

Norman realises he might be only a few yards away from George Mitchell aka Gordon Martin aka Gabriel Merkin. Who might, at this very moment, be watching the street, taking note of the cars that come and go, taking note of Norman's car that has just parked a few doors away.

'Do you think the children are there, inside the house?' Pippa whispers, as if she is frightened she might be overheard.

'I don't know,' replies Norman. 'I don't think so.'

A memory of the newspaper stories comes back to him as he speaks: when Gabriel Merkin was caught, he was using a lock-up workshop miles from his own house. That was where he worked.

'I don't think so,' repeats Norman. 'He didn't operate from home last time. Too much risk of being found out.'

'But they might be in there anyway,' says Pippa. 'We have to know.'

Willie gets out of the back of the car. He slams the door. He stretches. He comes around to the front of the car to talk to Norman, who winds down his window.

'What are you doing?' he asks Willie.

'Well, now we're here we might as well do something as sit here in the car biting our fingernails.'

'Like what?' Norman asks. He is irritated. He doesn't like the inference in Willie's tone.

'Like, see if he's in.'

'You can't just march up to him. You don't know what he'll do.'

'Well, what else are we going to do? Communicate with him by telepathy?'

'But what will you say, if he opens the door?'

'I'll tell him I'm doing a piece on rural communities for the paper,' replies Willie. 'I'll ask him what gave him the idea for starting a mobile library.'

And before Norman can say or do anything, Willie marches off up the street and up the drive, past the Bookwise van, to the front door of the neat little house.

'Oh my God,' says Pippa. 'What will we do if he goes inside?'

They have a clear view of Willie standing on the bottom step of the two steps leading up to the front door. They see him press the bell.

Norman's heart is beating fast by now, but it is nothing compared to what Willie's heart is doing. It is rattling away inside him like a steam train going at full tilt. Because, despite his air of bravado in front of Norman and Pippa, Willie is suddenly very frightened. What will he do if Gabriel Merkin opens the door and then invites him in? He can't remember what the guy did to his victims. Was it an axe? Or was it a chainsaw? His memory has been wiped clean. It is a blank slate. He can hardly remember his own name and all he knows is that he is terrified. He stands there with his old press card in his hand waiting for the door to open.

Nobody answers the door. There are no footsteps, no distant sounds of a kettle whistling or a radio talking. The house is silent.

Willie rings the bell again, with a fraction more confidence. The noise the bell makes is the noise of a bell ringing in an empty house. All the same he waits, an artificial smile glued to his face in case the door opens.

But it doesn't. Willie turns around after a moment and shrugs his shoulders so that Pippa and Norman, sitting pale-faced in the car, can see the gesture. Then Willie walks down the drive and on to the next house where he presses the front door bell. After a few moments, a woman answers. She's about forty-five and plump, wearing jeans and a tracksuit top, with fluffy slippers on her feet.

'Yes?' she asks Willie. Willie holds up his press card and says, 'Hi! I'm Willie Craig, from *The Northumbria Herald*. Actually, I'm looking for Mr Mitchell.' He so nearly says 'Mr Merkin', and stops himself just in time. 'Do you have any idea where I might find him?'

'Oh, him,' replies the woman. 'Why? Is there something wrong?'

'No, not at all,' says Willie. 'Not as far as I know. I'm just doing a piece on children's libraries for the paper.' He adds, in an innocent tone, 'Why? Do you think there might be something wrong?'

'Nothing to do with me,' replies the woman enigmatically. Then she adds: 'No, I don't know where he is. We never speak.'

'Not the talkative type, is he?' suggests Willie.

'I don't think we've spoken six words since he moved here.'

'Does he have another address?' asks Willie. 'A place of work, where he keeps his books, that sort of thing?'

'I wouldn't know,' replies the woman. 'But he's often away. That big van's been parked up for days. It's an eyesore. It shouldn't be allowed, it spoils everyone's view. And his other car's been gone for nearly a week.'

'What other car?' asks Willie.

'He's got a four-wheel drive. One of them with black windows that you can't see in.'

Willie thanks her and turns away. He gives Pippa a wink as he walks quickly past the car, and trots up the drive of the neighbour on the other side of Mr Mitchell's house. This time an elderly man opens the door. He has spectacles on a cord around his neck and a copy of the *Daily Telegraph* in one hand.

Willie starts his routine and the man listens, then replies: 'No, I've no idea where he might be. We don't see much of him. He keeps himself to himself most of the time. It suits us. We don't like noisy neighbours.'

'Oh,' says Willie. He can't think of any more questions to ask. Then the elderly man says:

'When you do catch up with him, ask him about his taxidermy.'

'His what?' replies Willie, who does not understand. Then he remembers what Gabriel Merkin used to do before he started embalming children.

'He's a very fine taxidermist. He once asked me in to look at his collection of stuffed birds and animals. The one and only time I've ever been in his house. He has real talent. He's very proud of his work, and rightly so.'

'I will, if I ever find him,' answers Willie. 'Well, thank you.' He turns to go back to the car, but the elderly man stops him.

'You might try his holiday place up in Kielder Forest.'

'What?' says Willie, turning back again. 'Where? Where in Kielder Forest?'

'Oh, I don't know. But when I was looking at his collection, I asked him where he got his specimens from and he said some of them were from up there. In the forest.'

'Where in the forest?' asks Willie. But the old gentleman doesn't know any more and seems content to end the interview. Willie walks back down the drive and climbs into the back seat of Norman's car.

'Oh, Willie, you're so brave,' Pippa says. 'Imagine if that man had opened the door. What would you have done?'

'Interviewed him,' says Willie in a cocky tone. He's feeling much bolder now than ten minutes ago. He tells the other two what little he has learned.

'Right,' says Norman. He feels upstaged by Willie and is anxious to prove that he too can be bold and decisive.

'Right what?' asks Willie.

'Let's go to this Kielder Forest place and look for him. Someone must know him. There must be pubs or shops that he uses up there.'

'I forgot, you're not from this part of the world originally,' Willie tells him.

'What do you mean?'

'I mean if you were, then you'd know how funny that sounded. Kielder Forest covers hundreds of square miles. There are hardly any pubs, or shops. It's just a whole lot of trees. If you didn't know the area, you could get lost in there for days.'

'You're not suggesting we just turn around and go home, I hope?' replies Norman.

'Oh no, we mustn't give up now,' agrees Pippa.

'Then what?' asks Willie. 'Go to the police? When we're this close to finding the children ourselves?'

Norman has an inspiration. It's what makes him a natural leader, he thinks to himself.

'Well, I can think of someone who won't get lost in Kielder. Someone who probably knows the place like the back of his hand.'

'Who's that, then?' asks Willie, still not catching up.

'The stepfather of Theo, the first of the missing children. That's what he does all day. He works in the forest. He lives not far from here. I can remember how to get to his flat. Geordie Nixon, that's our man. We'll go and camp outside until he comes home. He's the one who can help us now.'

Thirty-Nine

Geordie is back in the flat. He doesn't remember how he got there. The last thing that he remembers is reading the legend on the gravestone: how could that be? How could Theo's name be there, the years of his birth and death, when nobody knew where Theo was or whether he was alive or dead?

He sits at the kitchen table, waiting for the kettle to boil. Mary hasn't returned and he isn't surprised. He has the sense that everything he once knew is coming to an end. His life is unwinding like a ball of string rolling down a hill.

He knows now he's sick in the head. He sees things that aren't there. Of course he never saw that grey dog. Of course he never saw those lambs. And, above and beyond all that, he never, ever saw the name of his own stepchild on a mossy gravestone in the churchyard. So, he's sick in the head. Not to mention sick in the heart and, he suspects, sick in his body too. The leaden weight he feels in his limbs is present all day every day. The tiredness that will never leave him, so that even in his sleep he feels exhausted.

He wants to talk to someone about it. Above all, he wants to talk to Mary, but she won't listen now. He's tried talking to her, and even before they quarrelled she didn't really understand what he was telling her. It is as if they are standing on either side of an abyss that is widening all the time: each sees the other on the opposite bank, receding into a mist of misunderstanding and distrust.

The kettle is whistling and Geordie lifts it off the hob and puts it to one side. He has forgotten about making a mug of tea. He sits with his forehead resting on the cool pale wood of the kitchen table and asks himself: 'So what do I do now?'

There is an answer somewhere in the fog of his brain, but he can't grasp its shape or its meaning. He falls asleep at the table.

He sleeps, and then he dreams.

He is back in the forest. As he awakens in this new world, a sense of dread fills him. He knows this dream: it has come on him before. Even that may be a part of the dream itself. He is walking along a forest track. Now, for the first time, he recognises the track. He drove up there only the other day. In his dream, this doesn't seem strange, but quite natural. He knows that the answer to everything, all the alien sights and sounds that have been tormenting him these past few weeks, can be found at the end of the track. Weightlessly, he floats past the locked barrier. He crosses dark pools of water, but there is no sense of getting wet. He has no feeling in his body, but he can hear.

He can hear the wind rustling in the branches of the trees above him. He can hear the constant dripping of water from the branches. Now the track arrives at a clearing in the forest. At the far end of the track is a black shape. A building: a tower. Its dark silhouette is outlined against the sky. It is no longer daytime; dusk has arrived. Faint stars appear behind the Tower. Then lights come on in the windows: first in one window, then in another. The light is soft as if from a candle. There is someone moving about in the Tower. Geordie mutters to himself: 'Light in the forest. Light in the forest.'

As if in answer, there is a gentle laugh and then a teasing voice says: 'I'm waiting for you.'

The voice is like an electric shock running down his spine. Is it Theo's voice? Could it be Theo who spoke to him? And the voice continues to speak to him a little while longer, telling him what he must do.

The next thing he knows, there's the sound of someone moving around in the flat. His head jerks up. There is a terrific pain in the back of his neck from the awkward position he fell asleep in. He winces. He's dazed with sleep. It's light outside: a grey, drizzly day has dawned. He hears the sound again and in his muddled head he can think of only one explanation. He turns around in his chair and calls: 'Theo?'

Mary answers him from the room next door. 'It's me.'

Her voice sounds unfriendly. Geordie stands up and stretches, trying to loosen the tight muscles in his upper back. He rubs his hand over his unshaven cheeks. Then he goes into the room next door and sees Mary standing there, a suitcase on the floor beside her.

'Why on earth did you think it was Theo in here?' she asks angrily, as if he has deliberately set out to taunt her.

'I was dreaming,' he says.

'Oh.' She seems uninterested. The anger has gone out of her as quickly as it came. She points to the suitcase.

'I came back to collect a few things.'

Geordie looks down at the suitcase and then up at Mary again. Her face is tired and empty.

'Don't go,' he says to her.

'I've arranged to stay with Frieda for a week. That should give you time to find somewhere else to live, and move your things out.'

'But I don't want to go. I want us to be together,' says Geordie. He feels desperate.

'It's over, Geordie.'

Her words are so final. He asks – he knows it is exactly the wrong thing to say, but he asks it anyway, 'Are you going back to him? To Theo's father?'

Mary looks at him. He thinks there is contempt in her gaze, but maybe that's just his imagination.

'I've already told you that Theo's father can't be found.'

'Then why can't we try and make things work?'

'I've got nothing left to give. Not to you, nor anyone.'

For a long moment time is suspended as they stand there. Geordie's remembering Theo's name on the gravestone in the churchyard. He's remembering how he and Mary met. He's recalling how he managed to cut Mary loose from Frieda at the party in Jimmy's house, and how they started talking. What was it he said then that made her laugh? He remembers that she laughed but he can't remember her laugh. A whole host of memories follow, memories of the first time they went to bed together, memories of the two of them and Theo going to the Hoppings – the giant travelling fairground that comes each year to the Town Moor outside Newcastle. All these memories flash past him like the brightly lit carriages of a train as it disappears into a tunnel. Then nothing.

It strikes him suddenly that he may never see Mary again. It isn't just that he has upset her with his thoughtless, ill-chosen words. It isn't just that their relationship appears to have ended, to have lost its point since Theo went.

He has the feeling that Mary is withdrawing from the world. She believes her life is over and there's nothing Geordie can think of to say that might change her mind. He hasn't got the strength any longer.

'Goodbye, Geordie,' says Mary. He can't speak. He just stands there. She leans forward and kisses him lightly on the cheek. It means nothing; it feels like nothing. He is numb. She waits for him to say something. He doesn't. She picks up the suitcase and leaves the room. The flat door closes.

Geordie is alone again.

So that's it. It's all over. Geordie looks at his watch. It's only seven o'clock in the morning – too early to go and have a drink. He needs to make a plan. A plan: a map of his life with one arrow saying 'You Are Here' and another arrow pointing in the direction he must travel in. Some chance. He looks at his watch again. It's a quarter to eight in the morning. He's been standing in the middle of the room without moving for forty minutes or more. He's surprised he didn't fall over.

He goes to the bathroom and strips off and showers and shaves. Then he dresses again and goes back to the kitchen table. What now?

He ought to go to work in the forest. Now, more than ever, he needs money. He's one step away from a cliff edge so awful he doesn't want to look over it. A full day's logging will make him too tired to think. That's what he needs. His mind needs the emptiness that only real physical fatigue can bring.

But he doesn't go to the forest. He can't face being there. He feels the foreboding that comes on him when he goes into the forest, he feels it waking and he feels it dreaming. He must make a decision. He must do something. Time passes, and he doesn't move.

He hears someone outside the front door. Maybe it's Mary. Has she changed her mind? He doesn't think so. He goes to the door and opens it.

The fat bastard is standing there.

'Mr Nixon?' asks the fat bastard. Behind him is a younger man, whom Geordie recognises as the journalist who came to the flat with the fat bastard a few weeks ago. A pretty girl stands next to the journalist. Geordie sees her without the least interest.

'May we come in?' asks the fat bastard. 'I'm Norman Stokoe. We've met.'

'What for?' asks Geordie, not opening the door any wider. He could do without this. He really could do without the fat bastard and his friends. He's ready to throw them out physically if they attempt to come in. But then the fat bastard says something that changes everything.

'We know who took Theo. We know where he's keeping him. It's somewhere in Kielder Forest.'

Forty

And now the time for explanations has come and gone. When they first enter the flat and explain why they are there, Geordie doesn't show the least interest in Norman's account of how clever they have been in identifying Theo's probable abductor. But he does jerk like a man stung by a wasp when Norman mentions the name. Everyone recognises the name of Gabriel Merkin. When Willie explains why they believe Gabriel Merkin has hidden the children somewhere in Kielder Forest, Geordie simply says, 'Yes. He's locked them in a tower.'

The reply astonishes them; the look on Geordie's face as he speaks transfixes them. Pippa thinks she has never seen an expression of such pain; it is as if Geordie is at last recognising the reality of what has happened to the missing children; of what has happened to his missing stepson.

'How do you know that?' asks Norman in a frightened voice. But Geordie doesn't answer. Instead he stands up, his big frame filling the room. He is bigger than either Norman or Willie remembers him, a daunting, fierce-looking man well over six feet tall. He says, 'We can all go together in my truck,' without any discussion as to who should go, or whether they should go at all. It's unspoken between them that it's no good going to the police now. It's way past time for all that. The police are scouring the streets of central London, looking for the children huddled up in doorways, or maybe they are not looking at all.

'I have a car,' says Norman.

'You'll never get up those roads without four-wheel drive,' Geordie tells him.

'But do you know where we are going?' asks Norman.

'I know,' says Geordie, and the tone of his voice stops Norman in his tracks. He wants to ask: how do you know? How do you know they are locked in a tower? Which tower? Where is it? Why haven't you gone there before? But he doesn't ask all these questions because he knows the answer. Theo has been talking to Geordie. Theo has been talking to all of them, in different ways. He doesn't want to pursue the thought: it takes him to places he doesn't want to visit.

'We'd best get going,' Geordie tells them.

They don't argue. It's way past time for conversation. The day is getting on. If they are to do anything today, they must do it now. The idea of letting another night pass without finding the children is unthinkable.

Geordie's in charge now. It's his stepson they're looking for, his truck that's going to take them to him. Willie is glad Geordie's in charge. Willie thinks that if there were a physical confrontation with Gabriel Merkin – if they ever find him – Norman would look at his watch and say he had to get off to a meeting. To be truthful, Willie's not sure he would be much good either. He can still remember how his knees felt like jelly when he was ringing the bell of the quiet little house in Hexham. Pippa too is glad that Geordie is in charge. Theo is his child, she thinks. We are only onlookers.

Geordie's in charge and the dour expression on his face discourages any dissent.

They drive up the valley. As the truck passes through the

village of Wark, a crocodile of small children is filing off a bus, on their way home. They are laughing and talking at the top of their voices. Pippa sees Geordie look at them and then away again. She imagines he can see his own stepchild. They drive on up the valley, over the bridge at Bellingham and up past Newton and on through the wild landscape of small stone-walled fields, and grey cottages, and heather-covered hills, and dark stands of trees, the outliers of the forest that lies ahead. The road climbs and skirts the great dam wall of Kielder Lake and the truck roars on past this and in amongst the trees, into the forest at last.

Geordie turns off the Tarmac and the truck starts along the graded forest road. Norman is squeezed tightly between Willie and Geordie, and Geordie bangs his knee every time he changes gear. Willie is squeezed against Pippa, who is next to the door. In other circumstances, Willie would be very happy to be squeezed so tightly against Pippa, but now he isn't thinking about that at all. He stares at the wilderness of trees on either side, the acres of clear-fell, the grow tubes where new plantings of broad-leaved trees have been made. It's as if he has been here before, but he knows he hasn't. Norman too recognises something familiar in this bleak land-scape, but he doesn't voice his thoughts. The two rosy spots that normally bloom in his cheeks, a testament to his fondness for the good things in life, have disappeared. His face is pale and scared.

The truck grinds up the forest road and, on the right, they pass a strange tracked vehicle sitting forlornly on the side of a bank.

'That's my harvester,' says Geordie. 'I've been working here for weeks. Right next door to the bastard.'

Behind the harvester is a great field of felled trees, branches and smaller trees lying here and there as if a hurricane has knocked them over; shattered and split trunks standing like sentinels.

They round a long, slow bend between banks of bracken where the forest has receded from either side of the track for a few yards. Then the trees close in again. A few moments later, the road starts to narrow, and its surface becomes rougher and more uneven. Ahead, Norman sees a barrier across the road, and he sees the late afternoon sunlight glinting on the chains and the padlock that secure it.

'How do we get past that?' he asks Geordie, hoping that Geordie will shrug his shoulders and say something like, 'Oh, that's too bad – we'll have to go back.' Geordie doesn't say anything of the sort. He brings the truck to a halt and switches off the engine.

'Now we walk,' he tells them.

And nobody contradicts him because by then they are all beginning to understand that whatever they are looking for, it is at the end of this track. They climb down from the cab. They make an odd foursome. Geordie is dressed in jeans and a plaid shirt with a sleeveless fleece. He has work boots on his feet. Norman is wearing his grey double-breasted suit, with a cream shirt and a colourful tie. He wears black loafers on his feet. Willie is wearing jeans and trainers, with his suit jacket worn over a brown T-shirt. Pippa is dressed in what she always wears for the office: smart black jacket and trousers with a white blouse and high-heeled shoes. She takes a few unsteady paces over the rough ground and then kicks off her shoes and walks barefoot.

Geordie reaches up into the truck and takes out a bag of tools.

'What's in there?' asks Norman. Geordie doesn't answer.

Instead he says: 'If you want to follow, keep behind me and don't make any noise.'

They duck under the barrier and start walking along the track between the trees. Norman sneaks his BlackBerry out and looks at the screen. There's no signal. If there had been a signal, Norman would have rung Chief Inspector Saxon and asked him to come and rescue them at once, because Norman remembers this place. He's been here before in his dreams.

They walk along the track for some distance. They see tyre-marks in the soft ground weaving between the potholes and the pools of dark water. Norman wants to ask Geordie about them, but Geordie's face is set and Norman dares not speak to him. The track is narrowing once more, its edges crumbling, until it becomes a rutted path.

The afternoon is becoming evening. It will be light for a few hours yet. None of them, except perhaps Geordie, wants to be here when dusk arrives.

Pippa is trying hard to keep up, but now she can't go on. Her feet are sore and dirty and her trousers are soaking. She's exhausted and, worse than that, she's afraid. The atmosphere beneath these dark trees is affecting them all and Pippa, the youngest, is affected the most. Suddenly she sits down by the side of the track. She almost falls over.

'I must stop for a moment,' she says. Geordie turns and looks at her. He points at Willie.

'You, stay with her. Don't get separated. When she's ready to move, take her back to the truck. You'll be safe there.'

Willie doesn't argue. He sits beside Pippa as she sprawls in the bracken. Willie knows he ought to go on. He ought to be the first, not the last, to find whatever lies ahead. This was to be his story, the moment he has been working towards these last few weeks and, in another way, the whole of his life. How can he write his story if he can't write that he was first into the chamber of horrors? He is quite sure that there is a chamber of horrors, and it isn't very far away.

He stays with Pippa because Geordie told him to, and because he knows he cannot leave Pippa alone in that gloomy wood with dusk on its way. As he helps her to her feet, and they turn back towards the truck, he feels a profound sense of relief.

Norman and Geordie walk on. Norman, too, is tired by this unaccustomed exercise. He's tired because his legs are taking him somewhere he doesn't want to go. His shoes are wet through and thick with mud and they pinch his feet. A long way ahead, they see a dark shape beside the track. As they draw closer, it becomes a car; and a little later they see that the car is a Mitsubishi Shogun with tinted windows.

'It's his,' says Geordie. 'He's here.'

Norman looks behind him to see if he can glimpse Willie and Pippa, as if by some chance they have changed their minds and decided to follow. He would have been glad of the company, glad of any company. Geordie is not company. He does not speak apart from those four words at the car. Norman is reluctant to look at him. When he does glimpse Geordie's face, it is set like stone. But Willie and Pippa must be miles behind by now, and heading away from them back to the truck. The track climbs up along the side of a low ridge. Norman knows what is ahead: a clearing in the trees.

Five hundred yards beyond the Mitsubishi, the path crests the saddle of the ridge and the trees give way on either side to form a large clearing. It is evening now. Silhouetted against the sky is the shape of a tower, black against the red tinted clouds. As Norman looks at the Tower, the memory of his dream returns to him, but he does not know if he really dreamed of this place or if the place itself is like a dream; like a nightmare.

As they look at the Tower, a light suddenly springs out from one of the windows. It is not electric light: it is weaker, silkier. There is a clink beside Norman and he turns to see Geordie setting his bag of tools carefully on the ground. He takes out a hammer, and some other objects that Norman cannot make out.

'What are you going to do with those?' whispers Norman. But Geordie doesn't answer. Softly, they approach the Tower. The light in the window goes out, and then it appears at another window. They hear a cry, a child's voice saying: '*Please.*'

Geordie glances at Norman. His eyes are wild. He looks insane. At the foot of the Tower are stone steps that lead up to a wooden door. They climb the steps, Norman keeping close behind Geordie. He is beyond fear now; he walks like a man in a trance. Already he knows that at least one of the missing children is in that building and that he or she is still alive. He thinks they will find all three. He believes that, in a few moments, they will find Theo.

They are at the top of the steps. There is a stone bay and a wooden door. It is open. Geordie pushes it so that they can enter, and the door creaks as he does so. They enter an antechamber, lit by the pale evening light coming through a window where once there was only an arrow-slit. Norman wishes they had brought a torch. Then the gleam of a lamp appears beyond them and an educated tenor voice asks: 'Who is there? Is somebody there?'

Geordie stops still, the hammer dangling from his right hand, and Norman nearly bumps into him. The light approaches and they see a tall man, carrying an oil lamp in one hand, ducking to avoid the low lintel of a doorway on the far side of the room. The tall man holds up the lamp to look at them. Norman sees a pale snout of a face, a deformed, chinless face with dewlaps.

Trickles of saliva coming from each corner of the man's mouth, glinting in the lamplight. The man's strange head sits on top of a large, soft-looking body clad in jeans and a denim jacket. The newcomer smiles at them, showing his small teeth.

'I'm afraid I shall have to ask you to leave,' he says, approaching slowly. 'This is private property. You can't come in here.'

Norman feels a rush in his blood as if his veins are surging with sugar. He smells the scent of jasmine all around him. The tall man says, with more force: 'You *must leave*. Now!'

Geordie stands in front of him without speaking, the hammer dangling loosely from his right hand. Then he speaks: 'Where's our Theo? Have you got him? Is he here?'

Gabriel Merkin stares at Geordie. It is a stare in which surprise, recognition and terror are mixed together. Before he can reply, or react in any other way, something odd happens. Once again Norman hears that voiceless whisper in his head: *'I'm waiting for you.'*

Perhaps Geordie hears it as well, because he starts and raises his hammer to strike the man in front of him. The man turns and runs back towards the interior of the Tower. Geordie follows him.

Forward or back? Norman is terrified by the idea of following Geordie. He knows something appalling is about to happen. He's even more terrified of waiting here alone, or else walking all the way back to the truck in the dark. Almost blind with terror, he stumbles after Geordie.

Forty-One

It's getting dark by the time Willie and Pippa make it back to the big Scania. She's half-fainting from a combination of exhaustion and shame. She feels shame because she couldn't face what was in front of her; she feels she ought to have been able to travel the journey with Norman and Geordie right to the end.

They climb into the truck and Willie turns on the engine to get some heat into the cab. There's no fear of the sound of the engine being overheard. They must be a long way from the Tower House here and the wind is blowing in the opposite direction. They are a long way from anywhere. Pippa nestles in the crook of Willie's arm, her head on his shoulder. She is shaking: little shudders run through her body like ripples across water.

'I'm sorry, Willie,' she says. 'I dragged you back here. I know you wanted to be with the others.'

'Don't worry,' he murmurs. As a matter of fact, he's relieved he's back in the truck. He had felt as if he was walking in a dream back there, one with a bad ending. At the moment all he feels is grateful for the fact that they are both safe and warm. He locks the doors of the cab. They will be secure in here. The others should be back soon, with or without the children. He'll get his story.

Or maybe Gabriel Merkin will come looking for them.

The thought makes him sit upright for a second, trying to stare into the dark tunnel of the track. He finds the switch for the headlamps and flicks it on.

'What?' asks Pippa, half asleep.

'Don't worry,' says Willie. She murmurs something and is silent. Willie looks along the beam of light and sees nothing except the waving fronds of bracken and the branches of trees tossing in the wind on either side of the track. He kills the engine and turns off the lights and the heating. Pippa snuggles closer to him and after a while he too dozes.

His dreams are confused, but violent. He wakes with a start. There is a film of sweat on him. He starts to shiver. It may be late spring down below in the valley but, here on this tree-covered hillside, it is a chilly night. The stars are out and wisps of high ragged cloud occlude them from time to time, racing across the sky. His shivering wakes Pippa.

'What is it?' she whispers. Then: 'You're cold.'

'Ssh!' he tells her. 'I thought I heard something.'

They are both absolutely quiet. All they can hear is the noise of the wind rustling in the branches of the trees and moaning around the cab; and then it stops, as abruptly as if someone had turned off a tap. Then Willie hears a sound: a child's voice that sounds as if it is coming from a great distance.

'I'm coming!'

He can't tell from where the voice has spoken. It could be inside or outside the cab. It is like something heard on a radio, but the radio is not switched on. Willie stares at Pippa. He can see the whites of her eyes in the dark. *'What was that?'* he whispers, as if whispering might help. She shakes her head. 'I didn't hear anything.'

Willie gets a grip of himself. He switches on the headlamps again and peers into the darkness.

Nothing. Willie turns the lights off and winds down the driver's window to see if he can hear anything more.

Nothing.

But as Willie stares into the darkness, convinced that he can somehow hear better without the headlamps on, he becomes aware of small sounds. The sky has begun to lighten. It is not yet dawn. Dawn is at least two hours away, but the sky is paler to the east than it was. He hears the chirrup of birds in nearby trees that starts up suddenly, then dies away again. Then he senses movement along the track. In the dim light it just looks like different shades of darkness, as if something is there that wasn't there a moment ago. Willie strains his eyes but can't make out what he is seeing. He's sure that someone, or more than just someone, is walking along the track towards them.

He flicks the headlamps back on and the two of them stare along the beam of light. A many-headed shape becomes visible on the edge of the pool of light. The shape resolves itself into a man, with a child on either side of him holding his hands. The man is Norman. As he comes closer, they can see that his suit is stained and torn. His tie has gone. From below the knees down, his trousers and shoes are covered in mud.

The two children are visible now. The pre-dawn light is growing quickly and, as they draw closer, Willie and Pippa can see that the children are in a bad state. They are able to walk, but only just: as if it is the force of Norman's will alone that is keeping them upright. Their faces are thin and dirty and their hair is matted. Their dresses are filthy. It is just possible to make out from their clothes that they are two small girls. Their eyes have the blank stare of disaster victims everywhere. They see nothing except memories they cannot share.

Willie unlocks the cab doors and they both climb out and approach Norman. He lets go of the children who stop where they are, like clockwork dolls whose mechanism has just run down.

'What happened?' asks Willie. Pippa takes no notice of Norman, and rushes to the two children. She gathers them both in her arms.

'You poor darlings,' she says. 'You poor, poor darlings. Thank God you are safe. Willie, help me get them into the cab and put the heater on. We must get help. We need an ambulance.'

She speaks as if she has quite forgotten where they are: in the middle of a huge forest, miles from anywhere, where there are no phones or people or proper roads. Willie helps to lift the two girls into the cab. They smell awful. They are dressed in rags. One of them speaks: Willie thinks it is Karen Gilby.

'Please don't hurt us,' she says. Pippa hugs her.

'Nobody is going to hurt you,' she promises. 'Not ever again.'

Willie thinks that is optimistic of Pippa, but says nothing. He climbs into the cab and switches the engine on, so they can turn on the heating. Then he gets out again and finds Norman still standing there, with a dazed look on his face.

'What happened back there?' he asks Norman again. 'Where's Geordie? What happened to Gabriel Merkin? Was he there?'

Norman doesn't answer. He doesn't look much like Norman any more. The usual Norman expression – half calculation, half self-satisfaction – has been wiped from his face. He looks as if his mind has deserted him.

'And where's Theo?' asks Willie. 'Is he alive?'

At last Norman speaks and Willie is struck by the conversational tone of his voice, as if the two of them have just met at a drinks party.

'I'm having to revise my ideas about God. We were taught at my school that a true Christian turns the other cheek. Turns out that the way it works is an eye for an eye, a tooth for a tooth.'

None of this makes any sense to Willie. Norman is smiling at him, waiting for a reply, a witty rejoinder from Willie that will allow the conversation to continue. At the same time, he looks wasted by exhaustion and something else – an expression of horror that flits across his face as his smile switches on and off. Willie tries again: 'Where's Theo? Where's Geordie? Was Gabriel Merkin there?'

'I can remember the text,' replies Norman. 'Is it in Romans, chapter twelve? I think so. "Vengeance is mine, sayeth the Lord. I will repay." The God of Abraham is not forgiving ... He made us ... I can't tell you.'

After this enigmatic remark, Norman appears to close down. Willie wonders if he is in shock. It strikes him that he has a very difficult situation to deal with: two sick children, Norman out of the picture, and two people unaccounted for. There's no obvious way of getting help except by walking five or ten miles to the nearest public road. Willie doesn't fancy his chances driving the truck out of here. He's never driven anything bigger than a Ford Fiesta until now. He may have to, if all else fails, but he has a feeling he'll just crash the thing if he tries. He can't even remember how far they have driven to reach this place, or which roads they came by.

But what is he to do about Norman? The problem solves itself. Norman mutters: 'I must sleep.'

'Yes, you have a nice sleep,' says Willie, humouring him. If only he would go back to his everyday pompous manner of speech. Norman is in a state of fugue. Whether he'll ever come out of it, Willie can't tell. Once Norman is inside the cab, he falls asleep at once. Willie goes around to the other side to speak to Pippa.

'Are you all right?' asks Willie.

'Yes – but we have to get help for these two.'

'There's something I must do first,' says Willie. 'I can't get any sense out of Norman. We can't leave until I know what's happened to Geordie. And there's still another child missing.'

'What are you going to do?' asks Pippa.

'I'm going to walk along the track to the Tower House and find Geordie, if I can. And we have to find out what's happened to Theo.'

'But what if Gabriel Merkin's there?'

'Either he isn't there, or else he's out of action. How else could Norman have walked off with the two children?'

'Please be careful,' Pippa warns.

'Don't worry, I will. Lock the cab doors once I'm gone.'

A soft morning is dawning in the forest. The sky is a luminous grey haze. The air is warming up. It's going to be a fine day. A heavy dew sparkles on every frond of bracken and blade of grass. Willie is doing the bravest thing he has ever done, walking towards the Tower House.

In the growing light, the journey no longer resembles the exhausting march of the night before, stumbling along the potholed track with its deep pools. Now Willie walks along easily and his limbs no longer feel leaden. Although his heart rate is up and he is scared of what he might find, it is a different feeling to the blind panic that threatened to overwhelm him the night before. After a good while, he sees the Mitsubishi

Shogun in the distance. As he approaches, his apprehension increases; but at the same time he remembers, at last, why he's there.

He's there to get a story. He's there to change his life.

When he reaches the Mitsubishi, it's empty. He tries the door handle. It's unlocked, and when he opens it he can see the smart key lying beside the automatic transmission lever. Better still, there is another silver key attached to the key ring. With any luck, that's the key that will open the padlock on the locked pole barrier at the end of the forest road. Willie may not be able to drive the Scania with any confidence, but he can drive this car. As long as its owner doesn't turn up to claim it.

He pockets the remote and the silver key then continues along the track. The path climbs up a low ridge and then descends again into a clearing.

In the clearing is the Tower House.

Willie stops for a moment on the crest. The sun has burned off the morning mist and is rising over the tops of the trees. It has painted one side of the house a golden colour. The rest of it is dull grey stone. Willie pulls his digital camera from his pocket and takes a few shots.

It's an old place, an ancient place. It must have been built six or seven hundred years ago, thinks Willie, who didn't pay much attention to history at school. The grey and gold of the Tower looms above him. Even in the light of day it is a forbidding sight. It is a square building with battlements. On one side stone steps lead to a doorway where once there might have been a portcullis. Now the door is open, but there is no noise or movement. Willie reaches the foot of the steps. Then he stops.

Now is the moment when he will discover the last missing

pieces of his story. He swallows. He doesn't know if he can make himself go up those steps. He calls out: 'Hello?'

Then he curses himself silently. He's not a doorstep sales-man trying to find out if anyone is at home. He's a reporter. He's an investigative journalist, or he will be if he ever writes this story. He climbs the steps. The wooden door is half open. He peers in.

Inside is an empty stone antechamber. At the far end of the chamber is another door. Willie crosses the room and goes through a short passage that opens into the main room on this level of the Tower. It is a large stone chamber with two windows in one wall that allow some daylight in. Willie can see that, over the years, attempts have been made to render the room habitable. For example, one wall has been covered in wooden planks. It seems that someone thought if the room looked like a log cabin, it would feel more like home. The homely effect has been spoiled by a recent addition. Nailed to the planks is a man, his arms spread out on either side, his head hanging down. He has been crucified. Dark-red circles mark each palm, with a nail hammered through the centre. A bigger nail has been hammered through both ankles, shatter-ing bone and flesh. The head is drooping and Willie is thank-ful he cannot see the expression on the man's face, but what he can see is the crown of barbed wire that has been wrapped around the dome of the man's head, lacerating the flesh with scratches. On the floor at the foot of this *montage* are a few small puddles of dark blood.

Willie's heart stops, then starts again, racing with a ragged beat. He looks away from the crucified man and sees Geordie in the opposite corner of the room. He is sitting on the floor. He is alive, but he does not lift his head.

In the centre of the room is a long table – on a second look, it is three trestle tables joined together. Thirteen chairs have been placed along its length: six on either side, the thirteenth in the centre. Twelve of the chairs are empty. The thirteenth chair has an occupant.

It is the figure of a young boy.

Forty-Two

For a moment, Willie is frozen in shock.

Then he recovers the use of his limbs. He crosses the room to where Geordie is sitting, his back to the wall. He squats on his haunches beside him and asks: 'Are you OK?'

Geordie doesn't answer at once. The question is pointless, because it is obvious that Geordie is very far from being OK. But what else can you ask at moments like this? Geordie looks at Willie for a moment and glances down at the floor. Willie follows the glance and sees a hammer lying on the floor. The head is black and sticky-looking.

'He killed Theo,' says Geordie. His voice sounds rusty, as if he has been shouting. Willie doesn't need to ask who 'he' is.

'Is that Theo there?' asks Willie, pointing to the dead boy sitting at the table. The figure is like a high-class waxwork. It hasn't moved since Willie came into the room.

'Theo told me what to do,' says Geordie. 'Theo helped me.'

Willie stands up and backs away from Geordie. He can't be a hundred per cent sure that Geordie won't go for him with the hammer next. But Geordie seems exhausted, almost in a trance. Willie goes to the table.

The dead child is dressed in a white gown. His hair has been allowed to grow long, and Willie realises that this must have happened after the child was taken and before he was murdered.

He might have been kept alive in this grim place for weeks, or even months, before Gabriel Merkin finally took his life. Now he is still and pale. Willie has never seen an embalmed person before. This must be state-of-the-art embalming, because it almost looks as if the child is about to speak. Willie looks at the handsome face with its wide eyes fixed open. Have they been glued? He wishes they were closed. He feels the eyes lock on to his, knows that if he shuts his eyes he will see the face inside his head. He knows that he will remember that face for the rest of his life. He can almost hear the voice: 'Hello, Willie. You've come at last. What kept you?'

He backs away from the dead child and looks once again at the figure nailed to the wall.

How Geordie managed to nail him up there on his own is beyond Willie's imagination. Perhaps Norman helped him? Somebody must have helped because one man, no matter how strong or how berserk, could scarcely have held the body of Gabriel Merkin against the wall and then nailed his hands and feet to the planks. And where had the barbed wire come from, no doubt a contemporary allusion to the crown of thorns? Had that been in Geordie's bag along with the hammer and the nails? Was that what foresters carried around with them all the time? Or had some premonition allowed Geordie to prepare himself for this act? The implications of that were unthinkable.

Anyway, there is the focus of all Willie's hopes for the last few weeks, the child-abductor. The child-murderer: Gabriel Merkin. Whatever this man has done, the way he died is awful.

Willie can scarcely bring himself to look at the dead man – he hopes he is dead for his sake – but at the same time his reporter's instincts are aroused, despite the horror of the scene. He takes out his small digital camera and takes shots: first of the man hanging from the wall, then of the dead child seated at the table. He doesn't take any pictures of Geordie. When he's finished, he goes back to Geordie and asks again: 'Geordie, how are you?'

It's another stupid question, but Willy finds himself talking to Geordie as if he were the child, not the figure at the table.

'Can you just wait here for a while?' suggests Willie. 'I'm going to get some help. You just sit here and rest. It'll all be fine. You'll see. Nobody can blame you for what's happened.'

But Willie believes in his heart it will not be fine, that nothing about Geordie's life will ever come right again. He imagines what the police will make of this scene. He hopes he won't be a suspect in this man's murder. He's a bit vague about the law, but isn't he an accessory? And what about Norman? Aren't the police going to come to the same conclusions as Willie, that of the two other people in the room – the dead boy and Norman – it must have been Norman who helped Geordie carry out this awful re-enactment of a crucifixion?

There is no other rational explanation.

He tries to smile at Geordie, but it doesn't work so he leans down and pats him on the shoulder. Geordie doesn't react in any way. He doesn't look capable of standing up, let alone walking.

'I'll be as quick as I can,' promises Willie. Then he leaves the stone chamber with its awful burden of death, and finds his way outside. He stops at the top of the flight of stone steps to recover for a moment. He's quite proud of the fact that he hasn't fainted, or thrown up, either of which would have been understandable. He breathes in the fresh air of the forest. The sky is brighter now and white clouds are rolling in from the west. There's a damp feeling to the air, as if rain might be on the way. As Willie surveys the forest around him, the great bowl of trees that swells to the horizon in every direction, he realises that this is a beautiful place – not a comfortable beauty, but something all of its own. A wilderness. The sense of menace he felt the night before has vanished.

He heads along the path, and over the ridge to find the car.

The journey into the forest took an age, like one of those epic adventures of the fifteenth century when travellers, without proper maps, sought to find the edges of the world. Once Willie manages to squeeze Norman, Pippa and the two children into the Mitsubishi, the journey back down the valley is, by contrast, a tame little outing. Norman seems to have come to his senses. After a while he responds to Willie's questions, but with no great clarity.

'Geordie chased Merkin with his hammer into the main room. I was shouting something, I don't know what. After that I don't really remember what happened. Except that we found Theo, and Theo ...'

But then he stops and he can't, or won't, tell them anything else about what happened in the Tower House. He is very quiet. Becky and Karen are quiet too, except as they approach Hexham Karen seems to recognise her surroundings. She says: 'My house is near here. Can we go there now, please?'

'We just need to take you to the hospital first to make sure you're all right,' Pippa tells her.

'But Mummy doesn't know where I am!'

'We'll ring her from the hospital,' says Pippa. 'I promise.'

Willie's recollection of events over the next few hours is confused. They park in the hospital car park and nobody has any money for the pay and display machine. They head for the A&E department where there is a long queue. There is a brief altercation at the reception desk, where they are told to take a number and that there will be a two-hour delay. Pippa goes into overdrive at this point. She gives the unlucky receptionist the full force of her pent-up anger, and explains who the children are.

Once this has been sorted out, everything moves at high speed. A gaggle of doctors and nurses descends on the children and bears them away. Pippa wants to go with them but is told she can't, for the moment. She can't bear the thought that the children, scared and ill and confused, should be abandoned. But the nurses are taking care of them and she'll have to accept that her role in their rescue is now over. The Gilby parents are contacted, and the scenes that follow, the tearful reunion with Karen, can only be imagined as by then Willie and Pippa and Norman are elsewhere.

They are collected by a couple of squad cars from the hospital and taken to Hexham police station. There they sit for a long while. Then they are shown, one at a time, into a small room where they are interviewed on tape by two police officers. Sometime during this process, Willie loses his temper and points out to one of the officers who is interviewing him that none of them have either slept or eaten for twenty-four hours. This has no effect at all. He is sent back to a waiting room where, after a while, Pippa joins him, looking pale and tired. While they sit there, they see Geordie being brought in with a blanket around his shoulders.

'We'll be as quick as we can, sir,' says the stolid sergeant on duty at the desk, when Willie complains again. This isn't very quick and, to add to his annoyance, Willie's camera is taken from him.

'We'll have to treat that as evidence from a crime scene,' Willie is told.

'But I'm a journalist,' shouts Willie, his patience exhausted. 'I need those pictures for a story I'm writing.'

'What you are is a witness in a murder investigation,' says the sergeant. 'And I wouldn't be writing any stories for the papers just yet, if I were you.'

With a sense of shock, Willie suddenly understands his position. He can't write a word about what has happened without prejudicing his own position, or Norman's, and especially Geordie's. He's a witness at the least and an accessory at the worst. He's in limbo. No pictures and no stories, certainly not for the moment.

It is early evening by the time their immediate troubles are over. Geordie has been taken into custody. Norman, as a possible accessory to murder, is being detained for further questioning. At last Pippa and Willie are allowed to go, having promised not to leave town for the next few weeks. They've no transport. Norman's car has been collected from Geordie's flat by the police to have DNA swabs taken from it just in case it should turn out that he is the child-abductor and not the crucified man in the Tower. The police have collected the Mitsubishi Shogun from the hospital car park on a low-loader. Willie has been ticked off for driving it and contaminating a crime scene.

'What were we meant to do?' he asks angrily. 'Walk back to Hexham?'

There's no answer.

Willie and Pippa walk down to the station and sit on the platform waiting for the next train into Newcastle. They are both so tired by now they are almost beyond speech. Willie can't understand why he feels so deflated when really they ought to be celebrating. As the train approaches the platform and they both stand up, Willie speaks at last. 'Well,' he says to Pippa, 'we did it, didn't we?'

'I suppose we did,' replies Pippa. 'Those poor children.'

'At least they're back with their parents, now,' says Willie, forgetting for a moment that Becky Thomas's mother has disappeared.

'Well, they will be when the doctors let them out of hospital,' says Pippa. 'But they'll never be the same, will they? The man who abducted them stole their lives. I don't mean that exactly: he stole part of their childhood, didn't he?'

'I guess so,' replies Willie gloomily. He's not paying much attention to what Pippa says. He is thinking about his story, the one he can't write for the time being. They see the train approaching and stand up to board it.

They don't speak much during the journey into town. Willie is trying to summon the emotional energy to turn to Pippa and tell her that, whatever happens, they must stick together and they must look after each other. He knows he is about to lose her and he doesn't want that to happen. But he feels drained and empty. He can't do it.

Pippa believes that what happened in the forest is close to inexplicable: the three of them have saved the lives of two out of the three missing children against all the odds, and when the police couldn't find them. No, they didn't find the children: they were guided to them. It was a miracle of a sorts. She reflects that there doesn't seem to be much of a market for miracles these days. But since their return, they have been treated as possible suspects and not as the saviours of the children.

Willie is having similar thoughts. Their crusade to find and free the children has caused nothing but trouble. He's lost his job, and now it looks as if he won't be able to publish his story until after the trial, whenever that might be, of Geordie Nixon. He knows Geordie is likely to be charged with the murder of the man in the Tower House or, if he's lucky, with manslaughter. Willie still doesn't understand what happened. There's another dimension to all this, something he's unable to grasp. Why were the two girls still alive after all this time? How did Geordie know where to find them? He yawns suddenly. It doesn't matter, it's out of his hands.

'I'll need to think about finding a new job,' says Pippa. 'I can't imagine Norman will keep his position if he's a suspect in a murder case. It's so unfair. He was only trying to help. That's all any of us were trying to do.'

'I'll have to find work pretty quickly too. My bank balance is going into the red as we speak,' replies Willie, trying to make light of everything. He doesn't carry it off. As they leave the station, Willie is on the cusp of asking Pippa to come home with him. He wants to lie in bed with her again, his arms tight around her. It's not about sex – it's not just about sex, because the thought stirs him – it's about not wanting to let her go. But somehow he can't. It doesn't seem right. Instead he asks her, 'Can I see you home?'

'No, Willie,' replies Pippa. 'Do you mind? I'd rather be on my own just for now. I want a hot bath and a long sleep before anything else.'

'Well, I'll see you soon, I hope,' says Willie, with as much cheerfulness as he can manage.

'Yes. See you.'

But as they part to go their separate ways, each of them knows it's over between them. Their fragile romance has foundered on the rock of last night's events. Willie suspects that they will never meet again outside of a courtroom. As Pippa walks away from him outside the Central Station, Willie feels an ache inside him. It's not as if they've known each other for very long: but something that might have been very good has just been lost. The story got in the way. He didn't pay enough attention to what was staring him in the face: that a bright, pretty, warm-hearted girl was ready to share her life with him, or so it seemed for a moment.

Willie walks towards the Metro station, his hands in his pockets. There's still a chance he can win something from this mess. There's still a chance that he can have his story published. There's still a chance he can make a success of things.

Forty-Three

The police give Norman a hard time. They question him, return him to a holding cell, then take him out and begin all over again. Norman is very tired, and very confused. The more questions they ask him, the less he can remember.

'Did you know Mr Mitchell?'

'He's not called Mr Mitchell, his name is Gabriel Merkin.'

'Not according to our information. The deceased is called George Mitchell, he's a librarian and lives at number 23 Pinewood, Hexham.'

Norman tells them: 'That's his new identity, he was in the Witness Protection Programme.'

The detective who is questioning him looks bored, makes a note, and says: 'Well, we'll have to differ about that, won't we? Did you help Mr Nixon nail him to that wooden wall?'

'No.'

'We're finding it difficult to understand how Mr Nixon got the deceased up there on his own.'

'I can't help you.'

'Did you see Mr Nixon nail Mr Mitchell to the wall?'

'I can't remember,' says Norman. He almost wails his answer. The detective looks unimpressed.

'You can't remember? I'd have thought that's the sort of

thing you *would* remember. I'd have thought you would have difficulty forgetting something like that.'

They go around in circles, covering the same ground again and again. Norman is so tired by now that he can hardly recall his own name.

Then there's a long break. From what Norman can gather, the police are now questioning Geordie Nixon in another room, but he's not allowed to see Geordie. They don't tell him what Geordie is saying, but it seems Geordie must have claimed all the credit for crucifying George Mitchell because late that evening Norman is told he can go home. He is instructed to report to the police station again in the morning. He gathers the police are now treating him as a witness, rather than an accessory to murder. He's not allowed to take his car, which is still being dusted for fingerprints and searched for DNA. When he asks why, the detective tells him they just want to be sure he hasn't had any of the children in his car.

Norman realises that the police would really like to get him in the frame for the murder of Theo and the abduction of the two girls, but they're struggling with that one.

At last he's able to leave the police station, and walks home to his flat. When he's inside, he locks the door behind him, gets as far as the sitting room with the idea of pouring himself a large drink, sits down on the sofa for a moment and falls asleep for twelve hours.

He's awoken by the sound of the doorbell. It takes him a moment to get his bearings. He pats down his hair, adjusts his tie, and staggers to the front door. There are two men standing there. One is Chief Inspector Saxon. He's seen the other man at some of the meetings he's attended since coming up north, but he can't place him at first. Then he remembers. He's a very senior figure in regional social services: someone he would no doubt have known a great deal better if his job as children's czar had ever gone anywhere.

'Norman Stokoe?' asks the man. He puts out his hand and Norman shakes it.

'I'm Teddy Barnett. We've sat across the table from one another at various meetings but I don't think we've ever actually spoken. May we come in?'

'Of course,' says Norman. He tries to explain why he is looking so dishevelled. The two men listen politely but say nothing and Norman's explanations trail away into silence.

'Would you like some coffee?' Norman asks.

'No,' says Chief Inspector Saxon. 'We haven't got time.'

'May we sit down?' suggests Teddy Barnett.

'Do, please,' replies Norman. The chief inspector sits down first. Teddy Barnett is a little more hesitant. He perches on the edge of an armchair and says: 'We're here because we really need to get a better understanding of what you were doing with Karen Gilby and Becky Thomas. Chief Inspector Saxon is with the NCACU and I – as you probably know – am representing Social Services in this case.'

'I would have thought that was obvious. My colleagues and I were rescuing them from Gabriel Merkin.'

Chief Inspector Saxon and Teddy Barnett look at each other, and then the chief inspector says: 'We gather you made that statement to the police yesterday. Unfortunately, it was incorrect. The person whom George Nixon is alleged to have murdered was called George Mitchell. Gabriel Merkin died in Broadmoor Hospital some two years ago.'

The chief inspector gives Norman a steady look as he says this. The look says: I'll deny everything and you can't do anything about it.

'It's also very unfortunate,' Teddy Barnett adds, 'that you

309

did not inform Social Services of your interest in these children. I'm sure you know what the correct protocol is: you should have advised us of any knowledge you had of their whereabouts, and then allowed the professionals to carry out a risk assessment of the proposed intervention and take it from there.'

Norman is speechless for a moment. Then he says: 'We didn't know where the children were. Geordie Nixon guessed their whereabouts and he turned out to be right.'

'If he guessed, you could have told us, and we could have managed the situation in a professional and appropriate manner,' replies Teddy Barnett. He gives an apologetic smile as if to say: you ought to have known all this. You're the children's czar.

The chief inspector says: 'As it is, your vigilantism has so confused the evidence so that the only thing we can be certain of is that someone murdered George Mitchell. We don't even know yet who murdered Theo and abducted the two girls. It might have been George Nixon. He knew where they were.'

'It's regrettable,' says Teddy Barnett, 'that you didn't contact us or the police or preferably both. We're supposed to be working as a team, Norman, and your actions have certainly not been those of a team-player, have they?'

'We saved those two girls' lives. It was almost a miracle. No, it *was* a miracle. If we'd left it to you, they'd still be in that tower. They might even be dead by now.'

Teddy Barnett looks at the chief inspector again, and the chief inspector gives a slight shake of his head.

Teddy says: 'You don't have the training for this kind of intervention, do you? My understanding is that your role in the region was to be strategic, not operational.'

For once in his life, Norman has acted rather than gone to a meeting. And this is where it has landed him. He knows what is coming next.

'You waded into a situation about which you had no real knowledge. As a result, George Mitchell has been the victim of one of the most brutal crimes I have encountered in my whole professional career.'

'The children were the victims, not him.'

'That is a matter for the police, not you. You gave no consideration to his rights. You gave no thought to the risks of an intervention by amateurs.'

Norman doesn't answer. There *is* no answer to this. Teddy reaches into the inside pocket of his suit jacket and pulls out an envelope.

'I've been asked to give you this.'

He hands it to Norman. Norman takes the envelope, slits it open with his thumbnail and unfolds the contents. It's from the secretary of state and it advises Norman that he has been suspended on full pay while an investigation is carried out into allegations that he has been guilty of gross professional misconduct.

While he's digesting this news, the chief inspector stands up and says: 'We should be going, Mr Stokoe.'

'Going? Going where?' asks Norman in confusion.

'You have an appointment at the police station in about ten minutes.'

'But I need to wash and change,' says Norman.

'No time,' the chief inspector tells him. 'You can't be late.'

Teddy Barnett stands up too.

'Well, I'll leave the two of you to get on with that side of things,' he says. 'I must get back to the office. I dare say we will

311

meet again, Mr Stokoe, when we call you to give evidence to our own inquiry.'

Teddy Barnett leaves, and the chief inspector and Norman follow him down the stairs and outside to where the chief inspector's car is parked on a double yellow line. There's a driver in front and the chief inspector and Norman get in the back. It's only a short drive from the block of flats where Norman lives to the police station, but it gives the chief inspector enough time to lean across to Norman and say in a confidential tone of voice, 'Believe you me, by the time we've finished with you, Norman, your career will be history. You've only yourself to blame. I did warn you what would happen.'

'But we rescued the children,' replies Norman.

'You should have left all that to the police. We'd have got there eventually, and the whole situation would have been a damn site tidier than the mess you've left us with.'

The chief inspector sits back in his seat. Norman does not speak aloud, but he repeats the same words in his head: But we saved the lives of two children. It was a miracle that we found them alive.

When they get to the station, Norman is shown into an interview room and offered a cup of coffee. The chief inspector disappears and returns after a few minutes with an older, silver-haired man in a dark suit. Who this is, Norman never discovers, but he is obviously someone important. The chief inspector defers to him and seems a little awed.

'My colleague here has something to say,' says the chief inspector. 'I do advise you to listen very carefully, Norman. Your own future hangs on this. And other people's.'

Norman nods to show he understands. Although he doesn't understand. Then the silver-haired man speaks: 'Mr Stokoe, the coroner will send this case to the Crown Court and it is very likely that Mr Nixon will be put on trial for murder. There is a possibility that the coroner might decide, based on the medical evidence that will then be available to him, that more than one person may have been involved owing to the nature of Mr Mitchell's injuries.'

'It must have taken two people to nail Mitchell to that wooden wall,' interjects the chief inspector. 'And there was only you and the dead child in that room apart from Nixon.'

The silver-haired man glances at the chief inspector, who subsides into silence.

'So one way this could go is that Mr Mitchell would be tried and sentenced for murder, and you would be charged as an accessory. You may, or may not, have assisted Mr Nixon. You do not appear to have hindered him.'

Norman feels himself going cold with shock. He'd expected something like this might happen, but hearing the words spoken out loud makes it seem real for the first time.

'But,' says the silver-haired man, observing Norman's reaction and the colour of his face, which is now very pale, 'Mr Nixon could enter a plea of diminished responsibility. The jury might be persuaded that, in the intensity of his grief caused by discovering his dead child, Mr Nixon inflicted those injuries all on his own. A plea of manslaughter might be entered by the defence, and accepted by the court. As for you, the court might take the view that you were a passive witness, unable to intervene and in fear of your own life if you did.'

The silver-haired man pauses and looks at the chief inspector, who leans forward and taps Norman hard on the knee.

'My colleague is describing a scenario that might occur in an open-and-shut case involving George Mitchell. I gather the name of Gabriel Merkin was mentioned in some of the earlier taped interviews which, unfortunately, have been damaged by a technical fault in the recorder. We wouldn't want that name mentioned again, Norman, would we? It would make the whole situation so much more unpredictable and complicated, and we couldn't begin to say what might happen in those circumstances.'

The silver-haired man stands up. He says, 'I don't think I want to comment on what Chief Inspector Saxon has said. I leave it to your judgement, Mr Stokoe, as to how you want to proceed. On a personal note, I feel a great deal of sympathy for the father of the dead child. I would be happy to see him enter a plea of diminished responsibility, and I would like to think the CPS could be encouraged to accept that view. A lenient judge might not send him to prison at all, if he could be convinced there was no further threat to public safety. A simple Supervision Order might be made, and Mr Nixon could walk free after a year or two or even after a few months. In that scenario.'

The silver-haired man leaves the room. The chief inspector stands up too and says, 'We'll call you for interview in about an hour, Norman. Think over what we've said. Once you leave this building, all choices are at an end.'

The next hour is the longest in Norman's life. He wants to bear witness. Every part of him longs to tell the truth about what he saw in that room in the Tower. He heard – he believes that he heard – Theo come to life and speak to Gabriel Merkin. He thinks that was when Gabriel Merkin collapsed with shock. After that, Norman's memories are confused. He doesn't want to remember the next scene. The images of that are shut away in the darkest recesses of his mind.

He wants to bear witness to a series of miracles: the survival of the two girls, the fact that they were found, and Theo's apparent (and temporary) resurrection.

He wants the world to know the truth about Gabriel Merkin and he wants the police to explain why they never arrested him when they must have known – somebody must have known – of his new identity. Somebody apart from Norman, Willie and Pippa must have linked his presence to that of the missing children.

That is what he thinks for the first five minutes.

Then Norman starts to imagine how the cross-examination would go in court: 'You thought you heard a dead child speak, Mr Stokoe? Really? The medical examiner's report says he had been dead for weeks, perhaps months before you found him. Bear in mind you are under oath.'

'How did you know the children were in the Tower, Mr Stokoe? You say Mr Nixon dreamed about it. And are you telling us that a perfect stranger's dream was a good enough basis to go charging off into Kielder Forest?'

He might be done for perjury, contempt of court and accessory to murder all in the first half hour. At the very least, he would become an object of ridicule, pilloried in the national press. And he'd never, ever work again.

And then he thinks: 'Of course it's not just about me. There's Geordie to consider. If I make a fuss and start talking about Merkin, he'll be locked up for years. If Willie and Pippa and I just say we tracked George Mitchell down because of the Bookwise connection, Merkin's name need never come into it. And what does it matter now? He's dead. He can't do any more harm.'

For a moment he feels sick with self-loathing. He wanted to testify. He wants to bring the truth about Theo to hundreds, then thousands. Then millions.

But what did he really see in that stone chamber? He doesn't even believe it himself any longer. The whole Theo thing has been blown up out of all proportion. The boy is dead, and that's all there is to say.

The door opens and the chief inspector comes in.

'Well, Norman, are you ready for us?'

Norman forces a smile and gets to his feet.

Forty-Four

A week later, Norman calls Willie. Willie hasn't bothered to get in touch with the other two since the day he left Hexham. He has his own problems. He's behind with the rent and although he's started applying for jobs, so far he hasn't found any work. If he's honest, at the moment he couldn't hold down a job even if he found one. He can't seem to concentrate. His mind keeps flashing back to the moments when he entered the Tower House.

'We should talk,' says Norman, when Willie answers the phone.

'I'm not sure,' says Willie doubtfully. 'I've been to see a solicit-or and he says we should all stick to our own stories and not discuss them with each other until after the trial.'

'Don't be bloody silly,' says Norman, in a robust tone quite unlike the old Norman. 'Come to my flat for half an hour.'

'You're not in the office?'

'No I am not,' replies Norman with emphasis. There's something different about Norman's voice. It doesn't have that eerie quality it had for a while when they were all in the forest together. No – Norman sounds cheerful. He sounds *happy*. That seems rather odd in the circumstances. At first Willie tries to find an excuse to avoid going, but Norman won't accept any of his evasions and in the end Willie agrees to visit him.

Norman's flat is in a modern block in Hexham near the town centre. He can walk to Tesco or Waitrose or the chip shop in five minutes. Willie sees Norman as a Waitrose man, not a chip shop man. The flat itself is immaculately tidy: a gleaming, modern kitchen with a dining area, a sitting room with a large television set and a sofa and a bookcase. Norman greets Willie with offers of coffee, tea, or a glass of beer if that's what Willie would prefer? Willie refuses all this hospitality, sits down at the marble-topped kitchen table and waits for Norman to speak.

'You're wondering why I'm not in my office,' says Norman. 'I'm suspended on full pay until the court case comes up. Then there will be an internal review and I'll be fired.'

'How do you know they will fire you?' asks Willie. Then, with more indignation: 'Why would they fire you? You've just rescued two children. You're the children's czar, for God's sake.'

Norman smiles. He doesn't seem at all put out by his impending fate.

'The review will find that I ignored departmental protocol. The correct procedure would have been for me to inform the relevant Social Services department once we had found out where the children were, and then we should have let them get on with it. At the very least, we should have taken caseworkers from Social Services with us, and we should not have interfered with the children ourselves.'

'Is that what they think we did?' asks Willie. '*Interfered*?'

'Yes.'

'But how could we have told Social Services where the children were? We didn't even know ourselves until the last minute!'

'We found them, didn't we?' replies Norman gently.

'How are the children, anyway?' asks Willie. He feels a moment's guilt that he hasn't asked before.

'They're both still in hospital. I've tried to see them, but they're not supposed to receive visitors. One of the nurses told me that Karen cries a lot. Becky doesn't speak much, apparently. They've found her mother, but she won't be allowed to see Becky. She's not considered a fit person for her daughter to be with just at the moment. The nurse says she heard a social worker talking about finding a foster home for Becky, once she's out of hospital.'

Willie digests this, then says: 'I still don't understand why they would fire you. It's as if we're the criminals, not Gabriel Merkin.'

'Well, we broke the rules. I broke the rules. I was told I would embarrass the home secretary personally if I persisted with my theory that Gabriel Merkin and George Mitchell were one and the same. Of course, I realise now that I was wrong about that, and I've said as much to the police. But the damage is done. As far as my own department is concerned, I'm a pariah. My career there is over.'

'What do you mean, Gabriel Merkin is not the same person as George Mitchell? Of course he was. We proved it!'

Norman gives Willie a sad smile and says: 'No. We didn't prove anything. It was just my theory. We couldn't find where Gabriel Merkin was being kept and so we imagined – I imagined – that he must somehow have been freed and be the perpetrator of these new crimes.'

Norman shakes his head and repeats, 'We didn't prove anything, Willie. We just established a suggestive connection between the three children and the mobile library Bookwise.'

'But you said Chief Inspector Saxon said ...' Willie begins, almost shouting.

'Chief Inspector Saxon put forward various hypotheses to me, when we were discussing the disappearance of the children. But we have agreed it was a purely hypothetical conversation, and I have had to accept that there is no connection between Gabriel Merkin and George Mitchell.'

Willie stares at Norman for a while. Then he says, slowly, 'You've cut a deal, haven't you?'

'I don't know what you mean.'

'You've agreed to drop the Gabriel Merkin story in exchange for what?'

When Norman speaks again, his voice is almost inaudible. 'In exchange for not being an accessory to a murder. In exchange for Geordie pleading diminished responsibility and getting off with a few months in a psychiatric hospital or even walking away free.'

Willie says, 'But a half-decent defence lawyer could get those things anyway, couldn't he? What jury would convict Geordie of murder when he found his own dead stepson in that room? You've bottled it, Norman. What else did they offer you?'

But Norman doesn't answer. Willie stands up. His voice is full of disgust as he tells Norman, 'Well, if you won't tell the truth, I know who will. Me.'

'You can't publish anything until after the trial. You're a witness.'

'Maybe not. But then I *will* publish and I *won't* pull any punches.'

'If you want to tell the truth,' replies Norman, 'why don't you tell the truth about Theo?'

'And what's that?'

'That he was in my head. He was in your head. He was in the girls' heads. I think he even got into Gabriel Merkin's head.

How else could the girls still be alive? We all felt him. We all heard him. You did too. I know you did.'

Willie stares at Norman. Norman says, 'It was a miracle, Willie: a genuine, old-fashioned miracle. Divine intervention.'

'You're talking nonsense.'

'You must know who and what Theo is,' says Norman. He is smiling now and his voice has regained its former confidence. He reaches out as if to grasp Willie's hand, as if by doing so he can transmit his own belief.

But Willie's had enough. He avoids Norman's oustretched hand. He's on his way out of the flat. He's angry with Norman for inviting him here, angry with himself for coming. Norman's made him waste half a day, coming here just to hear rubbish like this. Norman's betrayed him. He's betrayed all of them. And then he goes all religious on Willie on top of everything else. It's not as if he hasn't enough problems already, without having to listen to someone who's obviously on the edge of a breakdown; someone who needs psychiatric help. Divine intervention? Miracles? Like turning Coke into Pepsi?

As Willie heads towards the front door, Norman follows him. He puts a hand on Willie's shoulder, the first and last time since they met, that he ever touches him.

'I may be silent about Gabriel Merkin, but I will testify to Theo. They won't silence me on that one.'

Willie shakes him off. He doesn't say goodbye. He leaves the flat, slamming the door with unnecessary force, and hurries away towards the station. In his head he sees the calm face of the boy sitting at the wooden table: the eyes that lock onto his and hold them.

Forty-Five

In the late autumn of that year, Willie is sitting opposite the senior editor of a well-known national newspaper. He is in a large office halfway up a tower of glass and steel, with panoramic views over the Thames.

'It's certainly a very unusual story,' says the senior editor, Mr Macpherson.

'I thought you'd think so,' answers Willie. He is wearing a new light-grey suit he has bought for these occasions, which he considers rather more metropolitan than his old brown pinstripe affair.

'My problem is,' says Mr Macpherson, 'that I can't get the facts to add up. You *say* that the man George Nixon killed was the serial killer Gabriel Merkin.'

'That's right,' agrees Willie.

'The trouble is,' says Mr Macpherson, 'you can't prove it. We couldn't publish a statement like that without evidence. And if we haven't got any evidence, then the political part of your story, the cover up to protect the home secretary, all of that just falls to the ground.'

Willie has heard this before, but he has to try, hasn't he? This is his big break, right here, if only he can make it happen.

'The police said in court that the deceased was a Mr George Mitchell. Same initials, I grant you, but that's the end of the resemblance. He was a librarian living and working in your part of the world who may, or may not, have abducted those children.'

'Excuse me, but of course he abducted them,' says Willie. 'I don't mean to contradict you, but who else would have done it?'

'Well, I can tell you in confidence we've had informal conversations with the police. They say it might have been this friend of yours, Norman Stokoe. But the crime scenes had been so messed up by you lot that nobody will ever know. The case was left open, wasn't it? Nobody has ever been charged or convicted for the abduction and murder of the boy, Theo.'

'Then where is Gabriel Merkin?' asks Willie.

'The police tell us that he died in custody.'

'Then we'll ask them to release the body, do a DNA check. We can do a Freedom of Information request.'

Willie's pleased by the way he introduces the word 'we' into the conversation. As if they're already a team. As if Willie has already accepted a high-flying job with the paper.

'The police say Gabriel Merkin was given a new identity in prison to protect him. Paedophiles and child-killers tend to have a hard time inside. It would have been cheaper to do that than to keep him in solitary confinement all the time. They do not divulge any details about people given witness-protection. It's exempt from FOI requests,' said Mr Macpherson, 'so we can't check any of that. Your theory is just your theory. You've no evidence one way or the other.'

'It's not just my theory,' Willie argues. 'It's Norman Stokoe's, too.'

The senior editor sighs, and pushes a hand through his hair.

'Ah yes, Norman Stokoe. The children's czar.'

'Well, not any more,' says Willie. 'But that was his job at the time.'

'It doesn't seem possible to find anyone who will admit to having employed him in that role. They never gave him a job description. Apparently he sat for months in Newcastle collecting his salary and, presumably, dreaming up schemes like the one he involved you in. Or abducting the missing children himself and then using you and that girl to muddy the water.'

'We found them though, didn't we?' asks Willie.

'It seems more like George Nixon—'

'Geordie,' Willie corrects him, but the editor ignores the interruption. 'Yes, this George Nixon knew where to find George Mitchell. You all followed him up there like sheep, as far as I can tell from the trial transcripts we've seen. He was very lucky to be allowed to plead diminished responsibility. After all, he was only the stepfather. At one time I believe he was thought to have been responsible for violence towards his stepson. Apparently the boy had all these marks on him when he was at school. Nixon got off scot-free in the end, didn't he?'

'Yes,' replies Willie. Geordie has been detained in a medium security psychiatric hospital.

'He was a lucky man.'

Then Mr Macpherson adds, after thinking for a moment, 'There is something in your story. It's very dramatic: melodramatic, even. I daresay our readers would lap it up if we could ever find a way of publishing it that didn't land us in trouble.'

'Thank you,' says Willie.

'You wouldn't be sitting here if I hadn't seen something in the story. You write well.'

'Thank you,' says Willie again.

'But then there's all this religious bollocks. Norman Stokoe's testimony in court was simply extraordinary. He said that the dead child – that Theo Constantine – spoke to him more than once and helped save the two girls. What did he say again?'

Mr Macpherson leafs through the manuscript pages in front of him.

'Oh yes. Here we are. He says he wants to testify that Theo is Christ come again and George Nixon was the instrument of his vengeance. Well, I should think the jury must have fallen off their seats laughing when they heard that.'

Willie agrees that it is, taken in isolation, an odd statement.

'There's a well-known phrase another journalist once used: "We don't do God",' says Mr Macpherson. 'On this paper, we do football; we do sex; we do the gossipy end of politics. But we don't do God. Norman Stokoe sounds very much as if he does do God.'

'He became a bit obsessive about that side of things,' admits Willie.

'Would it be unfair to describe him as – forgive the expression – a religious nutter?' asks Mr Macpherson.

'He wasn't to start with,' replies Willie. He is squirming in his seat at this summary of events that now seem so long ago. But he can't afford to give up. This interview may be his last and best chance of getting his story sold. If he doesn't succeed here and now, this very afternoon, Willie suspects it will all be over for his hopes of a career as an investigative journalist.

'The bottom line is, you can give us an eyewitness account of the recovery of two out of three of the children. We still don't even know why they were abducted. The medical reports say there was no evidence of sexual interference. But you can't really explain how you found them, or what happened in the ruin you found them in before you arrived. It's all speculation, or else the evidence of two very troubled juvenile witnesses.

Norman Stokoe's testimony is worthless. It's quite clear that the man is as mad as a snake.'

Willie groans inwardly. The problem is, he can't argue with this view. If the editor ever found out about the things he left out of his story, he might have expressed himself in even stronger terms. If he had heard the claim by one of the two girls that Theo came to them and spoke to them every day, even though the inquest showed he had been dead for months by that time. Or if he had heard Norman's assertion that Theo had so clouded the mind of Gabriel Merkin that he was unable to bring himself to murder the two girls.

Mr Macpherson laughs and pushes the manuscript back across the desk towards Willie, and then Willie knows it is all up.

'I must say,' he remarks, 'if Norman Stokoe was right and this was the second coming of Christ, it would be a bit rough, wouldn't it? First time he turns up he gets crucified, the second time he's murdered by an overdose of diamorphine.'

There's another short silence. Then the senior editor stands up and extends his hand out to Willie.

'I'm sorry, Willie. There's definitely something there, but there are just too many problems all along the line. Too many unanswered questions. It's not for us.'

Willie's wondering if now is the time to get down on his knees on the carpet and beg for a job. Instead, he shakes hands with the editor who hands him back his story and adds, 'But you do have ability. We're always on the lookout for bright young journalists. Leave your details with my secretary on your way out.' He sits down again. The interview is over. Willie turns to leave the office. The sense of defeat is terrible; he can hardly remain upright under the weight of it.

Before he reaches the door, the editor calls him back, saying:

'Of course, one of our competitors might take a more relaxed view about the lack of evidence. You might try one of the red-tops. You never know.'

But Willie's already tried speaking to the red-tops, and the digital TV channels, and some of the racier magazines. They've all reacted to his story in much the same way as this man. This was his last chance.

Willie thanks the editor for his suggestion and leaves. He makes his way out of the office and back to King's Cross to catch his train home to Newcastle. On the way to the station, he sees a skip outside a building site. He tosses the manuscript into the skip.

Forty-Six

There's a surprise at the trial. The medical evidence shows that the cause of George Mitchell's death was heart failure. He had a defective heart. The expert witness says, 'He might have died at any time.' The presumption is that the stress of being chased by a man with a hammer brought about the crisis that ended his life. But it is a presumption. The crucifixion was carried out on a dead or dying man.

Pippa watches all this from the public gallery, looking down on the courtroom. Geordie stands in the dock behind windows of reinforced glass. He looks white-faced and ill. Pippa can hardly bear to watch his misery. Below him sit the CPS lawyer and the legal-aid barrister defending Geordie. She watches Norman and Willie come in turn to the witness box. Norman's testimony is quiet and dignified. When he speaks about Theo, he speaks as if he doesn't expect anyone else to believe that a dead child could have influenced the events leading to the discovery and release of the living children in the Tower House. He speaks as if he himself believes his own testimony absolutely, despite interruptions from both the judge and the prosecution.

Willie makes a less favourable impression. He looks uneasy, not as if he is lying, but as if he himself is divided – as if he cannot quite decide what really happened. This uneasiness communicates itself to the rest of the court. The judge calls a recess and summons the prosecution and the defence to his chambers.

When the trial is resumed, other witnesses are called. The witness who is not called, who never appears because she is never found, is Mary. The police are trying to contact her, but it is as if she has vanished from the surface of the earth.

The proceedings are short and conclude with Geordie being convicted of manslaughter. A plea of diminished responsibility has been entered and is accepted. Geordie is not sent to prison. Instead he is placed under a supervision order and detained in a medium-security psychiatric hospital. He is not considered a risk to public safety.

For a couple of nights after the trial is over, Pippa cannot sleep. This may be the law, but is it justice? The image of Geordie behind the glass window, pale and motionless, haunts her for a long while. What did he really do except lose a child? Why is he the only victim in all this? She does not measure the life of Gabriel Merkin in her calculation: he had a diseased heart. He was a dead man walking. Perhaps that's why he liked to surround himself with dead children.

Gradually, her life resumes its normal course. She does not sleep well, but she knows she has things to do. At the top of the list is earning a living, since she has now received her redundancy notice from the department of state that once employed her and Norman. It is not hard for her to find work. Willie tells her this when they speak on the phone.

'A bright, pretty girl like you? You won't be out of a job for more than five minutes.'

This is true. Before long, Pippa's working in a digital marketing agency being paid twice what she was paid for sitting outside

Norman's office. It turns out, though, that Willie's remark had more then a touch of self-pity about it, for he remains out of work. He's even contemplating applying for jobs selling classified ads.

'It would just be to tide me over until something better turns up,' he confides to Pippa. 'Why don't we meet, anyway? I'd love to have a proper catch-up with you.'

But Pippa doesn't want to see Willie at the moment. She's busy moving into her new flat, a three-roomed apartment on the top floor of a large old house on the outskirts of Newcastle. She's busy learning about her new job. She hasn't the time to worry about Willie as well. Whatever spark there once was between them has been extinguished, at least as far as she is concerned. She suspects Willie just wants to cling to somebody before he is swept away on a vast tide of nothingness. She stops picking up his calls, and after a while they come only at long intervals.

She does see others, however. One bright autumn morning, she drives out to the small village where the Gilbys live. The air is soft but chill, hinting at the winter to come. Showers of leaves flutter down from roadside trees as Pippa drives along the quiet lanes. At the door of the Gilbys' house, she is greeted with a hug. As far as Mrs Gilby is concerned, Pippa is the heroine of the events at the Tower House. It doesn't matter that Pippa never made it as far as that dreadful room, she's the one the children remember: her, not Norman, or Geordie, or Willie.

Pippa follows Mrs Gilby into the kitchen and accepts a cup of coffee.

'How is she?'

'Oh, she's so much better now,' says Mrs Gilby. There are lines of strain about her mouth and eyes that suggest she herself has not yet made a complete recovery. The nightmares may have receded but they still grumble on at the back of her mind like distant thunder. 'She was wetting her bed a lot when she first came home. But she doesn't do that now. Hardly ever. And she's so much happier. Just look at her.'

She beckons Pippa to the kitchen window and she is able to watch Karen playing in the garden, unobserved. The girl is kneeling on a tartan rug. A kitten is next to her, washing its paws. Pippa can see a slight smile on Karen's face. Then she speaks, although what she is saying they cannot hear. She speaks, and then listens as if to someone's reply. Then she speaks again.

'She's been ever so much better since we bought her the kitten. She adores it,' says Mrs Gilby. But Karen doesn't seem to be paying any attention to her new pet at the moment. She is absorbed in a one-sided conversation.

'Who's she talking to?' asks Pippa. 'It looks like she's talking to someone.'

'Oh, it's just one of her little games,' says Mrs Gilby. She doesn't meet Pippa's eyes. 'I'm sure there's no harm in it. Come on and say hello. She'd love to see you.'

They go out into the garden. Karen doesn't get up. She is friendly enough when she says hello to Pippa, but Pippa is left with the impression that they have interrupted something. It's as if she, Karen's mother, the kitten, are all ghosts on the edge of Karen's world. What's real to Karen is someone or something else. Even as she speaks to Pippa – and her replies to Pippa's questions sound happy and confident – Karen's eyes slide away, as if seeking the approval of some other person nearby.

Pippa also goes to visit Becky. She is staying in a residential children's care home. She has not been reunited with her mother. Those whose job it is to map out Becky's future have decided that Mrs Thomas is not a suitable person to look after her. Pippa hears a little about this from the senior care provider, a middle-aged woman with a kind face, who tells Pippa: 'Her mother promised Rebecca's case manager she would give up the vodka, give up anything if she could have Rebecca back. But she's got no income apart from benefits and, most important of all, she hasn't got a safe environment in which to bring Rebecca up. She's in a shelter for the homeless at the moment. She's been told to clean herself up, get a job and reapply for custody in a year's time.'

The senior care provider gives Pippa a sceptical look as she tells her this, a raised eyebrow that suggests Becky won't be going anywhere in the near future, unless it's to a foster home.

Becky herself is calm enough when Pippa meets her. Her room is small and tidy, not unlike the bedroom she once had at home. There is a table on which several books have been left.

'Do you still like reading?' Pippa asks when they have greeted each other.

'Oh, yes, when I get the time.'

'Are you happy here?'

The child regards Pippa with a level stare. Then she answers, 'It would be better if I was at home. I can look after my mum. I've done that for a long time. But they won't let me.'

'Do you have friends here?'

'Where?' asks Becky in a sharper tone of voice. 'Do you mean in this room?'

She gives Pippa a look that is almost challenging.

'I mean in this care home.'

'I suppose.'

Pippa's longing to ask Becky her version of what happened in the Tower House. Why were the two children still alive?

But she daren't ask such a question for fear of the memories it might bring back. Nevertheless, Becky appears to have read her mind because she volunteers some information.

'He kept us alive until you came.'

'Who did?'

'You know.'

'But, my darling Becky, if you mean Theo, it couldn't be. He was dead before you ever reached that dreadful place.'

Becky shakes her head.

'He spoke to that man who took us there. The book man. He spoke to us. He must have spoken to you. How else could you have found us?'

Pippa starts to answer and finds that there is nothing she can say to this.

Becky adds, 'He speaks to *me* every day.'

And that's the last word she has to say on the subject. Pippa can get no further information from her and, as when she met Karen, she feels that Becky is waiting for her to go. She wants to be alone again, or at least without any human company for a while.

There's nothing further she can do for these children. They don't need her. She's not at all sure what they do need. They are unlikely survivors, but they *have* survived, and their lives will go on without Pippa.

Of course she meets Norman again, more than once. He rings her to apologise for being the means by which she lost her job. This is so un-Norman-like that Pippa cannot refuse when he suggests they should meet.

The rendezvous is the same atrium café in the building where they both once worked, and where Pippa once made daily sorties to fetch Norman his espressos and lattes.

Norman's different. He isn't wearing a suit and tie, for one thing. He's wearing a pullover and flannel trousers and he looks almost relaxed. That Normanish look of amused superiority has left him. When he speaks, it is to ask Pippa how she is. He doesn't talk about himself much and Pippa has to pry the information out of him.

'Oh, I'm applying for work in the private sector. I've had enough of being a civil servant.'

'Doing what?'

With a hint of his old asperity, Norman says, 'Looking after children, of course. Only, I want to be at the sharp end, not behind a desk. However it may not work out for me.'

'Why not?'

'Dirty work at the crossroads, I fear. They've applied to my old employer for a reference, and there seems to be some difficulty about that.'

Pippa is horrified.

'But how long have you worked for them?'

'The best part of thirty years. But it's what you do in the last ten minutes that counts, as far as they are concerned.'

Norman doesn't sound bitter as he says this. Then he changes the subject and asks after the two girls.

Pippa goes away from that brief reunion feeling that Norman is different to the Norman she first met. He is changing, but quite how much he is changing isn't apparent until she meets him again some weeks later at Newcastle Central Station. She's killing time at Starbucks, waiting for a client of her new agency to arrive. Today all she's meant to do is meet and greet, but maybe she'll be allowed to sit in on the discussions later. While she is waiting, a familiar figure goes past, carrying a suitcase. It's Norman, back in his more usual uniform of suit and tie. He's lost weight though; the suit hangs on him a little.

'Hello, Norman,' says Pippa as he walks past. He stops in surprise.

'Pippa! Are you travelling to London as well?'

'I'm waiting for someone. Have you time for a cup of coffee?'

Norman sits down at her table but refuses refreshment. He checks his watch.

'I can't stop long.'

'Where are you off to?'

Norman hesitates for a second. Then he confesses: 'I'm going to have a meeting with the diocesan vocations director in my old parish in North London.'

This means nothing much to Pippa and she says so.

'Pippa, it means I want to become a Catholic priest. This interview is the first step. Maybe, despite my age, I'll be accepted into a seminary. That's the second step.'

Pippa doesn't know what to say. Her face says it all instead.

'You're surprised,' Norman says. 'I don't blame you. A middle-aged man who's heard the call. It sounds as if I've gone a little bit mad, doesn't it? But I haven't.'

Pippa reassures him. He's not mad, she tells him. She wonders if that is true. But, as Norman continues speaking, she realises he's never been saner.

'I've changed, that's all. It happens to people and it's happened to me. I've realised in these last months that I never gave up the beliefs I learned at school. I thought I had thrown them away and moved on. But they were there all the time.'

Pippa is still catching up.

'Norman, I can't imagine you as a priest.' Then she adds, feeling that this doesn't sound very helpful, 'But I'm sure you will make a very good one.'

'Are you? I'm not sure at all. To start with, I'm having to

335

revise my ideas about God after what happened – you know – in that awful place.'

Pippa nods.

'I've realised that God likes sacrifices. It's not all sweetness and light. Far from it. That was what Theo taught me, in the Tower House.'

Pippa doesn't want to hear any more about the Tower House. Although she never went there, it still troubles her dreams from time to time. Norman checks his watch again and stands up.

'I've got to catch my train,' he says. Pippa stands up too, to say goodbye. She's not sure she'll ever see him again, but Norman pre-empts whatever parting words she was about to say.

'Theo brought the three of us together to find those children. Now there's no longer any reason for us to meet, and I don't suppose we will again.'

Pippa realises he's right. The bond that, for a moment, seemed to bind her and Norman and Willie so closely has disappeared. Now Norman is being sent on a different journey. Or maybe it's all his own idea. She can't be sure.

'Well, I wish you luck,' she tells him.

'Luck? I don't think that has got anything to do with it. This is what is meant to happen to me next. After that, I don't know. I wonder what he has in mind for you?'

To Pippa's amazement, Norman leans forward and kisses her on the cheek. That, more than anything else he has said or done, finally makes her understand how different Norman has become. Then she realises his last words to her require explanation.

'Who do you mean?'

But Norman has already turned away from her and is starting to walk towards the platforms.

'Who do you mean?' shouts Pippa after him. Norman is now part of streams of people converging on the automatic ticket barriers. Does he stop for a moment to reply to her question? She can't be sure, but she thinks she hears him call out a single word and then he is lost in a sea of bobbing heads moving towards a train that slides into the station like a long snake, the noise of its engines and the incomprehensible announcements over the public address system making further communication impossible.

Willie's attempts to reach Pippa by phone may have become less frequent, but he still calls now and again. The next time she sees his name on the screen of her phone, she decides to answer. It is perverse of her, quite the opposite of what she planned to do. Maybe it's because Norman told her the three of them were unlikely to meet again that she decides to prove him wrong and answer Willie's call.

'Hi, Willie,' she says.

'Pippa! Have you been away? I've been trying to get in touch with you for ages. I even wrote to you. Did you not get my letter?'

'I've been moving flat. And I've got a new job. You know how it is,' says Pippa, not feeling she needs to explain or apologise too much.

'Well, great to hear about the job. So how are you?'

They chat for a moment or two. Pippa finds she is uninterested in everything Willie can tell her and is looking for the right moment to end the call when suddenly he says something that captures her attention.

'Yes, so I've got this grant, haven't I? From Arts Council England. They're paying for me to go on a Creative Writers' Course somewhere in Scotland.'

'Willie, that's brilliant!'

'Yes, isn't it?'

'How did you pull that off?' asks Pippa. Willie explains that he has started writing an account of the last few months, but translated into a work of fiction rather than fact.

'I've changed all the names, of course, and a few other things as well.'

'Am I in it?' asks Pippa.

'Someone very like you, anyway,' says Willie. 'I sent them the first three chapters and they loved it. Well, at any rate, they promised to pay for this course.'

They talk for a while longer and the conversation ends with the agreement that it would be good to meet. But no definite arrangement is made. When Willie ends the call, Pippa feels happier for him. Willie's going to be writing stories. That's all he's ever really wanted to do and now at last someone's going to help him to do that.

There is one other person Pippa is longing to see, but he's difficult to reach, and that's Geordie. She has learned he is confined in St Mark's Hospital, a depressing-looking nineteenth century building near the North East coast. She tries a number of times to get an appointment and the question is always the same.

'Are you a family member?'

'No, but . . .'

'I'm afraid only family members can make an appointment to see him.'

'But he hasn't got any family,' shouts Pippa on the third occasion she tries. It makes no difference, says the person on the other end of the phone. Rules are rules.

At last, the regime Geordie is subject to is relaxed a little.

Pippa, describing herself as 'a close friend of the family', is allowed to visit. In her mind's eye she pictures one of those scenes familiar from the cinema, where she and Geordie converse through a barred window. The reality is rather less severe. The hospital is a dreary place with white painted walls and doors and miles of green lino on the floor. But Geordie's room, though small, is pleasant enough. It has a bed, a sink, a shower cubicle, a table and two chairs. She is allowed to talk to him without supervision. Geordie looks better than she expected. He has more colour in his cheeks, but then the last time she saw him was at his trial, so that isn't surprising. He doesn't recognise her at first, and she has to remind him how and when she came into his life.

'How are you, Geordie? I've been so worried about you.'

Geordie seems amazed that anyone might be feeling concern for him.

'Me? Aye, I'm fine.'

He doesn't know what to say next. He has no small talk and the conversation falters for a moment. So Pippa decides to tell him about the girls. Geordie is pleased.

'So the bairns are doing well? They're canny little kids.'

Gathering her courage together, Pippa says what she has really come to say.

'Geordie – I was so sorry about Theo.'

'Aye, Theo. Well now.'

He rubs his jaw with his hand and doesn't say anything for a moment. He looks out of the window. Pippa struggles to think of what to say. Then she asks, 'I don't suppose Mary has been to see you?'

'Nah.'

Another silence. Pippa is wondering if she can go now. She doesn't know what she thought might happen at this reunion, but Geordie is taciturn beyond expectation. Then it all changes because Geordie leans forward in a confidential way and says, 'She's lost. She's desperate, man, and she doesn't know what to do. I can help her.'

'Do you know where she is?' asks Pippa. But of course he doesn't. Nobody knows where Mary is or, indeed, if she is anywhere at all. Geordie looks straight at Pippa.

'Theo knows,' he tells her.

'Theo? Theo's dead, Geordie. We both know that.'

'He comes to see me. Every night, when it's quiet and the rest of them are asleep. He sits where you're sitting now and he talks to me.'

When he says this, Pippa feels the hairs rising on her forearms and on the nape of her neck. He's so matter of fact.

'He'll take me to her. I've just got to give it time.'

Pippa feels like weeping at the sadness of it all. But Geordie isn't sad. When he speaks about his dead stepson, his eyes brighten and he almost smiles. For a moment Pippa can glimpse another Geordie, the man he must have been when Theo was alive and Mary and Geordie still lived together. A man full of warmth; a comfort to those who knew him well. Now, he's as deluded as the others. He thinks a child long gone from the world can give him back his own life.

That night, Pippa has one of those dreams when you believe yourself to be awake at the time. She's lying in her bed in her new flat. The bed faces a window and the curtains are not drawn. There's a full moon and its beams shine down undimmed by the edges of ragged cloud. It shines upon her face and she dreams that its light wakes her. It is without surprise that she sees Theo outside the window. She recognises him instantly from the photographs she once saw of him. In any case, who else would be standing in mid-air in the moonlight, halfway between the sky and the earth? His voice is inside her head. It says: '*I'm waiting for you.*'

She feels an overwhelming urge to go and put her arms around him. She wants to tell him how sorry she is that he died. She wants him to know that she understands that his divinity – that state of grace into which all children are born – has survived his death. Then she remembers Norman saying – or perhaps he too is in her dream and repeating the words: 'This is a God who likes sacrifices.'

With a start, she wakes – this time it is real – and finds herself standing at the window. In her sleep she has climbed out of bed and opened the sash window to its fullest extent. She realises she has been on the verge of stepping out, three storeys above the ground.

The moon has disappeared behind black clouds.

Forty-Seven

Autumn passes away and then winter. It is not until the following spring that Pippa finds the courage to do something she knows she must do, if ever she wants to banish the memories that still haunt her from last year.

She drives up the North Tyne valley. It is a glorious spring day in early June. The sky is a soft blue, and white clouds drift slowly out of the south-west. She drives along the narrow roads that lead up to the dam wall. The hedgerows are full of cow parsley, and the may is blooming. In the gentle wind the white flowers toss and wave, so that if you half-closed your eyes you might think hundreds of children were standing there, waving at her, all dressed in white. Pippa drives up past the Kielder dam wall and leaves her car in one of the tourist car parks along the lakeshore. She's brought a pair of walking boots with her and a waterproof jacket, and she sets off along the forest road that she last travelled not quite a year ago, squashed against Willie in the cab of Geordie's Scania truck.

She walks up the long gradients between walls of trees and she breathes in the pure air of the forest with its scents of resin and new bracken. The forest is emerging from a late winter and small patches of wet snow still cling here and there to the sides of drainage ditches or lie in the shadows beneath the trees. It's not warm, but the sun is out, sailing through the sky above the forest. It is a more cheerful place than she remembers.

After a couple of hours, she comes at last to the locked barrier across the road. She ducks under it, and walks along the diminishing track. There are still faint tyre-tracks here and there: for a while there were police and other vehicles travelling along the track. But that was last summer and autumn and the traces of their passage are fading now. The track winds up the side of a ridge: this is new territory to Pippa. She never came this far the last time she was in the forest. She climbs the shallow ridge and on its crest she looks down and sees the Tower House.

Its stone is golden in the early spring sunshine. It is an ancient place. For a time its picture was shown on all the news channels around the clock. Now it is forgotten once again. Pippa descends into the clearing and looks up at the Tower. She still doesn't understand everything that happened here. Perhaps Norman was right and something took place that he called in his witness statement 'divine intervention'. If so, it was a divinity more akin to the Old Testament than the New: a wrathful, unforgiving, vengeful divinity. And yet lives were saved as well as lost. If there was a miracle here, it hasn't been recognised as one by anyone except those who were here. The rest of the world seems to have been rather annoyed by something that could not easily be explained.

Pippa sets these thoughts aside. She's thankful that the two girls are still alive. That has to be enough, in itself. She doesn't know how to believe all those people who claim to have seen a dead child, Theo, alive and speaking to them: Geordie, Norman, Willie, Becky, Karen. How could so many different people see him in so many different places? The answer is, probably, that he hasn't been seen by any of them. It is all nonsense. Nobody has seen him.

And yet.

She doesn't know whether, if Theo has survived somehow beyond death, this is a good or a bad thing, or whether the words 'good' or 'bad' even have any meaning in these circumstances. She only knows that she isn't prepared to deny absolutely, positively and rigorously that any such possibility exists.

She sits down on a heathery bank to rest for a moment. Around her is the great bowl of trees. She sees, without knowing all their names, Sitka Spruce, Norway Spruce, Lodge Pole Pine, Scots Pine, Willow, Birch and Alder. She gazes at the Tower above her, its walls bright in the sunshine. She gazes at the forest that covers the surrounding hills as far as she can see: it is no longer threatening. It is a wilderness; beautiful in its way. People bring their own fears and their own hopes to places like this.

Hearing a distant scream, she looks up and far above her she sees a cruciform speck. It is a buzzard, searching for its food amongst the dead and the dying. It slips sideways as she watches it, floating in the winds that blow endlessly in these Border hills.

W&N blog

For exclusive short stories, poems, extracts, essays, articles, interviews, trailers, competitions and much more visit the Weidenfeld & Nicolson blog at:

www.wnblog.co.uk

Follow us on

 and

Or scan the code to access the website*

*Requires a compatible smartphone with QR reader. Mobile network and/or wi-fi charges apply.
Contact your network provider for details.